PRAISE FOR AN... ...ION

"A strong, spare writer . . . ., *The Stolen Child*, will enjoy th... ...ty and fantasy."

—*Chicago Sun-Times*

"Charming, suspenseful, and even touching."

—*New York Daily News*

"[A] beguiling tale of those who love well, but not wisely, unspooling like a poem embroidered on the heart—ornate, painful, and true . . . While some readers might liken Donohue's penchant for mystical realism to that of novelist Alice Hoffman, any sweeping comparisons shortchange both writers, whose immense gifts bear separate and distinct literary imprimaturs. Still, he shares Hoffman's uncanny ear for capturing the libretto of childhood. . . ."

—*BookPage*

"Fused with spectral imagery and magnetic characters, Donohue's ethereal foray into the unexpected consequences of love, impenetrable depths of loss, and infinite possibilities of faith is a chilling yet affirmative experience."

—*Booklist*

"[A] strange and finely written novel. Donohue has a talent for using small details to draw his characters, and the result is a dark and unsettling story that takes hold of the reader."

—*Library Journal*

"Norah's unexplained origins form the enigmatic core of this story. . . . The novel movingly illustrates the quest for connection hardwired into every human heart."

—*Publishers Weekly*

Angels of Destruction

ALSO BY
Keith Donohue

The Stolen Child

Keith Donohue

Angels of
Destruction

A NOVEL

Three Rivers Press

NEW YORK

Published in the United States by Three Rivers Press, an imprint of the
Crown Publishing Group, a division of Random House, Inc., New York.
www.crownpublishing.com

Three Rivers Press and the Tugboat design are registered trademarks of
Random House, Inc.

Originally published in hardcover in slightly different form in the United States by
Shaye Areheart Books, an imprint of the Crown Publishing Group, a division of
Random House, Inc., New York.

Grateful acknowledgment is made to Brownlee O. Currey, Jr. for permission
to reprint "The Pelican" by Dixon Lanier Merritt (*Nashville Banner,* April 22, 1910).
Reprinted by permission of Brownlee O. Currey, Jr.

Library of Congress Cataloging-in-Publication Data

Donohue, Keith.
    Angels of destruction : a novel / by Keith Donohue—1st ed.
        p. cm.
    1. Widows—Fiction.   2. Girls—Fiction.   3. Supernatural—Fiction.
4. Psychological fiction.   I. Title.
PS3604.O5654A83 2009
813'.6—dc22   2008021277

ISBN 978-0-307-45026-5

Printed in the United States of America

Design by Lynne Amft

10   9   8   7   6   5   4   3   2   1

First Paperback Edition

For my brothers and sisters

Hope is the thing with feathers
that perches in the soul.

— EMILY DICKINSON

Einst werd ich liegen im Nirgend
bei einem Engel irgend.

One day I will lie Nowhere
with an angel at my side.

— PAUL KLEE

Angels of Destruction

January 1985

1

She heard the fist tap again, tentative and small.

From the cocoon of her bed, she threw off the eiderdown duvet and wrapped a shawl around her shoulders against the winter's chill. Alone in the house, Margaret took the stairs cautiously, holding her breath to verify that the sound at the front door was not just another auditory hallucination to disturb her hard-won sleep. On the fourth step from the bottom, she peered through the transom window but saw only minatory blackness and the blue reflected light of moon and stars arcing off the cover of new snow. She whispered a prayer to herself: *just don't hurt me. . . .*

Margaret pressed her palms against the oak to deduce the presence on the other side, without seeing, without being seen, and on faith undid the locks and swung wide the door. Shivering on the threshold stood a young girl, no more than nine years old, with a tattered suitcase leaning against her legs. Between the hem of her coat and the top of her kneesocks, her bare skin flushed salmon pink. She wore no hat, and even in the dim light, the tops of her ears blazed red through her fine blonde hair. A visible chill sashayed up the girl's spine, and her bony knees knocked and her thin hips wriggled as the shiver ended in convulsions of the shoulders and an involuntary clacking of the teeth. She flexed her fingers into fists to keep the circulation going. Beneath the threadbare plaid coat more suited for early autumn, the girl appeared no more than a frame of bones, all lines and sharp angles. Winter blew right through her.

"You poor thing, come in. How long have you been out there in the cold?"

Margaret Quinn regarded her visitor, then stepped outside to the porch, brought in the miniature suitcase, and locked the door behind her. What had seemed unreal through the open door now confronted her in the safety of the house. The girl stood in the foyer, thawing and shaking with tremors. Pinned to her cloth coat was a torn paper badge with three letters printed in an earnest and unsteady hand: N-O-R.

"Is that your name, child? You're missing something. That's no way to spell Norah. It's with an A and an H. Is that who you are? Norah?"

The child did not reply, but the heat had begun to work its way into her, loosening the icy grip on her personality. When she noticed the woman watching her, she grimaced with thin blue lips. Margaret busied herself, switching on the lights, through the dining room and into the kitchen, and the girl followed like a pup as Margaret struck a match and lit the woodstove and, with a kindling stick, shut the iron door. "Come warm yourself."

Old habits and dormant instincts returned. Margaret heated milk in a saucepan and spread butter on saltines. Perched in a chair by the woodstove, the girl unbuttoned her coat and worked her arms from the sleeves. When her severe glasses fogged with condensation, she took them off, wiped the lenses on the hem of her dress, and then promptly returned them to her nose. The blood rushed back to her cheeks and set them ablaze. Her eyes brightened, and without a word, she took the mug and gulped down half her drink.

"You'll have to excuse these buttered crackers, that's all I have. Don't get many children here."

The saltines vanished. The drained mug was refilled. The old house groaned and ticked, stirring from sleep. Behind her eyes, a light came on inside as she sat perfectly still and poised next to Margaret at the kitchen table, the two creatures considering one another in the enveloping warmth.

"Where did you come from? How did you get here?"

The coat slipped from the girl's shoulders, revealing a blue jumper with a yellow blouse and white kneesocks dingy from a hundred washings. Two mismatched barrettes held back her ragged hair, and a chalky rime glistened above her chapped lips. Contemplating her answer, she disappeared into blankness, and when she closed her eyes, small veins laced across the pale lids. Realizing the lateness of the hour, Margaret felt all at once her weary age, the heaviness in her arms and legs, the ache of her joints. A saturnine mood came over her. "Can you speak, child?"

"I was frozen," she answered in a phlegmy voice. "Cold as the point of an icicle." An old soul in a child's body, one of the preternaturally mature. In one swift swallow she finished her milk, and then she cleared her throat, the tones of her speech lightening an octave. "I hadn't had a thing to eat all night, so thank you, Mrs. Quinn."

Margaret wondered how she knew her name, and then reckoned that the child must have read it off the mailbox. The little girl yawned, revealing the jagged mouth of baby molars and holes, the serrated edges of her adult teeth piercing the gums at odd angles.

"You must be tired, my girl."

"Norah, with an A-H at the end. I feel like I haven't slept in a thousand years."

Both hands of the clock slipped off twelve. "There's an extra bed at the top of the stairs. But first thing we'll call your mother."

"I haven't any mother. Or father either. No one at all in this wide world. I am an orphan, Mrs. Quinn."

A sliver of sorrow cut through her heart. "I'm so sorry. How long have you been on your own?"

"Always. Since the beginning. I never knew my parents."

"And where have you come from? We should call the police to see if anyone is missing a child." She tried to remember the name of the detective—Willet was it?—who bothered her for months after Erica went missing. They never did find her daughter.

"I am not lost." The girl stared, unblinking.

The police are useless, she thought. "But how did you get here?"

"I have been looking for some place, and your light was on, and there is a welcome mat at your door. You were expecting someone."

"No one ever comes."

"I am here."

"That you are." On her fingertips, she calculated the years, thinking all the while of the possibilities. Her daughter had been gone for a decade, and the girl appeared to be just shy of nine. Old enough to be her own granddaughter, had such a child ever existed. Margaret led the girl upstairs to the empty room, which she rarely visited any longer, not more than once a month to run a duster over the wooden bureau, the desk, the bedframe. There had been many times when, suddenly tired of life, she sat on the edge of the mattress and felt unable to ever move from the spot. Sending Norah to wash her face and hands, Margaret stood before the closet, afraid of what might spring out, and reached in its dark recesses to pull out a trunk reeking of camphor. Under layers of too-large coats and a never-worn dress, she found a young girl's nightgown, creased and stiff. Norah wrapped herself inside the old clothes, crawled under the covers, and chirped her goodnight.

The question, dormant but habitual, arrived without thought. "Have you said your prayers?" She looked at the child's tiny head upon the pillow and saw in the faint light an unexpected answer to her own hopes. Switching off the lamp, she dared touch the child's soft hair, whispered "sweet dreams," and left the room to stand, breathless, outside the bedroom door. Listening from the hallway, unnerved by the presence of another, Margaret waited for the rhythmic breath of sleep, and nodding to the sound of the slumbering child, she padded back to her darkened bedroom.

2

The depth of darkness made the warning signs difficult to see. He was nearly upon the caution before he could read: Bridge Freezes Before Roadway, which made him laugh, for he had been cold a long time, and nothing would make him colder. Screwing his hat tighter against his scalp and gathering his scarf into the collar of his coat, the figure leaned into the breeze and strolled onto the bridge. The moisture wicked away from the chapped skin on his shaved jawline, and with every breath he drew, the air drove into the misery of his sinuses. The cold dried his eyes, and each time he blinked, he made warm tears which unsettled his ideas of order. No headlights approached; none had crossed his path that night. The bitterness of that late hour kept everyone indoors, nestled in their blankets and prayers to stay warm and safe. He stepped over the water and listened to the river, choked with broken ice, crawl and lap softly against the long steel shafts sunk into its bed. As he walked on, his heels echoed against the pavement, and when he paused, the world froze all over again.

Through the sad and fading town he moved in deliberate measure, past the shuttered windows and vacant storefronts. Down in the valley, the residual orange glow from one of the last mills huffed and dissipated like a lifting fog, as if hell itself were dying, going out of business. Once clear of the streetlights, the ambient light faded, and pinprick stars glowed through the crystal skies. In the corner of a constellation, an ember winked and traced a fleeting parabola. A cold night is best, he thought. Chances of encountering another soul grew more remote as the distance widened between the houses. He came across an old elementary school, a foursquare brick monument built during a more prosperous age, surrounded by a wrought-iron fence with a few teeth missing. Even through his gloves, the bars chilled his fingers. The vacant schoolyard echoed with laughter, and afterimages of playing children appeared like the ghosts of a half century ago. He drew in their memories, beholding nothing but these refugees of time.

Following his own sense of surety, he crossed through the woods and came to a small house whose yard lay protected by a split-rail fence. The darkened windows entrapped the sleepers and their dreams, Margaret and the foundling she had taken in. He circled round to the front and stood by the car parked in the drive to gaze at the porch and sheltering door. He knew the girl had finally found her.

Locked in place, he watched the old house while the air seeped into his marrow, as if he had been standing in the same frozen spot for days. Solitude had emptied him, and the quietus of three in the morning filled his mind with winter. Nothing more than the substance of prayer, the fear to complement hope, he tested the limits of his new form, shifting his weight from one leg to the other and cracking the stiffness in his muscles and bones to break the icehold. From next door, a tiny dog began yapping and bouncing to see through the window, its small head popping into view, steady as a metronome. He stared down the beast with one withering glance. To free his hands, he flexed his fingers in the leather gloves and touched the brim of his hat goodnight to mother and child asleep in the house. Before departing, he carved with his fingertip the name *Noriel* in the frost of the windshield, and breathing once upon the glass, he melted the word.

3

Paul had brought the baby at dawn, woke her with the fresh smell of talc and warm skin, the mewling bundle laid in the bed so close that Erica could tap her mother on the nose with a wild fist no bigger than a fig. Leaning over to kiss a bare sole that had escaped the blanket and then his wife's lined brow, he said goodbye before leaving for his job at the new clinic. The gesture reminded Margaret of the unexpected blessing of their daughter, granted well after all hope had been expended, and she knew that Paul, too, was surprised by joy and could not resist the cradle call. A gift each morning. Gathering warmth, she fell into a drowse, time escaping its hold, and saw her new baby, curious of all beyond her grasp. Lying in bed next to the infant, the new mother watched through the scant light her daughter's searching eyes, wide and bright as two moons, and the spastic flailing of kicks and stabs into the still air, as if Erica reached out to embrace the whole of life. A bright mystery and wonder in that gaze, creating the universe for herself by mouthfuls. That first year of her daughter's life, she worried that something terrible would happen to take away her baby. If Erica cried to excess, Margaret assumed the child was in mortal pain, and she could not be dissuaded by Paul's assurances about new teeth or a bout of indigestion. If the baby slept too long, Margaret would rush to the cradle to look for the beating pulse on the soft crown and the quick but steady rise and fall of the tiny chest. She fretted the child would die suddenly and forever, and only when she held Erica in her arms and felt the beating heart could Margaret truly rest. Beyond the two of them, the world itself was threat enough. *Sputnik* and the Hydrogen Bomb in the USSR. Charles Starkweather and Caril Ann Fugate on a killing spree in Nebraska and Wyoming. A school bus in Kentucky slid off a road and into a river, leaving twenty-seven dead. A fire at a Catholic school in Chicago took ninety students and three nuns.

Unrest in Cuba and Iraq, brickbats for Vice President Nixon in Caracas, bombs between the Chinese in Quemoy. She held her baby close while the television measured out the toll, wanting to protect her at all costs from evil and harm, accidental or intended.

As her daughter's infancy gave way to walking and talking, and the Fifties became the Sixties, she worried still that some illness or accident would interrupt the dream, and she kept a mother's watch on sharp corners, pennies on the floor, and the inviting holes of electric sockets. When she was three, Erica developed what Margaret feared were petechiae along the concave notch of her collarbone, a necklace of bloodpricks, and in her panic Margaret ran through all the thromboembolic dangers, only to be laughed at when her doctor husband diagnosed mild impetigo. When she was six, Erica jumped off a swing at school and lost her first baby teeth. At age seven, Erica fell off her bicycle and needed two stitches to close the wound in her chin. Paul patched her until she grew too old for his ministrations. But those few scares were the only bad things that had ever happened. Only the accretion of days and weeks and years eased Margaret's anxiety and threaded the beads of worry onto a stronger chain, and yet, no amount of love was store enough.

Awake that winter's morning, she decided that the child who had come as if summoned was a blank slate upon which, at this late hour of life, she might begin again. She longed to check on the sleeping girl but thought better of it. The house itself seemed to breathe the steady rhythms of slumber, coming to life once more at the hour of nine, which ordinarily settled into listlessness, lulled by the neighborhood emptying of children off to school and parents off to work.

She was used to moving numbly through the desolation of her life. Like the survivors of momentous devastation, she had patched her sorrow and moved on to some semblance of normalcy. And now the girl had come, and Margaret sensed the cracks in her will to abide nothing but the memory of her daughter. Everything, bad as it was, had been fine, bearable. But this morning, Norah had shattered the world.

4

On his way to open the Rosa Rossa Flower Shop, her neighbor Mr. Delarosa stopped by and banged on the front door, interrupting her reverie. After struggling down the stairs, Margaret stopped at the mirror by the front door to fuss with her hair and cluck at the puffiness around her eyes. Pasquale Delarosa was the last of the old-timers in the neighborhood who remembered her husband and daughter, and once Margaret was widowed, he had volunteered to handle the outside chores—shoveling the walk, pruning the boxwood, raking the leaves—in an act of charity and kindness that she repaid with cherry pies in the summer and rum-soaked fruitcake each Christmas. But he rarely visited otherwise, and his demeanor on the front porch suggested some embarrassment and trepidation for having gotten her out of bed.

"*Scusi*, Mrs. Quinn, so sorry to disturb you early in the morning, but I just wanted to check on you, see that everything is okay."

Gathering a fold of cloth to her neck, she motioned for him to come inside.

"No, no, I've got to open the shop. Two funerals this week. But there was a noise last night, late, and I thought I'll just go check on Mrs. Quinn, see she's okay."

The air chilled her bare ankles, and she gestured again to welcome him out of the cold.

"Round three this morning. My wife's dog was *pazza*, just bizarre, barking and chasing her tail, and you know she's old now and never gets up off of the bed, but something *boing* in her head set her off, and I say '*Fate silenzio!*' and threw a shoe, but yip-yap-yap, and my wife looks out the window, says there's someone in Mrs. Quinn's yard, like a monster, but I don't see nothing. But I get up this morning, she says go check on your way to work Mrs. Quinn, and I came over, look around, nothing. Not even a footprint in the snow. Only your car, eh? Frost everywhere, but a clear circle on the windshield, like someone threw a pot of boiling water, but probably nothing, eh? You're okay?"

"I didn't hear a thing all night, Mr. Delarosa, and I slept like a baby." She averted her gaze from his.

"You doing all right, then? I haven't seen you out on your walks so much."

"It's been so cold." Rubbing her arms, she pretended to shiver, and he took the hint, waving and saluting as he walked toward the street. Alone again, she smiled to herself and danced to the kitchen to ready a breakfast, dredging up from memory the distant recipe for pancakes. Halfway through stirring the batter, she realized there was no maple syrup in the house. Jam, perhaps, or powdered sugar. She wondered if the girl would mind.

UPSTAIRS, NORAH INSPECTED the bedroom. The missing daughter had left behind a bureau of autumn clothes, long-sleeved shirts, jeans, a rainbow of sweaters. Atop a small dish, six smooth pebbles collected from the beach. A pinback button with a dove perched on the neck of a guitar. Another that read *McGovern '72*. From an open pack of Teaberry gum, Norah unwrapped the last stick to find it shattered into terra-cotta shards. Taped on the wall above the bed were watercolor paintings—the woods on a snowy day, a bridge crossing over a roiling river, and a boy with long cascading hair who looked like a teenage Jesus. A crucifix hung above the light switch. On the child's desk lay a ten-year-old issue of *Time* with a picture of a stern Patty Hearst under the stark banner: APPREHENDED. A pad of blank white paper. Holding it aslant to the morning light, Norah detected the impression of the letters LV on its surface. The only other objects on the desk were four textbooks in brown grocery bag covers on which someone had doodled *Wiley* over and over, the name interlaced with flowers, hearts, a cobra of many heads. And more carefully drawn, the cryptic logo AOD over a pair of outstretched wings.

Inside the shallow drawer of the desk lay colored pencils pocked in the middle with toothmarks. A bundle of artist's brushes in different sizes, the camel's hair tips hardened into spearpoints. Norah pressed the end of one on the surface of the desk until the tip collapsed, the old paint puffing a cloud of amber dust. Hidden beneath a tangle of rubber bands and paper clips, a pack of cigarettes and a crisp book of matches. She took one of the smokes and put it in her pocket. The side drawers contained an archive of school papers, drawings preserved from all ages, notes, letters, a stray family photograph. She stared at one image of the three of them together beneath an artificial silver Christmas tree: the girl seated in a caneback rocking chair, her mother and father resting a hand each along the top rail, the image torn in two at the father and then taped together again. Buried deep in the jumble was a tablet filled with sketches—faces juxtaposed over desert roads, a girl in a pinafore floating over the horizon, a boy confronting a leopard from his quilted bed. She hid the portfolio under her mattress, saving it for closer study.

The aroma of pancakes rose from downstairs, and an unfamiliar grumble sounded in her stomach. She imagined, below in the kitchen, the woman stirring the batter, setting the table, preparing herself. The time was right for her entrance. Standing on her toes, Norah could just reach the bottom of the mirror by the door. She wet her fingertips in her mouth and combed her tangled hair, straightened her glasses, and practiced smiling. The light was perfect now. She would descend.

As she turned to call for the girl, Margaret was surprised to see Norah already on the threshold, dressed in her runaway daughter's tartan nightgown. In the morning light, they lost their place in time, for just a moment.

"So," Norah said, "you'll let me stay?"

5

Sean Fallon waited until nearly all of the other children left Friendship Elementary School, some running in knots for the best seats on the buses, others clumping in pairs and trios to walk. Standing in an alcove, nearly hidden under his parka and scarf, he watched the tough older boys saunter around the corners and disappear. Once safe to move, he pulled up his hood like a spy, hunched his shoulders to settle the weight in his backpack, and commenced the long walk home. Teachers hurrying to their cars paid him little heed. Even the principal nearly ran him over. An elderly man tipped his old-fashioned hat as they passed on the sidewalk, leaving behind an icy wake that made the boy's nose run and snot freeze above his upper lip. The wind blew against his face and through his hair, for the stranger carried winter in his coattails. New snow covered the ragged patches on the ground, softened the dense plowlines at the curbs and corners and the old trails carved along the sidewalks. Sean stopped now and again to trace his name on the powdered hoods of neglected cars, to run his gloves along an iron fence, to gently push the toe or heel of a boot to crack the glassy ice collected in miniature culverts and depressions. There was no need to hurry. His mother would not return from work for a few hours longer, and his father never came home.

Since the beginning of the fall semester, Sean had taken to meandering after school, unwilling to face his empty house after his parents' divorce. The desire for the comforts of nothing had become a habit of mind, and over the months, he cultivated his solitude. Alongside the woods, he allowed a measure of free imagination, enjoying the small discoveries of the natural world. Head bent to the ground as he walked, he had found the body of a flicker, the bright yellow wings neatly folded against the mottled gray torso and the band of red feathers. The shinbone of a fox or small dog swarming with red ants. And treasures he could keep: the perfect spiral of a giant snail's shell, a dozen rocks that glistened with quartz facets. A glass bottle with the year 1903 embossed on its amber bottom, a baseball card of Roberto Clemente, hero of the 1971 Series, a five-dollar bill and eighty-nine cents in loose change. A hand-size Bible caked with dried mud. Eyes raised to the skies and worries sloughed from his soul, he watched the changes of season, the air filled with leaves and birds and clouds. Many autumn afternoons he had witnessed the old lady who lived by herself, walking alone as well, looking for something misplaced.

The way home required him to either scale or duck beneath a rail fence at one end of the old lady's yard, put his head down as he traversed the open lawn, hop another fence at the property line, and trot straight to the fronting street. He did not like the risk, but the shortcut meant a mile saved, and using it had become a matter of principle. Each time he crossed the boundary, he recited, "Forgive us our trespasses, as we forgive those who trespass against us," not entirely sure what the words meant, which only reinforced their magic. From behind closed curtains, she spied, he was sure, waiting for the time when he might trip and fall, and she would come flying on a broomstick straight out the chimney top. Sean glanced at the kitchen window, bowed his head again, and then picked up the pace. Under his breath, he muttered another penitential prayer.

As he straddled the rail at the top of the second fence, Sean spotted the old woman and the little witch in glasses beside her. Hidden by the shadows, they lurked at the corner of the house. The lady stood stiffly wrapped in her greatcoat, a thick scarf wound around her throat, hair white as the moon, her face broken into angles dominated by a beaked nose. She watched his every move through merciless eyes. The ragged girl bounced on her toes, and when she saw his disadvantage she rushed forward.

"You're not supposed to cut through people's property." She wagged her finger in his direction, then waited, hands on hips, for him to untangle his feet. Half of her face was in darkness and half blazed in the sun, her features coming slowly into focus. Unsure of the rules of the game, Sean did not know whether to climb down to meet her or to retreat in haste across his footprints or to wait eternally upon the rail. A mourning dove, startled by the girl's voice, whistled and flushed from a sugar maple, crying as it rowed across the pale sky. He swung his leg over and crept down rail by rail as Mrs. Quinn stepped forward to confront him.

"You realize this is my yard?"

Stunned to be approached, he nodded. *She would lure him with warm gingerbread and then pop him in the oven.*

"What is your name, young man?"

"Sean Fallon, ma'am."

"How old are you, Sean? What grade are you in at school?"

"I go to third grade, and I'm eight and a half."

Norah sidled up to him, inspecting his face. "Ah, really? And when is your birthday?"

"August twenty-third."

"You're not eight and a half. It's only January. You're just eight and a quarter."

The boy blinked in the sunshine. *Or fatten him on bread and milk in a cage that hung from the ceiling.*

Mrs. Quinn stepped between the children. "I see you cutting through here every day. Sometimes twice a day—once in the morning, once in the afternoon. On your way to and from school?"

He looked at the snow between his boots. *And grind his bones to make her bread.*

"You'll take her with you from now on. And walk her home. She's in third grade just like you. Show up a few minutes early tomorrow, and take her to the principal's office. They can send me the paperwork to enroll her. Do you understand me, Sean Fallon?" With two fingers, she lifted his chin so that he could see her smile. Sean assented with a simple nod, and the two started to go back inside. Halfway there, she turned to the boy. "By the way, my name is—"

"Mrs. Quinn," he said. "Everyone knows who you are. Everyone knows who lives in this house."

Margaret pulled the girl to stand in front of her so that he might memorize her face. "And this is Norah." The girl squirmed beneath her hands and stuck out the tip of her tongue at him. "Norah Quinn, my granddaughter."

6

Piece by piece, they unpacked the few clothes from Norah's valise. As Mrs. Quinn inspected each article against the light, the girl described its history and her sentimental attachments, and then it would be folded into one of two piles: those that could be washed and mended to wear again, and the clothing that must be discarded—thrown away, or better yet, taken out back and incinerated in the wire-mesh barrel. Occasionally, she let the girl plead and triumph. A doll's execution was commuted. A white sweater with browned stains at the wrists was spared. Socks fit to be darned. But mostly, the orphan's stale things were simply too wretched.

"How can you live like this?" Mrs. Quinn asked, holding up a dull gray pair of underwear peppered with holes.

Norah twirled once and flopped upon the bed. "I have been lucky. I've been blessed."

"Let's find you something proper." She went to the closet and tugged out the cedar chest, which had been gathering dust for the better part of a decade. "These are old. You don't mind old, do you? From when she was your age, twenty years ago. If Erica's things won't do, I'll go shopping while you're in school tomorrow."

"Do I have to go to school? I'd rather stay here with you and help around the house."

"No, you have to stick to the plan. If anyone found you hanging around here, they'd wonder why you weren't in school."

"So why don't you take me?"

"I need to be invisible, at least for a while. Too many prying questions. The less they think about me, the better. If you're going to stay in my house, you must follow my rules. Tell them that I am a shut-in and cannot come into the school. Too many memories." Margaret opened the hasp and eased the lid on its hinges, then knelt before an open casket.

"Well, I don't need no Sean Fallon—"

"Hush." From the top of the treasures, she lifted out a prom gown and laid it gently on the bed. Thrilled by the taffeta, Norah leapt to the floor and peered over to see the inside of the trunk, balancing her small hand upon the woman's back. In the seven years since Paul had died, no one had touched Margaret so. Together they agreed upon a white blouse, a woolen skirt, a pair of Mary Janes, leather stiff. Near the bottom of the trunk, a thick embroidered poncho was draped atop the christening gown, pastel sleepers, and other relics of infancy. Mrs. Quinn ran her hands over the designs and smiled to herself, having nearly forgotten this prize. She displayed the patterns to the girl: two llamas stood on the hem, and behind them loomed the appliquéd Andes.

"My little sister brought that back from Peru one Christmas, and Erica wore it every winter's day when she was your age. You'd like Diane— she is as cunning as a crow, like you."

"It's beautiful," said the girl. Margaret flipped it over so the girl could see on the other side a stylized round red face surrounded by swirling wings or clouds. Norah's eyes widened. "Look, a seraph."

"Whatever are you talking about? It is the sun, smiling on us all."

"No, a seraph. You know, seraphim and cherubim."

"Stop talking nonsense." She gathered a pile of clothes in her arms. "Big day tomorrow, so time for bed."

The girl finally fell asleep, and Margaret ran the washer and dryer late into the night and folded the fresh laundry while the eleven o'clock news unspooled. Her muscles stiffened and she felt short of breath but managed to bundle all of Norah's clothes into a neat package, impossibly small, like a doll's outfits, the edges and hems frayed with wear and soft with age. She smoothed the pile and laid the girl's things against the bedroom door, as her mother had long ago when Margaret and Diane were children. Two stacks for two girls, but she inevitably mixed the sisters' clothes, and they would unjumble the socks and underwear while complaining to each other how poorly their mother knew her own daughters. Or else they'd steal one another's favorites without a word.

Diane would never understand why she had decided to keep the little visitor. Margaret barely knew her own reasons, responding more to the powerful pull the child exerted, as if she had been in her life all along. No one had come to the door despite ten years of prayer and pleading, and she would not refuse an answer, would not turn away the child. If it meant a few lies, she thought, so be it, though her sister would be shocked at the depths of her deception. From the hallway, ear tuned to closed door, she listened to Norah's steady breathing. She could still feel the warm impression on her back where the girl had touched her.

7

Winter mornings Paul would send her to school, bundled against the cold, and from their bedroom window, Margaret watched their daughter fling back the hood, unzip the overcoat, and rush to join her friends, her bundle of books hanging by a single strap. Erica had a life apart, outside the confines of their home, but her father never noticed until too late, when he was no longer her guide and protector. At age ten, she sassed him at the dinner table, a joke at first tinged with sarcasm, but soon enough she would roll her eyes at his faint attempts at endearment, his increasingly desperate maneuvers to win her back. The onset of puberty widened the gulf. She was running away, and he did not know how to bridge the distance between his adoring little girl and sullen adolescence.

From her vantage point behind the kitchen window, Margaret watched the children in the yard. She scanned the treetops in the backyard, remembering a kite Paul and Erica lost years ago, wondering if some tattered cloth still clung to bare branches. Perched high in a massive oak, a falcon screamed at first light, startled by the stranger blazing through the empty forest. The figure huddled deeper into his coat, tried to hide his identity.

The children raised their eyes, searching for the source of the piercing cry, and Norah pointed for Sean to follow the straight line from her mitten to the bird. A pair of crows, alarmed by the peregrine, gave chase, cawing raucously, harassing it until all three birds vanished over the scattering of trees.

Margaret calculated the distance and found the falcon in the sky, all the while rewriting in her mind the carefully crafted note requesting her granddaughter's admission into the third grade of the elementary school. In a panic, she had created a story about a broken family, the girl's mother with nowhere to turn, asking could they please send the proper forms home with the child, who was called Norah. Through three separate drafts, she attempted to affect an air of resigned acceptance at having to care for the poor child, and the final sentence was her coup de grâce: "We all have our crosses to bear." Over breakfast, Mrs. Quinn rehearsed the lie, counting on Norah to memorize the details and vouch for their authenticity. She folded the letter into the threadbare jacket pocket and stood by the door until Sean Fallon arrived as promised, and then watched them walk off together, the boy's furious pace making it difficult for Norah to keep up. The curtains at the Delarosas' kitchen window snapped shut, and Margaret knew her neighbor had seen the boy and girl depart. She would have to invent a story for the inevitable questions to come. Silence, old foe, returned to the house.

Coffee at hand, staring at the cereal bowl and empty juice glass across from her place, she wondered how she had let things get this far out of order. The girl had spent just two nights in her house, but already Margaret was willing to protect her with the most stunning untruth. As if she really were her daughter's daughter, whom she had already loved all of her life.

Had this been true, she would have walked with the child to school and proudly made the introductions. Walking had been her habit and comfort, even in the coldest part of the year, and ever since her daughter vanished, Margaret hiked everywhere, every day, along the country roads on the outskirts and, as her infamy faded, chancing to go as far as the cluster of shops and office buildings and brownstones down by the bridge that constituted the town proper. Those who knew her story claimed Margaret searched for some clue on these journeys, eyes focused on the ground or the detritus along the paths, seeking out a reason.

Over the course of the first few years following the disappearance, her husband had walked with her. They chose routes to quiet places with scant chance of encountering friend or stranger. Tramping through time, they followed deer trails or hiked along the bicycle path the town had carved beside a creek, rarely used by any cyclist. One hot summer evening, Paul calculated that they had circumnavigated the globe simply by following the same steps over and over again. Partners in loss.

Erica had come late in their marriage, an unexpected blessing after years of prayer for a baby, visits to fertility specialists, the most exotic techniques, and, finally, giving up entirely. Margaret had just turned thirty-seven when their only child was born, and Paul was a dozen years her senior, old enough to be his daughter's grandfather. He spoiled the girl despite Margaret's warnings, and when she left them, Erica broke his heart and felled him—not all at once, but slowly and surely as ivy chokes a tree. Four years later, he was gone too. A final exit. After she buried him behind St. Anne's Church, Margaret resumed her journey, walking the hills surrounding the valley to be alone, invisible, listening only to the wind or the arrival of the songbirds each March and their leave-taking each September.

Now age and the winter had enclosed her. The first deep aches infected her the past November, and by Christmas she could not bear stepping outside when the thermometer dipped below freezing. Strange pains afflicted her. Potted palms replaced her legs. Her fingertips tingled and then went dull. An elbow stiffened and would not bend. Bird-fragile, her bones seemed empty of marrow. A high wind would blow her to Kansas. Worst of all, a relentless fatigue settled in and refused all remedies of sleep or rest. She was a clock unwound and losing time. When the girl arrived, Margaret's first impulse was to find out the truth, send the child back to where she belonged, wherever that might be, but perhaps this was God's way, she thought, of answering her constant prayer. Some company, some restitution for all that had been taken from her.

All that must be done was to fool everyone—her neighbors, the school, and her sister, Diane, the only other family she had left. An eyelash circled in her coffee cup. She rubbed her palms over the tablecloth, straightening wrinkles visible only to the touch. "It is too hot in here," she said, though no one else was there. Opening a window, she heard crying in the air, the lonesome sound of one who should not have wintered over, but she could not find the peregrine all morning long. Nothing in the sky but blue brightness.

8

The interview with the principal took place in his cramped and humid office, the heart of the old Craftsman-style building tottering toward extinction. Atop the filing cabinets, a fern hung limply, fronds crisping to brown. Spangled on the walls, a gallery of photographs and banners marked the passage of his time at Friendship Elementary—the oldest sign, from 1970, welcomed him "on board." Despite the constant blowing heat from the furnace, he seemed frigid beneath his baby blue sweater, out of which peeped a yellow striped shirt and a navy tie with a pattern of repeating anchors. Principal Taylor read part of Mrs. Quinn's letter, glanced up at the girl across from him, who smiled every time their eyes met, and then searched for his place in the text. At last he reached the ending, his lips twisted into befuddlement as he muttered the phrase "crosses to bear." Norah hooked her wilting hair behind her ears and lifted an eyebrow when he turned his attention to her.

"Very curious."

"About what part?"

"About the whole thing. Your notorious mother. Your grandmother, Mrs. Quinn. Why didn't she just bring you in herself today?"

Prepared for the question, she told her first lie. "She is something of an invalid."

"An invalid? How can someone be somewhat an invalid? Do you even know the meaning of the word 'invalid'?"

Norah lowered her voice, spoke slowly. "Agoraphobia, I'm afraid." Seeing that her meaning was lost on the man, she restated. "A fear of the out of doors. Doesn't leave the house if she can help it."

"I know perfectly well, young lady, what agro—"

"She can't quite shake it. I'm a godsend, really. You can't imagine the strain of the simplest things. Groceries, taking out the trash, fetching the mail."

"And you are her granddaughter. What about your parents?"

"It says right there in the letter, Mr. Taylor. Are you going to make me say it out loud?"

"Yes, but—"

"Neither one of them really wants me, simple as that, I'm sorry to report." She looked directly at his eyes.

He dug into his desk for the proper forms, flipping through a multicolored stack of papers. "I suppose we can accommodate you, Miss . . ."

"Quinn." She leaned forward and laid her fingertips along the edge of his desk. Her nails were bitten to the quick.

"Right. Have your grandmother fill these out and sign them, and once your grades are transferred, you'll be official."

Norah sighed and bowed her head. "I've never been to another school before. Have you ever heard of John Holt and *Teach Your Own*? Homeschooling?"

Mr. Taylor looked up from the folder he had been inspecting. "You mean, your mother never sent you to school? Did she teach you at home enough so that you're even ready?"

He studied her eager, expectant face and then bent to his papers, brushing her away with a hastily scribbled note to the teacher. She could be the third grade's problem that day. In the margins, he jotted a reminder to call Mrs. Quinn, and then he added the letter to his overflowing in-box.

Norah flew down the hallway to her classroom, coat trailing like a windblown sheet, her sole-thin shoes squealing on the linoleum with every triumphant step. Catching her breath outside Room 9, Norah peered through the rectangular aperture cut into the door, as narrow as a window in a castle wall. Sean Fallon sat in the second row, fourth seat, and the nearest empty desk was in the third row, fifth seat, close enough for direct observation of him, far enough for her to go undetected. None of the other children spotted her face framed in the casement, for, scrupulous at their cursive penmanship, they watched their hands roll right-leaning spirals favored by practitioners of the Palmer method. Eight boys and twelve girls, and if no child was absent or out at the restroom, she would be number twenty-one, not as good as a prime, but a multiple of three and seven, two lucky numbers indeed. With these auguries in mind, she opened the door and marched directly to the teacher, presented her with the note from the principal, and stood like a willow hanging over her shoulder to read along silently. All of the children had stopped in their strokes. The teacher corrected her posture and stuck out her hand. "How do you do, Norah Quinn," she stage-whispered. "I'm Mrs. Patterson."

"Pleased to meet you," Norah whispered back, and shook her hand, pumping her wiry arm like a piston.

Mrs. Patterson unclenched and stood beside the girl, facing the twenty curious pairs of eyes peering out as if hidden inside twenty firkins. "Class, this is Norah Quinn, and she will be joining us, starting today. Why don't you tell us a little bit about yourself, Norah?"

Curious and ready to judge, the children straightened in their chairs, awaiting word from the new creature flung into their midst.

"I am almost nine. I like birds—anything that flies really—and leopards. I don't like Brussels sprouts. The last time someone gave me Brussels sprouts, I dumped them behind the radiator when nobody was looking."

The boys and girls laughed, but Mrs. Patterson's withering glare reproached them at once. "Where are you from, Norah?"

"Oh, I've lived all over, here and there. Right now, I live with Mrs. Quinn. My grandmother."

The second outburst of gasps and giggles could not be suppressed by a mere stare. Mrs. Patterson rapped her knuckles upon the desktop. "Class, plenty of children live with their grandparents, so I don't think that's any excuse—"

Two boys in the back pointed at Norah's old shoes and enjoyed a conspiratorial laugh. Sensing her control of the entire day ebbing, the teacher cut short the introduction. "All right, class, back to your circles. Norah, there's a nice seat over there by the window."

"If it's all the same to you, Mrs. Patterson, I would prefer that one in the back."

"Sit where you please, child. I expect the rest of you to introduce yourselves to Norah during recess, and I'm sure you'll all become fast friends. We won't be going outside today, as it is entirely too cold."

On her way to the fifth seat of the third row, she stopped to wink at Sean Fallon, and turning to the girl across from him, she asked, "Do you have an extra pen and paper, Sharon?" Without thinking, the girl held down her papers and opened the lid to her desk, and only when she had handed over the pen did she wonder how the stranger knew her name.

"I can read upside down," Norah said, and put her finger on the *Sharon* in the upper right corner of the page.

The morning passed quietly until the bell signaled lunch. Mrs. Quinn had neglected to pack a meal, so Sean Fallon gave Norah half of his sandwich, apple butter on white bread. Counting out her pretzel sticks, Sharon Hopper divided and handed over half. Gail Watts offered her a small carton of milk that she bought at her mother's insistence and threw away unopened every day. Mark Bellagio presented the greater part of a tangerine. Dori Tilghman, a shortbread cookie in the shape of a keystone. "They're called Pennsylvanians," she informed Norah, as if speaking to a student from some foreign land.

In the elementary school hierarchy, their table was far from the circle of popularity, though they were not the shunned freaks, merely the forgotten and the overlooked. The cafeteria hummed with the fall and rise of one hundred voices. Laughter rolled and slipped away. A shout rang out from a far corner, prelude to a chase around a table. Chair legs yelped across the linoleum, and a red-haired boy carried his tray to the trashcan, pulled out a paperback novel from his pocket, and leaned against the wall to read. At another table, a middle-aged lothario in a brown corduroy sports coat begged for potato chips from a gaggle of admiring girls. In a third direction, Norah spotted twin sisters licking pudding from plastic spoons, perfect mirrors of one another. All around her, the third graders traded stories about their friends and classmates, but she could not follow the gist of their gossip.

When the feast was over, Norah slapped her hands on the tabletop and thanked her tablemates for their generosity. Tearing a section from a brown paper bag, she folded the square into an intricate pattern, and taking care to tuck corners into fabricated openings, she blew into a tiny hole. Like an inflated balloon, the paper expanded into a hollow cube, which she served into the air with a pat of her palm. Sean watched the progress of the creation, hypnotized by the play of the trick. The children took turns batting it across the table like a volleyball, and when the cube came back round to Norah, she captured it in flight, brought it to her lips, leaned back her head, and with a steady puff of breath, kept blowing, spinning the box on one corner like a dreidel, until Mr. Taylor came along to snatch it midair and confiscate their fun. The children all cheered for her when, the moment his back was turned, she stuck out her tongue like a battle flag.

9

While the foundling was off in school, Mrs. Quinn wandered among the carousels of clothing in the girls' department at G. C. Murphy's. Winter coats had already been marked down after the holidays, even though the brunt of the season remained in prospect, and she chose a gray parka with faux rabbit fur trim for Norah. After selecting the coat, she was at a loss for what else to buy her, and wistfully fingered the corduroy jumpers and flannel nightgowns, remembering. Two decades had passed since she had brought Erica to Murphy's; 1965, simpler then, clothes, girls, everything. Her daughter's shade trailed her along the aisles—how she had loved shopping in those days. Taking her mother's hand, Erica had danced from display to display, coveting every bright color and wild design.

Lost in the past, Margaret did not notice the man in the camel hair coat who followed her around the store, stopping a few racks away when she paused to guess at sizes. He switched his fedora from hand to hand, anxious to be under the brim again. Whenever she looked in his direction, he stiffened like a mannequin and remained motionless until some other bright thing caught her eye. Conspicuous by his mere presence, he became inconspicuous by dint of will. He merged into the general background and disappeared in the thickets of hanging clothes.

The few other shoppers were women like herself. Widows, perhaps, but grandmothers surely, out hunting for birthday gifts or bargains to store away for next winter. They shuffled in a daze from bin to bin, and Margaret read in every face some suffering or disappointment, their hopes and dreams marked down, 40 percent off. She wondered if others saw the shame written in her eyes and scratched across her brow. The others, if they noticed her at all, must have recognized her as that woman whose daughter had run away from home, gotten into trouble, and never returned. Photographs of Erica had been in the papers and on television when the story broke, and even Margaret and Paul had once been on the front page of the local newspaper. If the women didn't remember the exact circumstances, they knew instinctively that she shared their heartbreak over irredeemable losses. But the little girl was her secret, and she clung to it with all the ferocity of untrammeled happiness. Margaret gathered in the parka, quickly chose a watch cap, scarf, and mittens in complementary red, and paid her way out of the store. She thought of crossing over to the Rosa Rossa Flower Shop to see her neighbor, but decided she did not feel like talking to anyone after all.

To get to her car on Robinson Street, she had to pass the diner where she and Erica had often stopped for an ice cream or to split a slice of chocolate cake. The air bit at her cheeks, and she felt hopelessly tired again. No harm, she thought, to step inside for a cup of coffee and warm up before heading home. At eleven o'clock, the place was nearly empty, so she picked a booth out of the draft. The decor had not changed from the 1970s, the same cracked vinyl flooring, burgundy booths, chrome fading to the sheen of silvered mirror, and the laminated menus offered the same choices—only the prices differed from her last visit. A waitress arrived as Margaret read from the selections, trying to decide if a piece of pie would upset her stomach. She could sense the young woman's presence, a dark mustard-colored uniform, glass of water set down with a thunk, silverware wrapped in a paper napkin dropped unceremoniously on the placemat. Margaret looked up just far enough to see the name tag: Joyce.

"What can I getcha, hon?"

Bring me my daughter at nine years old.

"Just coffee," Margaret said. "And—oh, I don't know—what pie is good today?"

"We have apple, blueberry, cherry, sour cherry, peach, pumpkin, lemon meringue, banana cream, coconut cream, though that's been here over two days. Nobody gets the coconut. None of the fruit is fresh this time of year, but the apples in the apple pie are real."

Echoing across the years, the girl's voice finally registered in her memory. Margaret had known her once upon a time, and instantly she averted her eyes, studied her fingernails. "Sour cherry, thank you. A small slice."

She watched the waitress walk toward the kitchen, just as she stared at all young women, trying to discern some sign of her own daughter in their faces and figures, a clue as to what Erica might look like now, how she might act, what she might feel or think. Trying to draw the particulars of Erica's life from the surface of others', she could not help but study them, their feathery haircuts, the fading fad for polyester disco clothing, the way they made older folks invisible. Young women had changed since the time she had been one of their tribe. More comfortable in their sexuality, hiding almost nothing, no garters, no wires or girdles, just open and brazen. The girl returned with a smile and set down the mug, milk and sugar, a forlorn slice of pie, the syrupy filling bright as blood.

"Excuse me," the girl said, "but don't I know you? Aren't you Erica's mother?"

Mrs. Quinn assented by her silence. The high school girl had aged a decade, but of course she remembered her well. All of her friends had disappeared too, when Erica ran away. They stopped coming around the house, so their faces were locked in time as teenagers, but she could still see the giggly teen in the careworn features.

"I thought it was you. I'm Joyce. Joyce Waverly, but you might remember me as a Green, my maiden name." She held out a chapped red hand to show off the wedding band and matching engagement ring. "I went to high school with Erica."

"Joyce Green." She remembered.

"So good to see you. Mind if I take a load off?" She pushed aside the department store bags and scooted into the booth across from Margaret.

"I'm married now," she said. "Seven years. One boy, and one on the way. His name is Jason, my son that is. I don't know what we'll call this one, maybe Mack Truck, 'cause I never even saw him coming till he knocked me flat. How are you, Mrs. Quinn? How's Erica? Haven't heard from her in ages. She still out west? Arizona or New Mexico, was it? I can't imagine living in a foreign country like that."

"She's still there," Margaret lied. She had no idea where her daughter was at that moment. "Doing well."

Her daughter's friend leaned across the table and whispered. "Did she ever get out of trouble? Is she married? Any kids?"

Mrs. Quinn sipped at her coffee. "Just the one. A girl. In fact, she's come to stay with me for a while." She nodded at the shopping bags. "I was just after going to the store to buy the poor thing some decent winter clothes—"

"I love little girls' things way better than boys'." Joyce Waverly had already begun pulling out the items. She held up the gray parka and brushed the fake rabbit fur against her cheek. "They don't have much call for coats and mittens down in the desert, you know."

"They're for my granddaughter," Margaret said proudly. "Norah. Norah Quinn."

THE STRANGER AT the booth nearest the door sat patiently until the waitress spotted him and wended her way. "Do you mind if I ask who was that woman? The one who just left? The one you sat next to and chatted with?"

"Mrs. Quinn?" Joyce lowered her pencil and pad. The man at the table looked kind and respectable, a bit like her grandfather.

"I thought so," he said. "It's been years since I've seen her."

"I was surprised to see her myself. We go way back, her and me. I was friends with her daughter Erica, and ever since that whole incident, she's been something of a hermit."

He fingered the brim of his hat resting near the sugar dispenser. "Ever since the incident."

"You remember," she said. "They thought that boy Wiley kidnapped her, but I say they ran off together. Everyone at school knew they were an item."

"Right, the incident."

The icy blueness of his eyes transfixed her, and she imagined how handsome he must have been as a young man. He kept his gaze fixed on her, and in her womb, the fetus kicked and fluttered. The man lifted his hand and held his palm over the hump of her abdomen. "May I?" he asked, and when she nodded, he laid his hand on the spot where the baby stirred, and Joyce shuddered with pleasure as the warmth radiated across her skin, a penetrating heat that spread into her body. The unborn child stilled as if he had soothed it to sleep. Withdrawing his hand, he leaned back into the booth. "So my old friend, Mrs. Quinn, was on a shopping spree?"

Flustered, Joyce kept on talking. "For her granddaughter, come to live with her for a while."

"Granddaughter? There can be no child."

"Oh, sure there is," Joyce said. "She showed me a new hat and coat. For Norah."

He chuckled to himself. "What a pretty name."

The baby kicked again at the sound of his voice, and wicked desire filled Joyce with a guilty pleasure. She twisted her wedding ring and looked hopelessly at the front door, wondering if anyone would come in.

During long division, as Mrs. Patterson worked on remainders at the chalkboard, Sean kept spinning around in his desk chair to make sure Norah stayed awake. Even when he was called to the front to demonstrate how to divide 400 by 6, he checked on the progress of her fatigue. Stultifying wet heat off the radiators made her drowsy, and she struggled to hold up her head in the cup of one hand. Her eyelids quivered, then closed in slow motion. Her head slipped from her palm, and then she recovered once before she could not fight off sleep any longer. With every inspiration, her nose whistled, and she began a purring snore, oblivious to the mathematics unfolding all around her. By tacit arrangement, everyone let her rest until art class began. Sean woke her with a whisper and a pad and colored pencils in hand, and she begged him to sit beside her at a table beneath the panoramic window.

She drew with a quick and certain hand, sketching out in a few deft strokes a tensed leopard, flash of tawny spotted coat, and teeth and claws as angry slashes. Cowering in the corner of the page, the gazelle caught in the split second of fear, legs bent, neck torqued as its head made a quarter turn too late toward the predator. Sean watched as she drew, tightened his body like the muscles in the gazelle's flanks. He smelled blood and fear. Lost in her drawing, Norah moved the colored pencils with grave concentration. Work complete, she set the paper aside, took another sheet, ripped it in half, and began folding precise creases.

Mrs. Patterson, making the rounds among the schoolchildren, paused to offer encouragement or advice to each child. When she reached the window and saw what Norah was doing, she broke from the regimen and strode to her, stopping close enough to cast a shadow over the table's pen-pocked surface, transfixed by the drawing of the attacking leopard and the delicate manipulations at hand. When she finished folding, Norah laid an origami crane beside her picture and immediately began work on another. Without a word, Mrs. Patterson slid the drawing into her hands, held it up in disbelief, and walked back to her chair at the front of the room. She considered the craftsmanship of the piece, still staring at its realism, and asked in a loud voice, "Where did you learn to draw like this?"

Norah did not look up from her origami. "I could always draw," she said, bending over another wing.

The whole class now focused on her paper folding as she built a third bird. When finished, she lined them up across the front edge of her desk, stood, and bent so that her face was inches away from them. She drew a deep breath and blew. The paper birds seemed to float in midair, falling up before fluttering to the ground. Each one landed perfectly on its base before toppling under the weight of wings. Sharon clapped first, then Dori and Gail from the other side of the room, and all at once, the entire class was on its feet, cheering and stomping with sheer delight. Norah stared straight ahead at Mrs. Patterson, challenging her to believe, waiting for the teacher to smile before she returned a broken beam of her own.

Norah watched Sean as he had watched her, and every time he noticed her looking his way, he flinched and reddened. The lonesome, like the mad, know one another on sight. She recognized his broken heart before she knew its cause, and he knew that she knew. Later that afternoon, she sidled up to him to walk her home. As they waited outside the door after the dismissal bell had chimed, Sean asked, "How did you do that trick with the paper birds?"

"Origami. And not a trick," she said. "What are we waiting for? It's freezing out here."

"I just like to let the big kids go first."

"Stick with me. They won't bother you." She grabbed his hand and pulled, running and laughing as they parted clots of children, and once they were through the crowd, the ice-cold air took their breath away.

Someone slammed hard against the chain-link fence, sending a tremor along its breadth, but no person could be found. They passed through cliques of students walking home along the quiet sidewalks and into the emptiness of three o'clock. A dog barked, invisible behind a tall wooden gate, and Norah shushed it with one curt hush. The distance between houses widened as the school grounds receded, and to get home, they took a shortcut through the woods, a bike path that ran alongside a drainage ditch, not more than a hundred yards long. Hidden by the bare forest of January, travelers were invisible from the streets and prying eyes. Usually Sean lollygagged at spots along the trail, peering over the edge into the frozen creek, dropping stones to shatter the ice along the banks, listening to the trees complain in the shifting wind. When they were alone, Norah stopped suddenly, looked up and down the path, and then produced a single cigarette from her pocket, holding it before him like a sacred artifact. She peeled off her mitten and took out a book of ancient matches.

"You're not going to smoke that!" Sean's eyes widened. "Smoking stunts your growth, that's what my mum says. You don't want to get stunted, do you?"

The flame flared blue from the sulfur, and the cigarette already hung from her lower lip. "I used to smoke a pack a day," she muttered, lighting up. Norah snapped out the match and threw it on the path. "Just kidding. I only want to show you this—" Forming an O with her lips, Norah exhaled a ring of smoke that widened like a ripple in a pond, and she blew another ring which passed through the first hoop, and then quickly, she exhaled a long trail of smoke that shot through both rings like an arrow piercing a heart.

Glee in his high voice, he asked, "Where did you learn to do that?"

With the toe of one shoe, she stubbed out the cigarette and then looked past him to the high thin clouds stretched across the winter sky. "I know lots of things," she said, and catching the interest in his eyes, she shrieked and tore off through the woods, her shoes skating across the snow and bare earth, and he did not catch up to her until they reached the back fence of Mrs. Quinn's yard. At a blind corner, they nearly crashed, and as he caught himself short by grabbing her shoulders, Norah screamed at the touch and laughed and screamed again, and he could see stars glistening at the back of her throat.

11

Having managed the most difficult part of their ruse, the beginning, Margaret and Norah looked forward to their first weekend together as a chance to slow the pace and get to know each other better. Come Saturday, the girl pushed open the woman's bedroom door with breakfast, burnt toast and strong coffee, and she sat at the foot of the bed while Margaret crunched and sipped, feigned delight on her pursed lips, and then Norah took the tray and washed the dishes while Margaret bathed and readied herself for the day. Conversation, which had been missing for years, filled the house, questions about school and friends, how nice that Fallon boy turned out to be after all.

Heavy footsteps on the porch, stomping snow from boot treads, announced the presence of the visitors before the first sharp knock. Norah surprised the couple standing outside the door as they unwrapped their coats and gloves. The man, a woolen skullcap over his bald head, seemed embarrassed to be discovered, but the woman craned her neck forward to take a closer look at the girl. "I'm Mrs. Delarosa," she said. "We're your neighbors. This is my husband, Pasquale."

"Hello, miss," he said, offering his hand. "Everybody calls me Pat. What's your name?"

Simonetta tapped him on the elbow for silence. "Is Mrs. Quinn at home?"

"Gramma!" Norah yelled toward the kitchen. "It's the next-doors come to call."

She waited a beat, and when Margaret did not arrive at once, Norah sped back and found her, flustered and uncertain, struggling from the easy chair. "Follow my lead," she whispered to her young confederate.

Waiting patiently in the foyer, the Delarosas offered a warm greeting. Simonetta handed over fresh-baked muffins in a wicker basket.

Pat presented a bouquet of Peruvian lilies accented by bright orange poppies.

"Pat, Simonetta." Margaret ushered them inside. "Where did you get these flowers in the middle of winter?"

"Blueberry?" Norah peeked beneath the gingham cloth.

"My granddaughter. Norah."

Lifting her hand to her mouth, Simonetta appeared on the verge of tears. "So she came back to you. After all this time. We pray for you every Sunday, and now Erica's come home. Where is she?"

"No, not her, just her daughter. Norah, this is Mr. and Mrs. Delarosa."

"Pleased to meet you."

"Oh." Simonetta shifted her enthusiasm. "What a lovely girl. You must be so happy."

Marking the passage of the bouquet, Pat Delarosa stepped closer. "You forget I have a flower shop. Flowers flown in from all over the world."

"You pray every Sunday?" Norah asked.

Bending to the girl's eye level, Simonetta took her hands. "For your grandmother. For your mother."

The women retreated to the kitchen to brew another pot of coffee. An explanation was hatched over blueberry muffins, elaborations on the story Margaret had prepared for the principal of the elementary school.

In the living room, Norah admired the arrangement in the vase. "Alstroemeria," Pat told her. "Don't tell your gramma but I had too many in the shop."

"She wouldn't mind. She's happy to have any."

"Hey, look here, I show you something you never known you seen. This kind of lily has twists at the bottom." He pointed to the resupinate leaves. "So what's the bottom is really the top, and what's the top is the underneath."

"Things aren't always what they seem."

"You have a favorite?"

"A favorite flower?"

"Your mama, she liked the scent of jasmine. I knew her since she was a little girl your age."

"Was she anything like me?"

Pat considered her question, taking her in as for the first time and straining to remember his earlier encounters with Erica. "She was a smart cookie like you, eh? And friendly like you. And Paul, that's her father you never met, she was the apple of his eye. A nice girl, too, and too bad what happened."

"Was my grandmother very sad when my mother left?"

"Sad? Oh, yes, heartbroken." The brusqueness of his confession caught up with him. "No, I mean, she was sad, yes. But happy now, right, that you're here?" Turning away from the child's gaze, he went to the window and looked out at the frosty lawn, his rough hands worried together. She did not move toward him but remained by the flowers and their fragrance building in the heat of the room. "I'm sorry," he said at last. "I don't mean to bring up such things, but we worry about her, your grandmother, kind of lonesome by herself. I keep out an eye, and my wife too. But you know, she don't ask much, and ever since your mother, well, she holds her heart to herself, eh?"

Norah approached from behind and stood next to him, staring at the bare winter scene. "You watch over her."

"Like a neighbor should. What's a neighbor for, anyhow? She don't go out much lately, and I worry."

"You make sure she's safe."

"Like the other night." With his chin, he gestured beyond the glass. "Simonetta, she hears something in the middle of the night, and I was dead asleep. But she says, Pat, Pat, and wakes me out of the bed to come see through the window, and I don't see nothing. But she tells me there's someone out in the yard. A man? Not so much a man, she says, an *ombra*. A spirit, maybe? Simonetta, she's so shook up and can't sleep, so I don't know."

He read the fear on her face, and bent down to her to speak in a low voice.

"Don't be too concerned with what she says she sees. She's from the old country, eh? Superstitious. Not important, what she thought she saw, only to say that a noise over here gets her worried. Then we see you and that boy coming through the snow. So let's go see for ourselves, and you know, everybody loves a mystery."

She reached out and touched him on the arm. "Until the mystery is solved."

Her touch alarmed him at first, by the overwhelming sense of rejuvenation he felt at the slight pressure of her hand. Most children dared not even approach him, and he could not place the feeling till later that night, in bed next to Simonetta, as he told her stories of the free and happy days of his own boyhood, tales he had long forgotten, and in the morning, Pat woke with shock at the wet patch on his pillowcase where his dreams had brought him to tears.

12

At dinner each night they went over the lies necessary to protect their fiction.

"You mustn't say you are an orphan," Mrs. Quinn began that Sunday night. "You are my daughter's daughter and she has sent you here to live with me while she is trying to patch together her life after a broken marriage."

"I will look sad when I speak of my father." Norah bowed her head to the mashed potatoes.

"You will behave yourself, that's what you'll do. Stick to our story. Your mother is staying in New Mexico to put her affairs in order."

"Is that what broke the marriage? Affairs?"

A wicked smile lit her face. "Yes, *his* affairs. No, no, you wouldn't know. You don't know, only that your mother felt it best, under the circumstances, for me to look after you for a while, and she'll send for you once she's on her feet again."

Norah speared a broccoli floret, considered its resemblance to a tree in summer, and popped it whole into her mouth. She crunched on as Mrs. Quinn spun out the rest of her tale.

"I can't explain you without explaining her away, and I can't bring myself to say it."

"That you never hear from her?"

"That I've heard from her exactly twice since she ran away." She eased herself from her chair, sighing as her knees ached, and left the room. Staring at the blank space across the table, Norah buttered a biscuit, and savored every crumb. Margaret returned clutching an envelope to her bosom, and with great ceremony undid the clasp and slid two items onto the tablecloth. A postcard stood on its narrow end and flopped over, and a thin sheet of paper hit the edge of a glass and fluttered like a leaf to the floor. Margaret could have been no more startled had she dropped a vase that shattered on impact, so Norah fetched the paper and stood at the woman's shoulder to read along.

"Thank you. This postcard came a few weeks after she left, and you see it's from Memphis." The picture on its face was labeled *Historic Elmwood Cemetery.* "Why anyone would send a postcard of a graveyard, of all things, I don't know. But I was so grateful to have it, although my husband was just livid. But Erica thought she was in love, so. Paul swore he'd get on a plane and fly right out there, and it was all I could do to stop him." A memory made her cut off the sentence. She picked up the letter and started reading it to herself. "They were long gone, you see. Nothing until this, four years later. Paul was dead by then, and I had given up all hope, well, almost beyond hoping, and then this. No return address, just a mention of the town Madrid, and of course, I thought Madrid, Spain. Who wouldn't have thought of Spain?"

"Spain sounds entirely logical."

"But this Madrid is a flyspeck town with the same name in New Mexico. I was tempted at first to give it to the FBI—especially since that man was shot—but she would have been arrested and ended up in prison, so I kept the letter hidden. Not a soul knows. I was too scared to say anything."

Without a word, Norah patted Mrs. Quinn on the hand and went to the den to retrieve the atlas. The book hid her body from nose to navel, and when she set it down on the table, a puff of dust rose and settled like silt. "There is old York and New York. London and New London. Athens, Georgia, and Athens, Greece. And at least forty-two Springfields," she recited while turning the leaves. "But who would have thought to look for Madrid in New Mexico?" Finding the vectors, she zeroed in on the spot. "Right exactly in the center of the middle of nowhere." Norah pointed to a dot on the map roughly halfway between Albuquerque and Santa Fe and read aloud the legend written along the road. "The Turquoise Trail, doesn't that sound beautiful? Now that you know where she is, why don't you go see her?"

"Who knows if she is still there? And who knows if she would even want to see me anymore? She's made no effort all this time. It's enough to know she was there. I can think she's still alive and well."

"But you're her mother—"

"She doesn't want me. If she hasn't told me to come for her by now, she doesn't want me in her life."

"But you should go while you can."

"That's enough for tonight. I only brought it up so that we might get our stories straight. Your supper's getting cold."

A truce struck, they finished their meal in silence. Later, side by side, they washed and dried the dishes, and after her bath, Norah curled her small body next to Margaret on the couch, and they read together under a circle of light until the bedtime hour. Well after midnight, Norah moved in whispers down the stairs, found the letters tucked inside the atlas at New Mexico, and read each word by starlight. And after she was finished, she tucked them back in place, closed the book, and began to cry. Outside in the moonlight, the one who watched the house drew in the wings of his camel hair coat and walked away.

13

Down in Washington, bitter weather forced indoors the ceremonies surrounding the second inauguration of President Reagan. The television news that evening showed empty streets, wind whipping plastic bags along the sidewalks, the grandstands silent but for the crisp fluttering of bunting. No recitation of the oath at the Capitol portico. No march down Pennsylvania Avenue. No shining city on a hill. Only the desolate cold.

The telephone rang in the Quinns' living room, a rare enough occurrence any day, all the more strange in the evening. Norah picked up the receiver and said hello.

"I'm sorry, I must have dialed the wrong number," the voice said.

"Who were you trying to reach?"

"Margaret Quinn. I could have sworn—"

"Oh, she's here. This is the right number. May I tell her who's calling?"

"My name is Diane Cicogna. With whom am I speaking?"

"Her granddaughter. Norah Quinn."

"Granddaughter?" A long pause on the line. "Tell your grandmother her sister is on the phone."

Before speaking, Margaret held the phone against her chest, composing what she would say. With a backhand wave, she sent Norah out of earshot to the living room and the rest of the television coverage. "Diane. I should have known you would call to commiserate. It is a sad day. To think they let a little cold spell—"

Norah moved her finger to the screen, aimed to touch Reagan's face, but a quarter inch away, a spark of static electricity leapt and zapped her. She sat back and considered his half smile. He seemed to understand what he was doing and to enjoy some tremendous personal joke on the rest of the people, the catch in his voice and cant of the head, the stardust in his eyes, and the shining pompadour. More pictures of Washington as a ghost town, patriotic theme music trumpeting as the credits rolled.

A quiz show began. Three people received an answer and had to compose the correct question, a concept that appealed to her philosophical nature, until she realized that there was only one solution. How much more interesting if there were a multiplicity of possible correct questions, just as in real life, where every question had an infinite number of likely answers, dependent entirely on where one wished the conversation to go. Margaret stayed on the phone the entire length of the program, and when the quiz was over, Norah turned off the TV to better eavesdrop.

"The reason I never said anything is because it happened out of the blue. . . . No, she just showed up here one night. . . . No, she's not planning on coming home. . . . Of course, I don't mind in the slightest, she's sweet. . . . I don't know when Erica will send for her, I don't know if she ever will. It hasn't been decided."

A long pause. Norah could hear a tiny voice shouting through the handset.

"That's fine, that's fine," Margaret pleaded. "But hardly necessary. No, no, no, I don't mind. Come. You're always welcome. No, great, come. Next month. You'll love her."

An even longer pause, an even more animated voice.

"I'm absolutely sick about it too. Such a faker, how anyone could vote—"

When at last she came into the living room, Mrs. Quinn looked older, the joy of the past two weeks drained from her features. She appeared as tired as she was the night Norah had arrived on her doorstep, but seeing the child again, she brightened and smiled, yet could not shake completely her distractions. Sitting next to Norah on the sofa, she stared at the blank television set.

"When I answered, I didn't know that was your sister."

"That makes you two even. She didn't know I have a granddaughter to take my phone calls. We'll have to be careful with her."

"Like a leopard. We'll use our spots to mimic the shadows."

Margaret nodded. "Something like that. She will be visiting for a couple of days in February, and I just now had a hard time with her. She's naturally suspicious. A born skeptic."

Gathering an afghan about her shoulders, Norah huddled into a ball and rested her head on Mrs. Quinn's lap. The woman sighed and began to stroke the girl's hair while a ticking clock measured their silence. She could not imagine her life without the presence of the child and wondered how she had managed to endure the emptiness that had preceded Norah's arrival. Not just the comfort of another breath in the house, not just the sound of footsteps in the middle of the night when the child crept to the bathroom, not merely the fact of her being. The ruse was more than a game; it was a way of gaining some mastery over what had seemed cruel and arbitrary. She questioned her conscience for the thousandth time and resolved to her own satisfaction her right to claim the girl, just as the girl had seemed to claim her, one the necessity of the other.

When Norah finally spoke, her tone reflected a shifting mood. "I'd like to invite Sean Fallon over to visit. Maybe after school or Saturday."

"He could come play and stay for dinner."

"I think having another child here will make it easier for my aunt to believe, and I can practice calling you Grandma with him around."

Margaret laughed and tapped her on the shoulder, signaling her to sit up. "You have a devious mind, Norah Quinn."

14

They fell in love with her. Each day illuminated some new aspect of her character that caused the children of the Friendship School third-grade class to wonder what strange creature had landed in their midst. Ordinary marvels abounded. She seemed to know just which questions to ask Mrs. Patterson to make their lessons clear and discussion lively. A pop quiz produced the unexpected result of perfect scores all around, an anomaly that puzzled the teacher well after her second cocktail that evening. A spelling bee dragged on past its appointed hour with no child left out, not even the recalcitrant boys who usually could not accommodate the spelling of their own names correctly. When Mrs. Patterson asked for volunteers for a dramatic reading, a surplus of eager hands shot up. The teacher took note of it all, the swift change in mood since the girl's arrival, the tonal difference between the dregs of post-Christmas school and the unexpected froth before spring. Sworn enemies buried their slingshots. There were no acts of violence, no bullying of the meek, no random or wanton vituperation of the ruling clique. A kind of harmony descended, and the other children recognized the changes brought by the new girl, who astonished them all by her simple and earnest desire to learn. Her crooked smile bestowed a spark of glee to January, as if she were lit within and could cast off gloom. She made fast friends with Sharon Hopper, Gail Watts, and Dori Tilghman, and brought them small treats of peanut butter cups or extra oatmeal raisin cookies or, once, old doll clothes rescued from the Quinns' hidden troves. During indoor gym, she was the only third grader who could shoot a basketball through a hoop hung ten feet high, and the force of her throw in dodgeball made every boy wary. And yet everyone could sense an innate gentleness in Norah, a lack of malice in word and deed, and more than any other quality, this they regarded as true virtue and were drawn to, even against their own selfish natures.

Mrs. Quinn, too, fell for her. Charmed by the girl and glad for her company, she felt at ease around Norah at once, as if the child embodied a second chance at being the mother she had always intended to be. The very sight of the girl's ragged hair or fogged glasses gave Margaret a thrill, and when the boy began coming around, she felt blessed beyond what she deserved. Unnerving at first, the sound of their two voices quavered in the house, the murmur about homework and classes and other third-grade girls and boys, the edgy debates over play, the squeals and shouts and laughter. The shock of the television or radio at four in the afternoon. What was it that Erica used to rush home for at that age? The vampire soap opera? *Dark Shadows?* The signs of their presence littered the ordinary complacency—coats on the hooks, boots puddling by the door, newspaper comics read and discarded. Two plates of crumbs, glasses filmed with milk. Skin of banana, bright coils of tangerine, core of apple, skeleton of grapes. Margaret was forever picking up their detritus, reordering her custom.

And yet, when Norah was off at school, the absence of commotion unsettled the new equilibrium. She wandered from room to room hearing the echo of childish laughter, anticipating a thump through the ceiling, a flash on the stairs, the front door yawning open and banging against the wall, heralding their arrival, and she welcomed them home each day with quiet relief, the joy in her heart bound by the briefest of smiles. As often as she wished them out from underfoot, Margaret also ached for them when they were gone.

Following the hot chocolate or an apple cored and quartered, they attacked their homework. Sean knew, by some gyroscope of the left brain, every mathematics answer, the difference at once among igneous, sedimentary, and metamorphic rocks, the dates and places of every Pennsylvania battle in the French and Indian War. Norah knew the magic of vanishing-point perspective, where the shadows fell in art by placement of the sun, how to draw without hesitation the confluence of the three rivers—Ohio, Allegheny, and Monongahela—and to distinguish in illustration what Sean would have drawn as identical flowers or birds. They helped each other through suggestion, competitive questioning, and cajolery.

Work completed, play began. Ever since the smoke rings and his baffled reaction, she had slowed the pace, lured him into her confidence with more ordinary games, and he savored her attention and company.

Norah preferred the outdoors, even in the dead of January, rolling out snowmen, cracking long icicles from the eaves and leaping away when the points threatened to impale, breakneck sledding, snowball fights, the stinging thrill of being cold beyond caring. For his part, Sean preferred to be warm and at the table, just the two of them, where he could teach her games. He revealed the trick of tic-tac-toe, unlocked the stratagem of checkers, the playful thinking of chess, so that in two weeks' time she unseated the master as often as she lost. Not having any siblings of his own, Sean brought over every game he had been given but rarely had the chance to play. They solved the mysteries of Clue, mastered the Rube Goldberg mechanics of Mouse Trap, and engaged in marathons of Monopoly, lasting hours over the course of several days. Once they tired of his games, they pillaged the closet upstairs and, hearts afire, played the game of Life, backgammon, and once, for nostalgia's sake, an Uncle Wiggily. But treasure lay in the attic, beneath a film of dust.

In a bright and brittle box lay Tip It, a balancing act. Players had to remove a single colored ring from one of three stacks while keeping balanced a plastic acrobat—they called him Mr. Tipps—who stood on the tip of his nose at the top of the pole, itself balanced on a fulcrum. Depending upon luck and destiny, the winner was the one who avoided spilling Mr. Tipps and sending the entire contraption crashing to the floor. At five in the afternoon, they had reached the crucial moment yet again. Sean had already won three times in succession and had taken a yellow disk away, just barely managing to keep the fellow from falling. Silence and cunning overtook any notions of sportsmanship; he passed the spinner to her with glee, and she, equally certain that any move was doomed, flicked the arrow and sent it circling madly around to blue. She picked up her plastic fork and pointed it at him.

"You know you're going to win no matter what I do. Why do you keep torturing me?"

"Just go," he said, then caught himself, swallowed, and smiled. "You never know. If you're real careful . . ."

"We can but try." Not budging from her cross-legged seat on the floor, she leaned over and slid the fork beneath the disks opposite from the direction the pole was leaning, keeping Mr. Tipps near her nose. With a saint's patience, she lifted the blue disk, and the plastic acrobat twirled like a pinwheel until slowing to improbable stability.

"You cheated!" Sean shouted. "It's impossible—there's not enough weight on that end. You breathed on him."

Her mouth was still an O. Glaring at him, she clamped together her lips, but the acrobat refused to fall, and then, closing her eyes, Norah made a new circle and began to gently blow. Mr. Tipps tottered, the pole shivered and slightly bent before heading back to the center until stopping at ninety degrees, and still she blew no harder than the air it takes to launch seeds from a dandelion puffball, and when the acrobat righted himself, steady and still, she inhaled, the wind whistling. Mr. Tipps spun counterclockwise, faster and faster till Sean grew dizzy just watching. When she sealed her lips, the whole apparatus clattered to the living room floor.

"The rabbis say that with every breath, God exhales an angel." Norah picked up the pieces and placed them in the box.

Eager to know the truth, he pressed the question. "How do you do that?"

The plastic man lay flat in her hand. Pinching his head, she picked him up and balanced his nose on her fingertips. "My grandmother's sister is coming this weekend. She will not believe without some proof."

Lightly blowing, she spun Mr. Tipps on her finger, and then setting the acrobat inside the box, she replaced the box top and slid the game beneath the coffee table. Though the afternoon light had weakened, she could read Sean's pure delight. Norah switched on a lamp, her hand and face suddenly radiant, and she reflected the glow on her friend. "We have to convince Aunt Diane that I am the real Norah Quinn."

"But you are Norah Quinn."

"She doesn't know that, and I want you to be my fearless ally. Partners?"

She spat in her palm and stuck it out; he did the same, and they briefly shook.

"And I'll need a spy to find out more about Erica Quinn. Do you think you could do that?"

A sly grin flashed on his face. "Happily."

15

The pain, a deep ache that coursed in the bones, began in her fingertips and toes and radiated into her limbs, across the ribcage like static electricity, up the spine and fused stiff the vertebrae in her neck. Margaret dared not move, but when her jaw twitched and the fire reached her skull, her face gave away the inner turmoil through the deep furrows on her brow and the panic in her eyes. Norah had been watching surreptitiously, glancing now and again from her book, and at last, she could bear it no longer. "Is there something wrong?"

"I'm a bit stiff." Margaret squeezed out the words. "This winter seems to have done me in. It never used to be this cold."

"Can I get you anything? Will you be all right?"

Margaret hummed an uncertain answer. Even the words were stuck behind her lips, caught behind the soreness that seemed to leach even to the teeth. For the first time, she worried about the symptoms of her ailment and wished she could ask Paul about the mysterious pain that threatened to leave her riven. Laying the book pages-down on the table, Norah rose and without another word quickened to the kitchen. Alone with her misery, Margaret grimaced and wondered what precautionary responses her sister might undertake should she find her hurting so. She wanted no fuss. Steeling herself, she pushed her toes to the floor and flexed the arches of her soles, and then fanned out her fingers, hoping to release the pressure by willpower. In the kitchen, a saucepan clattered on the stove and Norah sang to herself as she searched the spice cabinet. At least the girl is here, Margaret thought, and I will not have to die alone.

The notion surprised her in its sudden clarity and focused her attention away from the ache in the marrow of her bones to true reasons behind her deceptions involving the foundling child. Penitent and confessor, she forgave herself and pushed away the thought, merely grateful that it had banished the seizing pain and restored former feeling. By the time the child returned, a mug in hand, she could manage to move freely and accept the token of comfort. The scent of cardamom and cinnamon rose from the warm milk.

"My own special sleeping potion," Norah said.

Margaret blew across the surface and sipped the liquid. "Delicious. What's in it?"

"Family recipe. But you'll feel better soon and you should go to bed right away or you'll end up sleeping on the couch." Norah knelt on the floor beside her and found her place in the book, reading quietly as Margaret nursed the drink.

A pleasant drowse soon overcame her, and Margaret found herself half dreaming and dazed by the confluence of images merging in her consciousness. The boy Sean caterwauling as he chased Norah from one room to the next became a boy she once loved racing after her as a girl in a cherry orchard. Diane, all of four or five, holding her hand as they dashed across hot sand to embrace the cooling sea. The grieving walk around the world over these hills and through these valleys, the long solitary journey with a hundred things to tell her missing daughter, in her dream wishing her home. Through the haze, Margaret beheld the child reading at her knees. "Yes, if you'll lock up and take care of the house, I'm tired and will go to bed now." She could trust the girl to follow instructions, and in any case, Paul was in his study catching up on his patients' paperwork. "Goodnight, Erica."

Allowing her the mistake, the girl held out her hands to help Margaret rise from the couch, and kissed her gently on her papery cheek. Slowly, the woman took the steps to her bed and to her dreams. Norah switched off the lamp and courted in the dark the fear that she had arrived too late to save anyone.

Upstairs, hours after Margaret had gone to bed, Norah cracked the door to the woman's room to spy her sleeping, the covers drawn to her chin, and an extra blanket draped over her body like a shroud. Darkness obscured her features, but the body remained still, save for the slight lift of her shoulders with each breath. Illuminated by the hallway lamp, her left hand rested flat on the sheets against her chin. A lattice of veins snaked beneath the skin, her long, elegant fingers, and the wedding ring she still wore. Assured of the woman's peace, Norah snuck back down the stairs, unhooked her parka by the door, and stepped out into the night.

Frigid air attacked every exposed opening, stinging eyes and ears, burrowing into her brain through the sinuses and deeper into her lungs with every breath. She threw back her head to take in the stars, bright and sharp. Each exhalation formed a small cloud which dissipated into blackness. Norah fell to her knees and bowed forward till her forehead touched the ground, and her hood rose and fell over her head as she prayed. The one who had been following her moved from his hiding spot and drew closer, secreting himself amid the horns of the bare rosebushes that ran in a thicket along the Delarosas' property. Danger hummed in her ears, the menace made the short hairs on her arms stand on end, yet she remained steadfast in concentration and prayer.

Not far away from where she had prostrated herself, Sean Fallon awoke from a bad dream. He had been walking across a dry and open savanna, the African sun hammering at his vision, so he had to strain to see through the wavy heat the wonder of wonders: zebras and wildebeests as far as the horizon, with cattle egrets hitching rides on dusty backs, and small clouds of dirt as the animals wandered under a painful blue sky. At the edge of the plain, an ancient baobab grew, a twisted and gnarled sentry in the tall, dry grass; beneath its branches monkeybread had fallen at his feet. The low thunder of the cat rumbled from above, and he turned in time to catch the mad yellow eyes out of the shadow of spots, the teeth white and sharp against the liquid black mouth, claws flexed as it leapt at him, and he woke up, astonished to be in his bed in his room, the starlight seeping through the edges of the window blinds.

He unfurled the covers and got out of bed. His *E.T.* alarm, with a clock in the center of its belly, read 1:30 a.m. A voice compelled him to come out into the cold night, and he crept past his mother's room, down the stairs, and to the front door for his boots and overcoat. A shadow moved between the moon and the earth and raced past him at threatening speed. He hurried down the hill toward the Quinns' house, yet he almost missed her, bent to the ground, motionless as a dove on a rock, and he feared disturbing her. Curiosity trumped anxiety, and he crouched down close to her, so that he might speak softly yet be assured she would hear.

"What are you doing, Norah? You'll freeze to death."

She did not look up at him, and her words hit the ground beneath her face. "I am praying for guidance."

Sean looked to the silent house. All of the windows were dark, but the porch light glowed like a yellow eye. "Guidance for what? It's freezing."

She lifted her head and looked into his eyes. "For what can be done for Mrs. Quinn, what can be done for you. And what to do about the one who is following me."

He looked out into the darkness but saw nothing. "Someone's following you?"

"Someone's trying to stop me and take me away from here."

"But why would anyone want to take you away?" He raised his voice and sent the question echoing in the night air. All of her illusions—the stars that appeared in her mouth, rings of smoke, the things she moved with her breath—stood stark against the sinister aspect of the late hour. For the first time, he thought she might be something other than a girl. She did not answer, but bowed to the ground to continue at her prayers in a foreign tongue, filled with a savageness he could not comprehend. Beside her he stood for as long as he could bear; then, after insisting she go inside, he left for home in the small hours, vigilant for strangers, and edged under the covers to wait for the light of morning.

16

A squall blew in from Canada, bringing moisture from the Great Lakes and over the western hills, the first flurries tumbling around noon, intermittent as scouts, and by one o'clock, snow showers fell in sheets. In the driveway next door, Mr. Delarosa showed up early and unexpectedly, having closed the flower shop due to the threatening weatherman on the radio. A shroud of silence hemmed in the town, and on his way home, he saw the ice-encrusted figure near the bridge, mistaking it for a statue, until the snowman shrugged to clear his shoulders, and surprised by the sudden movement, Delarosa nearly drove the delivery van into the river. Just as she started to worry over the roads, Margaret was surprised by the sudden appearance of Norah and Sean at the front door, stomping their boots and shaking off their caps, dusting the snow from their coats.

"They let us out early," Norah announced. "And we want to go back out and play in it."

"Let me fix you something warm first, and you'll have to bundle up. Sean, do you want to call your mother and let her know?"

The children were gone for hours. At the window, Margaret kept watch through the crepuscular light, but saw only the blankets of snow rippling, falling so thickly and rapidly that the children's footprints had filled to shallow dents in the swale. She knew that something bad had happened as soon as she saw the two figures crest the horizon in the gloom, one limping stiff-legged, the other slowing to keep pace. As they neared, they looked like two snowmen indistinguishable from the white mantle, and Margaret felt the seeping wet cold, a panic quickening her breath, a sense that they would never make it home, too far to go. She threw on her overcoat and slipped into her boots to step outside, the porchlight halo swarming with snowflakes. The children drew closer and the details emerged; the struggling one was Norah.

"What on earth happened?" Margaret called out from the porch.

"She fell in the pond, Mrs. Quinn," Sean shouted from the yard. "Right through the ice up to her legs and she's near frozen."

In two bounds, she reached the child, bent to see her chapped blue grimace. "Get in, get in, and get out of those wet clothes. Are you hurt, girl? We'll get you warm inside. Norah, how could you be so careless?"

Her legs looked afire when they finally worked off her boots and pants, caked with silt and rock-stiff. She sat splayed on the edge of the commode, wincing with discomfort, as the steam from the bath made a cloud of the room. On command, she could wiggle her toes, but she balked at Mrs. Quinn's orders to take off her underthings. Her insistence on privacy went unspoken and was acknowledged with a sigh. As she left the bathroom, Margaret admonished Norah to stay put in the bathtub until she felt normal again. The girl sneezed and laughed to herself, waved goodbye with a red hand.

Downstairs, Sean melted and dripped on the mat in the foyer. He had removed his hat and mittens but otherwise remained a sentinel at his post, waving sheepishly at Mrs. Quinn. "Oh for heaven's sake, Sean, take off your coat and get warm—"

"Will she be all right?"

"You're sopping wet, and it's a blizzard out there. I think I have something of my husband's you could wear at least while I throw those wet jeans in the dryer."

Sean followed her upstairs, past the sound of Norah singing to herself in the bathtub, and changed into a worn blue flannel shirt that hung to his knees. As he rolled up his sleeves, he replayed the staging of her walk into the icy water and concentrated on the plot they had designed together. Wiggling his toes in the dead man's woolen socks, he could forget his discomfort only by focusing on the questions she had made him rehearse before she jumped through the ice. He left the bedroom and bumped into Norah as she exited the bathroom wrapped in a thick yellow towel. They exchanged a conspiratorial smile.

"Watch this." She pinched shut her eyes and twisted her lips into a grimace. A thin strand of mucus ran from her nose, and when she opened her eyelids, her irises glowed as red as cardinals. "Too much?" Afraid, he blanched and nearly cried out. She blew a raspberry and shut her eyelids again and then revealed a bloodshot pink. Holding up her left hand for his patience, she counted down a measure and then sneezed violently and loud. Giving him the thumbs-up, Norah sent him on his way.

"Do it like I told you," she said. "Like we practiced."

He grinned and slid down the stairs, skated across the linoleum in the foyer, excited to find her grandmother in the kitchen. The sight of him in her husband's clothes brought a flush to her cheeks.

"Was that Norah sneezing?" Mrs. Quinn asked from the stove. "I hope she doesn't catch her death of cold."

"Or double-p pneumonia," Sean said. "That's what my dad used to call it."

The boy rarely mentioned his absent father, and Margaret let the matter linger for a beat. "I phoned your mother, Sean. You'll stay here for the night, and if it isn't still snowing in the morning, she'll come take you home."

"We were just testing the ice to see if it could hold our weight, 'cause she said her mum was a great ice-skater and promised to teach us when she comes."

"She did, did she?"

"And I could hear it, crick, like stepping on a twig, and then crack, like a thunder. Before you know it, she was up to her knees, and I thought I was going to fall in too." He sat beside her at the counter, crossing his legs to make sure the shirt didn't ride up.

"With how freezing it's been, that ice should have been three inches thick. I walked that way for the past five years, and this time of year, it should be safe. But you did a good deed, Sean, thank you." She handed him a mug of hot cocoa, and watching carefully the level at the brim, he sipped at the steam.

"Is it true, Mrs. Quinn? About your daughter?"

"Erica?" Images from her history sped giddily across her mind. She did not understand the boy's question at first, thought he dug deeper than she allowed, then realized his meaning. "She could skate like the wind. As soon as it was cold, say, come December, Erica would be out on the ice every chance she could. And even on that bumpy pond, she could pirouette and, whaddyacallit when you fly on one leg with the other bowed behind your back? Grace itself."

He licked the chocolate mustache from his lip.

"And then one day, she just quit. Never laced a pair again. I don't know, maybe she just outgrew skating. A lot of things changed once she was a teenager."

"Boys, I bet."

Startled, she tried to focus on him, but his features were hidden behind the mug. "Boys, indeed. And don't you be getting any ideas when you're older, Mr. Fallon. A girl is vulnerable at that age, not knowing her own mind and body, willing to give her heart away to the first one of you hoodlums that pays the least attention, but oh you boys, you know your tricks, and it's not right, I tell you."

"Is that what happened with Erica, Mrs. Quinn?"

No, she thought, not just the boys, but Paul. His dark past. His desire to freeze time and keep her young and his own. They fought bitterly about the boys, not just Wiley Rinnick, but all of them. The first, just thirteen, hung around the house at dusk each night that summer, a cavalier on a bicycle. A handsome brown-eyed boy with a lock curling across his forehead that he swept away whenever he bent to talk with Erica. On an August evening, just before the start of high school, Paul strode like a bear to the curb where the boy was chatting with their daughter. Margaret could see them from the window—the boy slouching behind the high handlebars, Erica leaning against the mailbox, and Paul, the apex of the triangle. Words were exchanged, the boy pinning his curl to his scalp with one hand, his lithe body contracting under the sound of her husband's scolding, Erica straining toward him, tense with sympathy. Off the boy pedaled, never to return, and Paul just watched, helpless, as if on shore bidding a ship goodbye, till the moon brightened the evening sky.

She curled her fingers around the mug, felt the warmth escaping through the ceramic. From upstairs another fluttery wet sneeze roared through the floorboards. "That girl, I hope she's not caught her death. If you want to see Norah's mother, there's a photo album in the living room. Poor dear, I've got to take care of her now. You'll be all right by yourself, Sean?"

He nodded. Through the ceiling, their muffled conversation rolled from Margaret to Norah in the rhythm of a love song. He listened, anxious at the strange sound, before remembering his duty and padding off to study the pictures from long ago.

17

Here is Erica, bald and fat and toothless, naked in the grass. Here is Paul Quinn, making her fly, the baby a blur in the air, his fingers spread like branches for the catch. Here are Margaret's hands, one cupping the baby's head, the other rinsing soap from her daughter's potbelly. The baby's face startled by the suddenness of water. The toddler toddles. A circle of three-year-olds around a birthday cake, the candle flames white streaks on the gray tones of the snapshot, its edges scalloped and marked with runiform: Apr 13 61. Sean turned the page and the images sprang into muted color, washed out by the sun.

Here is Erica perched on a tricycle, ready to race past the edge of the frame. Topless at some summer spot, a beach house perhaps, sucking on a nearly empty Pepsi bottle. Holding up her first hooked fish, no bigger than her hand. The colors deepen, become more saturated. She is a ballerina, a Halloween black cat, a girl with one tooth missing. Close up she resembles Norah in some ways: the eyes one size too small, the pert nose, the planes of her jawline. Years go missing, unobserved.

Here is Margaret Quinn, twenty years younger, and next to her, arm around her shoulder, stands a woman close enough to be her sister, he thinks. Diane and Margaret pert in matching shirtwaist dresses, a burning cigarette in Diane's hand, a cocktail glass in Margaret's. Their lips brightly painted, their eyes shining with the glamour of summer. In one corner of the photograph, out of the depth of focus, the blur of a girl. He imagines her chasing the first fireflies of the evening or leaping through the sprinkler or being spooked by an unseen phantom. Then Erica, her back to the camera, looks over her shoulder at the lens. Spread across her outstretched arms is the Andean shawl with the sun aloft.

Here is Christmas morning, paper on the floor, the tree twinkling and forlorn. The barest smiles. The new white skates appear too heavy in her hands. Her father ungainly in a tight leisure suit, her mother done up in a beehive, two steps behind the times.

Here is Erica and her best friend Joyce times four—a photo strip from the new booth at Murphy's. From top to bottom: both girls caught in the middle of the giggles, Joyce's hand covering her mouth; Erica, three-quarters profile, fingers to her lips, and Joyce with her mouth wide open; now Joyce is smiling perfectly, Erica's eyes are shut; then flawless, cheek to cheek, happy to be fifteen.

Here is Paul Quinn, the final time, standing to the knees in a hole; above the ground, a cherry tree, its roots encased in a burlap ball. The camera has captured his little girl half out of the picture. She grips the trunk with such fierce determination that Sean reads first anger, then jubilation in her expression. Her hair hangs down past her shoulders in two curtains. Her body now looks like a woman's, not a girl's, the swell of small breasts against a tie-dyed shirt, her hips wider at the tops of her jeans, but more ineffably, her carriage—the way she squared her shoulders and lifted her head, in full cognizance of her strength and beauty.

Here he is, the boy at the class trip to the amusement park, barely noticeable, only in retrospect. The teenagers took over the merry-go-round, laughing, long hair flying, riding mad snorting ponies, an ostrich, lion, leaping deer. Just beyond Erica, who is centered in the frame, the dark-haired boy stares so ardently that his eyes nearly burn through the paper. There he is again, at the margins of a clowning group before the Tilt-A-Whirl, all eyes forward, devil's horns over the unsuspecting, but only this boy, cascades of brown curls, wearing a shirt with the peace sign, only he is gazing aslant at the object of his desire. And a final time, he stands behind Erica, arms clasped in front of her waist, both grinning out of focus as though photographed through a scrim of ice.

On the last page of the album, here is Erica's junior-year portrait, the one the police and FBI used, the one in all the newspapers and on television, the last known photograph. A formal coda to her childhood. A girl, becoming woman.

18

"She's finally asleep," Mrs. Quinn told him in hushed tones. "Poor thing. Her temperature is 102 degrees, and she's shaking and chattering like a bag of bones."

At the stove, Sean stirred the soup. While he was waiting for her to tend to Norah, he had raided her refrigerator, and a pair of grilled cheese sandwiches browned in a cast-iron skillet.

"You added a can of water?" Mrs. Quinn hovered over his shoulder, peering into the pot. "It's condensed, you know."

"I make my own dinner lots."

She patted him on the shoulder. "Of course you do." He looked so small in her husband's shirt and socks, a stickboy, elbows, hips, and shoulders sharp against the flannel. Fatherless child. She wanted to wrap her arms around him and rock and soothe him until his sadness went away. Standing on a stepstool, he had climbed onto the counter to take down the bowls and plates for dinner. She brought the silverware and napkins, two glasses of milk. They sat at an adjoining corner, saving a space for Norah, who would not be down.

"Your mother works late sometimes. You have to take care of yourself?"

"Sometimes." He slurped in a long fat noodle. "Monday, Wednesday, Friday. Saturday morning, sometimes."

"Do you get lonesome?"

"No, I kinda like having time to myself." He paused, remembering Norah's instructions. "Do you?"

"Get lonesome? Heavens, no . . . Sometimes."

"I miss my dad. Do you miss your daughter?"

She nibbled at the burnt crust, showering crumbs. "At first you miss them all of the time. You start to say something, call them for dinner, and then you catch yourself. Or you look up from the crossword or the soaps or your book expecting to see her in the doorway, but she isn't there, she isn't anywhere. And you wonder what is she doing this very minute, wonder if she ever thinks of you, or thinks of you as often as you think of her." Margaret looked at Sean. "Of course, your dad misses you as much as you miss him, but it's the same, isn't it, for us all? We go on not understanding how it happened this way."

He set his spoon down in the bowl and stared at the triangle of his sandwich. Beguiled by the memories he had opened, she went on talking to herself.

"All day long every day I thought of nothing but her. For months. To the point where I had completely lost all sense of anything else. Then one morning, Paul brought home a bunch of ripe cherries, picked them up at the farmers' market, and they were perfect. You know, just the cherriest cherries. Temptation. So I sat there, right where you are sitting now, and ate one, and the first sweet bite reminded me of summers gone by and when I was a girl myself, just a girl, and I loved cherries more than any other part of summer, more than blueberries or strawberries or even peaches. More than the Fourth of July or swimming at the shore or just wandering on a sunny day. I had forgotten how good fresh cherries taste. So I sat there and ate one after the other, and when Paul came back in the kitchen, he saw the pits piled high in a saucer, the nearly empty bowl, and me, my lips stained with sin. I couldn't resist, and there was a look in his eyes, a happy sadness. He was relieved that I had come back from the dead."

With the point of her bread she motioned for him to pick up his sandwich, and they ate in silence, the ticking clock accenting the rhythm of their thoughts. She pushed away her empty plate. The boy became an afterthought.

"You become more careful about letting in happiness, because if you do, and it leaves again . . . The everyday part of missing her was less acute in time, but it lingers, just waiting to strike like a panther. When Paul took sick, I had him to worry about, and when he went into the hospital—" She covered her mouth with her hand to catch her shame before it escaped. "I did not feel it as much as I thought I should, as much as I probably would, but you see, I was already numb. Erica had been gone three years, and he, he coped somehow, went on. And I think

I resented him a little bit his peace. Or how he managed himself, and I was angry, too, that now there was no one to talk to about Erica. No one like my husband."

Outside in the fading light, the snow fell in striations of white against the black, and through the window, Sean watched the particles pass through the faint light bending from the room above.

"Then a letter came. New Mexico. They were heading for California the whole time, but she got lost along the way, thank God. I expected her to have so much more to say, but it was just cold and factual. Not to a mother, but to a complete stranger, and that's when I knew they had brain-washed her, filled her head with their radical ideas. When nothing fol-lowed, I came to resent her again, came to wish—sometimes—that I hadn't heard from her, would never hear from her again because she chose to exclude me from her life, she chose to leave with him, she chose to reject me after . . . Still. If she walked through that door this very minute, all would be forgiven and restored. This is what love brings you to."

Tears welled in his eyes, and he tightened his lips, contorted the mus-cles in his face to avoid crying altogether, before turning away. She spoke his name, and he broke down. "He's never coming back, is he?"

She held out her arms, and he rushed into the space, laying his face against her breast, his small hard frame shaking with tears. With every breath he drew, he cried for his father. Margaret crushed his body against her body. "Sean, Sean, I am so sorry."

19

The man standing on the sidewalk in the bitter cold appeared to be regarding something only he could see, or perhaps he looked at nothing in particular but was merely listening to the sound of the wind, the passing vehicles sluicing through the slush, and the gentle susurrus as the showers landed upon the street, upon the parked cars, upon the meters like a row of cemetery crosses, upon the few souls stirring in the gloom. Had anyone paid more than cursory attention, he would have been puzzled by how long the man stayed in place absorbing the chill against his unprotected skin, in the folds and ridges of his coat, in the dish of his hat. But he was nothing more than a figure out in the snow to passersby, an obstacle on the sidewalk as they hurried home or made one last dash to the drugstore or the tavern. Madman, to be out in such a storm. He watched them come and go until at last he followed her into the bar at the corner nearest the bridge.

Few ventured into the night, and fewer still had sought out a drink. A man in a baseball hat stared at him from a perch at the rail and then renewed his acquaintance with a half-finished beer. A threesome—father, mother, son—munched on a plate of fries smothered in gravy. In the corner, a young woman appeared to be talking to herself, as the bartender ignored her and watched the basketball game playing on the suspended television set. Easy to find, the woman, even in the dimness of the bar, for her ears and nose glowed red from just having come in from the cold. Seated at the bar, she had draped her coat and scarf on the adjacent stool, so he chose the next available space, and she reached out with one hand to steady her garments when he sat. His coat was unbuttoned and hung like a robe around him, and with great care, he set his wet fedora on the counter to his right, and then turned to the left to see if the woman might acknowledge his presence. Not a nod or even a glance.

With a damp towel the bartender, a fellow called Jocko Manning, swiped at the space in front of the man. "What's your poison?"

"Something to take the chill off." He paused, considering the man's accent. "An Irish coffee."

When the drink arrived, he blew into it, and a cloud of steam formed and rose to his face, separating into two columns that wreathed his head before dissipating.

"Hey, look," Jocko said, "Santy Claus."

"Nice trick," the woman said.

The man swallowed a mouthful of coffee and set the cup back on the mahogany. "Do I know you?"

"I don't know, do you?" She studied him carefully, not the usual suspect for a bar such as this, and in that context, she could not place his face, though familiar. A type, she finally decided. Well dressed, polite, old enough to be her father. A gentleman who could be entrusted with her name. "Eve Fallon."

"Fallon." He shook her hand. "Do you have a younger brother? A boy around eight or nine years old? In the third grade at Friendship Elementary."

"That's no brother, that's my son."

"No, you're much too young."

She laughed helplessly. "You sure know how to flatter a girl who's about to start drinking."

Behind her the man in the baseball cap crossed to the bathroom, his eyes fixed on the threesome at their late dinner. On the television set, Duquesne tied the score, and Manning raised his fist in triumph.

"What brings you out," he asked, "on such a miserable night? Is Mr. Fallon with you?"

"Flew the coop." She toyed with a swizzle stick. "Last year, but it's not too bad. I mean, it's hard money-wise."

"I'm sorry to hear that, though I can't see how any man in his right mind—"

"Harder on my son because that rat doesn't even bother to call or visit anymore, and Sean's been kind of withdrawn. None of his little buddies from school come round anymore, and he was just listless for the longest time, like he wanted nothing more out of life."

The man ran his finger along the brim. "Children often go through a kind of emotional winter in times of personal crisis. But they are stronger than they seem. Resilient."

Eve straightened her spine and perched higher on the stool. "He'll pull through, I'm sure. There's this new kid who kind of sought him out just recently, it's so cute, a little girl. In fact that's where he is tonight, spending the night. First chance I've had to go out in ages, and wouldn't miss it. Cheers."

He lifted his mug to her glass in salute.

"Nice kid, from what I know of her. She's got a way of bringing him out."

"It wouldn't be that Quinn girl?"

"That's right, Norah Quinn. It's so sweet. Do you know her?"

"We're acquainted. But you do know the family history . . ."

"'Course I do. Her grandfather was my doctor. Nothing wrong with the Quinns."

"No dire implications. None at all. The child, I'm told, appeared out of nowhere. Do you know the grandmother?"

"Margaret? Not well, just to arrange the kids' get-togethers. Why all the questions?"

"Curiosity."

"Killed the cat, mister. What did you say your name was? Why are you so interested in the Quinns?"

Throwing a five-dollar bill on the counter, he reached for his hat. "I didn't, I'm not." Hiding beneath the brim, he rose to leave.

She lifted the glass to her lips and closed her eyes to take a sip. "Who are you?" she asked, but he was already gone. The door appeared to have never opened, and the other people in the room took no notice of his departure. "You know that fella?" she asked the bartender.

Engrossed by the basketball game, Jocko shook his head and flipped his towel to the other shoulder.

A moment's indecision scuttled any chance she might have had, for when Eve stepped through the doorway, she found nobody on the streets. The snow had stopped, and the temperature had dropped by ten degrees. Shivering, she walked as far as the bridge, within earshot of the waters far below lapping against the pilings. The sky, broken by clouds that hid and revealed the stars, closed heavily on her head, and she scanned the empty sidewalks for some sign of him. But the footprints in the snow jumbled into one inscrutable rutty path, and there was no diminutive man receding to the horizon, no coat and hat, not a thing. The doorbells jingled when Eve walked back in, and the bartender glanced once from the basketball game. The man in the Pirates cap had ordered a fresh beer. The family had finished their plate of fries and relaxed in their booth, fully sated, flipping through the jukebox playlist. The girl in the corner carried on her imaginary conversation. The bartender gave up on the home team and switched over to an Irish folk concert on PBS. Chilled and sullen, Eve cursed her ex under her breath and sat back on her stool, her whiskey sour acrid and foul. The stranger's coffee mug stood in place, and she was startled to find a thin slick of ice skimming the dark surface. Why had he asked about her little boy's friends? Thoughts of her son and his stillborn pain swirled in her mind.

Once upon a time, Sean had been just and fully hers, the child she bore, the infant at her breast in the middle of the night, the boy she taught to speak and walk, who began to leave her—imperceptibly at first, and then later he orbited into school and found friends, and she found the blank mysteries of his mind and heart too much to bear. This way of his becoming. The sense of loss of her only son washed over her, and Eve wondered whether Sean would ever be the same, whether the boy she knew and loved would ever come back to her.

Crossing the silent neighborhood at nine on Saturday morning, Sean was struck blind by the brilliant sunshine reflecting off the ice and snow. He squinted to see, cast his eyes first skyward toward the sun and then at the whiteness all around, shut his eyelids and chanced a few steps in comforting darkness, and then tried to focus on the path for as long as he could bear. His mother had warned him, before she left for work, to wear a hat with a brim, but Sean had ignored her advice, and halfway to Mrs. Quinn's, he felt he could not turn back despite the pain. Desperate for relief, he headed for the woods, though that route would add minutes to his journey, to find some shade, however sparse among the bare sweet-gum, hemlock, and oak.

Quiet at that hour and in such brutal cold, the forest sounded only of his passage, but at least he could keep his eyes open. He found it easier to concentrate on Norah and remember the outlines of their deception, the jump through the ice, the phantom illness. She would be waiting for him, eager for news.

Such conspiratorial thoughts hastened his steps, kindled his own eagerness to see her, and he did not notice the first bird alight on the path, ankle-deep in the snow some thirty feet ahead. Only when a second crow and a third landed nearby did he sense anything unusual. The crows seemed to watch as he drew near. Black feathers and jet beaks, fathomless eyes. Sean walked not four feet from the one on the ground before it hopped and winged to the others in the low branches, croaking a warning. He stopped beneath a beech and watched them watching him. The perfect exhilaration of solitude shattered, and he began to want someone with him. From a hole in the canopy another bird appeared, and then a pair glided between the trees to join the gang. Three more snuck up behind him, trilling and rattling deep in their throats. More birds flew in from every direction and settled in the trees or strolled about in the snow like a mob of priests in their cassocks, hands locked behind their backs, plotting some misdeed. As long as he did not move, Sean thought, they did not see him or pay him any heed. Fixed to the spot, he watched the dark assembly. One of the larger birds jumped from a low branch to the path, cocked its head left, then right, considering what might be done about the trespasser. The crow cawed once and filled the woods with echoes. The leader's caw set off a chain of vocalizations, a raucous call and response, and as it grew louder, the sounds joined together, mixing from cacophony to harmony. In an almost human voice, they spoke his name: Sean, Sean, Sean.

Beyond the murder of crows, on the point where the path of escape rose and crested, stood Norah, diaphanous in white, the glasses gone, the ragged smile replaced by perfect teeth, her hair brilliant as a halo. Through the din of his name came her voice, a simple command in a language he did not understand, and at the order, the birds stopped as one. The outliers in the high branches took off first, and then the others in twos and threes, chattering among themselves, lifted away muttering and grumbling, and he watched until the big leader hunched his shoulders and beat the air beneath his wings to disappear from the woods. When Sean looked back down the path to find the girl, she had vanished. A ring of perspiration dampened his scarf, and his hands were hot and moist in his mittens. He took one step on the rise toward her house. There was nothing in the woods. No sign the encounter had ever happened, and he did his best along the way to erase the impression that it had.

Mrs. Quinn answered the door, her eyes dark with shadows, fluttering nervously as she ushered him in. Her hands shook when she took his coat and scarf, and it took several moments before she could find her voice. "She's much better this morning," she said. "You kids gave me a fright. A fever and that cough, you'd have thought she would bring the house down."

With a quick hand she smoothed Sean's cowlick, and stopped to look at him for a moment. "She's upstairs if you like, but don't get too close and don't wear her out."

He was four steps up the stairway.

"And don't stay too long. She needs her rest."

He tiptoed into Norah's room and waited for her acknowledgment. Propped up against the pillows, she lay like a queen in her velvet robes, the down comforter barely revealing the contours of her thin body. Beside her on the nightstand teetered a pile of paperback novels—*Little Women, Black Beauty, Charlotte's Web, The Jungle Book*—and on top of the books a box of pastel chalks. Spread across her lap, an open sketchbook. He was surprised to see her there, wondered if she could be in two places at once. Norah started to smile before lifting her gaze from the paper.

"What news do you have, my spy?"

"Are you still sick? You want me to get some chicken soup?"

She raised her eyebrows and crinkled her lips in puzzlement. In the cathedral of her bedroom, sunlight rushed through the openings between the slats of the drawn blinds, suffusing the space with a pale yellow. Bedazzled, he did not know what to do next.

"How do you do those tricks?" He edged to the foot of the bed. "Where did you learn that magic?"

"Not magic." Bending to her drawing, she scribbled furiously, the pencil a blur in her hands. "Miracles and wonders. All part of the plan."

Uncertain whether to believe her or not, he fidgeted with a crocheted loop that threatened to unravel from the bedspread. He remembered what day it was. "Do you think the groundhog saw his shadow this morning? If he sees his shadow on the second day of February, that means six more weeks of winter. No shadow, we get an early spring."

"Hah! Superstition."

"You don't believe?"

"Don't mess around with matters of faith, amigo." From under the blankets, she pulled out *¡En Espanol!*, an old high school Spanish textbook with *Erica & Wiley* inked on the deckle edge of the pages. "I'm practicing my Spanish in case Aunt Diane quizzes me on New Mexico. And see—" On the sketchpad, she had drawn a large brown bird with a dead lizard hanging from its sharp beak. When he inspected the drawing more closely, Sean could see in the lizard's lifeless eyes three reflections of the sun.

"That's good," he said. "What is it?"

She flipped the pad around to her lap and added, with the edge of her pencil, a shadow cast by the bird's tail. "A roadrunner, see? You're probably thinking of the cartoon, but the real thing looks nothing like it. Only it is fast. Very, very fast."

"Meep, meep."

Without lifting her head, she rolled her eyes and stuck out her tongue.

"The part I like best," he said, "is when the coyote is tricked by the roadrunner into chasing it over the edge of the cliff. When he realizes he's standing on nothing but air, he looks at us—for just a second—before he falls. Just long enough to hold up a sign that says 'Help!' And when he falls it's always a long, long way down." He whistled the sound of a falling bomb. "Then a puff of smoke at the bottom of the canyon, and then he comes climbing out of a coyote-shaped hole all dirty and wobbly."

Norah picked up his story. "If he was standing on a rock teetering on some impossibly pointy point, that rock is going to fall too. But coyote falls faster than the rock, so that just as he climbs out of that hole, looking like a wreck and stars going round his head, just that moment, wham." She slapped her hand on the pad. "Wham, it crushes him again."

They both laughed at the memory.

"Just like life, amigo."

The furnace kicked on with a bang, and hot air curled through the registers, cooking the scents in the room—warm flannel and baby shampoo. The smell of her hair brought memories of his mother leaning over the bathtub, sleeves rolled to the elbows, working his scalp and then supporting the back of his head as he arched beneath the running tap to rinse, her hands caressing the last suds from his hair. He wanted to tell her about the crows, about seeing her in the woods, but he felt that she would just make fun of him.

"What do you know about her?" Norah asked.

"My mother?"

"No." Norah crossed her eyes. "What did you find out about my mother?"

"As far as I can tell, she ran away from home with a boy. And your grandmother still misses her. When she ate the cherries, she felt happy again, but not for long or for good. Your mother was very pretty."

"That's it? That's all? You need to find out more." The sheets snapped as she whipped them from her legs, and she slid out of bed to pace the floor, carrying on an internal monologue, gesticulating wildly, trying to contain her fury. Sean waited patiently for her to speak, but she spent her anger by pounding her bare feet upon the wooden floor. At a spot near the window, the floorboard creaked with her every footfall, and he amused himself by anticipating the sound with each turn about the room. He did not look at her but merely listened, and when she became aware of what he was doing, Norah stopped and stared at him. "What about her boyfriend? Did you learn anything about him?"

Sean hung his legs from the edge and pointed his toes to the floor. "He was darker and had long hair. And he liked the peace sign. And he was in love with your mother when she was a teenager."

"Did she tell you what happened to him? Did she say why he never came home?"

"No, I don't know. I guess our plan didn't work out so good."

She glowered at him. The furnace shut off and the ducts ticked as they cooled. Norah sat close beside him on the bed, keeping time with the pendulum of her leg. He watched her kick, vaguely disturbed by the nakedness of her feet and ankles. Because of her glasses, she did not look at him head-on, but craned her neck about thirty degrees to the right. He followed the angle, twisting to meet her eyes, and challenged her. "Why don't you just ask your grandmother yourself?"

"Because she already thinks that I am hers." When she parted her lips, the scent of gingerbread filled the space between them. "And I might just want to stay here with her."

No longer able to bear her closeness, Sean went to the window and pulled hard on the cord to the blinds, flooding the room with brilliance. "There is no easy way to miss it," he said. "Six more weeks of winter."

THE BIRDS SANG in their cage all morning long. An even dozen in a three-by-four case complete with artificial branches and covering leaves, the house finches were Simonetta Delarosa's babies. She came to the flower shop every day to coddle them with gourmet seed and bread moistened with milk, and had given each pair linked names from her favorite operas: the zebras were Romeo and Juliet; the Gouldians, Otello and Desdemona; the owl finches, Figaro and Susanna; the society, Violetta and Alfredo; the spice, Ferrando and Dorabella; and the star,

Guglielmo and Fiordiligi. Enraptured by the dazzling sunshine, the mates behaved as if a new spring had begun, flying and singing and preening for one another so much that Simonetta, long inured to their habits, took notice and sat by the cage and watched them carry on right up to the point when the visitor arrived.

As soon as he stepped through the doorway, the birds hushed and hid beneath the greenery. The man removed his hat and gloves, brushed his silver hair back with the flat of his palm. From behind the wire cage, Simonetta smiled at him, and Pat nodded through the glass of the walk-in cooler, where they kept the cut flowers cool and moist. The stranger circled the room, stopping to sniff at a bunch of tiger lilies, to finger a single violet face of a blooming dendrobium. He crouched next to the birdcage to peer inside. Simonetta tried to show him her treasures, but the birds cowered in the shadows no matter how she coaxed.

"They act like they're afraid of you."

"A stranger can sometimes have that effect on little creatures," he said. "Portents of uncertainty in their ordered world."

Pat wiped his hands on the front of his apron and advanced from the back of the shop. "Is there anything you're looking for?"

"No, no. Just coming in from the cold. Though those are beautiful orchids."

"My favorites. They come and go like magic, but while they last, they're like miracles." With a gaze approaching love, Pat considered the potted plants. "You from around here?"

The hint of a smile curled at the corners of his lips. "No. I'm with the State. I'm looking for someone. A runaway."

Rising to stand by her husband, Simonetta twisted her fingers together. "From the State? Who are you looking for?"

"A little girl," he said. "A runaway from an institution up north. I've come to find her and take her home."

The Delarosas drew closer, pressed shoulder to shoulder, and he stared at them, watching for their faces to betray their emotions, and then he laid his hat atop the cage to work his hands into his gloves. "A clever child, she might latch on to anyone. She might appear like an answer to a prayer, but every answer brings new questions, and every wish the hope for one more wish."

"We don't know any little girl," said Pat.

As the stranger placed his hat back on his head, he said, "You keep an eye out for her." And bringing two fingers to the brim, he bowed slightly and departed. The finches roared and sang in panic and threw themselves against the iron bars, and not until late afternoon could Simonetta manage to soothe the last of them, a star finch cowering in a high corner, and return the poor creature, thimble heart racing in her hand, to a safer perch.

21

All by itself, the front door opened with a creak after two quick knocks, and a three-note hello came ringing from the threshold. Norah and Mrs. Quinn rose from the table, their dinner going cold the moment they departed, rushing to greet their prodigal guest. The girl footed it more quickly, skittering to a stop just in front of the woman and her suitcases. Straightening from the waist, her Auntie Diane rose like a colossus, nearly six feet tall, her silver hair swept straight back in a thick mane, her face hard and divided into planes and sharp angles broken by a magnificent nose and fierce hazel eyes; shoulders thrown back, her spine a pole perpendicular to the surface of the world, her short boots planted as wide as her hips. Her coat, pink as a rose and with mother-of-pearl buttons, quilted her to the ankles, and fur-trimmed gloves gave her hands the appearance of brushed nickel. Norah had just enough time to take her all in before Margaret caught up to her. The sisters gasped, a small sigh of joy in recognition, and as they stepped toward each other, Norah pirouetted from their path, stood by silent and watchful as they embraced. Diane unclenched first, grasped her sister's biceps, and pulled away to consider her more carefully. The women smiled identical smiles, embraced again, holding four beats, long enough for Norah to begin bouncing on her toes. A draft sucked in the front door, which closed with a bang that startled them all.

"It's cold as the bishop's bum. I had forgotten what a godforsaken frozen tundra you live in, Maggie. You look good—what's all this talk about being tired?" She pivoted her head and stared at the child. "And who is this darling child? The sudden granddaughter you mentioned over the phone. The mysterious fugitive from way out west. Norah, is it? Norah Rinnick, I presume?"

"Quinn, actually. Norah Quinn. And you must be Great-Aunt Diane." She stuck out her right hand.

"My heavens, Norah Quinn." She turned to her sister. "She's every bit as you described on the phone. You're quite the shock, Norah."

"A miracle," Margaret said. "An answered prayer."

Diane pivoted around to the girl. "Well, since we're family, I must ask you for a hug. What do you say to your Auntie Di?"

The girl took a half step forward and found herself enveloped in a swatch of pink cloth, her face smashed against a great bosom concealed beneath a brassiere that felt like a birdcage. "Like Princess Di?" she asked, her voice muffled and small.

Diane's laugh erupted from deep inside her chest, and Norah was pitched backward by the percussion. "Just like Princess Di. The two great beauties of the modern age." She peeled off her gloves, handing them to Norah, and then with practiced formality, she disrobed coat and hat and burdened the girl. Norah staggered to the closet while the sisters linked arms and headed for the kitchen. "Be a dear," Diane said to the girl, "and take my bag to the room reserved for princesses." As she hauled the suitcase around, Norah eavesdropped on a bit of their conversation. "Oh, she is a dead ringer for him . . ." Him. Rinnick.

They warmed the plates in the oven and ate an overdone dinner a half hour later. Talk revolved around fatigue from the long drive north, snow at Somerset, but once through the tunnel smooth sailing; the terrible coldness of the winter, neither woman ever remembering temperatures so low for so many weeks in a row; the wretched state of the economy, Ronald Reagan, the collapse of the steel industry. To her astonishment, Norah was not the center of discussion. For the moment, she had ceased to exist. The sisters lingered at coffee, not yet willing to address the matter of the recent addition to the family.

After dessert, she went upstairs to bathe, and over the rush of running water, Norah could not spy so easily, though she tried listening through a glass pressed against the floor. All she could hear was the ocean. Washed, and dressed for sleep, she swept downstairs to say goodnight, finding the two women relocated to the living room, sitting at right angles to each other under a single lamp which cast a pale halo fading to black in the far corners. Like conspirators hatching a plot, they dipped close to each other, their faces moving in and out of the light and shadows, their voices near whispers and dripping secrets.

"Why, we were just talking about you, Norah," Mrs. Quinn said. "Are you clean as a whistle and ready—"

"Ready to blow?" her sister asked.

Norah wolf-whistled, and the women laughed. Mrs. Quinn held out her arms, and Norah hugged her, kissed her cheek, and then hesitated before Diane, uncertain of the protocol.

"I'm not going to bite you, child. At least not hard. Come here." She smothered her with a bear hug and a wet kiss on the ear. "I could eat you up." She held the child with one hand on her back and stroked her hair with the other. "We were talking about your mother, actually. Do you know neither one of us has seen her in nearly ten years? Just before you were born—"

"She ran away from home."

"That's right, muppet. Do you know why she never came back?"

"No, ma'am."

Dissatisfied by the answer, Diane held the moment, chewing her thoughts. "Well . . . her mother and her auntie miss her."

"I miss her too."

22

HUGE, read the first note. The postscript made him laugh and earned them both a twenty-minute detention. AND SCARY. When Sean unfolded the paper tossed his way, he knew that Norah was describing her great-aunt Diane. Caught sniggering by Mrs. Patterson, he was invited to share what he found so amusing with the rest of the class. He demurred, blushed, stammered into trouble. The teacher unfolded the message and misinterpreted the words as directed toward her.

After the dismissal bells trilled, Sean and Norah remained behind, fixed at their desks, waiting out their punishment, while at the front of the room, Mrs. Patterson graded papers, glancing up every so often, a bemused stare tempering the gravity of the situation. The red second hand on the clock face—MADE IN THE USA, ALLEGHENY COUNTY SCHOOL DISTRICT—slowed, wavered, threatened to stop entirely. Norah could count almost to ten between the ticks, and bored into mischief, she tried to attract his attention by clearing her throat, tapping her fingers along the pencil well on the desktop, sighing. He dared look back once, panic in his eyes, and for the last five minutes simply bowed his head and tucked it into the cradle of his folded arms. Excuses for their tardiness in getting home played out in the recesses of his mind. Never before had he been punished by a teacher, never asked to stay one minute after school.

Sentences served, they were dismissed with the admonishment to go and sin no more. Dragging their coats and bags behind them, the pair left the classroom to empty corridors stretching out to the front door. The school seemed alien and foreboding, and he pushed ahead, anxious to disassociate himself from the troublemaker. He pretended to be interested in the displays along the walls: the first graders' crudely fashioned poems to winter; lopsided snowmen built from cottonballs, spit, and glue; the second graders' paeans to Groundhog Day, now forlorn after the actual date had passed. The third graders' papier-mâché masks of African animals, his own clumsy antelope and Norah's toothy leopard. She called for him to let her catch up, but that only served to spur him onward. When he heard her flying toward him, he started to sprint, but before he had broken the traces, she was upon him, spinning him around so quickly that his bag flew from his hand and his coat whipped to the wall and dropped to the floor.

"I told you to wait up," she said.

"Get offa me."

"Are you mad because I got you detention?"

He met her stare with malice in his eyes. His face bloomed red and he spat out the words: "Go away. You're nothing but trouble since you got here."

"Sean, you're making a big deal—"

"Everything was fine till you showed up." Angry lines crossed his forehead as he flushed a deeper red, and he pinched his hands into fists. She struck quick as a snake, sinking her teeth into his shoulder, biting hard enough to break the skin beneath his shirt. Even as he jerked away, she clamped on and would not let go until he screamed out in pain and surprise.

"There!" she yelled at him. "There, now you have a real reason to be mad at me."

Fingers clamped on his shoulder, he stammered his reply. "What did you do that for? That hurts. You had no right—"

"I just wanted to talk with you and you ran away. I'm sorry, but you're not going to let Mrs. P ruin us being friends, are you?"

"You really bite hard."

"Sorry—"

"I'm still mad at you. I have to come by your house every morning and take you to school, and then you're all weird, and you know all these tricks and you won't share and you cheat and you keep secrets."

"I'm trying to apologize."

"Sorry isn't enough."

"You don't understand right now but you will. If you just help me."

"Why should I help you? You bit me. Why would you bite me?"

"'Cause you made me mad on account of a tiny problem, a bump in the road."

"But I never get in trouble. My parents would kill—" He caught the words as they tumbled from his mouth, choking on the memory of his father.

"Don't tell on me, okay? You can win next time we play chess."

With a grudging reluctance, he eased into his coat and shouldered his bookbag. A silent truce formed between them, and taking care to match strides, they walked to the front door. Outside a light snow fell dry and small. Norah pulled up her hood and tugged on her mittens.

Before they opened the door, he stopped to ask in earnest. "I won't tell anyone, but you have to tell me who is following you. You said that night that someone might want to take you away. Where to?"

"I don't know what he wants," she said. "But I am afraid. I don't want to leave."

They stepped into the empty yard. All of the buses and children were long gone, and just a handful of cars remained in the lot, their windshields dusted with powdered sugar. The snow ticked against hard surfaces and, in the hush of afternoon, sounded like waves of static. Heavy clouds diffused the light, softened every angle, and flattened perspective. Sean felt as if he were moving through a picture, the flakes white hatches on a gray background. Even Norah, next to him, looked like a paper doll.

"She's very tall," said Norah. "Aunt Diane. And intimidating somehow. Maybe it's the way she talks. You can almost hear the gears spinning in her head. She's thinking, boy. And I'm going to have to think faster and harder to keep up. And I'm going to need your help with her questions. You know what she called me? A fugitive."

"Like from the FBI?"

"Maybe I'm a Most Wanted Girl?"

They slowed to let a car pass before crossing the road to the trail through the woods. When they reached the other side, Sean grabbed her by the wrist. "Hey, maybe it's your mother who's the fugitive—"

"My mother would be nothing of the kind. Still, I'll need your help with Auntie Di. Come over tomorrow after school. We're still partners in crime, eh, amigo?"

"Just so long as there's no more biting."

She could not resist a smile. Taking her knapsack from her shoulder, she crouched on the sidewalk, unzipped a compartment, and rooted around the explosion of tissues, pencil stubs, and broken crayons. With a gentle hand, she scooped a small object and held it carefully in her palm, presenting to him a blue cup, delicate as porcelain, salvaged from a children's tea set. A pair of birds in flight, sharing a banner in their beaks, had been painted in expert hand on its surface, and but for a chip that marred its banded lip, it was a perfect miniature.

"This is for you," she said. "I've carried it with me for years, the only memory of my former life, but I'd like you to have it to say that we are friends. When I am troubled, I whisper a prayer into the cup and fill it with my wishes. You need it more than I do."

He hid the present from his mother, grateful for once that she came home hours later. In the silence of his room, Sean considered Norah's token, held the tapered bowl to his lips, and thought of all his wishes. He could not bear to whisper *father* into the cup, struck silent by the absurdity of her claims, by the failure of any prayer to bring about the desired answer. Why whisper when his heart shouted to no result? Still, he was glad for the gift, touched by the selfless gesture, and the teacup found a place of honor beside the circus cookie boxes filled with his collections of found objects. Later that night in the bathroom, he gingerly removed his shirt and stared at the red wound in his reflection. Sore to the touch, the ring seethed purple, and when he turned to get a better look Sean recognized the pattern her teeth had made. In the mirror, the bite mark looked just like a pair of wings.

23

The sisters circled around the subject of Erica, as they always had since her disappearance. From the very beginning Diane had suspected the truth, but she had remained circumspect those first few weeks in 1975 when nobody could be quite sure if Erica had run away or had been abducted or worse. The Quinns refused to believe theories proffered by the local police or later by the FBI, even after the confirmed sighting by the liquor store owner in Tennessee, the bedside description in Oklahoma, and the alleged confrontation with a waitress in a Texas café. Only when the evidence proved overwhelming could Margaret acknowledge to her sister that something terrible had happened to her daughter, and even then she maintained Erica's innocence throughout. After Paul passed away, the topic was rarely broached at all.

The summer following Paul's death, Margaret and Diane stole away together for a week at the shore, revisiting the beach house their parents had rented for a song when the girls were ten and eight. A weather-beaten clapboard, it seemed much smaller than they remembered, and the Atlantic too, less wild, less blue, everything diminished in scope and dwarfed by the decades of development along the coast. For four days they idled in the sun, doing nothing more arduous than soaking to the collarbone at low tide, watching the pipers dance to and fro, walking on the sand at sunset. On the fifth night, when the end of the respite began to touch their ease, Diane rustled a quarter bushel of steamed blue crabs, and they sat on the deck with their mallets and picks, a roll of butcher's paper to capture the shells, a six-pack of cold beer to wash down the tang of Old Bay.

"We haven't talked about him," she said, hammering through a big claw. "Not all week. It's okay, if you don't want to. . . ."

"Paul?" Margaret pried at a reluctant apron.

Diane reached out and touched her sister's forearm. "I know you blame him for Erica—"

"I miss him, I suppose, but I'm getting used to his not being there. He was going from me for so long that it seems like he left long ago. He didn't make her run away with that boy. If anyone's to blame, it's me. I should have stepped in between them, kept the peace. Talked to her like the woman she was becoming."

Diane sipped at her beer, the slick of condensation cool against her skin. "Keeping busy, then?"

Margaret tore off a lump of crabmeat and savored the salty taste. "The Delarosas have me keep their books, and I go downtown twice a week to volunteer at the Carnegie. I'll tell you a secret, I go by Mullins there, not Quinn, and nobody seems to know who I am. I like it that way."

With a strong twist of the wrist, Diane broke open another shell. "Well, I'm glad that you're moving on."

Leaning back in her chair, Margaret stared out at the ocean. A young family, a small boy held in his mother's arms, pointed out a dolphin breaking the surface and rolling beneath the waves. "Moving on? How can we move on? How can I ever forget for the rest of my life what my child has done? I pray every day for some salvation." She looked back at her sister and warned in a loud voice, "Don't touch your eyes. They'll burn all night from the spice on your fingers."

Using the crook of her arm, Diane wiped away her tears. Though she wished she could comfort her big sister, she realized she had no idea what swam in the depths of the body, what hopes and fears were fixed on her soul.

WHILE THE CHILDREN were in school on Tuesday, Margaret and Diane drove to town, past the shuttered mill, the workers drifting by the bars and the union hall. They stopped for lunch at the diner and wiggled into a booth. Diane curled her lip when she touched the waxy tabletop and the pads of her fingers stuck to the surface. Joyce Waverly noticed them and hurried over to say hello. "Mrs. Quinn, so nice to see you again."

"This is my sister, Diane Cicogna, come up from Washington, D.C., for a visit. Diane, this is Joyce Waverly Green."

"Green Waverly, Mrs. Q. Pleased to meet you, Mrs. Cicogna, though I think we may have met once or twice before when I was in high school. At a party over the house. How's that grandbaby of yours, Mrs. Quinn? She like that new coat?"

"Norah?" She held her eyes on Diane a beat too long. "Poor thing caught a cold over the weekend, fell through the ice down on Miller's Pond, but she's better now, thank God, though I was worried sick there for a while. How are your children, Joyce? How's the bun in the oven?"

"Keeping toasty. Tell the truth, my feet are already swelling up like pumpkins with toes. I don't know how I'm going to make the last trimester." Joyce shifted her weight from one hip to the other. "There's been something I've been meaning to ask you ever since you last came in."

Diane cleared her throat. "Are you one of the girls Erica ran with?"

"Don't know that I'd say it quite like that, but yes, we were friends, ma'am. Best friends, back in the day."

"Call me Diane. I wouldn't have recognized you, all grown up and a mother too. From the shape of you, you'll have a girl this time, carrying way up high like that. Of course if you had a spoon, some string, and a Gypsy, we could be sure."

Joyce smiled at the joke, took their order for club sandwiches, and left them in peace. A handful of other people dotted the chairs and booths, mostly solos staring at their meatloaf and mashed potatoes, former mill hunks working through the crossword or the salesclerk from Murphy's tackling the latest Stephen King. A pair of young nurses, immaculate in white, finished up nearby, talking about amnio and C-sections while dipping French fries into the last slick of ketchup on their shared platter. The prettier one hit the bottom of her glass to free the ice but sucked air, and they both laughed, split the check, and left. Diane gave them the skunk eye as they passed the table, but the nurses took no notice.

"The things some people will discuss over lunch in a public place. Delivering babies while decent people are trying to enjoy their minestrone." Diane laid both palms flat on the placemat, her engagement ring as ostentatious as ever. "What I'd like to talk about is that little girl of yours."

Tapping her nails like a metronome, Margaret shot a sideways glance down the row of tables to see if Joyce was coming. "Erica?"

"Tangentially Erica, but more to the point, this child Norah. Tell me again how she's come to stay with you? Out of the blue, you hear from your estranged daughter and then this illegitimate—I won't use the vulgar word—is forced upon you?"

"Not at all, not like that at all." She sipped from her water glass. "Just after the New Year, I got a telephone call in the middle of the night. She must have forgotten about the time difference, I'm always forgetting about time—"

The sandwiches arrived, stacked high and speared with colored toothpicks. Joyce Waverly set them down carefully before the two women. "Just let me know, ladies, if I can bring you anything else. Hey, I've heard news about your granddaughter. My cousin has a boy in third grade, and he says that the new girl is a real artist. Oh, what did he say? Better than Spider-Man, he says, better drawing than in the comics, and him loving Spider-Man more than Jesus, so it's quite a compliment. Since you last came in, I was wondering how's come Erica never mentioned a daughter when I talked to her a couple years back? Maybe I'm just not remembering right. Holler if you need anything, ladies."

They waited until she was out of earshot. "Better'n Jesus. Still the country out here, you ask me." Diane plucked the toothpicks from her toasted bread, held them like a picador ready to make the kill, and then tossed them to the rim of her plate. "So about Erica. What does she have to say for herself after all these years?"

Her sister finished chewing the corner of the sandwich, then wiped her mouth with the napkin, a dot of mayonnaise lingering on her upper lip. "At first, I didn't believe it was her and not someone else playing a prank. But she told me it really was her and she was in trouble, a different kind of trouble, and didn't know who to call."

"Didn't she give you some explanation?"

"What, that she's a wanted woman, that she's underground, hiding, that she feared she would be traced? Of course, she's sorry. But when your only child asks for help, you help. No questions. She said she needed someone to look after Norah for her while she got her life back together."

"Surely the statute of limitations has run out by now. Did you suggest that she might turn herself in and throw herself on the mercy of the court?"

"It wasn't a long discussion, Diane, and I didn't think about limitations, in fact, until you just mentioned it."

"But you at least told her about Paul, right?"

The waitress arrived to ask if everything was to their satisfaction, and when they nodded, she scratched her belly with the edge of her order pad. "I remembered what I wanted to tell you. There was a man in here the other day, a funny way about him, asking about you and Norah. Said he knew you from way back when. Very handsome and old-fashioned. Dashing, they used to say. Said he was a friend of the family."

Diane asked, "Did he call himself Jackson?" Margaret swatted the air in front of her.

"Never gave his name," she said. "Never saw him before or since. Just funny all of a sudden you come in and then someone asking after you. You had some unexpected company lately?"

"Very mysterious," Diane said. "We're fine, dear, really. Thanks."

The interruption gave Margaret a chance to think, and she bought more time by taking another bite of her club sandwich, bacon crumbling to the plate, and chewing slowly. Scrunching up her face, she removed the top piece of toast and removed the tomato slices. "Hothouse."

Between bites, Diane asked again. "So, how did she react when you told her that her father was dead?"

"As you might expect. They never taste right, hothouse tomatoes. I don't think she broke down and cried, if that's what you meant."

"After all that man put her through, no."

"He was only trying to protect her. You don't know that it wouldn't have been worse."

"Couldn't be much worse than her running off with a criminal."

"It can always be worse. There could have been a real confrontation. Threats were made."

"By Paul? Harmless old Paul?"

Margaret snipped off another piece of her sandwich. "By the boy. And besides, if it had gone any other way, we might not have Norah, right? This funny-looking creature, stick skinny, and an entire mystery. She needs me, at least for a while."

"Maybe you can threaten to keep her daughter." Diane laughed. "That might bring Erica home."

24

Tracks began at the edge of the bicycle path and cut on the diagonal through the maze of bare trees rolling into the hills, and the children bent to inspect the footprints: four toes and heel pad, the steps ten inches or more apart. Sean fingered the edges, and granules of snow rolled away in a miniature avalanche. Squatting next to him, Norah peered down the trail to the point where it vanished over the horizon.

"They're fresh." Sean spoke with authority. "Probably a dog wandering through."

"Not a dog," Norah answered. "No claw marks in these prints."

"Or a raccoon, I was about to say. Maybe a possum."

Norah followed their progress between the trees. "How long have you lived in these woods, Sean? All your life? The front paws of a raccoon look just like a human hand, five fingers stretched out. And claws, amigo. Possum looks like a raccoon only the fingers are more spread out, like you were playing piano. Claws too. This thing we're following is a cat. Or maybe a gray fox, though the claws would show up in the snow this deep."

"A cat? We're chasing after a cat?"

Norah waited for him to catch up, then bent to the print. "Definitely not Tiger or Fluffy. It's not a housecat, or if it is, then a really big cat, probably wild. But look how deep here. That animal weighs about twenty pounds, and look how it's walking."

"Like there's only two legs? Where did its other feet go?"

"A cat walks like this." She splayed out her feet and hands and slunk forward with an arched back, rolling each shoulder in rhythm, which made him laugh uncomfortably. "But a wildcat will put its back foot right in the middle of the hole left by the front one."

"A wildcat? Like a leopard?"

"If it's a leopard, I'll connect its spots. Bobcat, I think. C'mon."

They hurried through the winter forest, the snow fresh and undisturbed save for the solitary set of tracks and the windblown litter scraping along the surface, the papery oak leaves, the empty acorn cups, the feathery twigs snapped off in the latest storm. In the boughs, frostings of snow remained, and when the children brushed against low-hanging branches, powder would sluice off and shower to the ground in their wake. The scrub pines and occasional firs provided the only color, the rest dun or gray in the cold and damp. Deep in the forest, a rare quiet pervaded, the snow hushing all sounds but their own footsteps. He could hear her labored breathing, which reassured him when she hurried ahead out of sight, and he caught up by following the husky rasp to find her squatting again before a thrash of marks.

"See this deep impression here," she said, pointing to what looked to Sean like nothing more than two wide scrapes. "Kitty is tired. She sat back on her haunches for a siesta. Or maybe to watch a mouse skitter under a stone."

"What if it turns out to be a bobcat, Norah? What if we catch up to it?"

"Have a little faith." Her nostrils flared as she breathed deeply. "The game is afoot, my dear Watson. Well, come on, man!"

The afternoon faded to shadows as the trees grew thicker. Coming to a culvert between two hills, she paused and pointed to other tracks bisecting the cat's, showing him the rabbit run by the different patterns of footfall, the small front legs and the leaping pads. He expected blood on the trail, but the two animals had passed hours apart. Norah inspected the rough snow where the cat had casually sniffed the hare's scent and moved on. The sun dipped below the treetops, the upper branches splintering the sky into maroon and orange. The children climbed a path to the crest of the next hill, and she waved for him to stop and be still.

Silhouetted against the pewter clouds on the next rise about fifty yards ahead stood the cat in sharp relief against the snow. Its head cocked, nose in the air, catching their scent on the wind. A cloud cleared the setting sun, and the cat was bathed in light, its fawn-colored coat mottled with spots, the long white hair cloaking its paws and bristling at the tips of its ears and the bobbed tail. As quick as a breeze, it strayed into shadow and was gone. They could smell the tang of urine, hear the soft crunch of its getaway, and see its ghost standing on the vacant spot, fixed by magic and time.

"Listen, Sean. Tell me what you hear."

He heard nothing but the sound of his own breathing and the bare hour, the sound of the land in stillness.

Norah faced him, her eyes glistening, as if she were remembering some past pain, and she asked her questions in a care-laden tone. "Do you know about the atom bomb? The ones they dropped in Japan?"

Though he was not sure that he remembered any details, he nodded.

"There was just silence, like this, after the fires, after the sirens. Everything was still. Even the birds were gone. And those who survived walked around the destroyed city stunned to be alive."

The cat was long gone, he was sure, unlikely to come near the sound of her voice.

"I know a story that they tried to keep hidden," Norah said. "About Mrs. Quinn's husband. He was there, in Nagasaki, Japan, after the bomb was dropped, with the army's medical team. He saw the ruined city." As he listened to the details, Sean grew frightened, not only of the story about the young doctor facing so many dead and dying, but of being lost in the dark woods.

She finished in hushed whispers. Hunching her shoulders against the falling temperature, Norah pivoted on her heels and began to retrace their steps. Sean stumbled along behind her, nearly out of breath when he reached her side. They strode together, stepping in the prints they had made outward bound.

"Didn't I tell you it was a bobcat?" she said.

"I never seen anything like it," said Sean. "I saw a possum once crossing the yard, fat as you please, early one morning on my way to school. But a bobcat, wow. I had no idea they even lived around here."

"There's much you don't know and much that is hidden from you. Look beyond the surface, amigo." A phlegmy cough rattled her chest.

"That was so cool, but how are we going to find our way back when it gets dark?" He cast a worried eye to the skies. "Aren't you afraid of getting lost?"

She spat onto the snow. "Don't worry, it won't get dark."

"But the sun is already setting. You can barely see as it is."

Norah stopped and faced him. "Sean, if I say you'll get home before nighttime, you have to believe me."

He pleaded with her. "But it's sunset—"

"Where is your faith? If I wished, it would be bright as the noonday sun this very moment. Believe in me."

Having no other choice, Sean marched behind, following her through the trees, head tipped against the breeze, as relentless as a wave. Hidden nearby, the one who watched let them go. In his arms, the wild-cat squirmed and growled until his captor absentmindedly released his grip. In the opposite direction, the boy and the girl trudged home. Along the way she provided a running commentary on the forest, the names of the winter plants, the places where turtles slept and field mice hunkered down for the season. They passed a set of human prints, a man's dress shoes, leading in and out of a maze of paper birches, but she said nothing about the mysterious tracks. Out of the woods and onto the paths, she sang and whistled carelessly, distracting him from the passing time. When they arrived at his front door, he was astounded to glimpse the sunset horizon and the underside of the clouds glowing vermilion in the last gasp of the dying day.

25

When he was alone, Sean did not know what to believe. Caught between fear and fascination, he thought at first that she might be a magician, a witch, a devil, able to stop time or change her appearance at will or keep aloft objects with her very breath. But though she intended some deception with Mrs. Quinn, or at least her aunt Diane, she had no evil purpose he could determine. The evidence pointed elsewhere. What had she said? With every breath, God exhales an angel?

But if she was an angel, what about her wings? In almost every picture, they had huge white feathered wings that began between the shoulder blades and arced in triumph, curving until the tips nearly brushed the ground. Sean could not figure out how they got off the ground with such wings—some aspect of aerodynamics seemed all wrong—so he scoured his *Children's Illustrated Bible* and other books for pictures of angels in flight. Every image captured some static moment, and he could garner no sense of the wings in motion. The angels in books wore white robes and sandals. Some had starry halos behind their heads. Norah had no halo. Many angels wore their hair long and perfectly coiffed, as if having just come from the stylist. Her hair was a fright. Their faces were universally kind, impassive or gentle, and they were almost always depicted as men. How could she be an angel? She had no wings, no halo. Angels do not bite.

Flipping through his Bible, Sean discovered stories which featured cameo appearances by an angel. Jacob wrestles one and breaks his hip. In a vision, angels proclaim the holiness of the Lord, and one places a burning coal to the lips of Isaiah. An angel talks Mary into having a baby, and a heavenly host announces to the shepherds tending their flock that the babe is born and lying in a manger in Bethlehem. They are always proclaiming to people news from above. God's messengers. He wondered what message Norah had in store and why she was so long in delivering it. And then he remembered: she was no angel, but a child like him.

He wished there was someone to ask. Most mornings when home, he would think to ask his mother, but she had changed so much in the year since his father left. Always working, and when not at the job, she took care of a thousand household chores. Some nights when he was restless and could not sleep, he found her conked out on the couch, curled under a throw, the glow of the television flickering across the shadows of her face, and seeing her so, he longed to reach out and tuck her in, smooth her hair, wipe away the lines etched in her skin. Even in her dreams, she looked so unhappy that he dared not ask her about angels or say much about his new friend from school. He knew she would not solve his puzzles, only offer comfort or worry over his questions, try to fit together what would not be joined.

Still, it would have been nice to talk with someone about Norah.

Sean could ask his father, if he ever came back, although he was sure that some things, most things, would never again be as they once were. He felt that he would at least talk to him man to man; that much a father owes a son.

His teacher was out of the question. For five months, Mrs. Patterson had managed to ignore him because he was not the type of kid who would ever volunteer, and his answers, when he was called upon, emerged from his thoughts in such a soft voice that she had to ask every time for him to repeat, but loud and clear. Eventually, she tired of the routine. It was more expedient to call on someone else, and since he earned *Satisfactory* in every subject, there was no cause, good or ill, for her notice.

His friends—the kids at the outsiders' lunch table—were friends with Norah as well, and he couldn't ask about angels without arousing their suspicion or her retribution. On consideration, he realized that they weren't actually friends, simply the ones left over and out of place. Misfits. Until Norah came along, even they had rarely included him in conversations. On the playing fields at recess, the captains often chose him last or nearly so, an afterthought. Given the option, he ended up alone, tossing a ball against a wall, riding a swing into the bright and beautiful sky, or reading a book, his back against the yellow brick of the school building. He had only one true friend. The only person he could talk with about Norah was Norah herself. And he could not talk with Norah.

After brushing his teeth and wrestling into his pajamas, he went downstairs to say goodnight. His mother sat at the kitchen table, sorting through bills, the checkbook open in supplication. With her free hand propping her head, she bore a look he associated with taking a test—a mixture of concentration and frustration—but as soon as she caught his eyes, she managed a smile and put down her pen.

"Sweet dreams, sweetheart. Come and give us a kiss."

He shuffled over to her, his slippers whiffing on the carpet. She wrapped her arms around him and pulled his body close, kissing him gently on the cheek. His bitten shoulder ached under her touch, but he did not cry out or flinch.

"I saw a bobcat today," he said.

"Is that right? I've never heard of bobcats in these parts."

"Me and Norah tracked it down, followed its footprints through the snow and even got close enough—but not too close—to see its yellow eyes."

"You may be the luckiest kids in the county." She stroked his hair and pushed loose strands behind his ears. "You and Norah are good pals, aren't you?" He hung on to her, desperate for another moment.

"Mum, do you know anything about angels?"

"Angels, for heaven's sake." She traced a circle on his back. "When I was a child in first grade, there was a girl named Dorothy—"

"Like in *The Wizard of Oz*?"

"That's right, but everyone called her Dot, and she claimed she had a guardian angel that went everywhere with her. Said she could see this angel—although nobody else could—about the size of a grown-up with wings as bright as the sun, and this angel kept her out of trouble and so on. She went away for a while, and when she came back Dot told us that she had leukemia. She said the angel helped her through the treatments. Watched over her while she was a long time in the hospital, and we kids would go down there to visit and bring her books and juice, like that, and never once was Dot scared on account of the angel."

"And what happened to her? Dot, I mean?"

Mrs. Fallon twisted a curl around her index finger and stared straight ahead. "She died, I'm afraid. But the school had a painting done, a good likeness of her anyway, with Dot and her angel walking through a field, and they hung a sign beneath it with her name and the dates of her life, and it said something from the Bible. 'Blessed are they who believe,' or something like that."

"Do you?" His voice cracked and tears welled in his eyes.

"Oh, honey, I shouldn't have told you that story. Why don't you just forget all about it? Dream about what you have seen, not the unseen. What about that bobcat in the woods?" She held him until he settled, then sent him off to bed.

Blankets drawn to his chin, Sean fidgeted to find a warm and comfortable spot. In the dim light, he could make out the familiar shapes of objects in the room, and he spent a long time staring at the toy teacup Norah had given him and the books and games on the shelves his father had built. He wondered where his father was that night, worried that something bad would happen, and they would not ever get the chance to see each other again, though perhaps, he thought, one day in heaven after they both had died. Reunions were possible, he decided, in the afterlife when everyone gone and forsaken would have the chance to go over every harsh word and every word left unsaid, and such a possibility made sense of heaven, gave the idea some meaning and reason. Hanging on a hook in the open closet, his winter coat looked just like a pair of folded wings, ready to wear. Anxious, he rolled away toward the dim light at the window and felt a stab in his shoulder. Sean could not sleep and wondered if Norah was his guardian or had some dire message for him. *Has she come to warn me?* he wondered. *Is now the hour of my death?*

26

The sisters taught the girl to play gin, and she was winning every hand. Sometimes Norah would even lay down after picking up two or three cards, and the winners were astonishing: four queens and three eights; a straight flush to the jack of hearts. Margaret and Diane laughed with surprise each time, sipped their Irish coffees, and had another bite of the brownies Norah had baked with Auntie earlier that Saturday. The cards snapped as they were shuffled. Every so often, the furnace roared and bellowed for a few minutes, then the ducts pinged as the metal expanded and contracted. Like clockwork, Norah coughed abruptly just as the blowers stopped. Diane's turn to deal came round again, and as she passed out the seven cards, she asked what time they would be going to Mass in the morning.

"I'm not." Margaret began arranging her hand. "This weather is killing me. I'll kneel down and never come up."

Play began. Norah picked blind from the deck, discarded a two of clubs.

"Have you been to see a doctor, Maggie?"

Margaret drew a four of hearts, laid down a nine of diamonds. "No lectures, please. I had a doctor in the house for almost thirty years. It's nothing—arthritis, gingivitis, age-itis. An ordinary illness, life."

Diane took her sister's nine and left a five of clubs for Norah, who folded it into her hand and put down a second nine. Diane sneered at her. Margaret passed on the discard and drew from the deck, throwing down a jack of diamonds atop the pile. Diane scooped it up before her sister had second thoughts, and left the ace of spades for Norah. "I think I'll go anyhow, you don't mind?"

"Gin." Norah laid down three fives and four aces. "I'll go with you, Auntie Di."

• • •

AT THE PROPER TIMES in the Mass, Norah knew when to kneel and when to stand; she said her prayers in concert with the people in their pew; she sang every hymn without looking at the words in the songbook, though she stayed behind when Diane rose to join the lines for Communion. Head bowed to her folded hands, she knelt and waited for her aunt's return, sighing when the whole congregation sat as the rite concluded. The priest and altar boys processed to a choir of voices, and it was over. Had they been the first to leave, they might have noticed the figure in the camel hair coat at the back of the nave, guarding the door as if a sentry to another world, but he left before the final blessing. They bundled into their coats and headed through the massive double doors, the frigid Sunday air bone-chilling after the closeness and warmth of so many people.

"What say we go see your grandfather?"

"My grandfather?"

"Pay a visit to his grave. Awful lonesome in wintertime with so few visitors."

The others hurried to their cars, revved engines, sent thin clouds of exhaust into the air, and sped away. Diane and Norah waited till the last had left, then crossed the parking lot to the cemetery tucked behind a stand of sheltering firs. As they reached the gate, a crow lit out for parts unknown, a black smudge against the pale sky. A hundred souls or so lay buried by St. Anne's, and their stones and memorials rose like bergs on a rolling sea of snow. A caretaker had shoveled the main pathways, and here and there, a set of prints trailed off with dedication to a particular stone. Flowers and wreaths, some recalling the most recent Christmas, lay encased in ice, perfect until the first thaw. They meandered through the gardens, uncertain where Paul Quinn resided.

"You know, I've been meaning to steal you away from the moment I arrived. Just us girls. A chance to talk without you-know-who."

"But you've been here a whole week."

"Never alone with you, my dear. Just the two of us. Woman to woman."

Coughing into her mittens, Norah remained where she stood until the moment passed, stalling for time. "You could have asked me anything in front of Grandma. I would have—"

"You don't understand, you . . ." She collected her thoughts, strewn across the graveyard. "There are certain subjects I don't feel comfortable bringing up around my sister. For her sake, I bite my tongue."

"Once I bit a boy on the shoulder because he didn't believe what I said."

The red flash of a cardinal landing in a buckeye startled Diane, and the matter went missing. "So, child, are you Catholic? Your mother takes you to church?"

"I'm not anything, but there are lots of churches in New Mexico."

"Right, yes, New Mexico. I've been meaning to ask you about that—"

"And the Masses are the same, only Spanish." Norah held out her index finger spaced above her thumb. "I only know that much."

"You must have picked up something, since you're a native. Give us a bit of the old *español*."

"*Ojalá escuchen hoy la voz del Señor—*"

"Oh, *excelente*."

"Wait, I'm not finished. *No endurezcan el corazón*. Do you speak Spanish, Auntie Di?"

"*Un poco*. Where did you say you were from?"

"I didn't. I'm not supposed to tell you this, but my mother lives in a small town called Madrid."

"Like in Spain? The same name, how interesting. What is it like in Madrid?"

"Oh, you know, roadrunners and coyotes, mesas and cliffs and mountains."

"I thought New Mexico was a desert. Prickly pear and dunes—"

"No. New Mexico is three places in one. In the north, forests of juniper and huge snowy mountains, and in the central, the high lonesome hills. You're thinking of the south, *Tía*. Trinity site where they set off the bomb." Her voice changed, quickened, and the words seemed transparent. "Do you know what the man said about the atomic bomb? 'I am become Death, destroyer of worlds.' Robert Oppenheimer."

"How do you know such things, child?"

"I read about it in a book," she stammered. "I saw it on a plaque when my mother took me to White Sands. Angel of destruction."

At the mention of the cult, Diane felt faint, leaned over, and grabbed onto a headstone for support. With great effort, she bent her stiff knees and stared at the child. "Tell me about your mother."

"She is an artist. Paints bleak houses, the changing sky, the falling apart of lives in the middle of nowhere. She creates her art out of her sorrows."

"What is she like? Why is she there?"

"She is afraid to come home." With great excitement, she pointed to a spot just behind Diane. "There it is. . . ."

They stepped through the snow to Paul's grave. Six feet beneath the clay, Paul Quinn rested under a simple marker—an engraved name, the dates of his coming and going, a crucifix, and a caduceus. Diane remembered those last years with Erica, how he watched over her every move. By trying to protect her, he had driven her away. When her sister first called with the news, Diane had told Margaret not to worry, that the girl was acting out, typical teenage rebellion, and that she would be back soon. The last time Diane had talked with Erica, her niece confessed how much she hated her father, how much she wished both parents would just trust her to make decisions. How she would never be like them, keeping the truth from each other. And now both father and daughter were gone. To Paul's right a blank space on the stone for Margaret Quinn, end unknown. For a moment, they stared at the stone, not knowing what else to do or say.

"He was a good man," Diane said. "Basically. Did your mother ever talk about her parents?"

"My mother is like my grandmother. Most of her life below the surface. Her feelings buried deep in her heart. But the quietest ones often pray the loudest and bring their answers into being."

"Your grandmother nearly lost her faith when your mother ran away from home, and I can't say that I fault her. What kind of God allows the good to suffer, the innocent to be punished? I have my own doubts, but hers were greater, and from a greater cause. But she had moved on. She fashioned her own peace, until you came along." From the top edge of the stone, Diane brushed off loose snow, which stuck to her gloves. She clapped her hands, the muffled noise echoing from stone to stone. The scattered flakes glittered in the bright sunshine. "Why did your mother send you here? What happened to your father?"

"My father? One of the great mysteries of life. Maybe she thought it was time I met my grandmother? I don't ask, just do as I'm told. Oh, I thought of another one, just right for you."

"Another what?"

"A Spanish prayer. *Que los ángeles te lleven al paraíso.*"

"That sounds lovely, child. *Los angeles*—the angels, right? Not the angels of destruction?"

For the first time that day, Norah laughed deeply and fully. "It means 'May the angels lead you to paradise.'" Caught off guard, she grabbed Diane's hand and led her back to their car, giggling softly to herself, enjoying some private cosmic joke.

27

Dozens of hearts lay strewn across the dining room table. Sharp scissors. Tiny arrows. A pot of paste. The three of them judged and giggled when each new design was finished and presented. A light snow blew against the darkened windows. Beef stew simmered on the stove. Diane would be leaving in the morning, and they were already missing one another. The homemade valentines had been her idea, agreed to with alacrity, and they passed a pleasant few hours over doilies and red cardboard hearts.

"This one is for Sharon Hopper," Norah said. "Who believes but does not see. And this one is for Sean Fallon, who sees but does not believe."

"Believe in what, Norah?" Diane asked. "True love?"

Bent over her work, Norah continued sketching a cupid on the front of another card. "Most people say they want it and can't live without love. But they just don't know how to take or give it." She drew a pair of wings on the cherub and sat back to consider her efforts. "I heard that in a song on the radio." She stopped to glue the cupid to a cloud of cotton. "This one is for Dori, who sees and believes. Have you ever been in love?"

Margaret leaned over the paste pot, indicating to her sister that she need not answer.

"I don't mind," said Diane. "No, not the way I wanted to be. Never the passion I always thought I would feel."

"How about you, Grandma?"

Margaret stood and looked over their heads toward the stew. "Maybe we should be getting ready for dinner and stop all this talk of love for right now." She pushed back the chair and hurried to the stove.

As she gathered in pieces of cardboard, Diane spoke in a low confidential tone. "I wanted to forgive him. Before he passed. But Joe never said . . . he never gave me the chance."

"Forgiveness is the easy part," said Norah, three pairs of scissors in her hands. "Loving beyond the hurt is what will be hard."

Diane reached out and stopped the girl from moving. Tired of the chase, she challenged her in a rough whisper. "Who hurt you, child? Your mother?"

Laying down her tools, Norah flattened her palms upon the table, and when she spoke, her voice was colored by a strange monotone, as if reciting what had been learned by rote. "Never run with scissors, that's one of the rules. Always carry them points down. Look both ways for cars when crossing the street. Wait one hour after meals before swimming. I have been taught all of the rules for children. Danger. *Peligrosa.*"

Alarmed by the girl, Diane followed her to the den and the chest of drawers where the art supplies were stored. "You're hiding something about your mother." She lowered her voice to a whisper. "What has she done? Is she still a part of that cult? Did you run away from those people? The Angels?"

"Los Angeles?"

"Quiet, don't let your grandma hear."

Brushing past her aunt, Norah moved to the center of the room. She held her arms perpendicular to her sides and began to slowly pirouette, each sentence spinning to four corners. "There is no cult. Erica Quinn is no Angel. She is sorry for her sins."

Her aunt stepped toward her, caught hold of her wrists, and stilled her. "But why doesn't she come home?"

"We are all afraid of what's in our hearts. Wives afraid of their husbands. Mothers afraid of their children. Daughters afraid to come home. Maybe she is waiting for someone to find and forgive her."

Diane spoke in a calm, clear voice. "You are a strange creature, Norah Quinn. Where did you come from?"

The girl began to twitch slightly, holding back the answer. From the kitchen, Margaret called them to dinner, but Diane would not let go, her fingers digging into the girl's skin. "But couldn't you tell her? Couldn't you let her know that nothing matters more to her mother than seeing her child again? That she should come back home?"

"I cannot go where I haven't been called. And I don't want to go, I like it here. And Grandma cannot go. She is not well." As if her soul had flown away, Norah stared blankly ahead, her vision turned inward and awry.

"Why have you come?" Diane shook her once to claim her attention, instantly regretting her temper.

Margaret shouted for them again. "Dinner's on the table. Where are you? This is no time for hide-and-seek."

"Coming," Diane yelled. She lowered her voice to admonish Norah. "Next time you speak to her, tell your mother to come home."

"You could go," Norah said. "If you were careful. Safety first. Follow the rules. Never talk to strangers. Do not stare directly into the flash."

The sudden changes in the girl's manner worried Diane, and she began to fear for the child's mental state. Folding her arms around Norah, she held her tight and rocked her, ran her fingers through the child's hair until the trance broke. Over dinner, they talked about the excellence of the stew, the plans at school for Valentine's Day. All through the meal, Diane watched Norah closely for any sign that she had become unhinged. If she was telling the truth about her mother, Norah was ticking with stress, and Margaret could not be expected to deal with such a tightly wound being. Another heavy snow began to fall outside, and they all remarked at the persistence of an everlasting winter. Something was not right. Halfway through dessert, Diane announced that she had changed her mind—she would be staying with them for another week.

28

In the haze between sleep and wakefulness, he could not distinguish between the real and the imagined, what he conjured in his unrest, willed from his unconscious desire. Under his featherbed, his body retained the radiant heat from a long night's sleep, but Sean became vaguely aware of a chill infiltrating the room. Dampness settled like a fog from the ceiling, kissed his ears and nose and cheeks. Drawing the covers round his hunched shoulders, he buried his face in the pillow, but the cold air did not relent, and it pressed down upon him, reached beneath the blankets with icy fingers, and startled him from slumber. His first thought was that the furnace had shut off again in the middle of the night, but his lips were wet and tingling, and with a shiver he wondered whether a window had been left ajar and let the winter in. The notion that he had been so careless disturbed him, and he worried what his mother might say should she enter the refrigerated room. With reluctance, he opened his eyes and tried to gain some sight in the gloom. The shades had been drawn since bedtime, but he had sensed that more snow had fallen overnight and it was snowing still. A preternatural silence enclosed the space, and when he exhaled, a small moist puff of breath hung in front of his face. He kicked his feet and was shocked by the frigid sheets beyond his bare toes. A breeze, nearly visible in the blackness, passed over the bed, not from the window which he faced, but from behind him at the closed door. When he rolled over to find its cause, a hand covered his mouth and deadened his scream. The pressure took away his breath, and he felt that this must be what it is like to drown or be smothered by an avalanche. The thing in the room made no sound, and Sean came to realize that the hand would remain clamped on his face unless and until he stopped struggling and kept quiet. He shook his head sharply once and then stilled himself, opening wide his eyes to find some aspect beyond the hovering shadow.

"Good boy," the voice said. Male, not his father. A dark form filled the space between his bed and the door. His mother slept two rooms down and might not hear him or come quickly enough should he call out. "You will be quiet now?"

Each word arrived on a breath of ice which threatened to shatter in the air. A dozen thoughts raced through his mind—a robber, a killer, the devil himself. Someone come to take him away. He imagined terrible things, but he nodded his assent. The hand lifted from the boy's mouth. Sean coughed for air and to calm his spinning fear. Drawing an arm back to his side, the figure loomed larger, like a great bird of prey spreading enormous wings, or a wyvern coiled for the strike. "Just don't hurt me," the boy whispered.

"Sean Fallon—"

He was frightened by the sound of his name in the stranger's voice.

"—I have come to ask a few questions of you. About the girl."

"What girl?"

"Your little friend."

"Norah Quinn?"

"Yes, tell me the truth about Norah. Do you know what happens to little boys who do not tell the truth?"

Although he had lied plenty of times and gotten away with no real consequences, Sean nodded, certain that the stranger would see him more clearly than he himself could see.

"Good boy. Now tell me: who is it she says she is?"

Despite the darkness, Sean searched with his eyes for the blue china cup from Norah and found its place among his treasures, and he willed a short prayer into the bowl, hoping that she was right. He did not know the answer the man sought. A fit of loyalty seized him, and he did not reply. The figure in the dark expanded and his voice shaded deeper with menace when he asked again: *"Who does she say she is?"*

"Are you the one following her? What do you want with her?"

The man tacked another course. "Who do you think she is?"

"I don't know what to believe. Are you going to take her away?"

The figure shifted again in agitation. "What does she want with a boy like you?"

The question offended him, and Sean scowled in silence.

The stranger hissed and spat out his final question. "Has she told you anything about the Angels of Destruction?"

Images of angels floated in his mind. In flight above the shepherds and their sheep, announcing the Nativity. Michael and Gabriel from the *Children's Illustrated Bible*, photographs of paintings and statues and stained-glass windows. On the night table, a stack of books and magazines towered, filled with holes and missing pages from which he had torn and cut dozens of pictures for her. To give her wings. The visitor, he thought, might be some retribution for ruining the books. "Nothing," he said. "I don't know anything about Angels of Destruction."

"Good boy. You would not want to meet such an angel, and you never know what terrible things might befall a child who pretends to be what she cannot be. Be smart. You don't strike me as the type to believe in things you cannot see and cannot prove."

Such speculation frightened him more than the man in the room. He could hear his whispered prayer circling in the teacup.

"Everything is divided into two separate equal conditions," the shadow whispered. "Life that can be observed, the witnessed truth and reality of concrete forms and experiences. And on the other side, unseen rumor and faith. You know your father has gone away and you can feel the coldness in your heart, but what your senses tell you differs from all that cannot be proven. Anything imagined can be true. Angels and witches, love and hope—the list requiring pure faith never ends."

Sean wanted him to leave and, closing his eyes, willed him to disappear.

From the bookshelf, the porcelain cup began to vibrate and chime as if his prayer sped around the circle in revolutions fast and faster.

"Go back to sleep. Forget." The figure moved to the window and drew back the curtains. The snow was heavy now, bright against the darkness, and from that faint light, the stranger appeared nothing more than an ordinary man in a coat and an old-fashioned hat. "There'll be no school tomorrow, so sleep on, my boy." He moved quickly back across the room, his coat snapping like a flag, and at the door, he vanished to an airy nothing. The cold lifted, and warmth descended on the room once more.

Sean waited for a long time, listening to nothing, overwhelmed by a profound silence. Petrified by his vision, he could not move, could not run to his mother and have her say it was all a bad dream or offer either comfort or scolding. He considered all the possibilities and decided to act upon none. Baffled and tired, he drifted into a deep sleep, angels and devils dancing in his mind. His internal alarm woke him at seven, and though certain that all was not well, he could not be sure what part had actually happened and what was pure nightmare. When his mother arrived with the news that the snow was bad enough to close the schools, he managed to feign some delight, but as she left the room, he rolled over to face the window, wondering what might be beyond the drawn curtains.

29

For the first time, he was late. Sean had always been punctual, early enough most mornings to have a second breakfast while Norah puttered with a toothbrush or sought a missing shoe. When the clock sped past the appointed time, she started pulling at the drapes, searching the dim light for his approach. But he was late. Flurries lingered in the violet sky, falling atop the previous night's snow cover, but no tracks led to the door. She had not missed him. At ten minutes past, Norah pestered Mrs. Quinn to call the Fallons, but there was no answer. At fifteen, she begged to go to school without him. Had she been in the habit of checking the weather, Margaret may have turned on the radio or television to hear about possible closures, but she was out of sorts, distracted by the sense that she had left open a window or door somewhere, sometime. The night before her sister, too, had acted peculiar, eying Norah as if she deduced their deception.

"Do you think you could find your way alone?" When the child rolled her eyes, Mrs. Quinn had her answer. "Go then. Go. He's probably home sick for the day."

Norah knelt on the sofa to watch through the large picture window, pressing her nose against the glass until her breath completely fogged the view. On the wet panes, she traced wings and daggers with her fingertip until the heavy warmth inside the house made the condensation evaporate, leaving nearly invisible drawings on the surface. No sparrows darted across the sky. No cars minced along the snow-covered asphalt. No children tromped toward school. Their absence from the scene made melancholy the snowfall, emptying the world of life, and Norah reveled in being its only witness. She drew the curtains and found Mrs. Quinn in the kitchen, stirring oatmeal. She stood quietly at her elbow, hoping to attract her attention, hesitant to disturb her daydream. "May I go to school now?"

Without looking up, Mrs. Quinn said, "I thought you were already gone. Dress warm and don't dawdle on the way."

The girl circled her arms around the woman's waist and felt Margaret lean back slightly into her embrace. The warmth of the child's face lingered in the small of her back long after she had gone.

As she hurried into her boots and parka, Norah peered through the window by the front door. Snow fell more heavily than when she first took notice, and the motion of the storm entranced her. For the first time that morning, she wondered if school had been postponed or even canceled, and that, she thought, would explain Sean's absence. Wrapped in her warmest clothes, she stopped by the hallway mirror and checked her appearance: the gray coat and red cap and scarf set off her pale complexion, and when she removed her glasses, she appeared a different creature altogether. A pink lipstick lay on the sideboard, tempting her. On impulse, Norah drew a wide smile across her lips and covered her mouth with the scarf. She sped by Margaret and nearly knocked over Diane, coming downstairs lost in another morning's drowse, and burst through the front door into the snow, letting it shower upon her upturned face. Each wet fat flake felt like a kiss.

The snowplow, which early in darkness passed over their street, had pushed mountains against parked cars. Old footprints, from the paperboy perhaps or some other wanderer, were disappearing from the sidewalk. A squirrel had hopped from a bare maple to the cover of fir, leaving behind a follow-the-dots. Otherwise the yards were clean again, covered with a seamless white quilt. Like a pioneer, she carved a trail through the virgin snow. When she reached the back fence, she looked back at the pattern her feet had made. In the distance a mother called her son, "Eddie, Eddie, you forgot your hat," and then the door slammed shut, a pause, then shut again. The woman's voice seemed to come from miles away to pierce the prayerful silence like a cough in a cathedral. Norah moved farther from home and into the woods. Nothing stirred save the falling snow, and nothing sounded save its falling. A bough complained with an arthritic creak, and then the nothing returned, insinuated itself into her soul, and emptied her into itself. Swallowed by stillness, Norah felt the dread of her own existence in creation, and she craved reassurance of separateness from the storm and felt the need to go, to move somewhere, anywhere, to resist the eddy and flow around her. Like an aviator from some silent film, she wiped her spectacles, threw her scarf over her shoulder, and set her course. Beyond the bicycle trail, she turned right on the road to school. Each cross street she passed lay deserted, blank of all signs of life except for a few wisps of chimney smoke, imagined families around imagined fires. She came at last to Friendship Elementary. Encircled by a black iron fence, the enormous yard flowed as a white sea surrounding the island of the building. On a normal day, buses would be idling in the parking lot, coughing smoke and sulfur, and children would be clotting the doorways as teachers waved them in, already thinking of day's end. But devoid of people in motion, the school lost its energy, became just another place, yellow bricks darkening with moisture, windows fogged opaque. Norah curved away from the front door and headed to the playground. Ringed by trees, the broad fields lay empty, and she walked to a fence surrounding a slab of concrete that, when uncovered, had fading lines for hopscotch and foursquare, a wooden seesaw warped and gray, a rusty swingset with half the seats missing. Children dared to sneak in on weekends or on dusky summer evenings, though trespass was forbidden by a chained gate. Norah tested the lock, held her breath, squeezed between the bars, and stepped into the smooth clean yard.

Snow spilled like excelsior when she grabbed the monkeybars. Climbing to the top, like a crow in the nest she scanned in all directions, wishing that Sean were with her, enjoying the soft day, the light wind, and the loneliness of so much nothing. The horizon vanished as the low clouds hemmed in the view. She felt trapped inside a swirling snowglobe, particles in the sky fine as ash settling on everything, the fallout of the ruptured clouds. Treading softly, she investigated the four corners of the enclosure, slipped down the sliding board into a drift piled high as autumn leaves. She plopped on a swing, snorting when its dampness leached through the cloth of her pants. Cold and wet, she stomped angrily across the pavement. Her movements obliterated the false surface, and everywhere she stepped she left proof of her presence. Her feet ached in the boots and her legs stiffened. Tired of the playground, she circled round to the other side of the school, encountering no other soul, and climbed the bottom rail of the iron fence and held onto the bars. A patina of black paint and red rust clung to her woolen mittens. Nothing stirred but the squalls of snow, which now seemed an ordinary part of the everyday air.

Norah closed her eyes, lifted her face to the sky, and let the drops dapple her skin and tighten her lips. She felt a shadow pass nearby like an image from a dream. In the quiet, footsteps approached, and she snapped open her eyes to frighten him, only to discover the world white and blank as paper. Muttering at her own folly, she removed her glasses and wiped the moisture with the end of her scarf. Flakes lit upon her lashes. She blinked and beheld the figure on the other side of the fence.

He was elegance. From the leather gloves holding the iron finials to the camel hair coat snug against his frame. At the collar, out peeked a silk scarf, and on his hat, the snow clung to the brim and sharp crease like butter on a knife.

"You startled me," she said. "Sneaking up on a person with her eyes closed."

Leaning over the rail, he bent down to face her at eye level and chuckled when he saw the pink slash of her mouth. "You startled me. On such a day and at this early hour. What are you doing out here all by yourself?"

"I came to school, but there's no one here."

"There is no school today. Didn't you get the good news? Too much snow." His face softened. Patches of snow rested on his shoulders like epaulets, and his hair was salted where it stuck out from beneath the brown fedora. "You look cold, very cold."

"I like being cold."

"But not too cold. Wouldn't you like to get warm?"

She took one step back and considered his smiling eyes. "You aren't going to take me back with you, are you? I don't want to leave her."

"Margaret? I know all about Mrs. Quinn too." The man straightened his spine and looked toward the school building, blinking his eyes, either from the blowing snow or some private embarrassment. He seemed larger, as if a radiant energy grew inside his chest.

"Never talk to strangers," she said. "Don't cross the street in the middle of the block. Just Say No."

"Since there is no school, maybe you might want to come with me and get warm."

"What are you doing out in this freezing snow?"

"I'm a snow man myself, of sorts, lost in it every chance I get."

Norah's nose began to run, and she wiped it with her sleeve. She hacked out a cough, mucus rattling in her chest.

The man twisted his features into a half frown. "And just who are you, little friend?" He bent closer to the bars, close enough for her to see into his eyes. Where her reflection should have appeared on his pupils, nothing but misery, and she knew at once what sort of creature he was. The depth of his emptiness scared her, and she looked away. In the sound of his very breath blew a cold wind over the icy tundra. She could sense the glacial river pulsing in his veins, the utter silence of the transparent frozen heart. In the wink of an atom, the clap of his hands, her time would cease to be. "Tell me who you are."

"I am an angel," she stammered. "A messenger. A nothing become something so that they may see and understand. The time is at hand."

"I have been following you and know where you have been. What time is at hand? The end? Whose end?"

"I am not sure."

"Does anyone know that an angel has come?" Around them the snow undulated and sank to the ground. He reached between the spaces of the gate and grabbed her thin arms, pulling her toward him fiercely. Her body slammed into the bars and her face pressed hard against the cold metal. A rabbity cry escaped from the back of her throat. "Have you told anyone you are an angel?"

"Sean, a boy, suspects. But he doesn't believe. No one else yet."

"Tell me why you are here." He tightened his grip. Drops of blood bubbled from the corners of her mouth.

"Because she wanted me to come. Margaret Quinn." She was losing her breath. "She called me into being."

"And yet you have told the boy. Why have you broken the first rule of safety?"

"Sean needs to be saved too, but he does not know how to ask. None of them do. They no longer truly believe."

"You're not very smart, Norah Quinn. I could crush you right now and nobody would know. You cannot stay here, do you understand? You cannot become an angel for those who do not ask."

She could not answer. Blood streamed from her nostrils, and her eyes rolled white. An anguished moan rose from deep within.

His skin reddened, and he began to shake as he lost his strength and stability. Through clenched teeth, he asked again. "What makes you think that anyone needs to believe in angels?"

"All need some reason to hope, to believe." Twisting her shoulders, she escaped him and stepped back from the fence.

The man appeared powerless and beaten. Trapped by the bars that separated them, he could not reach her and was frozen in place. The ground beneath him rumbled, and around his form a brilliance gathered and intensified with each word. "You are a fool. They will not believe you without some sacrifice from you. You cannot stay with her. You cannot stay with the boy. You must destroy your world to save theirs."

There was a flash as brief and brilliant as a thousand suns bursting at once, and then too quickly he was gone, before she could speak another word. Vanished into a fog of snow. When she could no longer perceive his form, it seemed to her that he had never been there, as if he had been a snowman she had rolled and patted and molded in her mind, a shape that melted away quickly when she forgot him for just that one moment. Soon even the impression he made in the snow would be gone.

With the back of her sleeve she wiped the blood from her nose and lips, and then she rolled the scarf over her mouth to begin the walk home. As she left the schoolyard, she was humming tunes Mrs. Quinn had sung around the house, songs from her daughter's childhood, when she would bathe Erica in the tub or gently push her on a swing. Lost to the music of her imagination, she almost failed to notice that someone had built a snowman in the middle of nowhere. Wound round his collar was a silk scarf, and on his head was a rakish brown fedora. A few children apparently had braved the storm to create it, and at the sight, she burst with laughter.

He was giving her a final chance, and she knew what must be done. The time was at hand. The stranger had been one of them—a destroyer of worlds. Angel of destruction.

30

Each student cut a slit into the top of a decorated shoebox to ready for valentines. Mrs. Patterson relished the mayhem and enjoyed picking one or two children to spy upon as they navigated the crowded aisles in search of best friends or private crushes, tokens of affection in hand. She loved to see the smiles of the giver and the recipient, and even cherished the disdain on certain faces, particularly the boys, reminding her that they were growing up and would soon be beyond such innocent gestures.

Caught between the nostalgia for their youth and the desire to put such childish things behind them, the third graders moved like sheep in search of the shepherd. Some secretly loved the ceremony and saw the cards as tokens of genuine affection, but the more cynical or shy signed the cheapest store-bought cards—emblazoned with cartoon characters making gentle puns—with just their name or desultory or ironic greetings. An occasional oath toward an enemy. Two of the more notorious claimed to have forgotten completely the special day, which drew the silent approbation of the class. When Mrs. Patterson signaled the exchange, Norah stood first, hefted the lid to her desk, and started the rite with such joy that nearly everyone forgot their trepidation. Red hearts beat a tattoo on box after box.

"This is for you," Sean Fallon said, waiting for her at his desk. "Open it."

Sliding her index finger under the fold, she broke the seal, removed the card, and flipped it to see the face. A collage of dozens of birds, photographs clipped from magazines, illustrations stolen from old books. Bird by bird, she scanned the surface, covered so densely that space barely existed between any two wings. Eagles in flight, two swans at swim, nesting plovers, a redwing blackbird screaming from a cattail, songbirds in their singing, vireo, cardinal, mockingbird, a hummer humming in the corner. A cartoon roadrunner sped across the bottom edge. Inside in his early cursive: *Birds fill the air, when you are here. Happy Valentine's Day.* She felt like throwing her arms around his bony shoulders, smothering him until he cried. Looking up from the words, she saw his unabashed hope, his bright smile. A smile that said the world will one day crush such a boy, but not today, and she kissed him lightly on the lips. It lasted less than a moment and all of his life, one quick kiss. Looking around to see if anyone was watching, Norah handed him her card in the same motion, but he was too stunned to open it, so she took it back and pushed the valentine into his makeshift mailbox. He was the last to finish the circuit and take his seat, wondering if his collage was recompense for the china cup she had given him.

After the card exchange was over and the children counted out their love notes, Mrs. Patterson passed around a box of sugar hearts with red messages embossed on pastel surfaces: Be Mine, 4ever, Hi Cutie, How's Tricks? The candy tasted like sweet chalk. Thus content, the students could be drawn back into their lessons. She tapped them into submission with a wooden pointer. "Who's ready with their report?"

A groan, the shuffling to order, papers out upon the desk. In honor of the holiday, they had been assigned to write an essay, to be read aloud in class, on any aspect of Valentine's Day. Four or five eager hands rose in the hot, dry air, and Mrs. Patterson chose Norah Quinn. Wrapped in Erica's old Peruvian poncho, she clutched her pages and advanced to the front of the room, pivoting at the teacher's desk to face her classmates and read:

"Who was Valentine? How have we come to make this day a celebration of love? Why all these hearts and cupids?

"The past is no more certain than the future. Little is known about the real Valentine, only this. There may have been two. Both were martyrs who died for what they believed. Both lived and died long ago. The first Valentine was a priest in the Roman times when the emperor outlawed marriage for young soldiers. This was done so that they would be more devoted to fighting than to their sweethearts. But Valentine felt sorry for those men and married them in secret. When the emperor found out, he had Valentine killed! Off with his head, chop. Sometimes love means sacrifice.

"The second Valentine was just a man who had been falsely imprisoned. He fell in love with the jailer's daughter and had to smuggle love letters in secret. He signed them from 'Your Valentine.' These two stories are legends, and not much is known about Saint Valentine.

"The day of February fourteenth is related to love and fertility rites of the pagans. The pagans were people who believed in more than one god or sometimes none at all. This love and fertility rite is the time of the marriage of Zeus and Hera. The Romans thought they were gods, but they were wrong. It is also the the feast of Lupercalia, when the boys of Rome ran naked—*am I allowed to say that?*—naked in the streets, striking women with a leather strap. This custom was continued by the Christians. In the Middle Ages, during the coldest part of long winters, it became a day when men and women sent each other notes of their true love. These were the very first valentines. Though boys no longer ran naked in the streets hitting ladies with straps.

"It is a day to look forward to the end of winter and death and to celebrate a new beginning. The Middle Ages poet Chaucer said, 'For this was on Saint Valentine's Day, when every bird comes to choose his mate.' "

From his seat, Sean Fallon blushed as the class politely clapped at the end of her presentation. Stunned again by the girl, Mrs. Patterson applauded too, then said, "That was just lovely, Norah, but what about the cupids? You mentioned in the beginning you were going to talk about the cupids."

Norah pulled at the fringe of her poncho with nervous fingers.

"You know," said Mrs. Patterson, "the little angels with the bow and arrows? Shot through the heart with love."

Sean watched Norah closely, fearing she might stop time or turn her eyes a fiery red.

"There are no cupids, Mrs. Patterson," she said. "They're just made up."

The teacher's laugh was pitched between amusement and derision. "Surely you don't believe that. No naked cherubs with the power to make you fall in love?"

Working her fingers along the hem, Norah blanched when the first chuckles emanated from the seats nearest the window, rolling across the room in contagion, a wave that would bounce and echo back if she let it reach the far wall. She straightened and squared her shoulders, fingers flying madly through the fringe. Her voice deepened, and she spoke stone-faced. "I would not joke about things invisible to see, for while there are no cupids, angels walk among you."

The laughter stopped, threatened to rise again if she paused.

"I am an angel," she said, "come to tell you the time is at hand. I am a messenger. Beware the others—the angels of destruction—who walk and watch among you. The seven who serve the terrible will of the Lord to punish the faithless. The *Malake Habbalah*: Kushiel, rigid one of God; Lahatiel, flaming one of God; Shoftiel, judge of God; Makatiel, plague of God; Hutriel, rod of God; Puriel, fire of God; and Rogziel, wrath of God. Besides these named, their number is legion. Four and forty thousand to come to dwell among you, wreaking judgment."

The children's faces had turned to ash.

"But the Lord is merciful and full of forgiveness. He has sent his messengers ahead to beg your faith and trust. You will know us by the light of the heavens in our eyes."

She took off her glasses and opened wide her eyes. All of the children leaned forward in an attempt to see what constellations might be swirling in her irises. Sean was startled by how small her eyes appeared, how she seemed reduced, more vulnerable, a mere child like the rest. He prayed for her to stop. Norah spread the wings of the poncho and said again, "I am an angel of the Lord."

Shouts of "Norah, stop" from Mrs. Patterson went unheard, the hosanna made of her name until it became a remonstrance, and she did not notice the scrape of the teacher's chair against the floor, nor the footsteps as she approached, calling her name, insisting, begging her to *"please just stop."* Norah did not quit until the woman's hand clasped her shoulder, and glowing, she was led back to her desk, past her stunned and silenced classmates, until seated, she slumped back in the chair. She shuddered and her limbs convulsed as though a shock ran through her nervous system, and then at once, the strange trance ended. Within seconds, her eyes were closed, and exhausted, she slept until the lunch bell rang. As the other students filed off to their meal, Mrs. Patterson asked Norah to stay behind.

"What on earth came over you?"

Norah folded her hands, offered no explanation, prepared herself for punishment.

Mrs. Patterson softened, thought of the girl as hers for the moment.

"Are you all right, child?" Receiving no answer, she said, "I can't have such episodes in my classroom. I will have to tell your grandmother about your disruption today, and the principal as well. We just can't have it."

Norah paid no heed to the threats of discovery, and in fact seemed pleased that the news would soon reach her home and spread like fire through the town. The plan to save Mrs. Quinn had been put in motion. Norah strolled to the cafeteria like an empress, and the children stopped to whisper as she passed, the rumors of her brazenness trailing her like threads loosed from a caftan. The others were waiting for her at the dining table, suddenly the center of the room, beaming with joy. Only Sean seemed troubled by her confession, but he kept his fears to himself. After the celebratory meal, her classmates queued to escort her back to class, and later to walk home with her, just to be close to the light they had newly discovered.

BEFORE THE CHILDREN were due home, the phone rang. Had not Diane been trying to nap in the upstairs bedroom, Margaret would have let it go. But she picked up the receiver, and at the sound of Principal Taylor's voice, Margaret drifted into true fear. He spoke of episodes and disruptions, counselors and psychologists. During their conversation, she thought immediately of the other two times panic had gripped her so. The first was when they told her about the explosion and she finally understood that Erica was gone. The most recent had been about Paul, not the day her husband finally died, that was more relief buoyed by a sloughing sorrow, but the moment of his diagnosis; the two of them faced the doctor confirming what Paul had long suspected. She shuddered at the finality of the news, the shockingly few days left in the game, and the paucity of remedies. There would be none. He had been through it with her the first time such dread arrived. But now there was no one to help her. Diane would be heading back to Washington, and Margaret would have to face the coming danger all alone. She prayed again for some help.

"There is something wrong with your granddaughter," the principal said. "She stood in front of the class and announced she was an angel of the Lord, and threatened that there would be fire and plagues and forty thousand more angels. She frightened the other children, not to mention poor Mrs. Patterson. I'm not even sure this girl is legally registered in my school, Mrs. Quinn, and on top of that, all this trouble today. You need to do something about Norah."

The child's claims did not bother her. Children are capable of believing anything and telling the most outrageous lies with unerring confidence. No, her fear was where such a story would lead. Norah had to escape scrutiny and stay out of trouble. If the right people pulled the right thread, their ruse might unravel, and in the end, the girl would be taken away. She hung up the phone and stared out at the blank landscape through a rime of frost etched on the glass.

A figure materialized out of the whiteness, and in the afternoon light, she first mistook him for a ghost, her husband coming back to her, but as the man approached and came into greater clarity, his features shifted beneath his brimmed hat, and he seemed in his gestures more like her father or what she imagined her father would have looked like had he aged into late life. He moved as if on ice, gliding to her, filling the windowpane with his form, the camel hair coat, the jaunty scarf, his face kind and creased, his hair yellow against the snow, blond as the boy she had known and loved long ago, before Paul, and his countenance changed again as fleeting as a thought and he became all that she both desired and dreaded, moving toward her. From afar, she heard his name on her lips voiced across space, penetrating the glass. *"Just don't hurt me,"* she whispered a prayer, and in reply his voice sounded *Norah* in her imagination, so she closed her eyes until he was gone. Banished as suddenly as he had been summoned. Margaret collapsed in a chair by the window, staring at the failing light of four o'clock, numbed to the nothing of the world beyond the thin glass panes. She was sitting there still when the door flew open and in slipped a cold breeze, followed shortly by the child. Wordless, Norah came to her in a moment of need and threw her arms around Margaret's shoulders and laid her head upon her breast.

BOOK II

October 1975

1

Down the highway they flew, bound for destruction. Fearing they would be chased, they charted a southerly route, moving in an unexpected direction, plotting along a crescent line through the Bible Belt, then shooting across the western wasteland to Vegas, and on to rendezvous with the other Angels in Berkeley. When the rising sun broke upon her face, Erica cringed and shielded her eyes. For a moment she did not know where she was, and the landscape racing by the window confused her further until she turned to find Wiley fixed on the road ahead. She remembered having dozed off an hour or so after their escape, and now in the brilliant morning, the night's events came rushing to mind—Wiley in the bedroom, the gun, stealing past her father—and her pulse thumped in her temples. Sunlight streamed through breaks in the treeline, sawn into shafts that pulsed like a strobe.

"Where are we?" The croak of her voice surprised them both. She cleared her throat and asked again.

"West Virginia somewheres." He put on a thick bumpkin accent. "Over the hills and through the woods."

In the branching light, Erica had to angle her wrist to shield her eyes. "Near anywhere?"

"Morning, Merry Sunshine." *Stop that,* she thought. It sounded old, something her father would have said, and put her off the mood. "You missed the first strip mine," he said. "Bastards took half the mountain like blowing the top off someone's head and scooping out the brains."

"You are gross and disgusting. First thing in the morning, to be talking like that."

The car whined as it pushed up and over a bare hill. "Are we near anywhere else a girl can find a little privacy?"

At the next straight stretch of road, he pulled over and stopped the engine. Along the berm, a mist filtered through the ferns and tall grasses, spilling out from between the trees, and pooled ankle-deep where Erica stepped from the car. She looked into the alien fog, then back at Wiley in the driver's seat, wishing he would get out, too, and keep her company. Behind a sheltering oak, she pulled down her pants, squatted, and waited to relax. The morning air chilled her bare bottom, and when the car door opened and slammed shut, she reflexively peed. When she stepped out from behind the trees, she saw him leaning against the hood of the Pinto, pistol in hand. "What are you doing?"

"Protecting you. From the wilderness. You never know what creatures live in them thar hills."

"My hero."

"We've got to put some road behind us, babe."

A rabbit paused in the middle of the road behind them, and Wiley raised his hand and pointed the pistol between its two erect ears. "Pow," he said, and chortled. They got in the car, tires chewing grass and gravel as it slid onto the road. Sleepy again, she leaned her head against his shoulder.

The clock on the dashboard ticked off the passing of another hour. "How long you think we got? He's waking up, getting ready for his day. You left the note, right?"

"Don't worry. He'll be thrilled I left early for school. Like he finally got through to me about my grades. People'll believe anything when they think they're the ones causing all the changes."

Flexing his fingers around the wheel, Wiley appeared to be formulating his next question rather than listening to her answer. "Your mum comes home by dinner today—"

"Trust me, it'll be tonight. They won't think to call Joyce about me sleeping over till tomorrow. Even if the police figure out what happened, we'll be long gone."

"Twenty-four hours, baby. They wait twenty-four hours. Vanished." He flipped down the visor, twisted it to the right to protect against the slanting morning sunlight. "And we will move through the people like fish in the sea." A few miles later, she fell asleep again. Shadows cast by the trees raced across her face, and patches of October sunshine flattened her features, eyes closed and mouth agape, so that she appeared two-dimensional, a pie plate, a cartoon. As they drifted south, he'd steal a glance from time to time, and seeing her so, he was dumbfounded by the way she became a caricature of her waking self. He was already wondering if she had what it takes to be a true revolutionary.

2

She loved to play with his dick, and that was the beginning and end of all her trouble. The first time had been on the bus back from a school trip to Hershey, late at night. She took off her sweater and laid it like a blanket across their laps, and as the wheels rolled and bumped along the turnpike, she slid her hand undercover and unzipped his fly, exposed and fondled him, all the while talking of roller coasters and Ferris wheels, how the whole town smelled of chocolate and how such sweetness was bound to cloy after the initial thrill. She kept up the conversation to throw off the other kids in the seats around them, and he kept staring at his reflection in the darkened window, enjoying her attention even more by having to feign disinterest, when every molecule was focused on her fingertips until he could stand the caresses no longer and tore his gaze from the black landscape to kiss her and gently pull her hand from beneath the cloth.

"But Wiley . . ."

"That was nice," he said. "Too nice for a time like this." He leaned his head against the glass, and Erica sidled closer, resting against his shoulder, quietly allowing time and space to roll by.

From the beginning, she had loved to hear him talk; the passion in his voice made him seem older, part of an antic generation passing away from fashion. A Sixties boy in a Seventies world. They had been together that entire school year, his last, but her crush on him began the day she entered Forward High. How different he had been—scrawny and quiet—but even then she could sense his radical intelligence, his arms filled with forbidden books by the Beats and Baudelaire, political buttons on his knapsack, and the decals and posters inside his locker door. His heroes were Thomas Merton and James Baldwin, Che Guevara and Bob Dylan. Zigging Left while most everyone else was zagging Right. And when, between his junior and senior year, he shot up four inches, grew out his hair, and started favoring clothes from thrift shops and surplus stores, he matched a renegade spirit with a dangerous look. Though the student body itself was resolutely white and middle class, he affected an air of being a citizen of the world, a brother to all mankind. His senior thesis was on *Bury My Heart at Wounded Knee: An Indian History of the West*, and beneath his graduation gown he wore a bright red dashiki emblazoned with the slogan "Don't Rock the Boat . . . Sink It!" She gladly said yes when he first asked her out, she gladly said yes to his every question, and the deeper her commitment, the greater grew his self-confidence, so that their quest for identity became enmeshed with desire and pleasure. They could no more separate from one another than cast off any other outward sign of who they were groping to become.

Letters had been arriving in his mailbox for months, recruitment propaganda from the Angels after he had answered a mysterious ad in the *Painted Bird*. Typewritten and mimeographed, the pamphlets bore titles such as "All that's Wrong with America," "How Big Business Calls the Shots," "The Atom Bomb and the Coming Civil War," and other diatribes. When Wiley wrote back, the reply came from a man who called himself Crow, whose first letter was a call to arms: "The Twelve Objectives" on a letterpress broadside. The need for destruction in order to save the world. The Angels would take up where the Black Panthers, the Weathermen, the Symbionese Liberation Army, and all the other revolutionaries had failed. In July the summons arrived from Berkeley: Come join the Righteous Ones.

All through that summer after his graduation, she was tempted and impulsive. The thought of running off with him jolted her sexuality. She wanted to please him, to make sure he would really take her away with him. At the swimming pool, she'd skip her fingers down the front of his trunks and giggle at how such a simple gesture could arouse him even in that cold water. Hearing his arrival at the curb in front of her house, she'd flash him from the upstairs window, just to see him shake that brown mane and stare in wonder at her brazen decadence. They carried on when they could in the back of his brother's Pinto, or became wild things in the woods with hidden creatures watching, or had mad sex on his basement sofa as Mrs. Rinnick slept upstairs, and once in her parents' bed when Paul and Margaret had gone into the city for the Civic Light Opera.

"Has that boy been here?" her father asked the next morning over cold cereal and the newspaper.

"No," Erica lied.

Her mother, who had been crossing from the refrigerator to the stove, stopped in stride and looked behind her daughter's back at her husband hidden in the comic pages. She paused for the briefest moment to absorb the certainty of the lie, and hoped that Paul would accept the answer.

He licked his fingertips and turned the page. "Just that some things were different when we got home. The big popcorn bowl in the middle of the sink."

Erica ran her finger along the edge of her juice glass. "I watched a movie. They showed *The Graduate* on Channel 11."

From the cupboards, her mother cried out, "On television? How could they?"

"If you're talking about the naughty bits," Erica said, "they censored it like everything else in this fascist country. It's just the human body."

"One of my beers is missing," her father said. "I'm sure there were four cans and now there are only three. You wouldn't know anything about that, would you?"

Clapping the tabletop with her palms, Erica leaned forward. "I don't know anything about your precious beers. Maybe you drink more than you should. Maybe Mom just couldn't take it anymore and decided to have a little cocktail. But I can't stand the swill. You know what beer tastes like? Plastics. And if you want to make accusations, go ahead and accuse me, but I didn't do it."

"Honey," Margaret said. "Nobody's accusing anyone of anything."

"Dad is like the FBI sniffing around for clues. Shoot first and ask questions later. What do you have against Wiley anyhow?"

Snapping the newspaper into shape, he folded it in half and pressed the crease fresh. "I only wondered why one is gone." He modulated his anger, and an idea strayed to mind. "Maybe I lost count." After their daughter left the room, Paul finished his coffee and went to his wife and dried the dishes. "I smelled him in the bed," he told her, and reaching into his pocket, he produced a sandwich bag with the roach ends of two joints. "And these were in the trash. What does she take us for? Fools?"

A sinking weight filled Margaret's lungs and she sighed to expel it, but could not separate panic from the sorrow at coming trouble.

3

A whisper and fingertips on her bare skin. "Let's go."

She blinked her eyes and saw him hovering above, his long hair curling down and framing his dark face, his shoulders broad as wings. Her dream of flying over the house had been interrupted, so she drew deeper into the pillow, tried to get rid of him and fight back to sleep.

"Let's go."

Slowly aware of his physical presence, she arched her arms, stretched her fingers, wanting him to lie on top of her in the bed, to join her in the warmth of the blankets. She spread her knees apart to make a space for him, but he was not there. Instead, he tugged at the top of the sheet.

"Erica, let's go."

Wiley stripped the covers and gazed at her bare arms and legs, the sharpness of her hips outlined beneath the cotton nightgown. Sorely tempted but no fool, he lifted her by the shoulders to sitting position and gave her a moment to understand the situation. They had been planning this escape for months, and she was supposed to be awake, ready and waiting, not caught between dreams and reality.

"The time has come," he said, hoping she would respond fully. He cocked his elbow to capture the moonlight on his wristwatch. Ten minutes after three. In one motion, she crossed her arms, grabbed the hem of her nightgown, and with a twist pulled it over her head. Naked to the waist, she flashed a wicked grin and licked her lips. "Aren't you going to wake me with a kiss?"

He leaned into her, cupped his left hand beneath her breast and stroked her hair with his right. In the pale light, her skin glowed blue, and he nearly missed her mouth when he bent to kiss her. "Time to go, Sleeping Beauty."

"Avert thine eyes, Prince Charming."

By the time she finished dressing, the spell had vanished, their gid-
diness turned to fear, not only of being caught by her father sleeping just
down the hall, but a general dread of the first steps of their long-distance
runaway. The rake of her nails on his back startled him, and a gasp leapt
from his throat as he wheeled to face her.

"Let's go," she whispered, and over her shoulder, she slung a macramé
bag crammed with necessities. A week before, they had snuck out a suitcase of her autumn clothes, which now nestled in the trunk of the stolen
car. She led the way, pushing open her bedroom door into the darkened
hallway, the sound of the old man's snores penetrating the walls, and Wiley
had to cover his mouth to still nervous laughter. At the top of the staircase,
she stopped and tugged on Wiley's shirtsleeve. "I have to pee." When she
saw the panic in his eyes, she reassured him. "I always go just before a long
trip. You don't want to have to stop before we get going. Besides, he won't
wake up. Sleeps like a dead man."

Waiting for her in the vestibule at the bottom of the staircase, he
thought he heard someone knocking at the front door, the soft rapping
of a child, uncertain perhaps at waking the household at that deep hour.
He hooked the lace curtain with one finger and peeked through the side
windows. No one. The wind. The sound of his own heart jumping against
his ribs. He did not hear Erica sneak behind him, and when she touched
him, he let out a short whoop. Overhead the bedsprings creaked as the
body rolled over. The faint glow from the bathroom illuminated a thin
patch of the hallway at the top of the stairs, and the drone from the fan
underscored the silence.

"I left the light on in case you gotta go. Long trip, baby."

He rolled his eyes.

"Seriously, if he wakes up in the middle of the night, he'll think I'm
in there. And he'll just tie it in a knot and wait. Never knocks, never dis-
turbs the queen on the throne. Then he'll get tired, and just go back to
sleep. I wouldn't be surprised if he's still in bed when my mother gets
back tomorrow night." She danced a four-step jig. "Let's go already." He
stumbled over the bottom step and sprawled, nearly knocking her over.

The moon and stars lit the way around to the backyard. They climbed
over both fences, and just once she looked back at the bathroom window
shimmering like a lighthouse beam. She felt like an emigrant pulling
away from the shore with the certain knowledge that she would not be

sailing home again. Not now, not ever. For a moment, she let go of his hand, and he raced on ahead across the dewy lawn, stopping only to look back for her. Erica glanced over her shoulder, pulled by the sharp tug of all she had known, by the memories of happier days with her parents. By the pain she was about to inflict. A deep sadness nearly stopped her, and had the house shown any sign of life, she would have turned back. Wiley called softly, and her soul jumped and raced to his side. Cutting through the new bicycle path, the trail ended at Friendship Avenue where he had parked the stolen Pinto. Wiley opened the hatch to stow her knapsack, and in the back, obscured by their suitcases, sat a shotgun, a .22 rifle, and a box of shells atop an old Pittsburgh Steelers stadium blanket. Swaddling the guns, she tucked them in for the night. They were well down the road before Wiley reached under the steering wheel and eased out a Colt revolver he had secured in his waistband. He handed the gun to Erica, asking her to stow it in the glove compartment.

"What was that for?"

"In case the old man woke up."

"What would you have done?"

"Waved it in his face. Scare him."

"What if he refused to let me go?"

"Shoot him."

She wondered if he was serious or impressing her through false bravado. It was already beginning to feel too late to go back, so she breathed deeply to settle any second thought. As they passed the Friendship School, she rolled down the window and shouted into the night: "Angels of Destruction!" Tipping his head through the driver's-side window, he echoed her with a curdled yowl. The headlights reflected off the lenses of a pair of round glasses, but they never saw the figure along the road. Against the school's wrought-iron fence, a lone young woman heard their cries and laughed to herself in the darkness.

4

She imagined what it would be like. With the sun beating on the windshield and the cars droning down the highway, she daydreamed. His eyes intent upon her face, watching her eyes, her mouth, following measure for measure whatever she had been saying. Lord, even she could not remember what had been said, but he listened, could no doubt recount their words together, whereas she lived in the flow of time, lost to sense and fixed on impression. She imagined how his hands would feel upon her bare skin, gently tracing the contours of her hips, remembering, rediscovering, how he would look and drink her in, the rough friction of his chin, his thundering pulse. The gasp as she coaxed him inside, how she would find his pleasure points with her nails. He speaks her name, she draws him even closer. *Any closer and I'll be in back of you*, and they laugh at the old joke. And laughing together they feel closer. Not so much his nakedness and certainly not hers. She did not imagine how they looked now, but saw them young and perfect. How when he said her name now, it seemed at once a surprise and a comfort, reenchanted from their past, a time she rarely thought of any longer, and the words from his lips, each syllable delicate and uttered again for the first time. Margaret. Maggie. My own. And traveling home to Paul, she realized the differences between the two men, though she had long thought them so very similar in kind: in how they spoke and joked, and complemented, through their passion for her, the strange disassociation she felt around most other men. Paul was her type, she had decided, because of how much he reminded her of her first love, Jackson. But until she had seen Jackson again, she had not realized how dissimilar the two men were. Perhaps she had overlooked the character and shape of their souls.

It had been a mistake, she thought, to see Jackson again after all these years, after life had played out as it inevitably and relentlessly does. The phone rang on an early September afternoon, the slack hour between lunch and Erica's arrival home after high school. When she picked up the receiver expecting Paul, dry cleaning or dinner menu on his mind, she was shocked to hear Jackson say hello, his voice rip through the wire and worm into her brain. She knew it immediately, even after decades, and the sound of her own name as he said it pierced her to the core. Margaret weakened, sat and listened as he explained, affecting nonchalance, how he had run into her sister, Diane, and her husband, Joe, one evening at the Old Ebbitt Grill, how they had recognized each other, despite the gray hair and vicissitudes of time. The Cicognas insisted he join them, and they had pleasantly strolled through the memories, and talked mostly about you, Margaret, you, and when he had asked, Diane wrote down the number, said you would be glad, and why not pick up the phone, he finally decided. It would be wonderful to catch up. Are you ever in Washington? Let me take you and Paul and what's-your-daughter's-name to a night on the town.

At the mention of her husband, Margaret reclaimed the intervening years. Paul, yes, Paul. They chatted about jobs and kids and aches and joys. She took his number, promised to call when they were in town, though truth be told, we don't come down to D.C. so often anymore, but if so, I will arrange a visit. She hung up the phone just as Erica walked in, sweater tied around her waist, perspiration glistening on her bare neck. So young. She wondered if her daughter was having sex with that boy. His dark curly hair long as a girl's. The loose-limbed way he walks around the house, insouciant, challenging Paul. The fresh brow, bright eyes, the tightness of his skin along the jawline. She could imagine them wild together, but just as quickly banished the image, or at least erased her daughter from the naked picture. Surely, they did it. Things are so different now than when she and Jackson were young like them. Sex was more furtive, fugitive, sudden. Nowadays they take their time, find a place, and imitate what could be seen any night of the week at the movies right in their hometown. She and Jackson had never even been completely naked together. Nowadays they waddle bare as babies in the mud, weave flowers in their lover's hair. Born too early in this misbegotten century. But still. He was wonderful in those days, not that Paul was not passionate in his own way. But Jackson had loved her so, foolishly so.

At dinner, she dropped the notion into the conversation, and deftly, the idea became his at once. "Diane's got a birthday at the beginning of next month," she began. "I haven't seen her in ages. Maybe the three of us—"

"But, Mom, I've got school, and Wiley and I have plans."

"Busy time at the clinic, dear," Paul said, and without missing a beat, "You should feel free to go, though. Have some alone time—"

"Wouldn't think of it."

Erica quickly interjected. "We can take care of ourselves. Go. Have fun."

It had been fun, she told herself as the car sped her closer to home, surprised by the sound of her own voice. I would have slept with him had he asked, would have thrilled at his slightest touch, would have done everything we never did. She had forgotten how she had loved him. Would have jumped into bed with Jackson the way Erica hungers for that boy.

They had shared an innocent lunch. He looked elegant and handsome. Funny how men can get better looking, distinguished, gravitas, even though their heads are as gray, lines as deep, waists as soft, but we just get older. We live more in our bodies than they do. Boys give them up as young men, discarding the body to live inside their minds. But girls and their bodies become women and live in the same skin. Jackson and Margaret's conversation flirted with the edge of feelings, but never too far. In fact, Jackson nearly teared up when talking about his late wife, his son off in college, but she knew by his frantic suppressed joy that he had come to see her again; had she said the right words, they would have ended up in a tangle of blankets and regrets. Turning off the exit in the fading light of dinnertime, she wondered if Wiley loved her daughter so, and perhaps she had been too hard on Erica of late. She should get between her husband and her daughter before one or the other goes too far. Jackson had said, you broke my heart. Not in recrimination, more in sorrow for the passing of all time. And he had said, but it is sure great to see you again, you haven't changed, although they both knew this was a lie or a wish. Why hadn't she leapt yes when he asked her to run away with him when they were kids? How foolish to ask, to say now what should have been said then. She wondered what pledge of love Wiley had promised her daughter. Seized by the notion that she could save Erica some heartbreak, Margaret thought of nothing but her daughter, walking on the sharp edge of change.

Dusk bowed to darkness. Paul had switched on the porchlight for her. Leaving her bags in the car, she hurried through the door to ask, even before hello, where is Erica?

5

It all went down in 1968. In April, a man shot Martin Luther King in Memphis, and he saw the faces black and white steeped in mourning for all hope. Two months later, they killed RFK in the Ambassador Hotel in Los Angeles. Wiley studied the photographs in *Life* and *Look* of the stunned busboy on the floor cradling the fallen man, the flood of light on his face and his right hand closed in a fist, to the somber farewell days later, when the funeral cortege from New York to Washington passed through towns crowded with ordinary people waving goodbye. And later that summer the riots, the burning of the cities, and the police beating the shit out of the protestors in Chicago. The war in Vietnam, and dead bodies on the television set every night during dinner. The old man talking back to Cronkite or Nixon. "Those hippie bastards, look at 'em, they think they're better than everyone else, think they're better than the boys going over there and getting shot up." At the dinner table, his father focused past his wife's shoulders to the blaring television in the other room, while she just sat there with the funny pages, working out the puzzles.

That summer he followed his older brother onto the roof over the carport where Denny had gone to smoke purloined cigarettes without fear of being caught. He'd climb through the open window and shimmy across the gently sloped peak to light up in the August evenings, the days already closing early, the sun setting one minute sooner each night. Wiley caught him just before Labor Day, the soles of his sneakers framed by the curtains, and through threats and cajolery, he was allowed to join his big brother, but Denny swore he'd kill him if he breathed a word.

Through late summer and into the autumn, they sat on the roof every clear evening after supper. Under the stars, the brothers' conversations drifted in a desultory way from the fate of the hometown Pirates that season to the petty tyrannies of their father and the depthless mysteries of their mother. Four years older and in high school, Denny controlled the flow of their colloquies, seeking never to ruin the ambience of cigarettes in the blackening evening. He'd blow smoke rings and philosophize on the virtues of the Stones versus the Beatles, Dylan acoustic or electric, and whether Hendrix improved "All Along the Watchtower." Or the strategies for getting the girls to go all the way—though Wiley understood his brother's monologues to be theoretical rather than experiential. Acolyte on the roof, he was shunned everywhere else by his brother, ignored or picked upon, so that he came to regard these stolen moments together as the only authentic and genuine part of his life. When the subject of politics arose, he listened intently. Denny explained, weeks before the '68 election, that while Humphrey might take the North, George Wallace would win enough votes in the South to give the presidency to Nixon. "Crackers will have their day."

"What do you mean, crackers?"

"White people who don't like Negroes. Didn't you know George Wallace is an old-line segregationist? Ever see those pictures of a firehose blasting a bunch of people, just knocking 'em over into the street? Doesn't like black folk mixing with whites. I'm not sure our old man wouldn't vote for Wallace, if he knew the union would never find out."

Wiley considered the possibility for the first time. The notion that his father might have a political life seemed preposterous, but, the more he thought of it, Denny's judgment appeared right. He was, after all, a high school boy.

"You don't think it's a coincidence, do you? That the people trying to change all that, they're shot dead. JFK and Malcolm X and Martin Luther King and Bobby Kennedy. All shot dead." He blew a cloud of smoke into the dark sky. "Don't you know the fix is on, man? That the whole scene is rigged?"

"What are you talking about?"

"I'm talking about CIA, man, the Mafia, the FBI. They're watching us all. You don't think it's some whacko with a rifle all by himself, do you? Come right up to the president and bang? No way. You gotta read the real papers, and you'll see. There was more than one gunman at each of those assassinations. All a big conspiracy. Don't you think it's odd that first King, then Kennedy—just when he's on the brink? Keep the black man down, keep the poor man down. Keep the fodder going for Vietnam. Poor boys in body bags."

"You're kidding, right?"

"Wish I was, partner. Wish I was. Things gotta change, man. You ever hear of the Black Panthers? You thought the riots were bad, wait till the revolution comes."

"The revolution?"

"When the black man and the poor man and every man who has been beaten down will rise up. Going to be wild, and you don't want to be on the wrong side of that war, let me tell you." Tossing the lit cigarette over the side, Denny watched the glowing ember sink into the neighbor's yard. "Tell you what, though. If you're going to wake the tiger, you better find yourself a long stick."

A kind of anger raced through his limbs, and he felt emboldened by the sudden thrill of this new sensation. At eleven years old, Wiley began planning for the revolution.

6

Nose to nose with the stolen car, the police cruiser glistened, and a Virginia Commonwealth trooper stood, his booted foot resting on their bumper, as he scanned the woods and deserted country road for some sign of the driver. Blinking, Wiley emerged from between the pines and with one hand waved a friendly hello as he fastened his belt buckle with the other. The policeman did not return his greeting but scrutinized the boy as he climbed the sloping ditch, stopping at the top to pull his long hair into a ponytail and square his shoulders. "Looks like you caught us," Wiley said.

"This here your car?" He dropped his foot and removed his stiff-brimmed hat, revealing a docked circle in his crewcut hair. Not much older than Wiley, he looked puzzled by the circumstance.

"We had to take a break. Call of nature." Beneath Wiley's feet, the carpet of pine needles felt soft and slippery through his old sneakers. He began to wonder if the policeman had already searched the Pinto. "Sure, this is my car. Well, my brother's actually. Listen, I'm with my sister. She was desperate. Isn't against the law to use the bathroom, is it?"

The trooper did not drop his stare, though his lips twitched briefly. "Your license and registration, please."

As Wiley reached for his wallet, he realized that the registration card lay in the glove compartment, probably just under the barrel of the pistol. He imagined the scenario: beat this hick cop to the draw, hold the gun on him while Erica tied him up. They'd leave him in the woods bound and gagged till someone noticed he hadn't come in from his shift. Be long gone before they found him. If the son of a bitch went for his gun, he'd have to shoot first. Get off a round, their only chance. The trooper sprawling across the road, blood leaking from the hole near his heart. After handing over his driver's license, he stepped around to the passenger side and pretended that the door was jammed.

Her hello broke the stillness. The men turned their heads as she strode through the high grass below them. Erica brushed twigs and leaves from the seat of her jeans, then waved to the men, and the young policeman took one step in her direction, hand instinctively cocked to his holstered sidearm. When he saw her struggling to find a foothold on the grassy bank, he moved to her, one arm outstretched like a lifeline, and as she took his hand, Erica watched Wiley go for the glove compartment. A vision of the gun flashed in her mind. Instead, she saw him grin triumphantly and flash the registration card. She grabbed the policeman's other arm at the top of the incline and hoisted herself to the road, holding on a moment longer than necessary and thanking him. Above his shoulder, high in the cloudless sky, a turkey vulture rode the thermals, circling and inspecting the landscape.

"I found it." Wiley walked over to them, carrying the card like it was made of glass. "My brother's car, like I said. Just driving our baby sister back to college."

The trooper took the card, bent his head, and strained to read it, unable to concentrate.

"Hollis," she said, remembering a girl from their hometown who had gone there.

"Hollins? Y'all are a far piece off target. Your sister you say?"

Wiley edged closer. "Came down from Pennsylvania."

"Can see that," the policeman said. "Liberty Bell tags. How'd you all wind up over here if you was going to Hollins? You already missed it."

She touched her fingertips to her cheekbone, and his eyes followed the motion. "We got directions from a friend."

"Either y'all went too far south, or he ain't much of a friend. You lost. Don't want to be lost in these parts. I come up on your car, thought something bad happened to you when they's nobody inside. These some untraveled roads, miss."

Wiley tried to establish a position in the conversation. "We decided on the scenic byways."

"Scenic, all right." The three of them surveyed the horizon. Oak trees showed a touch of brown among the fading green leaves, and the maples burned yellow and red. Framed against the cold blue sky, the colors hinted at the splendor a week or two away. The vulture traced a lazy course, graceful as a kite sailing amid the clouds. Erica looked away to study the two men, and when she returned her gaze to the sky, the bird had vanished, swiftly ascended to the heavens. "Lonesome here," she said.

The trooper nodded. "Lonesome, yeah. When you're out by yourself in the middle of nowhere, only soul in the world, just wind and sky. You never gonna meet another body ever again, or you get that heartsick feeling that nobody knows you like you understand yourself, and never will. Lonesome is right, and lost, like you all." He put on his hat, tamping the crown till it fit snugly.

"We sure are glad it was you," Wiley said, "and not someone else coming along to tell us we were lost."

"You never know what's coming down the road, which's coming out these hills. Folk here might be called hippie hunters, and take one look at that long hair a-yours, and could be trouble. Down these parts, we got a respect—"

"Maybe I should get a haircut," Wiley offered. "War's over, after all."

Twisting his mouth to spit, the policeman did not answer at first, but seemed to resurrect a story from the depths of his mind. "On this selfsame road another car stopped 'cause it was lonesome and private. Two kids, hippie kids, but they was just high school sweethearts, not brother and sister like you. Neckin' in the car out in the woods there when something unholy come up on them. The boy was mutilated like a catamount caught him, though some say it was the devil hisself. You all are in college and don't have much truck with the devil, do you?"

Erica caught bits of the forest floor in the comb of her fingers. Taking a step toward Wiley, she longed to reach out and take his hand, but sensing her intent, he inched away, a wild uncertainty in his eyes.

"The girl just vanished. Word is she is a sexual prisoner of a man out there in the mountains, but I say we have ourselves a killer, either in these parts or passing through. But, no ma'am, I wouldn't want to be lost, unprotected so to speak. Ain't nothing worse."

The falling angle of sunlight stippled the road with the outlines of leafy branches, and when the breeze blew, the shadows danced across the pavement. The policeman handed back the license and registration and then turned to Erica, holding his gaze upon her features and her hair feathering across her face. She pulled a flyaway length together and tucked it behind her ear, keeping the tresses in place with a crooked finger. His stare alarmed and fascinated her; she had not noticed before how his gray eyes strained toward blue, but perhaps that was a trick of the radiant hour. "Don't get so hankerin' for lonesome that you find yourself lost." To an attentive Wiley, he gave directions to Roanoke, and as the Pinto eased away, they left the trooper in the middle of the road. In the rearview mirror, or so it seemed to her, the young man reflected an unearthly glow that brightened as the figure diminished.

SHE THOUGHT OF it as their wedding night, or akin in spirit and symbol, the first night they would share a bed to sleep next to each other and wake up together in the morning. In the game she was playing, a great leap forward. Off the highway on the Tennessee side of Bristol, they found a Mom-and-Pop motel that backed onto neighborhood streets where children called and hollered to one another in the early hours of the evening, eking out the last bit of play and nonsense before going to bed. She shut the drapes, wrapped her arms around her man. "We made it," she said. "Despite the freaks, we got away."

"The police have seen us. We'll have to get rid of that car," he told her. "And be more careful. Don't want to be caught."

"Still," she said. "You liked it. Out there in the woods, like a wildcat."

He kissed her and began to paw at her clothing, but she pushed away gently and patted him on the chest. "Why don't you stretch out? I want to get a shower, get ready."

In the cramped bathroom, she unwrapped a thin bar of soap, inhaling deeply to discern any aroma. There was none. She laid out her cosmetics on the counter, arranging her lipstick and deodorant and tweezers just as she had at home. A small plastic bottle held a few ounces of her mother's lavender shampoo, and Erica caught her scent. She unrolled the red camisole bought just for this evening and hung it on the towel rack, the silk crimson as a wound spilling over the white terrycloth. In the mirror, she pondered an oily patch across her forehead and gazed into her tired eyes, and then cocking her left shoulder to the reflection, she admired the backward tattoo of the intertwined AOD and angel's wings.

That policeman had liked her, she decided, and the old man at the front desk too. He had leered at her, tried to look down her shirt when she bent to pick up her bag. She was pleased to know that men outside of her hometown, men other than Wiley, found her desirable, and as she stepped into the shower, that knowledge heightened the pleasure of soap and hot water. The lavender would last a few days, and then she would be gone for good. Indulging herself, she stood in a cloud of steam long after she had made herself clean. Wrapped in a towel and brushing her hair in front of a wiped circle in the mirror, she turned the handle and pointed at her reflection. "Pow," and then the wide smile spread like a bloodstain. She slipped into her camisole and stepped through the doorway. Sprawled across the bed, Wiley snored into his pillow, a slick of dirt where his sneakers scraped the coverlet, his hair twisted over his face and around his neck like a noose. She turned off the overhead light and in the soft glow of the table lamp, she watched him sleep, so much like a child in his dreams, a little boy lost, that she could not bear to wake him.

7

Try to remember, walk back to when it began. Paul at crack of day, eyes heavy, coffee, oatmeal, stocks and sports, her note on the counter. Childish hand, like his own mother's: "Test today, off early. Remind Mom about staying the night—Erica." And when Maggie asked, he could not recall the name of the family where she was staying. One of her friends from school, the chewing-gum girl. When pressed for details, he could not picture a face. Exasperated, Margaret went to bed without him. And then the cycle begins, walking through his day, steady stream of patients at his practice, moving from examining room to examining room. A chart. Eyes, ears, throat, say aah, take a deep breath, good, another, so many beating hearts begin to sound alike. A day like every day, people anxious to tell or hide their problems, bodies moving through time, the bright advance, the dark decline. When does it break down, this getting old, when do we rest from our aging?

Paul sat in the darkened living room counting remembered patients, hours after his wife had fallen asleep. Like sheep, children by the dozens, earaches passed among classmates, or sibling to sibling, a river of bacteria. One punctured eardrum as rank as death. Baby with colic, young mother worn and jumpy. Fear for that child, that woman. He remembered a boy who every semester came to school all black and blue, bruised as overripe fruit. The father and mother taking turns. The nuns who brought him in wanted the parents arrested but those days were so different. Farmer with shingles, a constellation on his back. Salesman who could not outtalk cigarettes. Mrs. Day and her migraines and nightmares. Miss Jankowski: this small lump, here doctor, feel it. Nothing more than a milk gland, but still, a referral to ease her mind. Breast no bigger than an apricot. Eve Fallon worried that she was infertile, trying for years, frightened that he might leave if they don't get that baby so long awaited. Arthritic woman his own age, nothing to be done, the inevitable. And I seem to be forgetting the simplest things, he says to himself, but not the past. Just the other day he thought, for the first time in decades, of the playhouse in the woods where his sister Janie and he would hide and use the doll's china dishes. Pinecones and needles on the plates, water drawn from a cold stream and served in fragile porcelain cups small as thimbles. And he could easily call up the face of a little girl dying in Japan at the end of the war. But where have I put my glasses, the keys, the grocery list, my new friend's name? Where have I put my mind?

His own father, born of another, more stalwart century, spent most of his life clenched and stoic, but the end, the end in madness. Senility. Did not recognize anyone in the last days, brothers and sisters around the bed, the June birds singing at daybreak, look of sheer terror at the strangers in his room. His own children. Am I going this way?

Paul could not remember what his daughter had said. I'll be spending the night tomorrow at . . . what was the name? A color, yes. Red, no, nobody's last name is Red. Brown? White? Black? Try to form her face as she says it. Nothing but a jaw working the chewing gum. Sometimes he cannot remember what Erica looks like as a teenage girl, cannot reconstruct her features in the haze of his imagination. How long had it been since he had really looked and taken in all the changes, the woman she was becoming? Much better when they are young, when love is so much clearer. Too hard these days, and it comes back to him, her head bent, lifting, hair parting, her eyes, her smile. Had she smiled at him when she said the name? Yes, Green. Joyce Green, that's it. He uncapped his fountain pen and wrote the name on a prescription pad so that he would remember it in the morning and not forget to tell Margaret. Must talk with Erica when she comes home, about the boy, maybe I am being too harsh.

The windows rattled. He pried himself from the easy chair and went to look out, peering past his reflection at the waxing quarter moon floating in the cloudy sky. A cold front had been promised, and here it was, pushing high winds ahead, bending treetops and scattering leaves. "Hold on to your feathers," he said, just as he had repeated for so many years when the wind blew up in Erica's company. Not lately, but when she was young, she would laugh each time, neither of them certain of the maxim's meaning or significance. He could see her now, in his arms a child of two or three, the happy surprise of the wind startling her as she breathed it in, the flushed cheeks, delight in her eyes, and she burying her face in the crook of his neck. "Hold on to your feathers," he said, "or you will fly away." Paul Quinn took one last look at the moon, the stars, and the streaming clouds before climbing the stairs one by one to his bed.

8

In the parking lot of Bearden High School in west Knoxville, they watched the juniors and seniors drive back from lunch. Wiley had already switched their Pennsylvania tags with a set from Tennessee, which he held in his lap, tapping his nails against the raised metal letters. They waited for some student to make a mistake. From the passenger seat, Erica noticed the boys in their Bulldog jackets, the girls neat and perfect, walking like fashion models back to their classes. Or gaggles of friends excitedly sharing the latest gossip, goofballs horsing around, hoods smoking joints or cigarettes. A pair roared in on a motorcycle, the boy in black leather, the girl's long brown hair trailing like a horsetail.

"Look at them," Wiley said. "Clueless rich kids."

"I remember the first time I saw you in high school. Squirt, always had your head in a book."

"Come the day, they won't be ready."

"What'd they call you? Little Mao? 'Dare to struggle, dare to win.'"

His shoulders sank, and his expression darkened.

"You're not upset, are you? 'Cause look at you now. Big strong man." She wrapped her fingers around his biceps and waited for the anger to pass. The traffic slowed to a few stragglers, the last of these a blue and white Plymouth Duster that inched into the space fronting their car. "You've got to time this right," Erica said. "Not before she gets out, not after she closes the door, but just as she steps out."

He honked the horn, startling the driver exiting her car—a teenage girl in a denim vest and white peasant blouse, beads spangling to her navel—who froze when Erica pushed open her own door. "Hey there. I'm Nancy. Nancy Perry." Erica came around, stopped at the bumper, flashed the peace sign.

The girl let go of the door and took three steps in their direction, intrigued by the sudden disruption of her routine. Peering over the top of her sunglasses, she moved forward, bell-bottoms dragging along the asphalt, the eagle feathers that hung from her belt stirring with each step. "Nancy Perry?" Despite her uncertainty, the girl let Erica approach. She jumped nervously when the driver's door clicked open, and Wiley stepped from the car, grinning and showing her his teeth. His appearance must have spooked her, for she tensed for flight.

"My boyfriend," Erica said. "He's a freshman at Tennessee."

"Looks like you're the last one back from lunch. No hurry to get to class?"

"Gym," she said, and shrugged her shoulders.

He was nearly upon them both. "Hey, nice belt."

The girl blushed, bowed her head.

"I haven't seen you around," Erica said. "Thought I knew all the cool kids."

She shielded her eyes and tried to remember if she had seen them before. "I kinda keep to myself."

"Oh really?" Wiley moved closer. "What's a girl like you doing all by yourself?" He reached out and flicked at a feather on her belt. "Maybe you want to come for a ride with us, angel?"

The invitation surprised all three of them. For a moment, the bohemian girl mulled the offer, her eyes glistening as she ran through its connotations, wicked with excitement, but then she looked away to the building. Erica waited for the answer too, wondering at his intent, and when the girl waved shyly and went on her way, relief replaced anxiety. "See you in school," she hollered after her. Once the girl was out of sight, Erica smacked Wiley on the shoulder and arched her eyebrows.

"Never mind that," he said. "It worked, didn't it? Scared so stiff, she forgot to lock the door. I'll see if I can get it started."

In their glove compartment, there were a dozen yellowed mimeographed sheets emblazoned with the AOD logo: "How to deal with the Pigs," "How to free the Masses from American Imperialism," "How to beat Big Business," "How to buy a Gun under an Unassumed Name," "How to hot wire a Car." Wiley unfolded the page, and by the time Erica had screwed on the new plates, he had brought the Duster to life, popping up behind the steering wheel full of unbridled pride. They wrapped the guns in the Steelers blanket and threw them in the back with their gear, and then took off to find the western highway. In the ashtray were a half dozen joints, which they lit up and smoked one after another, leaving Knoxville behind in a reefer cloud.

They spent the night in a ten-dollar motel near Nashville, where the night manager begged them to listen to his latest song, crooning sad lyrics and strumming an out-of-tune guitar, painted cobalt with a dozen flaking white stars. Everyone had a dream to sell, some story about what had gone wrong. The man with the blue guitar reminded Erica of her long-gone Pap, her mother's father, who used to strum an old ukulele and make up ditties for her delight. She had not thought of him since he passed away, when she was nine.

Thrilled by the first of their crimes, Wiley was a terror in bed, starting up again just as she began to doze, and a third time after that, which left them famished and light-headed near midnight. She pushed her foot against his bare back. "Get us something to eat, would you? Something real. A burger and a shake." He rolled over and lifted his eyelids to see her stretched out naked as a concubine on a seraglio couch. "Chocolate," she said.

From the moment the flimsy door banged shut behind Wiley, Erica savored the quiet and her privacy. She picked up his dirty socks and underwear, threw them in the sink with a dollop of lavender shampoo, and washed as best she could, wringing out the clothes and hanging them from the shower-curtain rod. His white briefs reminded her of holiday bunting. The domestic ritual brought an ease to her thoughts; she hummed a few bars from "Get Down Tonight" and waggled her hips in time. He hated that kind of pop disco, but she liked to secretly dance to its insistent rhythms. The song was company, but not enough. Tired of her own voice, she clicked on the television and lay on the rumpled bed.

Some old movie in black and white, all shadows and crazy angles, quick crosscut shots of men looking for someone: a man runs through a series of dark tunnels, a storm drain beneath city streets. The police are chasing him, shots are exchanged. Wet down there. Like a cornered animal, he looks fearful and desperate. Disembodied German voices echo from all sides. A staircase appears at his shoulder, and he looks up to freedom, climbing as fast as he can—is he shot?—till he reaches a grate above his head. Pushes but it stays stuck, and then on the darkened street, a miasma of mist and shades of cold gray. A wind howls. His hands unclench from the iron grid, fingers emerge through the holes, stretching, reaching for the salvation that will not come. Mere hands reveal the heart.

Outside, a car pulled into the gravel parking lot, diverting her from the story, so she went to the window, fussed with the double curtains to peer into the night. A man emerged from the car, lurched as he stood, then staggered right to her window. Through the glass, he looked straight into her eyes. Old enough to be her father, but younger than the real thing. A shot rang out from the movie, distracting her for an instant, and then the man at the window had disintegrated. She checked again the bolted door, the latched chain. Heart pounding, Erica slid into bed and tried to refocus on the movie.

Two men ride in an open jeep, chatting amiably, and pass by a stylish young woman who refuses to acknowledge them.

"Let me out."

"There's not time," the man in uniform says.

"One can't just leave. Please."

The driver stops. "Be sensible, Martins."

As the man grabs his suitcase and leaves the jeep, he says, "I haven't got a sensible name, Calloway."

A sensible name, Erica thought, and laughed over her inspired choice of Nancy Perry. The girl in the high school parking lot had no clue that the real Nancy Perry was martyred for the cause in a shoot-out with the police in Oakland, California.

Martins leans in a nonchalant manner against a cart parked by the road to wait for her. The camera locks on the approaching woman, cool and elegant and beautiful, walking along a gallery boulevard lined with glorious leafy trees. Crazy music begins to play, and Erica wonders what on earth can make such a weird noise, somewhere between a harp and guitar but with vibrato. Angels on acid. The man waits and waits. The woman walks by, passes him, walks on without even glancing in his direction; she wants nothing to do with him. Walks past him, right past the camera, and out of his life, and he just stands there and watches her go, that mad music the only sound till he flicks away a match, and then "The End" in white letters on black.

Daddy would have known what that music was, would have told her all the trivia connected to the film, the other movies the actors appeared in, the name of the man with the expressive hands, and the meaning of it all. Too late. Suddenly cold, she pulled the blanket over her legs. Had she the courage to ask her father, he might have explained, too, the reason behind Wiley's invitation to the girl back at the high school. Come along for a ride. The thought of another creature in their bed swept over her like a winter storm, and the room began to shrink and close in on her. She turned on all the lights. The wet clothes in the bathroom dripped against the porcelain tub. That drunk would be coming any minute now to burst through the locks and chains to abduct her. She plucked out a thread from the covers, unraveled a stitch. Mother will be furious. Leaping from the bed, she pressed her ear against the door to listen for footsteps.

9

As he tucked the pistol in his waistband, Wiley flinched when the cold barrel brushed against his bare skin. Careful to leave the car door unlocked, he crossed the empty parking lot to the restaurant, adjusting his gait so that the gun would not slip to the ground or peek out from behind his denim jacket. A bell tinkled when he opened the door, and the clerk behind the counter glanced up from his paperwork and nodded. The menu along the wall displayed a raft of choices, but Wiley kept his head down as he approached and did not look at the man, focusing instead on the handle of the pistol bulging against his jeans. "Two burgers, no, make it three. And a large fry."

The clerk, a thin white man with a regular boy's haircut, sighed and straightened his stack of papers, taking time to staple a cash register tape to the topmost page. "We're closing."

"Sign outside says open to midnight, and by my watch, that's another ten minutes."

The man glanced over his shoulder at the leftover items on the warming rack. Wiley followed his gaze, spying through the service opening another employee, a young black man in a white apron, intent on scraping the flat grill. "Looks like your lucky day," the counterman said. "How about a ham and cheese, a junior roast beef, and two fries? I'll charge you the same."

"You serve plain hamburgers, don't you? I mean, fella comes into your establishment should be able to order anything off the menu, as long as you're open. That's your business, right?"

The counterman leaned forward, his lank hair falling across his brow. He looked older, maybe late twenties, wrinkles foreshadowed around the eyes, with the kind of pallor that comes from too much time under fluorescent light. "Listen, bud," he said. "We're out of cheeseburgers. Now, I can give you what we have, or you can just split and go somewheres else. There's a McDonald's up the highway, may be open if you hurry."

"I was just saying—"

"You want what we got, or not?" The man raised his voice, and from the kitchen, the cook wiped his hands on the apron and marched toward the front, disappearing from Wiley's view for an instant, then crashed through the swinging doors, glowering.

"Sure, sure," Wiley said. "I'll take whatever you got." He laid a five-dollar bill on the counter, and the cook and counterman grinned simultaneously at some inside joke. Wiley took the bag of food and his change and started to leave, then remembering, he turned on his heels. "Oh yeah. Two large shakes. Chocolate."

"Shake machine's closed," the cook said.

"We're closed," the counterman said. "Why don't you go on now?"

Wiley approached them, face red with anger. "Look, man, all I want is—" He flinched when the cook slapped his hands upon the Formica. "My girlfriend had her heart set on a chocolate shake."

"Ain't that funny, Carl," the counterman said. "Girlie boy says he has a girlfriend."

No conscious choice registered in the seconds it took to put down the bag and draw the pistol; rather, the movement, which he had practiced so often in the mirror, was accompanied by a strong sense of déjà vu. The gun leapt into his hand. The two men behind the counter, surprised as Wiley, did not know what to think or how to react other than to twitch in recognition that they, too, had been in this scene before, played out in their imaginations, and could remember what to do: when the bad guy pulls a piece you reach for the sky, like in a cartoon, and that is how they found themselves, hands in the air, a pistol waving madly back and forth between them, waiting for their cue, hoping he would not shoot. But he did not speak, this long-haired boy with fury in his eyes. He seemed stunned, too, by the suddenness of the moment and the dangerous act. They waited, mumbling prayers.

He debated which one to shoot first. If the counterman, the cook might panic and jump him, and from his size and demeanor he appeared the tougher of the two and more likely to make a move and perhaps disarm him. Of course if he shot them both, no one would know which had been killed first, although the sequence would matter in his own conscience. He imagined the pull of the trigger, the flash, the bullet through the brain leaving a clean hole in the skull, and then the body's surprised collapse. Then the other one—he had decided by then that the counterman would go second—the other man would cry out in shock and have an instant's panic before he, too, would snap alert at the report of the pistol and flinch as his soul flew homeward. A cool trickle of sweat ran down his spine.

"Carl," Wiley said to the cook. "Carl, that's your name, ain't it? You know how to make a milkshake?"

Carl nodded. His paper hat was soaked with sweat.

"Well then, Carl, you make me two chocolate shakes while your friend and I wait. Don't be all day, Carl. I'm thirsty." He clicked and locked the hammer, and Carl moved like a robot to the machine. Then Wiley turned to the man at the other end of his gun.

"You shouldn't have been such a miserable prick. You should've treated me like any other customer. Brother, either you are with us or against us."

"I'm sorry," the counterman said. "Please. Don't shoot me."

"What's your name?"

"Barry," he said. The first tears rolled down his cheeks.

"Barry, you got a good reason why I don't shoot you for being such a prick about making a chocolate fucking shake? A simple fucking chocolate shake?" The first bite of power felt sweet in his mouth. He had been bullied so long that the moment of control gave him revenge upon all the boys who had ever taunted him, and the sight of Barry weeping filled him with joy.

The counterman's nose began to run, and sweat dripped on the counter. He wiped his face against his shirtsleeve, never lowering his arms. "I've got a wife, and a baby girl—"

"Barry, Barry, Barry, you got to quit that crying."

"I'm sorry, I'm sorry." He drew in a few deep breaths. "I'm not crying."

"Nothing worse than a crying fascist. You and your wife and your baby girl and your manager clip-on tie and your five-dollar haircut, and you lording over Carl back there and you thinking you're better than me. Well, fuck you very much, Barry." The handle of the gun tingled in his grip, but his hand no longer trembled.

The cook set the two cups before him, fished out two straws, and placed the lot in a bag. When he had finished, Carl stared at the counter, mumbling a penance. "You don't want to shoot that gun, friend. Don't ever start down that road. That road leads you straight to hell." He stared, unblinking and steadfast as an owl, hoping to break down the boy's will.

"Thank you, Carl. This is your lucky day. I am sorry to have to do this, so be sure that I mean no harm to you. Your day will come, brother, when you are truly free. I am on your side. Tell them the Angels spared you. Do you have a rope around here, maybe a roll of duct tape?"

Fixing his gun on Barry, he watched him tie and gag Carl, and then Wiley bound them together to chairs in the storage room amid the gallon drums of ketchup, the cardboard cartons of toilet paper, the solvents and cleaners. At seven in the morning, the day manager found the cook and the counterman taped back to back, alive and livid. The milkshake machine had frozen, and the night deposit bag was missing, but by the time the police arrived, the Angels had flown. They were veering southwest, slouching toward Memphis.

10

As he left for the clinic in the morning, Paul finally remembered his note on the table and told his wife that it was the Green girl who had invited Erica to spend the night. Margaret called the Greens and discovered that Erica had not been there, no sleepover plans, and when the daughter Joyce came to the phone, it was clear that she had played no part in the subterfuge. Are you sure? Margaret had wanted to ask, could you check again? Instead, she left the note on the kitchen table and slowly took the stairs to her daughter's room to see if Paul had made some mistake, perhaps he was wrong, and their daughter had come home late and merely slept in; she imagined the rumpled quilt, the slumbering body, Sleeping Beauty curled in the bed, but no. She feared even before opening the door what the room would reveal. Quiet as a burglar, Margaret searched through the dresser drawers, investigated the closet, and took inventory of all that was missing.

Erica had left, and Margaret knew she had run off with that boy.

As she tried to picture Wiley's face, she realized how little they really knew about him. Early on, Paul had disapproved, as he always had with whomever Erica dated, and because that displeasure manifested itself every time the boy came around or at the mere mention of his name, they did not see or talk with him as much as they could have, should have. As tangential to the main frame of their lives as the postman or the newspaper boy, Wiley was a rumor. A glimpse, a wave, and then gone again. And after the time Paul had found the spent joints and smelled the boy's presence in their bed, after the accusations and demands, Erica never mentioned him again. But crediting her mother's instincts, Margaret knew her daughter secretly continued to see her lover, knew that she was with him that very moment.

Finding no hard proof in the bedroom, she closed the door and tried to remember the boy's last name—Bannock, Babcock, Riddick, Rinnick. There was only one listing in the telephone book, so she dialed S. Rinnick and let it ring seven times before hanging up and jotting down the street address. She drove across town to one of the older neighborhoods, modest brick houses built for the mill hands, with old cars parked along the curbs, tiny yards choked with toys and dead grass. The wind chased her up the walk and blew across the porch. The night before, that same wind had rattled the windows so fiercely that she woke in the middle of her dreams and could not fall asleep again till her husband joined her, slipping in quietly so as to not disturb her, tossing in his private restlessness. Margaret banged on the door, and when nobody answered after she counted to fifty, she knocked louder and waited. A shower of beech leaves eddied in the corner of the porch. Across the street, a young woman in round glasses peered from the front bay windows and then withdrew as suddenly behind the curtains.

The boy who answered from behind the stormdoor reminded her of Wiley, but he did not seem to recognize her, and she guessed that instead he must be the brother. When he cracked open the door, a blast of heat from inside nearly bowled over Margaret. He wore blue flannel pajama bottoms and an old sweatshirt with PITT stitched across the chest. His feet were bare, and his hair stood out from his head in a tremendous, unkempt mane. Without a word, he motioned for her to come in, and she entered into a dark wood-paneled foyer. "I'm Margaret Quinn. Erica's mother."

With a shrug, he bade her follow, his soles smacking on the waxed floor, her mules clicking as they walked down a long hallway. Due to the house's northern exposure, the walls wept with dampness, and as Margaret passed by the front rooms, they, too, seemed perpetually dark, the furniture old and rotting. Bright paintings of flowers in vases and cherries spilling from a bowl hung in the hallway, though in the weak light, the effect only compounded the sense of dreariness. The boy pushed open a swinging door, and a flood of artificial light shone like salvation. In the kitchen, the ceiling lamp cast its glow on an oaken table and an older woman in a faded red bathrobe hunched over the morning's newspaper. She glanced up at Margaret, then bent to her reading, finishing her sentence and sticking her finger on the paragraph.

"Mrs. Quinn," the brother said. "Guess why she's here."

Mrs. Rinnick curled her upper lip and snarled at her son.

"About my car, I 'spect," he said.

Margaret offered her hand, but when she realized how committed Mrs. Rinnick was to her spot in the paper, she withdrew. "I'm Margaret Quinn," she said. "I think your son may be seeing my daughter."

"Denny here? That's a laugh."

"Not Denny. Your other son, Wiley."

A lemon-bite look crossed her face. "Wiley ain't here."

"Yes, but that's why I'm here. You see—"

"Make yourself useful, boy, and ask Mrs. Quinn if she'd like a cup of coffee. Or maybe she's a tea drinker. She looks like the kind of lady that drinks tea and that 'stead of coffee. Put on the kettle, Denny. Bags in the cupboard. Have a seat, Mrs. Quinn. Do you do the Jumble?"

Margaret pulled out a chair and joined her at the table. "Nothing for me, thank you, Mrs. Rinnick. I'm afraid I've come here on rather serious business. You see, your son Wiley and my daughter Erica have been going stead—"

"Pretty girl. Now I know who you are. You're Erica's ma." Mrs. Rinnick became more animated as each word hit the mark in her mind. "I'm Shirley, pleased to meet you."

"I wish it had been under better circumstances, Mrs. Rinnick."

"Call me Shirley, everybody does, 'ccpt my old man. You don't wanna know what he called me. Called me the Black Hag, how'd you like that? Clogged arteries and he topples over dead right there in the mill john, serves him right. It's so nice to finally meet you face-to-face, and oh, I can see where she gets the good looks. Apple doesn't fall far from the tree, does it, Denny? You know that girl he brings round here? Well, this is her ma."

"We met," he said.

"Maybe you can help me," Shirley asked. "Do you have any idea what TEELA might be?"

With her index finger, she moved invisible letters about in the air in absolute concentration. Margaret watched in dull horror until the kettle steamed and whistled and the boy took it off the boil.

"Mrs. Rinnick, this is something of an emergency. My daughter is missing and I think she may be with your son. Wiley."

Denny set a mug of tea in front of her. "Do you take sugar? Milk?"

Shirley wrote TEALE in the margins of the newspaper, and then struck through the effort. EATLE did not work either. "I wouldn't worry. He's off gallivanting around half the time, off to Pixburgh to meet with the other boys in that club of theirs and that. God knows what they're up to."

"Comes the revolution," Denny said.

"Maybe you know your son, but you don't know my daughter. She lied to us. Said she was spending the night at a friend's house and never came home."

"Probably just snuck off. You know kids these days. Free love and that?" She cackled and her upper plate slipped. "Tell you what, they didn't have that free love in my day. Everything has a price. Ain't that right, Denny?" She wrote LATEE and scratched that out too.

"Wouldn't know, Ma. You never did say if you want anything for your tea."

"I just want to know what your son has done with my daughter!" Margaret shouted. "Not milk or sugar or tea or puzzles. Where are they?"

Shirley laid down her pen. "No need getting your drawers in a knot. I'll let you know if I hear—"

"Please do, yes." She stood to go. "Sorry, I'm just worried."

Pursing her lips, Shirley looked stumped, as did her son standing behind her contemplating the puzzle.

" 'Elate,' " Margaret said as she rose to leave. "Try 'elate.' "

11

Caught inside a long leafy tunnel of trees lining both sides of the winding road mile after mile, and though the foliage shone with new colors, the repeated patterns of·the forest had a soporific effect. Erica tried to doze, but she was too nervous, made skittish by his story. Well after midnight he burst into the room, clutching two bags of food, his face flushed and dotted with perspiration, and as he wolfed down the sandwiches and sucked up the melted shake, he told her about Barry and Carl, the pistol, the tears, and the bag of money—the whole story, laughing when he relayed the cook's words of warning. "Don't go down that road," he mimicked the deep voice. Each time she looked over at him behind the wheel, she replayed the scene and his unhinged excitement. On scant sleep, he woke her early in the morning, jittery with adrenaline, anxious to be on the road again. His passion, which had so excited her during their half year together, threatened to boil over. The gun in the glove compartment ticked like a hidden bomb.

The sudden snap of violence and Wiley's enthusiasm made her wonder what might have happened the night of their escape had her father heard them. Daddy stumbles sleepily into the hallway, his hair disheveled and chin unshaven, fatigue etched around his eyes and across his brow. Trapped in half-consciousness, he cannot speak as he puzzles over the sight of the boy in his house at that hour and the backpack strapped to her shoulders. Gun in hand, the barrel like an elongated finger, Wiley slowly intones the speech he had rehearsed. *She's coming with me, don't try to stop us.* Daddy reaches out for her. Like the time at the shore when she was five or six and wandered out into the sea with him. Pummeled by the surf, she held out her hands to be rescued, and her father made the same gesture, arms outstretched, fingers grasping as desperately as the man's in that old movie, and he repeats it on the stairway in her imagination. He stretches but cannot reach and shouts no! Wiley fires the gun, malice in his heart mirrored in his eyes. In slow motion, the bullet corkscrews through the air, at its tip a tiny demonic face winks with every revolution, striking her father in the breast pocket of his sky-blue pajamas from just the Christmas before, and the cherry-red stain spreads like a sunrise as he hurtles away from her. In the driver's seat, Wiley was singing along to the radio, oblivious to her thoughts. For a moment, Erica wondered if he had in fact shot those two men at the hamburger joint, and if murder was the reason they took off before dawn, if Carl and Barry were dead in the meat locker.

A flock of ducks crossed the sky, and Wiley pointed out how they circled to approach a landing. He slowed the Duster, calculating where the birds had found water, and pulled over to the side of the road. Behind a screen of pines, a small lake rippled. From beneath his bucket seat, he grabbed the bag of money and his pistol. "Come with me." The lakeshore was dotted with a few fat mallards—hens brown to blend in with the fading vegetation, the males ostentatious in their formal suits and iridescent green heads—waddling to the safety of a depression in the grass, complaining of the interlopers with every step. Wiley led her to the edge and plopped the night deposit bag to the peaty ground, and then he pulled out the pistol from his waistband.

"What are you doing with that gun?"

The shot rang out, and all the ducks took flight in a cacophonous panic, quacking and beating their wings. At the ground by his feet, a wound in the earth seeped water. The recoil from the shot forced his arm to a ninety-degree angle, and Erica traced the path from his shoulder to the barrel. A wisp of smoke curled from the gun and dissipated. "Are you crazy?" she hissed. "What if someone hears us?"

"It's locked," he said. "And no knife will cut through that mesh cloth. I wish I'd asked them for the keys." Rocking back on his heels, he let his arm drop to his side and listened. All was quiet save the gentle scrape of a few falling leaves and the waves lapping against the grass, and the ducks circled farther out on the lake, bright orange feet sluicing as they settled on the surface. He angled his gun again, closed one eye, and tried to determine the proper vector.

"Get closer," she said. "It's not like that bag is going to shoot back."

Glaring at her, he bent to one knee, put the muzzle against the metallic surface of the bag, turned his head away from the blast, and pulled the trigger. The flock beat their wings and flew off for good. The shot sent a shower of paper into the air and knocked the bag into the shallows. Wiley raced to retrieve it, his sneakers sinking in the mud, and found that the bullet had torn a hole as big as his fist. Poured out on the grass, most of the money was ruined—half blown apart, and many of the salvageable bills were singed or waterlogged. He yelled out a string of obscenities.

Erica put her hand to her mouth to stifle her laughter. "You shot the money."

"It's not funny," he said. "Stop laughing at me."

Wading into the duckweed, she helped him salvage what could be saved, ninety-seven dollars in all. They lined up the bills one by one to dry and upon each laid a small rock, and the sight reminded her of a cemetery, rows of grassy plots dotted by headstones. He paced the waterfront looking for stray survivors, and she stretched out on the bank, the warm sun soon drying her bare feet and evaporating the beads of water that had collected like dew in the fine hairs of her forearms. Through closed eyelids, she could sense the changing light, and on her bare skin feel the falling temperature, and when she stirred from her rest, Erica was not surprised to see an expanse of clouds swallowing the blue sky.

"Looks like rain," she hollered at the distant boy, who poked a stick at something submerged at the water's edge.

They pocketed the damp money and trudged back to the car. Every few steps, he looked back over his shoulder at her, scowling whenever he caught her smirking. When he touched the wires together, the Duster's engine failed to turn over, and daring her to so much as giggle, he tried again; it whirred and clicked but would not start. She folded her arms, refusing to offer any solace, and watched a ladybug crawling across the windshield. Six segmented legs swam across the glass in crazy desperation, no pattern or plan but escape. The moving circle stopped, the wings flared and then folded, and she wondered why the ladybug did not simply fly away, since it could. After the third unsuccessful try to start the car, Wiley banged out and popped the hood, tinkered for a while, pretending with parts he did not know. Red-faced in the driver's seat, he tried a few more times, but the engine was dead. Muttering and cursing like a lunatic, he pounded out his frustration with his fists on the dashboard while she just stared, impassive, through the glass, fascinated by the erratic path of the bright and tiny insect.

12

At three in the afternoon, a line of thick gray clouds cruised in on a cold western wind, and Erica and Wiley headed leeward, anxious eyes on the horizon, fearful that they would be caught in the coming rain. Dotting the far shore of the lake, a few toy houses clung to the hills, never appearing to draw closer. After bundling the rifles in the blanket and burying the package beneath a pile of leaves, they donned their backpacks and hiked through the silent woods, hoping to reach shelter before the downpour. She followed the trail he blazed, calling out for him to slow down when he marched out of sight.

At the top of a rise, she found him squatting on his haunches to inspect in the undergrowth hanks of gray fur scattered in random patches, grim reminders of some death on the spot. With a long knobby twig, Wiley stirred through the detritus, overturning matted leaves, attempting to discover the buried squirrel or rabbit, but nothing else remained. No bones, no blood. Whatever had been caught had departed with the predator, a fox or owl perhaps. A day or two and the clues would disappear as well, blown by the wind, washed by the rain, or stolen by some woodland creature to line its bed. Resting her hand upon his arm to steady herself, she bent to join him and felt the electric tremor on his skin just before the first dazzling fissure of lightning.

Drops struck the dry leaves in irregular explosions, a budding threat of what was to come, the rhythm building and flattening out as the rain beat harder and more steadily in a rolling percussion. They moved with quick, earnest strides, trying to keep themselves dry, but the rain fell heavily. Their long hair clung to their scalps and shoulders, their clothes puckered against their limbs, and their feet squelched in their shoes through muddy puddles. The water seeped into their knapsacks, doubling the leaden weight on their backs. By the time they reached the first cabin, they were soaked to the core. Wiley pounded on the wooden door to be heard above the roaring storm.

A young girl, about nine years old, opened the door. She was stick-thin, her face a plane of sharp angles. Her fine, fair hair hung straight to her shoulders, though mussed on one side, as if she had been reading all afternoon and holding up her head with one hand. Fogged with condensation, her glasses obscured the brightness in her eyes. Unrolling her free arm like a wing, she welcomed them inside wordlessly.

They dropped their wet packs on the floor and gathered their bearings. Table lamps had been lit against the gloom and made the curious objects in the room appear yellowed with age. On all four walls, mounted animal heads stared back at them: two deer bristling with antlers, a black bear, a colossal ram with spiral horns. Whole fish glistened with shellac, swimming on wooden plaques. On the mantel, a fox flushed a bobwhite, a raccoon raised one paw forever above the mystery of a box turtle emerging from an acrylic stream. A red, white, and black Indian blanket woven in simple bold geometry had been thrown over the back of the wide sofa. A dressmaker's dummy stood in the corner, wearing nothing but a necklace of feathers; in another corner, an old-fashioned velocipede rested its handlebar against the wall like a loitering dandy. In a globed terrarium, a pale blue skink dozed beneath a blossoming white orchid. On the wall above hung a shadow box containing sixteen different bird feathers pinned in place. Another box showed eight desiccated butterflies, wings pocked with holes and tears. Glass-fronted bookcases were stuffed with old fairy stories, children's tales, the *WPA Guide to Tennessee*, *A Brief History of the Natchez Trace*, *Birds of Appalachia*, and an oversized Geneva Bible open to Ecclesiastes, a thick underline at chapter 7, verse 4. Erica and Wiley circled the room, taking it all in, dripping slowly on a corded rug, and when they realized the child had disappeared, they stopped marooned in the center.

"I'm cold," Erica said, and drew close. Wiley made no move, offered no sign or word of comfort. A chill slithered up her jeans and down her blouse, so she wrapped her wet arms across her chest and shivered.

The girl came back with two thick towels and a pile of folded clothing in her arms and handed Erica a pair of slacks and a black sweater and Wiley a red plaid shirt and dungarees. "You may have to roll those pant legs, mister. He was taller than you," she said. "You all can take turns in the bathroom, but please be quiet. Mee-Maw's having a lie-down in the bed. She always tires when it rains so."

Dressed in the strange clothes, Wiley and Erica sat near the hearth to dry by a newly made fire, and the girl brought them bowls of clear broth. She said hardly more than what was necessary and seemed content to make them warm and comfortable. Daylight waned, and the window-panes were steeped in darkness. Complicities of fatigue and stress, the hypnotic fire dancing before him, and the close and musty air in the quiet room caused Wiley to fall asleep against one wing of the easy chair, and as soon as she noticed, the girl crept to his side and laid the Indian blanket across his lap. Erica watched this simple kindness with a waylaid sympathy, and then rose from her chair to study the curiosities in the glass cabinet until she became entranced by its enchantments. Taking down a book of fairy tales, she settled into the facing chair and soon dozed as well, her hands fixed to the pages of dreams. Outside, the rain hastened the fall into night. A door creaked open from the back of the house, then shut with an exclamation. Erica and Wiley awoke just in time to see an older woman, bent slightly at the waist and blinking in the light, enter the room and stop to focus on the strangers by the fire. "You're back," she said. "We've been expecting you."

13

There in the afternoon, the hour when Erica usually came through the door on school days, passed without her. Margaret busied herself, checked the impulse to wait by the window, and muttered the same wish over and over as she wandered through the house attending to imaginary dust and scrubbing again the same spotless stovetop. After her strange experience with jumbled Shirley Rinnick, she had come home and dialed Paul at the clinic. He advised to check with the high school whether Erica had shown up for classes, and if they could not locate her, Margaret was to wait for the appointed hour when their daughter was due. "If she's with that boy," he said, "and cutting class, I'm sure she'll show up like usual to make it seem like she was in school all day." The hour came and went, and no sign. "Surely she'll be on time for dinner," Paul told her when she called again. How can you be so calm? she thought, but years of living with him prevented the question from coming out. Instead she walked a mile inside the house, praying like a nun.

At four, a flock of starlings landed in the front yard, paraded like an undertakers' convention through the dying grass, and through some telepathic signal flew off en masse.

At five in the afternoon, nothing happened.

Paul would be home shortly and would know what to do. She sat beneath the kitchen clock to outwit time and force the hands to move faster. Outside a van door closed, and she saw Pat Delarosa walking up the grade of his lawn, a bouquet of yellow roses in his arms.

Fifteen minutes before six, footsteps clopped across the wooden porch, and then a quick knock. Fear froze her to the chair. But before the visitor could depart, she rose, dreading the possibility of a policeman, hat off in respect, sent to break the news, something awful, an accident, the hospital, please not the morgue. Through the side window, that boy appeared again, the brother, what-was-his-name? Wiley's brother. The older one. Give me a clue, she thought.

"Mrs. Quinn? Sorry if I'm interrupting your dinner."

"Dennis, come in." Still dressed in the University of Pittsburgh sweatshirt, he shuffled into the house. "Can I get you something? A cup of tea, perhaps?"

"Never touch the stuff," he said. "Makes me jumpy."

"Come in, come in." She led him to the living room. "Have a seat. Have you heard from them? My husband should be home any minute."

"The thing is, Mrs. Quinn, I have some sorta bad news. Not really bad, but . . . I think I know where they are. Not where exactly, but I think I know what happened."

"Is everything all right? Is she okay?"

He leaned forward in the chair and stared at the floor. "The thing is, Mrs. Quinn, my car is missing. My Pinto."

You'll have to drive him to the point, she told herself. "And you think Wiley took it?"

"I know he stole it, 'cause he kept asking me if he could buy it from me, and I kept saying no, and, well, I know about the Angels."

"Angels?"

He raised his head and looked her in the eyes. "Wiley, he's into some pretty heavy stuff. You know about Patty Hearst?"

"The bank robber they captured a couple weeks ago? The heiress?"

"And the Symbionese Liberation Army."

A car pulled into the driveway, the headlights sweeping across the front window, and the boy stopped, allowing Mrs. Quinn to decide whether to wait for her husband rather than hearing the tale told twice. They arranged themselves on the edges of their chairs, backs ramrod straight, and cocked their heads to face him full on when Paul entered the living room. At first, his expression failed to register any difference, but gradually he came to realize who the visitor might be and why he was sitting next to his wife, whose eyes were fixed upon the very air, anticipating a story that floated in the space between them. Paul slowed the motions of his ritual, carefully folded his overcoat and balanced it on the top rail of a rocking chair, which pitched backward, then righted itself, and then he smoothed the gray hair at his temples, and thus ready, he moved swiftly, like a predator taking down the prey, to shake the boy's hand and offer an introduction.

Margaret spoke to him in a formal tone reserved to mildly shock his intermittent memory. "Dennis is Wiley's brother. You remember I told you over the phone that I went to see the Rinnicks this morning." Her husband sat beside her and stared at the boy. "He's come to tell us about Erica."

"You have some news?"

Denny cleared his throat and began again. "Do you remember when they kidnapped Patty Hearst, then it turns out she's been brainwashed into being one of them?"

"Are you saying Erica's been kidnapped?"

"No, not exactly. Wiley kinda talked her into going with him. To join the Angels. The Angels think that the people need to rise up and start a class war. A revolution."

She asked, "Why are you kids always talking about a revolution? Against what?"

Ready to pounce directly from the chair, Paul leaned in tense and anxious. "But I thought that was all over. The authorities caught Patty Hearst."

"It is all over, man. Vietnam is over. SLA. The old days are gone, no more people marching in the streets. All went up in smoke."

Paul looked at Margaret for an answer. "What are these Angels?"

"Angels of Destruction," Denny said. "Wiley found out about them through an ad in one of those underground papers, and he wrote to the PO box in the ad, and the guy starts sending him pamphlets and that. Propaganda, literature."

"So he wants to be an Angel?" Paul asked. "He got Erica into this cult?"

For the first time that evening, Denny laughed. "Well, I wouldn't call it a cult, exactly. Might be some guy in his garage with a mimeo machine he stole from his high school. When he wasn't home, I'd go in his room sometimes and look through his stuff, and it was a trip." From his pocket, he pulled out a sheet of yellow legal paper. "This is the kind of stuff the head of the Angels says: 'No doom is ever executed on the world, whether of annihilation or any other chastisement, but the destroying angel is in the midst of the visitation.' They call themselves the Angels of Destruction, and they are here to start some kind of holy war."

Paul bent forward and buried his face behind his hands.

"After the news about Patty Hearst, Wiley got a long-distance call from this guy named Crow. And yesterday morning, I wake up and find my car is gone and my daddy's old hunting rifle and shotgun, and all the money stole from the coffee can at the back of the kitchen cupboard. My mum don't want to admit it to herself, but—"

"Where are they going?" Margaret asked.

"I have no clue. He never said. Bound for heaven or bound for hell."

"She's gone," Paul said. "He took our baby. Call the police, Margaret, and have them meet us at this boy's house."

While the Quinns readied themselves, they left Denny alone, small and uneasy in the easy chair. Arrangements made: the dinner taken from the oven to cool, neglected, in the baking dish; Erica's room quickly scoured for further clues; Paul's blood pressure medication best not forgotten; the tangled conversation with the police; coats on, and where did I leave those keys? She had a moment alone with Denny in the foyer while Paul searched his slippery memory. Margaret cleared her throat and asked with a hint of fear, "What did this Crow person say to make them run away?"

Before he spoke, Denny licked his dried lips. "Wiley told me: the time is at hand."

14

Mrs. Gavin's imagination had tricked her into believing that her prayers had been answered. Earlier, in the muffling warmth beneath her comforter, she heard their voices through the drowse, and some trick of longing conjured them. Before the strangers in the living room, she took off her glasses, pretending to stop a tear, and in that instant, could deny the truth before her and arrest relentless, unforgiving time. No matter. She would improvise her way back to reality.

"No, Mee-Maw, these are the two—"

"You were expecting us?" Erica asked, and chuckled nervously.

Rain tapped against the windowpanes, falling in sighs through the pines surrounding the cabin. It drummed the surface of the lake where they had stopped and fell upon the ducks huddled together on the cold shore, and rain beat on the stolen car, rivulets spilling through the cracked window on the driver's side to soak the blue velour seats and carpets. Through a makeshift hill of fallen leaves, the rising waters soaked the swaddled and buried guns. An absolving, cleansing rain that threatened to fall forever. In the space between the question and the answer, the rain fell, and the four of them listened to a new sound entering the world.

"No," the woman said. "You're not who you were supposed to be, not who I thought. You'll pardon me."

Wiley stepped forward to offer his hand. "Our car broke down out by the lake, and we got caught in the storm. Your granddaughter here opened the door and let us borrow these dry clothes. I'm Wiley Ri—" He caught the name before it completely spilled from his mouth. "Ricky. Ricky Wiley, and this is . . . Nancy Perry."

"I'm Una, and this here is my grandmother, Mrs. Gavin." The girl sidled up to the old woman. "Mr. Wiley and Miss Nancy need a place to stay for the night. Can we, Mee-Maw, can we keep them? For the night. It's raining tadpoles."

Acquiescent, Mrs. Gavin wrapped her arm across Una's shoulders and drew her near, holding her so for just an instant. The overhead light reflected off Una's round glasses, obscuring her eyes, and from across the room, Erica and Wiley could not read any emotion in that temporary opacity. As soon as her grandmother spoke, however, Una could no longer restrain a wide smile. "Of course they can stay, of course. Miss Perry, Mr. Wiley, if you please. I was just fixing to make our supper, but we can stretch a stew to four, and I won't send you out on such a night with the heavens thrashing the earth. You'll stay."

Mild objections were raised and gracefully rebutted. Mrs. Gavin threw more carrots in her stew, set the covered pot to simmer on the stove, and with the weary patience of the long-suffering cook, she mixed a buttermilk dough, then dropped rough spoonfuls on a cookie sheet. The heat from the oven suffused the kitchen and spilled over into the whole cabin, and when the biscuits began to bake and the stew was uncovered for a stirring, the smell of the dinner triggered a Pavlovian reaction in her guests. They could be heard from the fireside, small exclamations punctuating their concentration. Puffs of flour sifted through the air when she clapped her hands against the apron and went to announce the service. Una and the visitors were in a triangle, knee to knee to knee, huddled over a deck of cards, a game of War afoot, the child clutching the thickest of three stacks, satisfaction shining on her face.

"Come and get it while it's hot," Mrs. Gavin said. "Cold butter won't melt if you tarry."

After Una's blessing and amen, they tucked in, grateful for the homemade meal. Ravenous, Wiley speared hunks of lamb and potato and tore them from the fork with his teeth. Between bites, he sopped biscuits in clots of gravy, eating so quickly that it spilled from the corners of his lips. More determined to savor the fare, Erica picked like a bird for the choicest pieces, and as she chewed, the flavors reminded her of winter nights at home with her parents at the dinner table, but she did her best to squelch the thought. In the chair beside her, the little girl watched her every movement, and when Erica's features stiffened, Una reached out to bring her back into the world. "I would've beat you," she said. "I had all the good cards, and it's my best game. What's yours, Miss Nancy?"

Gathering dust in the attic: Monopoly, Parcheesi, backgammon, Chinese checkers, Mouse Trap, Tip It, Clue, Life. Her father loved the last one best of all. The tokens were tiny plastic cars with six holes for pegs, blue for boys, pink for girls, which you acquired by chance. One time he had a carful of pink pegs and asked with a wink, "Where to, ladies?" and her mother had given him the funniest look, acknowledging some story hidden behind the gag. Erica imagined he had a dark and risqué past, dancing girls and nights afire. "Life," she told Una. "The game of Life."

"Hah!" Mrs. Gavin banged the flat of her palm on the table hard enough to lift the flatware. "Game of life, indeed. It is no game, let me tell you, but a jigsaw that you never can finish. Always a couple of pieces missing, or one that fits in nowhere, and the cover to the box is gone, so you've no picture to offer a clue as to what it's supposed to look like."

Without stopping his chew, Wiley answered her. "I've always thought of life as a struggle. Marx said, 'Once all struggle is grasped, miracles are possible.'"

"Groucho Marx said that?"

Erica smiled at her confusion. "Groucho Marx said that 'the secret to life is honesty and fair dealing. If you can fake that, you've got it made.'"

"Never mind," said Wiley. "Marx was wrong. It's from Mao's *Little Red Book*."

With a clatter, her spoon slipped into the bowl. Mrs. Gavin squared her shoulders and looked him in the eye. "Are you a Communist, Mr. Wiley?"

"Me? No, ma'am, I'm an American, but I do believe there's a revolution coming where the poor will rise up against the powerful. Some people see it as a race war, but it is really a conflict between the classes, the oppressed versus the wealthy. And I truly believe that there will be much bloodshed on the streets before there are equal rights for the poor, for women, for people of all colors. The apocalypse is coming, and the new creation first requires the destruction of all that is truly wicked, and a cleansing of our sins. We've got problems in this country. Black men in Watts without jobs, poor people living like dogs, Tricky Dick Nixon in disgrace, gas shortages, and Whip Inflation Now buttons, and all you see is the rich man in the country club, the white-shirt crewcut Baptist, the jelly-doughnut-eating Mormons, the cannibalistic Catholics—"

Nothing but gape-jawed silence answered his outburst, and it seemed for a time that not a word would be spoken ever again. Erica stole glances at Mrs. Gavin, still and wild-eyed as she tried to digest his meaning, and at Wiley, who was reeling in his tongue. The three adults were hemmed in by their private fears of saying the next wrong thing. Only Una remained implacable and went back to her stew with gusto, pausing between bites to ask, "Are you a preacher, Mr. Wiley? A man of God?"

"No," he said, with a smile. "I am lapsed."

Erica leaned over to confide in the child. "A few days ago we met a man who told us not to pine after being alone in case you might get lost, and Wiley here, Mr. Wiley, he met a man who said if you take a man's life, you are bound to carry it with you for all eternity. Everyone has some holy message inside, some desire spoken only in their prayers."

Inching closer, Una asked, "Are you a child of God yourself, Miss Nancy?"

From the head of the table, Mrs. Gavin cleared her throat, and the subject was changed. They talked about the colors of the autumn leaves, what happens to the ducks and other birds when it rains, and how quiet it was so far removed from other houses and the road. An apple pie appeared miraculously from the antique pie safe, a percolator bubbled with fresh coffee, and a game of cards resumed as the night settled into its quietus. When the hour drew late, Una was sent to ready herself for bed, and Mrs. Gavin disappeared soon after, only to return with the child, who handed out two sets of flannel pajamas.

"Goodnight. I'm so glad you found us and decided to stay," Mrs. Gavin said, and then suddenly stepped forward to Erica and embraced her and the child together. Surprised by the gesture, Erica tightened her grip and pressed against the child's face, inhaling the scent of baby shampoo from her fine blonde hair. Off to bed they went, and from behind the closed door hummed a brief muffled conversation and the rhythm of a prayer, and later still, the melody of a cradle song.

"Who did she think we were?" Erica whispered in the dark.

He rolled to his side to face her. "A couple of ghosts."

Tucked above the width of the great room was a narrow loft, and Erica and Wiley climbed a short ladder to find twin beds head to head beneath the cantilevered eaves. "It's like we're sleeping under a giant letter A," Erica said. The rain beat against the shingles, and they crawled into one bed together and fumbled at each other's clothes while trying not to fall from the mattress. He clipped her nose with his elbow. Her left foot got caught between the bed frame and the wall. When they finally calculated the proper positions, they stopped short and breathlessly held each other still when a door opened downstairs and a nightlight snapped on to illuminate a corner of the hallway. Mee-Maw sighed to herself, then shut her door without turning the knob. They tensed and waited to hear the creaking of her bed. "Maybe this isn't such a good idea," Erica said.

"What do you mean? It's always a good idea, and besides"—he thrust himself inside her—"I'm already there."

She turned her head away, gritted her teeth, and tried to relax her clenched legs. It was all over within minutes. Working her hands flat against his chest, she pushed him away, gasping for breath. Her flannel top stuck to her skin, warm and moist with perspiration. Sated but clueless, he rose, pulled up the pajama bottoms, and flopped into the other bed. "We'll be gone in the morning," he said. "And who cares what those people think?" Within minutes, he was fast asleep. Erica listened to his irregular breathing, the whistle in his nose sounding like a siren; she listened to the rain drip and the house groan and tick as the wood cooled in the passing hour. In the unfamiliar space, she lost the persistence of vision and the faith of her own sight. She closed her eyes and tried to imagine again the wedding in a ritzy chapel in Las Vegas, Elvis and his child bride, the rendezvous with all the other Angels in San Francisco. Magical city. Indelible pictures of her childhood. At Una's age, Erica had seen on television images of the Summer of Love, long hair and wild protest signs; the fallen soldiers arriving home box by box; on her father's desk, the *Esquire* magazine of Kennedy, Kennedy, and King standing among the gravestones; the riots in the streets, and flowers in gun muzzles, the boys and girls who believed they could change the world. She worried that the game would be finished before she and Wiley could get the chance to play, the revolution over before it had really begun. Her hero would have no one left to save.

Restless, she rolled out of bed, and feeling with an outstretched palm along the unfamiliar wall, she found her way to the ladder and climbed down. Though she could not see, she felt the glass-eyed stares of the mounted trophies along the walls, the raccoon chittering from the mantel, the weight of the antique globes and heavy furniture scattered about the room pressing in on her. She shut her eyes, pretended to be blind, remembered her daddy on the bright green lawn, a kerchief stretched across his eyes as he stumbled and chased a circle of girls, all screaming with delight, at the birthday party the summer she turned seven. Did he ever catch a soul? At the corner where the kitchen met the hallway, she flicked on the light switch. Standing in front of her was the apparition of Una, stock-still in her white nightgown, the light streaming through the gauzy cotton to silhouette her thin body, nothing more than sticks bound by wire. "Jesus," Erica said, "you scared me half to death. How long have you been there?"

Without her glasses, Una appeared much younger and more vulnerable, her green eyes blinking in the sudden light, the midnight look of the awakened caught between dreams, her pale skin reddening at the cheeks from leftover warmth of the bed. When she spoke to Erica, her voice cracked in tremolo, her words seemed wounded. "I heard you ascending from the loft and thought you couldn't sleep."

"Descending. You're right. I'm sorry. A strange house and a strange day."

"Shall I make you a potion? Hot spiced milk is what Mee-Maw always makes me when my thoughts are running away."

Erica nodded and went to the fireplace, wrapped a blanket around her shoulders, and sat by the window, listening to the rain spatter against the glass. By and by, the child arrived, walking with measured steps and holding at arm's length a mug, the spoon clinking against the ceramic edge. The milk smelled of cardamom and honey, and at the first sip, Erica felt relaxed and full of sleep. Una sat in the next chair, curled her feet under her, and made a tent of the white nightgown over her knees. They whispered to each other in the dark.

"This is just the thing. I'll be asleep in no time."

"It's a magic potion. Mee-Maw cackles when she's stirring, calls it her brew, like she's a witch."

"Your grandma said she was expecting us?"

"She goes off in her own thoughts sometimes. Imagining what ain't here."

After stifling a yawn, Erica took a long swallow. "You live here just the two of you? Where are your parents?"

"Lest you want to sleep down here in the parlor, you best get on up the ladder. That potion will have you dreaming in a few minutes."

Fatigue raced through her veins like quicksilver. Her muscles felt like pulled taffy. Ordering her legs to move, Erica trudged back to bed, and when her head landed on the pillow, she slept like a baby, endlessly rocking, gone from this world of cares.

15

"Here is a riddle I almost forgot to ask you," Shirley Rinnick said. They had been requested to wait downstairs while Paul and Denny checked Wiley's room. "When is a thought just like the sea? Do you know? Today's Jumble question, do you remember? You helped me with 'elate.'"

The sea. Maybe they've gone to the sea, Margaret thought. Forget all this crazy talk of revolution, they're just in love. They've eloped and gone to the Jersey shore, maybe, or Maryland, or Virginia even. The tide roaring in on the sand. Funny how after you're there more than a day, the surf gets in your head, your blood, in your legs. Tug of the sea for days after you go home. Remember Jackson running in the morning on the strand.

"I used the A and the T from 'elate,' if that helps you. When is a thought just like the sea? When it's . . . ? Two words, Mrs. Quinn."

He loved you, that boy. Jackson. Romantic then, but now? Let's go to the ocean, he proposed, and stare all day at the waves.

"Mrs. Quinn. First word is one letter, and that's usually an A, so I'll give you that."

Middle of fall, like now. All of twenty. Go stare at the waves.

"Second word, six letters. When it's a blank."

Erica is not like me. She would go, if asked. Yes. That's where Paul went wrong, trying to keep her close, he held on too tightly to Erica. She went not just to be with this boy, but to go. To be free. Margaret looked at the woman across the table. "A notion."

"Right you are, right you are," Shirley answered. "How did you get it so fast? I didn't figure it at first, but the sea is the ocean. Not always the same, but still—"

"You think they're just on a getaway? You said they'll be back by Sunday night," Margaret snapped at her. "He wouldn't have forced her to go? I saw that room of his. Wiley is an angry child."

"I always do the Jumble, every day. Keeps the mind sharp."

"What about the stolen car?" Margaret asked. "The guns, the cash from your hidden coffee can? How do you explain that, Mrs. Rinnick?" Kidnapped my daughter, she thought, and ran away, probably to get away from his crazy mother.

"A notion, an ocean."

Oh be quiet, you stupid fat cow. Erica is missing and your son is to blame and all you can do is rattle on about some puzzle?

"A sharp mind is the key to life. If you have your wits, you have everything. You could lose an arm or a leg—"

She wanted to say: *Shut up, you crazy bitch.*

"—or even be paralyzed from the neck down, but as long as you have your mind, you're still alive, now aren't you? The mind has a power to solve life's puzzles. You just concentrate long enough and you make up the answer. What's the matter, Mrs. Quinn, still worried about your daughter? They've run away."

Before she could reach over and strangle the woman, Margaret noticed the red flashing lights through the window. She hurried to open the door, usher in the two policemen to Paul and Denny, upstairs in the younger boy's room. The officers seemed discomfited by the circumstances, unsure of what they sought, and why they had to miss their dinner for a couple of runaways. Columns of teetering books lay all about the floor, books spilling under the bed, hiding between issues of newspapers and magazines, *Rolling Stone* and *National Lampoon*. Drugstore paperbacks, political screeds and works of philosophy. Ginsberg's *Howl*, Kerouac's *On the Road*, Conrad's *The Secret Agent*. Sandwiched between the mattress and the box spring were a few well-thumbed *Playboy*s and a forgotten manual, *How to Make a Bomb in Your Basement*. Three of the walls had been painted black, and on the fourth, the painter had stopped midstroke next to the window and abandoned the project. The old white coat looked yellowed by smoke. Posters filled the space above the unmade bed: Lenin under the words "Acid Indigestion," a white rabbit on a chessboard surrounded by psychedelic shades of blue and pink, a Wanted poster with mugshots of all the people involved with Watergate, and one of Patty Hearst as Tania, wielding a machine gun with a hydra-headed snake in the background.

When the younger policeman opened the closet door, they all saw stenciled in gold spray paint the AOD logo, with wings. Margaret had seen that design before but could not place it, though in truth the kids had so many cryptic symbols that often signified nothing more than the desire for peace, love, or bliss. Signs with no meaning. Still, she could not stop trying to remember where she had seen those wings and could not concentrate on the conversation from the other side of the room. Her husband argued quietly with one of the policemen. Out of his element, she thought. Away from the clinic, he projects nothing of the mastery when playing the doctor. The wise old man gently counseling the smokers and the drinkers who will not quit, the mothers who neglect vaccinations for their children and wonder why they are sick, the boy with the bad heart, the girl who refuses to speak. They look up to him like a good priest, rabbi, magician, miracle man. The truth was he had slowed to complacency, a year past the normal age for retirement, one slip from malpractice.

"Most of the time," the older policeman said, "runaways like this call their folks in two, three hours, a couple of days, a week, tops. 'Course, the longer it goes . . ."

She whispered, "I have been such a bad mother."

"But I don't believe," Paul said, "that she would just run away like that—"

"Of course, we'll follow up, Mr. Quinn—"

"I'm a doctor."

Margaret spoke in a loud voice. "She was in love, love. Love makes you do crazy things. Well, not you . . . but some people. Erica." Every head in the room spun round to stare at her. She clapped her hand to her mouth. When is a thought just like the sea?

"Without an actual crime, there's not much to do but send out an alert. And wait to hear if anyone's seen them, but I wouldn't worry, Mrs. Quinn. Most of these kids think the world's going to be one way, turns out the world is something else. If you have any other thoughts about where to look . . ."

"I have absolutely no idea," she said. And the voice inside her head kept time with her answer—a notion, a notion, an ocean.

16

When he tried to wake her and she would not get up, Wiley shrugged his shoulders, slipped into the old clothes of the missing man, and shinnied down the ladder from the loft, following his nose to the source of its enchantment: bacon and eggs and coffee on the stove. The old woman and her strange granddaughter had already risen, dressed, and set the table for a feast: sliced bananas and poached pears ripe and juicy in porcelain bowls, a column of toasted homemade bread next to a perfect stick of butter, brimming jam jars, and a honeypot in the shape of a beehive. His mind wandered back across the room and up the ladder to his sleeping beauty, but let her rest, he decided. She had been through a lot in the past few days and seemed distressed by some malady he could not name. Let her sleep, and maybe she would awaken in a better mood, and besides, he did not want to wait to eat a minute longer. His hostesses did not trouble to ask but invited him instead to have a seat, get comfy, do you take sugar, Sugar?

Breakfasting at the rough pine table with the old woman and her granddaughter, Wiley imagined himself as a hero among the plain people. Mao dining with the proles, Che among the Cuban peasants in hiding from the Batistas, Lenin in his Siberian exile plotting what is to be done over borscht and glasses of strong, hot tea. The Gavins could not take their eyes off him, clearly admired him, and he felt a current pass among them. He was dangerous, valiant, a man of true principles, and these poor people looked upon him as savior, champion, destined for history.

Morning sunlight shone through the windows and altered the aspect of the room. What had been foreboding at night and in the gloom of rain now appeared merely old and forlorn, as tired as the fading year. The stuffed menagerie became a piebald zoo, the animals moth-chewed and dusty, their glass eyes clouded without the dancing reflections from the fire. The great wooden globe was cracked and fissured, the paper peeling, a bare white patch where Greenland once lay, a curling lip off the coast of Chile. A cherry bureau which doubled as a desk was topped by a silvered mirror, which mangled one's impression in brushstrokes of clouds and obscurity. But the breakfast table shone with wax and groaned with food, which Wiley ate with guiltless pleasure. Erica did not wake all through second helpings, through the casually peeled orange, through the third freshening of the hot black coffee. She slept through scrubbing up; through his indifferent tour of the library, through his perusal of the vibrant color plates in *Birds of Appalachia*. Tired of the yellow warblers and pileated woodpeckers, tired of waiting for Erica to get out of bed, he found his jacket on a hook by the side door and went out into the late morning to find their car and see what could be done with a new day's patience.

She had been dreaming that the rain had stopped and the sun was shining, that when the shot rang out, she took off with the flock, their wings beating, voices crying in one great rush, and she rose above, could envision Wiley on the banks of the lake, gun in hand, and as he fired again, the cook exploded as the bullet hit his chest, saw him falling and the money erupt from the hole, saw the bills float in the air like oak leaves caught in a swirling breeze against the sun burning above. And then the pop and the flash as he fired again into her father and the money burst into air, burst into flames, and the body—Daddy—drifting in the dead man's float on the water, of no more consequence than a discarded sail, and she could not move from overhead as the birds scattered in panic.

When she could finally summon the strength to lift her eyelids Erica did not know where she was. The wooden beams in the rafters looked like timber from a cross in a church, then the upside-down ribs of a boat above her head. Disoriented, she closed her eyes, tried to remember, and then came the voice of the girl. "Miss Nancy, wake up," she was saying. Who was Nancy? Wrestling an invisible weight upon her, she turned her head to the side and searched for the child. She wanted someone—her father, her mother—to come rescue her from this strange bed but could not find the words to cry out. Pebbles lined her throat, and paste caked at the corners of her eyes.

"Wake up, Miss Nancy." Una stood by the headboard, a full glass in her hand as an offertory. Erica sipped once, then fell back on the pillow and closed her eyes, sighing at the mattress's tender embrace. "You have to get up, Miss Nancy. The morning is well spent, and Mr. Wiley left without you. C'mon, we'll fix you a queen's breakfast. It's past tin."

Tin, ten, *Tinnissee,* her memory came back to her, worthless and ragged. "I'm sick," she said. "The world has fallen on top of me."

"Try." Her thin arms strung with exertion, Una lifted her to a sitting position.

The bed pitched wildly on a storm-spun ocean, and Erica fought to right her balance and steady the whirling room. The child clung to her, and after a few deep breaths, Erica could focus and tempt her body to pull back the blankets, lift her knees, and swing her hips. When her feet hit the bare floor, she stopped to rest. "What do you mean?" she asked. "He left without me?"

"Gone to get your car, he says. Told me to tell you he'd be back as soon as he could get her started." She giggled at the word "her."

Erica rocked to steady herself and try to stand. "I don't think I can make it down that ladder. Too wobbly. I don't know what's wrong with me."

"You need some food in you, is all. Come along, and I'll watch over you."

Caution guided every step till they reached the safety and comfort of the kitchen. At the stove, Mee-Maw concentrated on the frying eggs and did not notice her company until the chairs scraped across the floor, but when she saw how poorly the girl appeared, she set down her spatula and raced to her side. With a cool hand, Mrs. Gavin felt the temperature of Erica's brow, tutted to herself, and fetched a glass of orange juice. "Drink. You're coming down with something."

"I feel bored-out, empty. One side of my face is so tender it hurts."

"A flu or pneumonia, considering how long you was out in that cold rain."

They fed her dry toast and then cosseted her in front of the fireplace, a warm blanket on her lap, a glass of tepid ginger ale on the tableside. Una was charged with making a fire and hurried through her tasks of finding matches and kindling, stoking the flames with her breath, anxious to be not too far removed from Erica's side. Mrs. Gavin hummed at her chores, washing up another skillet and pouring cold coffee down the drain, and every quarter hour, checking in on the mummified girl, punching up a throw pillow for her neck, and straightening the already straight blankets. On her threadbare throne, Erica could not fall asleep, but found herself instead restful and contemplative, watching the dancing fire and thinking of the friends she had left behind in high school— what would Joyce Green think of me now?—and the buzz in her hometown once they realized that she had gone and done it, had the nerve after all, and good for her, she got out and is following her heart. Like a hospital nurse, Mrs. Gavin came and stuck a thermometer under Erica's tongue, and the little girl squatted on a hassock in front of her, staring intently at the glass stick.

"You ever seen," Una asked, "a cartoon where the sun is shining so hot and the red line on the thermometer goes higher and higher the hotter and hotter it gets till splat! Right through the top? I used to think blood was inside. Mee-Maw likes to say when she is mad it makes her blood boil. But I ain't never seen that red line move in a real thermometer. Fact, you can't hardly see that line at all lest you look just so. Like a lot of things in this world, you might miss seeing what's there at all, lest you are looking the right way."

Squinting to catch the light in the angled glass, Mee-Maw announced, "A tick over 101 degrees. We should get you back to bed." From outside, the sound of a distant shot echoed through the mountains, stilling the conversation for a moment. Mrs. Gavin paused, considering the possibilities.

Erica pulled the blanket to her shoulders. "No, I want to wait for Wiley."

"I'll leave you entertain our company," Mrs. Gavin said to her granddaughter and wandered back into the depths of the cabin. The girls played cards to help pass the time. Una taught her rummy and gin, taking most of the tricks as her opponent struggled to recall the rules and strategy of the games. As daylight began to fail, Erica grew tired and waved away the deck, and Una boxed the cards and sat quietly. Sleep overshadowed her patient like a cloud. Keeping vigil, Una chose a book to read quietly, the delicate turning of the pages a comforting sound. Awakened by the gasping interruption of her own breath, Erica drew in the sudden darkness of the room. The only illumination came from a short lamp casting a halo, under which Una sat. When the blankets rustled, she rose to Erica's side.

"How long have I been sleeping?"

"An hour or so. You called him Wiley before. Mr. Wiley. I thought his name was Ricky, but before you fell asleep you said you had to wait on *Wiley*. Why wouldn't you call him by his Christian name?"

"Did I? Must be the fever. How long has he been gone? Ricky, I mean."

"All day." Una knelt in front of her patient's chair and rested her hands on Erica's knees. "You think he's ever coming back for you?"

An ache spread and flooded her joints and muscles. The stiffness pinched her shoulders when she shrugged. "I don't know," she said, surprising herself.

17

The car had melted in the rain. Wiley hiked back through the woods to locate the place where they pushed the Duster off the road, though he could not be certain in the bright new day if he was following the right path. He found the lake by following the sounds of birds in flight, and he found the clearing and the path to the road. But no car. Impressions from tire tracks in the waterlogged ground provided evidence that it had been there, but he could not figure out how or why the dead car had moved. And without the landmark of the car, he could not remember where they had buried the guns. Perhaps someone else had found the Duster, he thought, managed to start it, and driven off, or perhaps a tow truck, called by the police, had pulled into the space and dragged it away. Or perhaps his bearings were all wrong. He walked a half mile along the highway, then retraced his steps and investigated the side of the road in the other direction. Certain that he remembered the clearing, Wiley returned to the trail and stood at its apex, overlooking the lake, willing the car to return. He strode to the shoreline and looked for signs writ on water—perhaps it had become unmoored and floated away and now rested submerged in the bottom silt. Nothing but mallards feeding on duckweed, and caught in the tall grass, the tattered flag of a ten-dollar bill fluttering, drying in the sun-blistered air. Farther along the shoreline, the waters lapped against the abandoned canvas bag floating like a sail from a drowned boat. He sat on the slant of a downed tree and stared at the sunlight dancing on the water.

The stillness of the afternoon reminded him of the last time his father took the boys hunting. They tramped up to Potter County and the canyons carved into the mountains, bivouacking in the cabin of a friend of a friend from the mill. Denny must have been twelve, and Wiley, at eight, labored under the heft of the rifle. A killing frost had long since come and gone, and the November dawn arrived steel gray and loaded with moisture. The threesome waited in a blind fifteen feet in the air, and the gun in his father's hands, the same rifle now missing, looked like a cannon. Wiley prayed that no deer would pass through the parameter of their sights, and just as he settled into the belief that his wish would be granted, a gunshot cracked the silence. The buck, shocked by the impact at its shoulder, coughed blood and bumbled into the brush. His father climbed down first, Denny following closely behind, and by the time Wiley had negotiated the makeshift rungs, they had caught up to the deer. His father grabbed the antlers and hoisted the head for his sons to see the raging eyes, the heaving flanks, and the tenacious instinct to fight surrender. And life stole away without gesture. Wiley's stomach rebelled and he threw up behind a chokecherry tree. A sharp knife greeted him on return, as his father prepared to field dress the animal. Lifting the point skyward, he turned to the boy. "Son, all things must pass and give way to the next, whether by your hand or God's. If you're going to go hunting, you got to be ready that something will die, and if you are scared of death, you've no place being here." Wiley wiped his mouth with the back of his hand and knelt next to his father.

A drake called across the water, and he remembered where he was. Erica would panic when she heard about the missing car, and he dreaded the scene—that perplexed squint threatening tears, the rush to accusation and despair: How could you let this happen? What will we do now? That crazy old lady must have a vehicle stashed somewhere on the property in order to get off the mountain for food, clothes, and other necessities. He could probably score the keys while Moo-maw and that imp slept and be down the road hours before the cock crowed next morning. Or they could hitch to Memphis and take their pick of cars. Or he could leave now, by himself, were it not for the money and his bag back in the cabin. Erica was just not as resilient and resourceful as he had expected; in fact, she was too stiff about the whole thing. Not a real rebel, not a true revolutionary, certainly no Patty Hearst. Hell, that high school chick—sexy girl in the round glasses—from whom they stole the car was probably more radical, and why had Erica given him such grief over his invitation to her to join them? What did Erica expect, really, that she would be his one and only? Did she think that her life would be remotely like the one they had left behind? The revolution's coming, baby, and we need to give our love away. "I am too young to die," he said aloud, and the ducks on the lake replied with strings of nervous chatter.

Taking the pistol from his jacket pocket, he stood and sighted down the barrel at the nearest mallard and squeezed the trigger. The retort masked the splash of the round on the water's surface and the ensuing frenzy of the birds. "Next time!" he shouted into the air. Reorienting himself, Wiley headed back to the road in search of the buried guns. Eyes to the ground, he tried to remember their hiding place, wandering like a man who has lost his glasses only to find them atop his head, and when he stumbled at last upon the package under the pile of leaves, some measure of hope was restored. Unwrapping the sodden stadium blanket, he was dismayed at the wet arsenal, which he would have to break down to clean and dry, but the weapons, at least, could be salvaged. Guns cradled in his arms, he began the long march back to the cabin, mulling every step of the way what he might say to Erica.

18

A week after their daughter left, Paul awoke at his usual early hour, showered and dressed, and announced at the breakfast table that he was going back to work. "Just for a few hours," he told her. "I've got patients." Staying at home with Margaret for those seven days proved more than he could manage, both of them anxious for police reports that never came. He left the house only to prowl his daughter's haunts and interview her dead-end friends, all the time obsessing over the unanswerable why. The high school students proved unhelpful—blank looks, shrugged shoulders, no confessions forthcoming. Beneath their stonewalling, he felt certain that they knew the truth but chose to protect and romanticize the pair, for even the most cynical longed for Erica and Wiley to get away with it.

Unsure of how to comfort his wife, how to read in her resolved stoicism hints of hope or despair, Paul kept to their tacit understanding. They had unraveled all possible plots and decided that they simply did not know, would wait, and wait they did. She ate little, slept less. Sometimes she would catch him watching her, certain that her lips had been moving in the running conversation she had with herself. And he knew she could not bear his internal pacing. He felt her madness creeping into his soul and rejected it, leaving her to tend the phone, isolated as a lighthouse keeper.

Margaret did not argue with his decision to return to the clinic, but let him go without a syllable of protest, relieved when he finally shut the front door behind him. His worries had grown by accretion till he was made gravid by his thoughts. Long after she was alone in the house, she went to the window to check for his car in the drive, and a scree of leaves danced like ghosts in the empty space. Those first few days had been a horror to bear, the godforsaken vacancy in their house, in their lives, the slow realization of how utterly missing she was. The detective, who came by their place the morning after the encounter at the Rinnicks', had said that most missing children return within hours, at worst a day, but if Erica hadn't returned—and she had already been missing three days by Margaret's reckoning—the percentages diminished. Being realistic, he had said, pretending reality offered any solace. Each day, as soon as the hour was decent, she telephoned the police station, then again in the afternoon, and then again in the evening until everyone remotely connected with the case simply avoided her altogether or took a message, until finally telling her to simply wait, and wait she did, her sorrow mingled with self-recrimination and regrets. Mrs. Delarosa sat with her for two hours the first day, one hour the second, and zero by week's end. Word had spread through the town, and neighbors came calling, to help they said, but Margaret sensed the morbid curiosity of each good Samaritan who drew close merely to measure how she would feel if in Margaret's situation. Or, worse still, the unspoken accusation: what kind of mother would let her only child run away? She resolved not to allow such judgment any purchase. She never cried once when another soul was around, and she was blessedly alone until Diane arrived to keep vigil with her.

When Margaret opened the door, the two sisters collapsed into each other's entwining arms. As usual Diane swept in, done up in the latest fashion—a high-waisted red tunic dress with contrasting black and white Bakelite bangles on her wrists. But as soon as she was with Margaret, they were young girls again, confederates against their long-gone parents and the history of their husbands, chained by DNA and five thousand nights and days together. No one else could understand the degree of loss, and their presumption of empathy allowed them to move at once to frankness.

"You look like hell," Diane said. "I'm so, so sorry."

They hugged each other again and then broke off, holding hands as they crossed into the kitchen. Margaret unwound the story, unpacked the scarce details about Wiley and the Rinnicks, and uncovered a shocking paucity of any real clues. A sort of progress was achieved in the telling— for Margaret, the unburdening of her confusion and loneliness, and for Diane, the opportunity to feel useful again to her older sister. At three in the afternoon, they began to sketch out their plans for that night's meal, for how long she might stay. And after dinner and drinks, after Paul finally begged off to bed, they sat in the living room sipping white wine, the television on but soundless, and took up the matter again.

"Do you worry that she's never coming back?"

"I am trying not to think about her at the moment."

"Some distraction is called for then. Let's play a game."

"I don't want to play a game. The police haven't called today. Why don't they call?"

"Not cards. You always cheat at solitaire, and you're only cheating yourself, you know. How about the crossword? I'll get the newspaper."

"That awful Rinnick woman. She drove Wiley to it. Bad blood always begins in the womb."

"Don't say that, Maggie. You can't blame yourself for Erica's hormones." She finished her wine and set the glass down on top of a magazine. "Love makes us do wicked things."

"What does she know about love? She's still just a girl."

"Now you sound just like Mom again. Those kids may not know a lot about life—the daily tricks to just get through the boredom and disappointment—but don't say the young don't know about love. It's the only thing they do know. From that first blast of air into a baby's lungs, they come into the world hungry for it, clamoring for affection."

"Don't be ridiculous. A baby cries because she's hungry for mother's milk. Needs a diaper change. Or is startled, maybe cold."

"No. Right from the beginning, we're wrenched from the one true love. The womb where that baby has spent every moment for nine months, listening to the music of the mother's heartbeat. And then the baby is pushed out in a fit of crying, on its own now, always looking for the missing piece. Where is my mother? Cold? Hungry? Crying for love, from the first day that's all we know. She's in love. *Amour fou.* She went willingly with him."

"That's just lust, just raging hormones."

"You ought to know enough not to confuse sex with love. One's the happy accident of the other. What about that boyfriend of yours down in Washington? I know you saw him, Maggie—"

"Jackson," Margaret whispered. "I'll call Jackson. He'll know what to do." She reached for the telephone, watched her sister tiptoe away the moment she began to dial.

19

The setting sun lit the underside of the clouds, reflecting glory on the bowl of the sky, suffused with gold, magenta, and pewter, even white renewed in its brilliance. From the top of a hill, Una watched the colors bend to evening as she waited for the approaching figure to negotiate the path through the woods. From afar, he looked like some Hindu deity, extra arms protruding from his sides, but the closer he came, the more clearly his appendages were revealed: in the cradle of his left arm, a shotgun broken down at the nexus of stock and barrel, and in his right, a rifle carried upright like a soldier's. Una studied the sky, then the man, calculating the time and distance, hoping he would come upon her while light remained for him to notice her and not react in fear or surprise. Beyond in the vale, the cabin lights blinked on window by window.

Wiley had planned to hide the guns on the property near the cabin and wake up early the following morning to clean and dry them properly in a private place. The girl had doubtless seen the pistol hidden in his jacket, but there was no need to alarm her or the old woman any further with a display of more firepower, no reason to spook them, for he had reckoned on their trust and help in getting out of these hills. Though he had not discovered where she hid it, they would need to borrow or steal the old lady's car. Or, if Erica objected to the idea, ask the old lady to drive them into town or out to the highway at least, where they could hitch a ride to Memphis and find another set of wheels. But when he saw Una come flying off the hilltop, earnest arms pumping and feet smacking the ground, he scrambled for some explanation. Breathless, she stopped short to wait, rested her hands on her knees, and lifted her mad red face to meet his gaze. "Mr. Wiley," she panted. "Thought you'd never come, but you best be quick. She's been asking after you. She's real sick."

He wanted her to slow down, so he rested the butt of the rifle on the ground and spoke in a calm tone. "Who's sick, Una? Your gramma?"

"No." She rose to her full height. "Miss Nancy. She's been sick all day and fearing your return, just burning up."

Slinging the rifle to his shoulder, he followed, and as they neared the cabin, the aroma from the kitchen stove filled the air with carrots and herbs, rendered chicken fat, egg noodles on the boil. The soup flowed like a stream through the pines and deepened his hunger, for he had been all day in the woods, chasing after the phantom car, without a scrap of nourishment. In a dark corner of the porch he braced the guns, and took three bounds to reach the kitchen, wrenched the heel from a loaf of fresh bread, and dipped it into the soup, stuffing half the mess into his mouth. Wiley was still chewing when he heard Erica clear her throat, and turning, saw her swaddled in the rocking chair, hair lank against her scalp, her eyes vanishing into sockets dark as bruises. After dunking the other half crust into the broth, he went to her, mouth full, and knelt at her side, laying the back of his hand against her hot skin. "You look awful. What happened to you?"

She licked her dry lips and waited till he choked down his swallow of bread. "You're back. I was beginning to think you had abandoned me."

"I wouldn't leave you." Like a young boy, he threw his arms around her and buried his head against her breast.

With grave difficulty, she raised her free hand and stroked his long hair. "Why were you gone so long?"

"I lost the car. I went back to the place where we left it, but someone took it, or it rolled off on its own into the lake. I looked all day but couldn't find a trace."

Clamping her fingers on his skull, she lifted his head to look into his eyes. "Someone stole our car?"

Mrs. Gavin, who had been eavesdropping by the bookcase, emerged from behind them. "We'll have to call the police—"

"No," they said in unison. Wiley offered up an explanation. "It wasn't our car, but a friend's. I don't have any papers, don't even know the license plate number."

"But your friend, he will be angry if—"

"We traded cars," Wiley said. "His Duster for my Pinto, because we were going so far. So you can't call the police."

"I'd get in trouble," Erica said. "I'm only seventeen. But we're off to be married. We're headed west to elope, but I'm underage back home. Please don't call the police."

From the other side of the room, Una spun the globe with a slap of her hand. "Married?" She skipped over to them and smiled at Erica. "Mee-Maw, did you hear? That's the most romantic thing I've ever heard. Like Romeo and Juliet. Are you two madly in love?"

The question went unanswered, but the notion satisfied Mrs. Gavin, for the matter of notifying the police never arose again. Erica joined them at table for the blessing of the soup, though she could manage only a few spoonfuls of broth.

Rather than subject Erica to the climb to the loft, the Gavins rearranged their sleeping habits, Una bunking in with her grandmother, and the invalid moving to the child's small bed in the far corner of the house. Though he objected to being alone, Wiley reconsidered and withdrew to the loft, collapsing on the bed. The buzz of his snoring overhead made them all giggle with disbelief. Una fixed another dose of the sleeping potion and brought in the warm mug, tucked the covers round her charge, and sat at the foot of the bed. Together, they stared at the stars streaming in the black sky painted across the window. Away from the city lights, their luminosity increased. As a lifelong habitant of the room, Una knew the names of the fleeting constellations and enjoyed pointing out the more definitive ones for her, then waited for Erica to finish her spiced milk before turning out the nightlight and bidding her sweet dreams.

The darkness encouraged Erica to whisper. "I was just wondering what you might think, lying here every night, the whole of creation right outside your windows."

"The heavens above, the earth below."

"Do you miss your parents? When are they coming back?" Erica asked.

The girl rose and stood in the doorway. "I never did say."

"I miss everything," Erica said, and then rolled over by a quarter turn into the balm of sleep.

20

Erica did not recover the next day, or the one that followed, nor the entire time they were sequestered at the cabin in the Natchez Trace. Her symptoms followed a pattern established early on: an unrelenting fatigue that no amount of sleep could conquer and a low-grade fever unassailable by chicken soup or drugstore remedies, with a rising temperature in the afternoon, dipping at sunset, causing her to complain of the chills and request extra blankets abed or in the parlor chair where the daily dose of hot spiced milk would be delivered by the cherub of the house. This cycle induced a gradual ennui or emptying of passion, although that, too, drew scant complaint. Though her appetite had deserted her, the thought of food sometimes made her sick. She occupied her few waking hours with the books in the glass cabinet, games of chance and imagination with Una, and, when her energy waxed, short strolls around the grounds.

At first, Wiley was solicitous, worried over her health and well-being, preaching caution. He spent the first few days of her infirmity carefully disassembling the rifle and shotgun, cleaning and oiling the guts and letting them dry in the sun, and then, with some difficulty, refitting the pieces. The Gavins, used to men with rifles out in the country, paid him no heed. October played fair and mild, and he enjoyed being outdoors with a task that required his solitary attention and concentrated effort. But as evening passed to a lonesome night above in the loft, and the next days followed with no signs of progress, he grew agitated and restless. Mrs. Gavin sometimes left them alone with her granddaughter, driving off in an old white Rambler, mysteriously produced from a hiding place, and returning several hours later loaded down with groceries or, once, a quarter cord of firewood stacked in the back. Grateful to have some useful purpose, Wiley helped her unload supplies, eying the car and coveting the keys. For the most part, however, he went off on his own. He took to hiking the trails around the lake, pleased to be among the birds and small animals amid the fallen leaves. Some days he ventured back to the spot where the stolen car had been parked, prowled through the brush and along the shore for some clues to the Duster's disappearance.

To test his marksmanship, he took the rifle with him into the woods to wait for something to move, shooting at the birds that chanced his way, killing one with a single bullet through the breast. After huffing through the underbrush, he found the body, cupped it in his hand, and brought the winged thing to eye level. The cowbird was limp but stiffening with rigor mortis, its feet curling around a missing branch, its wings poised for departure. Wiley waited the rest of the afternoon for something bigger to kill, but the forest creatures grew wary of his presence and nothing flew or crawled or crept nearby. Back at the cabin, he asked Mrs. Gavin whether Erica needed a doctor but was rebuffed by her assurance that the girl simply needed some rest, let the body do what the body does best.

Day by day the sickness whittled away the sense of momentum they had built for the journey, and as the date passed for the planned rendezvous with Crow and the rest of the Angels, Wiley's mood darkened in captivity. As long as she could not travel, he felt bound to stay, but he needed to make some outward sign of his commitment to the cause, a radical break to counteract the domestic and quotidian turn his life had taken. He was a warrior in a just cause, different from his contemporaries who had given up the fight. Buried each day in the *Little Red Book*, he began to meditate on what distinguished the bold rebel from the apathetic masses, and he concluded that he needed to demonstrate his dedication to a higher calling. The ascetic warrior moves against the times. Wiley decided he would shave his head as a rite of passage and cast off the trappings of the common crowd. He approached Mrs. Gavin with a request to borrow her car, explaining his need to drive into town and find a barbershop.

"I'll cut it," she volunteered. "You want a shaved head? I do my granddaughter's hair."

A quick look at the girl's ragged mop did nothing for his confidence, but he capitulated under the circumstances. Mee-Maw made him wash his mess of curls but instructed him to leave it wet, and draping a bath towel across his shoulders, she brushed it out like a horse's tail. Snipping the scissors in the air above his head, she asked again, "How much should I take off? The whole head, Una?"

Wiley cricked his neck to spy her from one eye. "As much as you want," he said. "Pretend that I'm on the run and don't want anyone to recognize me. Pretend I'm a desperado in need of a new identity."

Drawing the hair together in a thick rope, Mee-Maw sawed through the hank, and after separating the final strands from his scalp, she raised the coil into the air like a warrior claiming her coup. Una gasped at her grandmother's audacity and the realization of the time it had taken the boy to grow such a pelt. With a final flourish, Mee-Maw tossed the hair on the newspapered floor and, steel slicing through air, set to shaping the uneven ends, all the while humming a lullaby. The frenzied blades slowed to a more calibrated pace, and when she heard her grandmother turn on the razor, Una ran off to herald the news to Erica but could not find her in the bedroom or the bath, so through the front door burst the breathless child.

Una shielded her eyes against the sun with the flag of her hand. "Miss Nancy, Miss Nancy, come see." But her friend was not sitting on the porch as usual. The girl called again twice and, receiving no reply, launched an elliptical orbit around the cabin. Under a willow, leaves silvered and clinging to weeping branches, Erica perched on the beam of an ancient sandbox. As soon as she saw her there, Una stopped short, anxious that her next step might be off the edge of the earth. She had not thought of the sandbox in ages. Her father, or so she had always heard, built it for her before she was born, hauled the white sand and lumber braces, now weatherworn to gray. As a toddler, Una spent many hot summer days under the willow, watching the feathery leaves and graceful limbs dance in the breeze. By six years, she had forsaken the spot altogether and its sway on her emotions. Rain and wind had flattened the sand into a bowl-shaped depression, and lichen and woodworms had claimed the timber. The tips of the branches overhanging the sandbox had burrowed into the surface, as though desperate for water beneath a desert. Some old toys lay in the sand—a red plastic bucket bleached on one side to salmon, a doll stretched out and staring blindly into the sun, a rusty watering can with a sunflower nozzle. As she approached, Una noticed that her friend was using the shard of a broken china dish to carve lines in the sand.

"I loved that tea set," she said, her voice tinged with longing.

"I had the same pattern," Erica said, then bent her face back to the sky and closed her eyes. "Wonder what's become of my old toys." She had taken off her sweater and knotted it around her waist, exposing her bare arms and shoulders to the sun. Una sat down beside her, skin against skin, and aped her pose, lifting her face to gather in warmth. The willow branches broke the sky into a mosaic as blue as the shattered dishes. "I'll bet you were out here every day in the summertime. I used to set up my tea service with all my dolls and stuffed animals in these teeny, tiny chairs, then I'd make my daddy come to tea, and you should have seen him try to sit there—his knees would be sticking up over the tabletop—and the little bone cup in his big hand."

She glanced over at the child, who seemed on the verge of tears. "Miss Nancy. I've something to ask you, if I dare."

"We have no secrets, you and me. You've been taking good care of me these past weeks."

"Lest I do you further wrong, I should ask." Her voice quavered. "Are you an angel? An angel sent to us?"

The willow shivered in the breeze. Erica averted her gaze to the fractured sky. "What makes you ask such a thing?"

"Your wings." She fingered the tattoo on Erica's bare shoulder. "And Mee-Maw says."

"This? This is just a symbol me and Mr. Wiley had done. A sign of our love for each other. But what has Mee-Maw been saying?"

The girl did not want to answer. She picked up a china cup and flicked at the sand clinging to its edge. "She said maybe you was sent from heaven to deliver us a message about my mama and daddy. That's why we have to keep you here till you give us word and not let you go lest you leave without us knowing." Una frowned and drew a spiral in the sand. "But I don't believe her, though I do as I am told."

"Knowing what, Una?"

"Knowing where they are. My mama and daddy."

"You said they would be coming back soon. What happened to them?"

Una shook her head. "That's what Mee-Maw told you, but I know better. They run off when I was a baby, run off to Canada because of the Vietnam War, and left me with my grandmother to watch over till they come back."

"I didn't know." Waves of empathy and confusion rolled over her. "The war's over, though. They'll be back soon."

"No, they're dead, ain't they? They'd have sent for me if they were alive. Or called or wrote. That's why you've come to us. You are an angel of truth—"

"I'm not sure there are really such things as angels."

"I prayed for you to come. And to tell me why. And to stay with me."

Erica could not think of any other way to silence the girl than to hold her close and rock her, soothe her hair. "We came here by accident, Una. What makes you think they are dead?"

Wrestling with her conscience, Una finally spat out her confession. "I had a prayer to God every night to bring them back, and if not, if they are never coming back, to send a message with his angels."

"But I'm no angel."

The sunshine beat in waves, and they huddled beneath the willow, hoping they could be saved, and listened to the birds. Una knew every song by heart and distinguished for her among the mockingbirds and waxwings, the wrens and the jays. Far off near the lake, over the long marsh grasses blowing in the wind, a redwing blackbird flew to land on a solitary tree, called out, and waited in the stillness for a reply that never seemed to come. Una held a china cup, blue and small as an egg, next to her chest.

"The sun's making me feel much better, how about you?" Erica spoke at last. "Let's go in and see the others."

"I forgot! Mr. Ricky got a haircut. I came out to tell you—" She stood and swiped the sand from the seat of her jeans. "He got scalped."

When she entered the cabin, Erica saw for herself and did not know whether to laugh or cry. Shorn of his long hair, he looked younger, like the children from her elementary school days, but also somehow more menacing, the angles of his skull outlining the set of his jaw, the slightly Neanderthal slope to his forehead, his eyes all but disappearing into the wide expanse of skin. He looked as handsome as a killer.

"That's him," Mrs. Gavin said. "My boy, Cole. Your father, Una. He looks just like the boy that got away."

21

The sleek black telephone in the living room rested on the table by the sofa, and the beige telephone in the kitchen hung on the wall like a barnacle. Both waited silently taunting her each time Margaret passed by. Ring, dammit, ring. On the other end, she imagined, a hand reached for the receiver, and then the caller reconsidered and withdrew. She waited for word from the police, for Jackson to fulfill the promise he had made two weeks before, for Paul to ring up from the clinic to check in—nobody ever called—and she was a virtual prisoner in her own home, forced to lock herself away from the gossip, the stares, and the whispers. She waited for Erica to pick up that phone to let her know she was coming home or at least that she was still alive. There was no one to call her Mother.

Diane offered some distraction, some company, someone to keep the daily household running. Swooping in from Washington, she took care of all that had been neglected—leftovers molding in the fridge, the darning pile, the bills unopened and unpaid, and the doctor brushed and dusted and sent off to tend the ill. Diane did the shopping, answered the dry cleaner's persistent phone calls, scrubbed a line of silt from the bathtub, and polished the neglect. When she had restored order and there was nothing left to do, she began to pick away at the ice around her sister's fears.

One melancholy afternoon, she asked, "What's your worst nightmare?"

"Do you ever think that she is dead? She could be lying in a ditch somewhere, or in a shallow grave, behind a Dumpster, or at the bottom of the ocean."

"I prefer to think of her alive and will do so until proven otherwise."

"I don't mean to be morbid. Just preparing for the worst." Margaret blinked, bringing into focus the far wall, blinked again, and blankness.

Her sister reached out. "Of course, that's one of many possibilities, you're right. She may well have gone willingly, and they've eloped. One expects a honeymoon period when the bride incommunicado forgets that her poor mother is worried sick."

"I wish you wouldn't talk like that. If you're going to talk like that, I wish you wouldn't talk at all."

"Then let's talk about your husband and what this is doing to him."

"I tried to make peace between those two. Tried to get him to understand—"

"He blames himself."

"I don't want to talk about Paul."

Diane switched tactics, opting for a little humor. "I can always change the subject. Have you ever thought of getting a pet? We never had one growing up. Mom always thought them too much work. But a pet would be someone to keep you company when I'm not around."

"Where are you going?"

"You seem like a cat person, but then a cat can be aloof at times, and you're no better off than when you started. A dog might do the trick. Long walks through the neighborhood, fetch your slippers. But a dog is a lot of work and distraction. Birds are always nice."

"You never told me you were leaving."

"A canary is a first-rate singer. Or house finches. Have you seen all those singing finches at the Delarosas' shop?"

"What will I do if you go?"

"Or how about a parrot? A parrot will talk your ear off. Not a real conversation, mind you, but they can be trained to have an impressive vocabulary."

A sharp knock unnerved Margaret, and she excused herself and rose to answer it.

Diane kept on talking. "Illusion of a conversation makes them ideal companions, for a parrot will only tell you what you have already said. That could, if viewed through the proper lens, be considered affirming by some."

"I do not want a parrot," she shouted in the foyer.

"You should get that door before he gets away."

Through the side window appeared a middle-aged man in a dark gray suit, white shirt, and a narrow red tie. He shifted his weight from foot to foot, hopping with impatience like a runner on the blocks. Margaret opened the door, and the suit showed an identity card with a photograph laminated next to the name. The man in the flesh bore only a slight resemblance to the man on the card. "Harry Linnet," he said as she read along. "Mon Valley resident agent with the Federal Bureau of Investigation. Is this a good time, Mrs. Quinn?"

"Come in, come in." She ushered him to the living room. "You have some news about Erica?"

"Sounded like you were in the middle of a conversation."

"I'm Diane Cicogna, her sister. We were talking about a parrot."

"A parrot?"

"Yes, they make excellent pets, don't you think? Someone to talk to when you're alone?"

"I guess, but they only say what they've been taught to say."

"That's their advantage over husbands."

He pulled at the knot of his tie and followed the women inside. Agent Linnet waited until the women sat on the sofa before claiming the outer inches of the easy chair opposite. "The Pittsburgh office sent me over to talk with you about your daughter, see if the Bureau can help. Actually, they were asked by headquarters down in Washington to look into this. You must have friends in high places. How long has it been?"

Jackson, Margaret thought. He said he had a friend at the FBI. Still loves me in some small way. "That was thirty years ago."

Linnet frowned and snapped open his memo pad and took out a ballpoint pen. He dared not look either woman in the eyes. "I'm sorry. How long since you noticed your daughter was missing?"

"Twenty-two days. I was away, visiting my sister in Washington, as a matter of fact. My husband was supposed to be keeping an eye on Erica."

"The truth is, nine times out of ten, a girl that age is a runaway. Had she been acting strangely at all before her disappearance?"

"Tell him," Diane said. "Tell him she was in love. She ran away with the boy just like you would have if—"

"It wasn't a matter of courage."

"Courage, Mrs. Quinn?"

"It was the boy. What teenager doesn't act a bit strange when she's in love?"

Diane spoke over her. "You're wrong there. Love is always a matter of courage."

Linnet thumbed through his notes. "This boy, Wiley Rinnick, you disapproved? Had he been acting differently at any time before they went away? Were they in any way political? Would you consider him in any way dangerous?"

"What are you driving at?" Margaret asked. "What are you suggesting?"

"Nothing, really. Just, in your estimation, does he pose a threat?"

With a clap on her knees, Diane drew his attention. "Not a threat, sir, but a promise. He has absconded with my niece."

Linnet nodded and put on a grave face. "Of course, of course. But I meant threat in a more general sense. These are strange times, Mrs. Quinn. Just last month, there were two assassination attempts on President Ford's life. Two troubled women. Women, for the first time in our history, and you would be doing your patriotic duty if you know anything about any threats your daughter or her boyfriend may have made against the president."

Diane slid forward on her seat. "That's what this is all about?"

"No, she's not political," Margaret said. "No more rebellious than any other teenager—"

"I have to tell you, Mrs. Quinn, I've already been to the Rinnick house, and there's some evidence that your daughter's boyfriend has some un-American ideas. I've already spoken to the borough police, and I've spoken to your husband. He seems to think the boy is a radical."

"My husband thinks everyone who dated my daughter was a radical. She's not an enemy of the nation. She's missing."

Focusing somewhere below her chin, he sucked on the cap of his cheap ballpoint, leaving a dot of ink on his lips, and she felt exposed and crossed her arms across her breasts. She wanted to stand, go to the phone and call her husband to come home at once and be with her, but the agent held his gaze on her, his eyes focused on her folded arms. "Mrs. Quinn," he said, "I don't mean to suggest . . . It's my job to rule out the possibilities. We're all concerned about the president, after all."

"Do you know anything about my daughter?"

"Can we go to the bedroom?" Linnet stood and buttoned his jacket, holding the memo pad in front of him at belt level. "Have a look around at what Erica left behind?"

Her daughter's bedroom was as still as a sanctuary. The bed had been made, of course, but the only item Margaret had removed was a round pink case that held birth control pills, which she had discovered that first day, and pocketed from her husband. The several doses remaining she had flushed down the toilet in private. Diane and Margaret watched Linnet poke about the room, opening drawers and fingering the contents. Diane whispered in her sister's ear. "This creep is making me uncomfortable. Ask him if he has information or did he come just to make these ridiculous accusations and to leer at us?"

Linnet provided a running theory of the case as he snooped. "Without an actual crime, Mrs. Quinn, they'll be hard to locate, and his brother Dennis is unwilling to press charges against Wiley. Says he lent him the car. Erica's underage, but barely, and the truth is thousands of teenage girls run away each year, escape old mum and dad. Or run off with some boy, or worse. Little to hold them in a little town." He angled a writing pad to catch in the falling light any impressions on the surface.

Like a firehouse alarm, the phone rang downstairs, and Margaret raced to answer it. Diane waited at the top landing, trying to eavesdrop on her sister's end of the conversation while keeping an eye on the detective. Under the illusion of privacy, Linnet stuffed an article of clothing into his jacket pocket, and the flash of robin's egg blue stood in relief against the dark wool as he thrust his hip forward to shut the bureau drawer. A claret stain of embarrassment rose and receded before he would look at her.

Margaret returned, out of breath, clutching Erica's latest school portrait. "That was my husband. He told me to be helpful and give you whatever you want. He also said you came for this." As she handed over the photograph, she felt a parent's pang of apprehension and remorse, wondering what this stranger would do with the image of her daughter.

"There's nothing here," Linnet said. "Your husband told me you have a theory. They're headed for the coast. Jersey, maybe, or Maryland."

A notion, an ocean. "I don't know where she is, it was just a stupid guess. Please find her."

He studied the photo for a few seconds, glancing quickly at Margaret to trace the familial resemblance. "We'll send this out on the wire to our field offices, ask them to share it with the local police. Keep an eye out." He winked. "But I don't want to get your hopes up, Mrs. Quinn. It's a big country, and far easier to disappear in than most people imagine. Our best chance is that your daughter and her lover run into some trouble, nothing serious, but enough to get the local police involved. And then they think to give us a call. Missing people are missing for a reason. Some get lost, run into some nasty character, and stay lost. Some of these girls are just afraid to return home, and I'm hoping that's the case with Erica. That she'll come to her senses and give you a call before it is too late. But, if she's decided to stay lost for one reason or another, she might just vanish." He held up the portrait. "Sometimes this is all we have to prove they were ever here." He tipped his hat at the top of the stairs and jogged down to the door and out into the street, leaving the women quite alone.

"Did you see him wink at me?" Margaret raised her eyebrows.

"He took something else," Diane told her. "Snuck it in his pocket. Panties, I'd say. Pervert."

For the first time in weeks, Margaret laughed. She clutched her sister's arm, and they sat on the edge of the bed, giggling until tears came to their eyes.

22

Waking in darkness, Erica sat up in bed and realized that Una had failed to bring her the nightcap of warm milk. Every evening since the arrival, they had shared the ritual, and just the smell of cardamom triggered an overwhelming desire for sleep, and she always drank the potion to the dregs, a trail of spices climbing the inside wall of the ceramic mug. But Una had passed over the moment that evening, her neglect linked to the fuss over Wiley's shorn head. The sight of him shocked Erica initially, but when she touched the short bristles, she thrilled to the new sensation and could not resist running her palms over and over the coarse nap, the skin and bone. The old woman, likewise, could not stop staring at him, her son's name loose on her mouth as she whispered what she had wrought, if only in appearance. Like Frankenstein's Prometheus: *it's alive.* Or the ghost made flesh again. Una did not know what to think or how to act, for she had betrayed her grandmother under the willow tree, let slip her desire and extracted the truth, their plot unspooling like a skein of yarn batted by a cat.

"You could pass for Cole," Mee-Maw had said, and then to Erica, "And you are growing more like her each day, pale and thin as a Madonna."

"But they're not, Mee-Maw. They're not them. We should ought to let them go."

"Whisht, child." Her eyes were lit with rage.

They passed an uncomfortable meal talking about the changing weather, the cool winds bringing in the real autumn. Wiley rubbed his scalp between courses, pondering his new haircut with his fingernails, grinning like a tot whenever he strayed into the field of Mrs. Gavin's be-maddened glances. When the dishes had been cleared, Erica registered her old complaint once more, the tiredness coming on despite the hours in the healing sun, perhaps too much sun, and she let herself be led to the child's room, where the rite of story and prayer continued, falling asleep as Una read Aesop's fable of the fox and the stork. When she awakened hours later and remembered there had been no sleeping potion, Erica put a hand to her cool forehead and thought her fever had broken.

Kicking the quilt from her legs, she crawled from Una's tiny bed to hunt for the ladder leading to Wiley, but the room was dark and the hallway darker still. With arms stretched and hands extended, she closed her eyes and gingerly felt her way along the wall, step by step, until she reached the sharp edge of the corner. Her bare feet stuck to the wooden kitchen floor, and she counted the paces to where the parlor was supposed to begin and where she expected scant starlight to offer better illumination, but when she opened her eyes, Erica saw that she had entered a narrow curiosity box. All around her, the room's strange objects swelled and crowded close, pinning her to the center of the space. A huge globe rolled off its pedestal, its axis threatening to impale her. A riderless velocipede cranked its pedals in mad abandon, spiraling in figure eights around the dressmaker's mannequin, which arched its back like a magician stretching arms toward the hearth, where the fireplace sparked, then roared with flames. The creatures on the walls blinked to life: the deer head strained to escape the wall, a raccoon, trilling with ecstasy, scooped a crayfish from the acrylic waters, and a bird spread its cottony wings to fly once around the room before settling atop the bookcase. A pane shattered, and the butterflies escaped the shadow box. The glass doors popped open and the books tumbled in single file from the shelves, fanning their pages in freedom, their contents spilling out word after word, uttered in their authors' voices, then falling like road signs into jumbled stacks of hot type. She stood in the middle of a pinball game, her gaze bouncing from bumper to bumper, like a toy in a penny arcade. A pair of giant eyes filled the picture window, the wizened head tilted for a closer look, and Mee-Maw screeched like a witch. Projected on the far wall were the larger-than-life faces of the Virginia state trooper pining for her, and Carl and Barry from the diner, talking with one another in hushed tones. Superimposed over their features appeared circular targets, and the shots rang out from behind her, the points piling high with each hit. A fierce wind roared through the trees outside, and the voices of her father and mother blew in, bored into her ears, and drilled into her brain.

Una descended from the loft, her wings unrolled and shimmering like an angel's. Not the celestial kind, but a watcher, more sinister and threatening, as though the heavens had been emptied out and they roamed the earth in misery, unsure of their mission. She walked toward her, arms outstretched, crying *Mother*. The bohemian girl whose car they had stolen soared beneath the eaves, abandoning Wiley in the bed, shorn and spent, his life draining between his legs. Luminous and foreboding, she spread her wings to span from floor to ceiling and from wall to wall. In her hands she cupped a radiant fire, shielded its brightness in the knot of her fingers, and then released it all at once until the light and heat filled the room to sweep everything from its path and send Erica tumbling into the fathoms, falling up into the limitless sky. She reached out to be saved, and then cried once and collapsed to the floor, where he found her in the morning, dropped from the sky in a crumpled heap of bones and hair.

"We are getting out of this place," he said. "Let's go." Wiley bent over her and slid his hand beneath her shoulders, but she did not recognize his face without the curtain of curls. Sharp against his skin, his skull flashed, and she thought he was dead. She had fallen away from him to the bottom, drowning in an ink blue sea pressing on her body and soul. Parting the blades of water, she emerged gasping and unsure of her whereabouts, cast away and waking in the middle of an endless ocean.

"Let's go, Erica. We should have gone long ago."

Lifted to a sitting position, she wrapped her arms around Wiley's shoulders and pulled him to her, kissing the stubbled hair behind his ear, his jaw, the arch of his cheekbones, his lips, hungry for him, waking from a century of slumber, and he returned the embrace, filled with relief, and welcomed the tang of her skin, the pressure of her limbs, the course of her hair spilling into his hands.

Together they saw the child watching from the kitchen. She had just awakened, her hair a bird's nest of knots, and trembled with suppressed indignation. "You called her Erica. I heard you." Wiley helped Erica to her feet, and she leaned against him for strength. The child quaked like a banshee, her eyes darting from face to face, her hands balled into fists. "You've been lying to me all along—"

Wiley said, "We're leaving. Today."

"Mee-Maw won't let you go. She'll never let you go. She'd kill you first—"

"Una." Erica stepped toward her, but the girl inched backward. "You're right. We're not who we say we are, but that doesn't change anything, Una. That doesn't change how I feel about you. We had to lie to protect ourselves, to protect you. We had to pretend to be someone else."

"Mee-Maw says you are them come back."

"I'm not Cole Gavin," Wiley said. "I'm not your father. She's not your mother."

"We are not who you want us to be."

The girl looked away, up to the ceiling, folded her arms and brought her hands to her collarbone, hugging herself and fighting tears. She crossed her feet, rested the right upon the left, gripped by the power of her own desperate confusion, gnawing at her lip, anxious for rescue from herself. Groping to become one of them. An uncertain angel. Erica held her close and felt the wild thump of her own heart drum against the child's ear.

NO PROTESTS, NO negotiations, and no threats from Mrs. Gavin when they told her they were leaving, only a hint of resignation when she asked if they were sure, if it wasn't wiser to wait a day or so to see if they were well and fit for travel. The Gavins' old Rambler station wagon had been hidden beneath a paint-splattered canvas in a locked shed, but once Wiley insisted that she drive them to town to catch the next bus heading west, it was uncovered and prodded till it started. Mrs. Gavin busied herself with the child while the fugitives packed their gear. She gave them a duffel bag in which to stow the broken-down guns, and cooked a last meal before their departure. She refused any payment for her hospitality, and on the road seemed preoccupied by the driving and occasional car passing the other way. Littering the roadside were strands of brown oak and poplar leaves, and when they pulled into the parking lot of a general store, the tires crushed a swath and ground the leaves to dust.

The bus stop outside Parker's Cross Roads was nothing more than a bench beneath a small sign in the shape of a racing hound labeled "Dixie." Tickets were purchased at the counter inside amid the dusty goods, the sweating soda cooler, the rows of cigarettes and ammunition, and plastic-carded fishing lures and wicked hooks. Arranged neatly in a rack next to the cash register, an army of stacked pamphlets trumpeted in red capitals: HAVE YOU BEEN SAVED? ARE YOU BORN AGAIN? THE

COMING ARMAGEDEON. Wiley took the last of these, spread the folds like a roadmap, and chuckled over the contents as the clerk filled out their receipt for the bus to Memphis. He paid with a singed twenty-dollar bill and with the change bought four Cokes, which they took outside to drink. "How much time to your bus?" Mrs. Gavin asked.

"Three thirty," Wiley said. "Under an hour, give or take. You don't have to wait."

"We'll set awhile. I just like to be off the road afore dark. Can't see as good as I used to. You remember when I first laid eyes on you, thought you was my Cole."

"I'm not him."

"No." She shook her head slowly. "No, you ain't. If he comes back to me, he will not leave me like this. The prodigal son returns humbled and is given the fatted calf."

The chrome gas pumps reflected shards of light. The day's temperature had reached its apogee, and a cool breeze foretold the chill night ahead. Erica tied a sweater around her shoulders, fighting off the lingering aftershock of her fever. Pressed to her side, Una took short sips from her bottle to make her soda pop last and thus forestall their farewells. "Will you write me a letter? I will write you back." She slipped her a label with a PO box address.

"I'll send you a postcard, okay? Next place we go. And when we're all settled, I'll write you again."

Hidden in her jacket was the small china cup she had rescued from the sandbox, trimmed in Wedgwood blue, painted with two birds in flight, holding up with their beaks a tiny banner between them. Una pressed it into Erica's palm. "I'd like you to have this to remember me by. You won't forget me?"

She hugged the child one last time and nodded.

"Can you tell me your real names? Romeo and Juliet?"

Erica did not reply, but stared down the road for a long time. When Mrs. Gavin finished her Coke, she stood and signaled to her granddaughter. Goodbyes and thank-yous, an awkward embrace, and then they got into the car and drove away. When the Gavins had disappeared, he checked his wristwatch and announced they had another twenty minutes to wait for the bus.

"Imagine that little girl, all alone with that old woman, and never knowing what happened to her parents. I feel sorry for her."

"Don't," Wiley said, and then threw his empty bottle into the trash. "She was trying to get you hooked every night. Love junkie. That's how much she wanted to make her own dream come true. They would have kept you forever if they could." Worse fates were possible, she decided, and better ones. Waiting for the bus, she resolved to rekindle her feelings for Wiley, to choose to be happy, to will herself to give in to his schemes and wild notions. She resolved to be what he wanted her to be, to change as he had changed. A silent laugh flared in her chest and rippled through her throat and echoed in her brain. The idea of forever seemed an impossibility, like love itself, or finding your way ashore from the middle of an ocean, or returning to earth after being abandoned at the top of the sky, blue as the cup resting in her hands.

23

Diane nearly bumped into the postman on her way out the door, and after apologies were exchanged, he handed her the mail and tipped his cap goodbye. In her haste to get back home to Washington, she passed the bundle on to Margaret, who laid the mess atop the sideboard by the door. Joe had been calling nightly, missing her, and at her sister's insistence she prepared to make the long drive back. Golden light dressed the morning, and the sisters, glowing white, lingered by the car packed with her suitcases. Reluctant to take her leave, Diane held her in her arms and would not let go. "You call me the minute you hear anything. You call me any time you need to talk, night or day."

Crushed by her sister's embrace, Margaret could only nod.

"She'll be back," Diane said. "I'll keep you both in my prayers."

Though she had her doubts, Margaret thanked her and stood in the street till the car vanished. With a sigh, she walked into the foyer and swept the mail together and laid the lot on the table. Already missing Diane, she fetched a cup of tea and sat to sort the junk from the bills. At the bottom of the stacks lay the postcard. On its face, a photograph of a Victorian funereal statue, a grieving stone angel in the foreground framed by bare branches in the wintry background. *Historic Elmwood Cemetery, Memphis, Tennessee* ran the caption.

What kind of person would send such a morbid picture? She flipped over the card and the sight of her daughter's handwriting struck her in the solar plexus: "Do not be blue, for I am finally happy. Goodbye, and do not try to find us." Without understanding, Margaret managed to read it twice before the first tear hit the saucer's edge.

. . .

ANOTHER PICTURE POSTCARD sent from Memphis arrived in the rural post office box but was not retrieved until the week of Thanksgiving, when Mrs. Gavin came into town to buy a small turkey. The photo on the front showed a downtown streetscape at dusk or dawn, a few stragglers talking in doorways, marquees glowing, and a lonesome car parked curbside. *Beale Street* and a progress of musical notes in the upper left corner, and *Home of the Blues* centered in the bottom. Una did not know why such a card had been chosen for her, but she kept it many years.

> *Dear Una,*
>   *Drat, I messed up with this postcard and meant to send this one to my mother and the one with the angel to you, for you are the true angel and I will always remember you. See, I told you I would write and will write again.*
>   *"Miss Nancy"*

24

They did not speak a word to each other the entire time in Arkansas. From the moment Wiley and Erica crossed the Mississippi to five hours later when they skirted Fort Smith on the western border, they stared out the windows at the passing pavement and had nothing to say. The day, which had started innocently, sweetly, perfectly, had degenerated into rancor and frustration. He fumed in the driver's seat, strangled the steering wheel, met her eyes only by accident. Cowed by his rage, she resented him, grew bored by his pettiness, found his attitudes and reasoning more than slightly absurd. No hope for peace existed while they were locked into the bucket seats and speeding down the road. She put her bare feet up on the dashboard. He drummed his fingers for an hour. They needed to stop and have it out or seek forgiveness from each other, but the urge for redemption gave way to the desire to put as much road as possible behind them.

The car, a red Ford Torino, made the journey tolerable, that is, the car was clean, comfortable, handled the road with ease. They had stolen it the night before, their second evening in Memphis, and rejoiced in their good fortune. Behind locked doors, the keys in the ignition sparkled like gold, and all Wiley had to do was jimmy a hanger behind the window while she stood watch. From Beale Street, he drove straight to their hotel and sailed in, had the valet park the car in the garage, bold as you please, pretending they were two newlyweds enjoying an expensive gift from Mom and Dad. The thrill of the crime gave them a sense of invulnerability, and they ordered room service, beer and barbecue, throwing around their money and pretending to be who they were not. After the night's debauch, she woke up first early in the morning, and letting him sleep stretched out in a cruciform, Erica left the hotel to explore the city on her own. Stepping into the sudden light, she was unencumbered by the hovering presence of her familiars. The fatigue which had crept into her soul lifted with each step along the sidewalk. She had been overtired by solicitude and had borne too much the kindness of strangers. An hour or so in her own company, she felt, would refresh her spirit. At the corner, a bus ingested passengers, and she ran to join the line.

The route wound from the city center up Third Street before turning right onto Walker at Gaston Park and into a leafy neighborhood, and with no particular place to go, she watched the changing housing patterns, the cars below, her fellow passengers. She had never seen so many black people together in one place and drank in the different skin tones from high yellow to burnt coffee, some folk with hair straight as her own, other's cut scalp-close like Wiley's and brittle stiff, still others under halos or helmets of hair, one man's Afro high enough to hide a tall black comb with five long teeth and the hilt shaped like a fist. Despite her stares, no one tried to speak with her, though one or two people looked back, and when their eyes met, she felt they could see inside her soul, so she immediately averted her gaze, ashamed. Two seats in front of her, an older man flinched at what he saw through the window, removed his fedora, and brought it to rest over his heart. Erica strained to see the object of his reverence and realized that they were passing a cemetery, and on impulse, she pulled the overhead cord to signal the driver to stop.

Among the stones and statues, she wandered, dallying beneath the spreading elms and blazing myrtles continuing on all the way to the Victorian cottage at the northern end and its small gift shop, where she bought two postcards and stamps, and sitting in the quiet of the Confederates Rest, she wrote her messages. From across the green, a woman in round glasses and beret pretended to be reading from a small book, a woman who reminded her of the radiant angel of her dreams. She looked like the girl from Tennessee whose car they had stolen, and the woman she imagined that first night standing in front of the Friendship School as they raced past. When she finished writing the second postcard, Erica rose to cross the leaf-strewn lawn and speak to the stranger, but the figure had disappeared. After searching the forest of headstones and carved memorials without any luck, she caught another bus back to the hotel. Not gone but two hours.

Though it was nearly noon, Wiley was still asleep, naked in the bed, a bare foot peeking from the covers, and smeared across the white sheets and pillowcases were crimson streaks the texture of dried blood, evidence of some gory struggle in her absence. Suicide, she thought, and I am the ghost upon the scene to lament the loss of one so young, no chance for the life expected, no revolution, no glory, no retirement to the wilderness, no babies crawling across the bare earthen floor. Romeo, in error. But when she slipped her hand beneath the covers, he stirred and pulled her to him, the spice of last night's barbecued ribs still on his lips. Her trailing arm brushed against his erection, and she smiled at him in the half-light pulsing through the drawn curtains.

"But we should be quick," he said as he tugged at her blouse. "We have to get out of this place."

Without his mane of curls framing his face, his head appeared like a dish on the stick of his neck, beet red from his exertions, his eyes wide, blank and unblinking, a hint of cruelty in his unchanging visage. His neck corded, a tremor ran the course of his shoulders, and his biceps twitched. She let him rest his weight against her bones, and he shivered, stopped, exhaled like a boiling kettle. As he relaxed, he felt heavier, and the slick of perspiration between them felt clammy against her skin. She patted him on the bottom and he rolled off.

"How long have you been up?" he asked.

Using her open palm, she fanned her face. "For hours. I already went out—"

"Out? By yourself?" He propped himself by his elbow and stared at her.

"To this cemetery. Historic Elmwood. I took the bus."

"You shouldn't go out by yourself."

"I needed some time alone. Nothing happened. I just sat there in the quiet with all those gravestones and all those souls underneath. Just sat in the sun to think."

"About what?" He licked his lips. "Why do you need to think?"

"That morning you found me on the floor, I had been dreaming. The whole house was a nightmare, all those creepy things coming to life, coming to get me. I dreamt of my mother and father. And saw Una. Do you know she thought we were angels, real angels, because of this?" She traced the tattoo on his shoulder with her fingernails. "And I dreamt of that girl from Tennessee you wanted, only they were like angels. I saw her before on the night we ran away, and I'm starting to think there are angels everywhere."

Wiley groaned and pushed his head deep into the pillow. "You think too much. You let your imagination run away. Don't be going out without me."

Leaping off the bed, she found her discarded jeans and hoisted them up her legs. "I wanted to send a letter. I promised her I'd write."

"Who?" He was out of bed too, hands at his hips.

"The little girl, Una." The full-length mirror on the open bathroom door held her reflected gaze. Her illness had taken some weight from her frame, except for a tiny potbelly. She sucked in the bulge as best she could and studied her profile. "And my mother. I sent a card to my mother so she wouldn't worry—"

"You what?" He rushed to the chair, flung on his pants and shirt.

"So she wouldn't worry. I couldn't stand her waiting like Mee-Maw for someone who isn't coming back. Just to let her know, but I didn't say anything, just not to try to find us—"

"Jesus, Erica. They'll start looking right here once they get your letter. What were you thinking?"

They fought while packing to leave, fought on the elevator and in the checkout line in the lobby, fought in the car as they tried to find their way out of the maze of Memphis. He swore at her, called her unthinking, stupid, clueless. She absorbed the shocks with scant rebuttal, sniping back until they were high over the Mississippi River and the trestle shadows began skipping across their faces like the beat of a folksong. Halfway across, on the Arkansas side, a slick of algae bloomed in a broad arc in the muddy waters, and caught in the trash and muck, an anhinga, slick as a snake, labored to swim, and watching the water bird's efforts, Erica could no longer bear the sound of Wiley's voice. Or her own. They did not speak again until they reached Oklahoma, where they shot a man.

25

"Where are you going with that gun?" Erica wanted to stop him before it was too late, but she did not know how.

In Garrison's Creek, Oklahoma, they had parked in the lot of a clapboard Mom-and-Pop roadside market with a pair of Esso gas pumps around back and a screendoor entrance that read *Open* though the place appeared deserted. All still for twenty minutes, no customers in or out, not a bird in the sky. In the front seat of the Torino, Wiley popped out the cylinder and inserted a moonclip with six rounds and tucked the Colt revolver inside his jacket. He reached behind the seat, fumbled with the blanket, and soon produced the shotgun, handing it to her as tenderly as an infant passed between them. "Take this," he said, "and wait outside as lookout. If you see anyone coming, you stop them, and if you hear any trouble inside, you come in blazing like Patty Hearst."

"But Wiley—"

"Don't but me. We're out of money, spent it all living it up in hotels and room service, and now's your chance to show you're ready. For the revolution. Comes a time in everyone's life where they must act instead of just thinking. This is your opportunity. Don't let it be your only chance."

A quartet of houseflies sunning themselves on the wooden columns stirred halfheartedly when Wiley stepped on the porch, and then they lurched back to the same sunlit spots, not even bothering to move when Erica took her post by the door. Wondering why he was taking so long, she stole glances at the scene inside. He pretended to be shopping the meager inventory. A jar of peanut butter, a loaf of bread, a quandary at the rack of jerky and pemmican. Laying the goods on the counter, he watched the man rise from his stool, put down the notebook he was writing in, and transfer the pen from his right hand to his left to ring up the prices on an old-fashioned cash register, an ordinary man, not particularly pleased or disturbed to have a customer in the heel of the afternoon, merely anxious to return to whatever he had been writing. With a ding, the total appeared and the register drawer sprang open, and the man looked up to announce the sum and found the one eye of the pistol staring back at him.

"Count it out, mister, all of it, and put the money in a paper bag."

The man did not move but fixed his gaze on Wiley, committing the details of his face to memory. Since he had not spoken to a soul in hours, he cleared his throat and licked his dry lips. "You look like you just come out of, or are going into, the service, boy. How old are you anyway? You wanted something all you had to do is ask, so put up that Colt and I'll oblige."

Wiley thumbed back the hammer and locked it in place. "I'm not putting down nothing. Just put the money in the bag. Do it."

"Son, I'll give you one chance to redeem yourself in this moment. Never point a gun at a man unless you fix to shoot him, and never shoot a man without the will to kill him, if need be. Now, I don't believe you have the desire to shoot that Colt in your hands."

"Shut up." He wagged the pistol at him. "Do what I tell you—"

"There can't be more than seventy, eighty dollars in here. You reckon a man's life is such a paltry sum, you go on ahead. Like I said, had you first asked, I'd a given you what you need, no questions, but you do me a harm, and the price of my life is your soul."

"Shut up. You think I won't shoot you over seventy dollars, but that's where you're wrong. And if you are willing to spend your life at such a price, you place little value on it."

"You share my disdain for life, son. But do not sell your soul so cheaply."

Through the screendoor, Erica could see them arguing, so she fingered the pull trigger and slipped inside, brandishing the shotgun. The man behind the counter heard the door squeal on its hinges, saw the shadow enter the room. He remembered the pen, snug in his hand, and lifted it to make one final point. The shot left a quarter-sized hole in his shirt, hitting the pectoral muscle and passing through his back below the right scapula, twisting his frame like a boxer's jab. Without the noise and flash, he may not have realized the first shot, but the second, coming from the front of the store, felt like the sting of a host of wasps, the birdshot peppering the side of his face and blowing a hole through the hanging display of poker cards beyond his shoulder. The second shot echoed the first, a call and answer, the quake and the aftershock. The man fell to the floor, his face and neck bubbling blood, and Wiley and Erica froze, wondering what had possessed the other, the instant passing back and forth in hard stares, inscribing itself on the memory like a name on a stone. She cast off the wickedness that had leapt into her hands and dropped the shotgun with a clatter.

"You killed him," Wiley screamed at her.

"I thought he was going to shoot you. Is he dead?"

Holding the pistol like the end of a rope, Wiley pulled his way forward, peering over the edge of the counter at the body on the floor, a red blot blossoming from the man's shirt, the skin on the side of his face and neck flensed and tattered. In his clenched fist, the pen rested between sentences. One of the man's shoes was untied, causing Wiley to reflexively check his own laces before he clambered over the counter and emptied the till, pausing long enough to stuff a handful of Hershey bars in his pocket. "He appears to be dead, but that was a pen, you idiot, not a pistol. We better get out of here in case someone comes, or he decides on resurrection."

Disbelief cemented her to the spot, the fear that if she moved, the present could not be rewound to the moment before the gunfire, and further still to morning, when she last found Wiley irresistible instead of loathsome and dangerous. If she stood still, she could will time's revolution counterclockwise and halt the hurtling motion into the awful future. Wiley brushed past her, barking to pick up that gun and follow, but she did not move, and he was gone, leaving her alone in the store with that bloodied man, dead or dying. In a dusty corner by the flour and sugar and faded canned goods, the girl materialized. Neither smiling nor frowning, the girl appeared before her to reproach with silent witness, eyes round and knowing behind the crooked glasses. They watched each other across the room, hesitant to move or speak and break the spell. Una fingered the hem of her jacket and rolled on the balls of her feet. "You better go," she said, "lest he leave you behind like an abandoned child in this forsaken place."

Erica intuited that the apparition might vanish if she took her eyes off the girl. "I wrote you, like I promised. But I always meant to ask: what was your mother's name?"

"Mary." She smiled at the word. "Mary Gavin. Now go while you still can."

In the parking lot waited her accomplice, and Erica turned her head to see if the car was still there. When she looked back, the child had flown. With a sigh, she picked up the shotgun and raced to the car. The screendoor whined, then slapped shut in her wake, and the houseflies buzzed in chaotic loops. Following the country road south to its source, Wiley bumped along for a few miles, shaking with adrenaline while she sweated in the heat and curled like a baby bouncing against the passenger door. "Angels of Destruction!" he hollered out the open window.

"Stop," she said.

"Baby, in a war there's bound to be some casualties—"

"No, please. Stop the car."

"Erica, we got to get out of here. We can make it to Oklahoma City by suppertime and be as invisible as two ghosts—"

"Shut up and stop the fucking car. Now."

In the dust just off the deserted road, she managed just in time to pull back her hair, lean out through the open door, and retch into the dry brown grass.

26

Lost, not all at once, but in stages of suffering, the girl vanished into her own oblivion. Gone was the ebullient spirit she must have had before the long stay in the hospital, replaced by an imposter, an eggless shell. The child in the bed opened her eyes for the first time in a week as Paul pushed the morphine through the syringe and into her bloodstream. In her eyes, cognition at his act, a mix of shock and gratitude for the mercy he bestowed before she went to sleep for good. She was the seventh and last of them to endure beyond bearing. Though they were under orders not to treat the radiation-sickness patients at the Nagasaki Prefecture medical center, but merely there to observe and advise the Japanese doctors, Paul knew the seven were dying and no amount of rest or penicillin or vitamin therapy would ever cure them. Sent a month after the bomb, the Army Medical Corps had missed the worst of it, the utter devastation. While the city itself looked as if it had been stomped on by the gods, the dead had been buried. The thermal burn victims, the maimed, and the injured took priority in the immediate triage, and then those with highly penetrating radiation—the *hibakusha*—whose debilitations varied widely began arriving. Paul witnessed the delayed effects in some patients, initially asymptomatic, but who showed up days or weeks later. A woman whose hair fell out in hanks. An elderly man with a crosshatch of burns on his back. Dozens complaining of fatigue. A husband and wife who both started bleeding uncontrollably from their mouths one morning after breakfast. They all thought themselves survivors, but the unfortunate who crowded the wards could not outrun the slow poison in their bodies.

He had written just once of the mercy killings. A heartfelt letter to his sister Janie back in the States, and it was her reply that had lain hidden in his files since 1945. She had offered consolation and assurance— "you were putting them out of their misery"—so that when he finally came back home, he could leave the horror behind him. Returning to his new wife, Margaret, and his small-town general practice, having safely buried the memory of the seven euthanized patients, he talked in vague measures about Nagasaki, chose not to dwell on the past, but to move on as quickly as possible to the normalcy he craved.

Penned in old-fashioned handwriting on nearly translucent paper, the letter from his sister seemed like a relic unrelated to his life's story. He had no memory of it when Erica confronted him the night she came back from her high school trip. He had no idea why she was waving the thin sheet like a toreador's cape. Misplaced, forgotten, the words brought back the anguish of his decision, the memory of each lethal dose. After reading the letter, he folded his hands over the paper and closed his eyes, and a vision appeared of the young Japanese girl, wrapped as if for the grave beneath the thin hospital sheets, her life and pain draining away, a wry smile on her lips as if she dreamt of the summer days before the shattering blast. Paul did not see his own daughter's distress, her confusion over this damning evidence, and that look in her eyes that said she had already found him guilty before he could speak.

Erica stood across from him in front of his desk, suddenly tall and imposing. Her face was red and raw from crying.

"It was just after the war," he told her. "And the patients were all in such excruciating pain. They'd never get better, so—"

"How could you do such a thing? I thought you took an oath. First, do no harm."

He rose and walked to the door, closing it with great care. "Please keep your voice down," he told her. "Your mother doesn't know."

"Doesn't know? You never told her? How could you?"

"I thought it best—"

"Never told her you killed those people? I don't know how you could keep such a secret from your own wife, not a word in all those years. And your own daughter?"

He shut his eyes again, and the Japanese girl walked into the room in a white kimono bruised by plum blossoms. He could not understand the words she was saying but her tone was clear. He opened his eyes and leaned his back against the door. "Your mother and I were just married when I got called up. I never thought I would go, I was too old, you see, but they needed doctors."

"To save people, not to kill them. What's the matter with you? Husbands don't keep such secrets from their wives. Not the ones they love, but maybe you never really loved her enough to trust her."

"I just didn't see what good it would do. I didn't want your mother to be afraid."

"To think the worse of you?"

Paul stepped toward his daughter, seeking forgiveness. "It was a world ago, Erica."

She stormed past him, swung open the door, and ran off into the night.

And when she ran away for good, he remembered the day she had found the letter, saw it as the beginning of her break from them both. Already growing up and outside her father's desperate love, she turned to the misbegotten boy and his crazy ideas. She became lost to him, not all at once, but in stages of suffering until she, too, vanished. Just as they all were going from him. Those he had once loved.

27

They thought the malady might be the residual poison in her system or traces of the drug that had caused the sleeping sickness in west Tennessee, a relapse brought on by the shock of the accidental shooting, or a bad case of fatigue after more weeks on the road than planned, but whatever the cause, she could not stand the rolling nausea that struck with such force and tenacity. Under slow descent of dusk, they made it as far as the town of Shawnee, where she threatened to turn herself inside out if he didn't find her a motel bed for God's sake, where she could lie at anchor and get some sleep, for the flatland tilted at the horizon and the rising moon spun like a top. The next morning was no better, for the nausea returned, and she hung her aching head over the porcelain bowl in their six-dollar room. She felt dizzy and hot, drunk and dying, dead and about to be born. Because he hankered for doughnuts, Wiley left her flat on the floor, her face mashed against the cold hard tiles and praying to be taken from this life of such abiding misery. And she prayed for forgiveness, unable to get rid of the vision of the gunshot man, replaying the scene till she could see clearly the pen, and not a gun, in his hand, and she must have known as it happened, she told herself, that the first shot had come from Wiley; in that split second necessary to pull a trigger, she had realized her mistake, was penitent in the act of commission, but panic overwhelmed her judgment. I'm sorry, so sorry.

"Are you okay, lady?" A woman's voice enriched by the acoustics of the bathroom. "Wake up if you hear me."

Opening one eye, Erica first saw the soft deer-brown shoes, the white-stockinged ankles and strong calves beneath the hem of a maid's uniform. In a rush of motion, the legs disappeared as the woman bent to her knees and lowered her head. Her thick black hair was drawn back severely, stretching the skin at the temples, and her eyes, black as holes, revealed no more information than her placid features. She reached out and brushed Erica's hair away from her face. "Have you been drinking? Drugs?"

"I am sick."

"Do you need any help? A doctor?"

Suddenly aware of her nakedness, she drew in her limbs, curling into a tight ball. "Can you get me some of my clothes?"

The maid stood outside the door while Erica dressed, and when the door cracked open, she smiled and held out her arms to guide the girl to a chair. "You feeling better? You're white as a snowman. You had anything to eat today?"

Erica swiped at the air. "Nauseous."

"Ginger ale and peanut butter crackers," the maid said, and then left to fetch them from the vending machine just outside. When she returned she found Erica slumped in the chair. "Eat this. Old Indian medicine."

"You're an Indian?"

"Lenape. You heard of the Delaware tribe?"

"You're a long way from Delaware."

"No, I'm a local yokel. My guess is you're a long way from home, though. What's your name, child?"

"You can call me Nancy. What's yours?"

"I'm Josie." She pointed to the name badge pinned to her smock. "Get something inside you, child."

She nibbled at the edge of a cracker and sipped the can of ginger ale as Josie made the bed with the crisp economy of one who has dressed thousands. When Erica was little, she would follow her mother on wash day. Laundry basket perched on her hip, Margaret climbed the stairs with folded sheets and laid them out upon the dresser and then stripped the beds. Behind her mother's back, the girl jumped on the bare mattress, giggling as she positioned herself dead center, still as a soldier, and Margaret would pretend not to see her, pretend she was not there, then snap the sheet in the air till it billowed overhead like a sail, like the falling sky, to cover her body. Thus hidden, she would not move, suppressing all laughter, and her seeker would say, "What's this lump?" with gentle hands pulling and tweaking and massaging the tiny shroud till Erica rose up like a ghost shrieking with laughter, the sheets wound around her like a caul, born again into the world.

Josie smoothed the blankets with her palms and pulled up the covers as if she were saying goodnight and tucking in that same child, and then she sat on a corner to face her. "You're getting some color back, good."

On bitter February days, Erica would complain of flu or fever, or if the temperature outside dipped near zero, Margaret would consent with no fuss, telling her to stay home from school, shutting off the lamp again, and she would lie in darkness, buoyed by the warmth of her bed, the bitter cold pressing against the blinds, sometimes falling asleep again till nine or so, and then call for her mother. Margaret brought tepid ginger ale or pale tea, the crackers, a bowl of chicken noodle soup for lunch. Afterward a story or the morning paper's comics read together on pillow tops. Palm to the forehead, a reprieve. By four o'clock, the winter's day slowly weakened to dusk, and they'd cuddle on the couch for an old *I Love Lucy* rerun or *Mr. Rogers' Neighborhood*, and worn out by her purloined leisure, she would nap until her father came home from the clinic. Now she wanted nothing more than to have this stranger stay with her, wrap a blanket over her in the chair, and remain until she could fall asleep.

"How long has it been?" Josie asked. The question, having no referent, confused her. "You are expecting?"

"Me?" A calendar whirred in her mind. "Expecting what?"

Folding her hands together, Josie drew in a breath. "Two months gone, I'd reckon. Don't you know?"

"What makes you think I'm pregnant two months? Some old Indian magic, in touch with Mother Earth?"

Pleased with the girl's sass, Josie laughed and rocked back on the bed. "Some old mother magic. Three babies of my own, though they're old stinkers now, but it was always the same. Sick as the dog's breakfast, but the moment passes, once your hormones settle."

"I'm not having a baby, just a little bit sick."

"Are you sure you're not just a little bit pregnant?"

She searched her memory. Her period should have come while they were at the Gavins' house in the hills. But no, surely she would remember if it had. Last time? Her friend Joyce Green had asked her to come swimming—one last dip of summer—and she had to be off cycle to risk the pool. She had missed two. "I'm only seventeen," she said.

"I could be wrong. But you got the look, and the morning sick-ness. Best you find a doctor. How old's that boy you're with? When I first seen him, he looked like an army man, that short hair, but that boy's no warrior—"

"He's eighteen."

"—just a boy with a gun. I seen what's in the back of that red car, if that is your car. Where you two from?"

"Back east. Pennsylvania."

"Girl, you got to get yourself back, no matter how far away, how hard it is. Go see a doctor first, take care of that baby."

"My father's a doctor." She looked stricken. "Jesus, I can't believe it."

"Jesus ain't got nothing to do with it. Go on home, child." Josie pat-ted her hand. "Listen, you're worried 'bout what your mama will say, what your daddy will do. Sure, they'll be angry at first, how could you have done, and let me get my hands on that boy. But they'll come around, and nine months, you show them that li'l angel, they'll melt away and forget and forgive. Take up their burden, that's their job, your mama and dad. Get that boy to get you to a doctor, and get you home before you're too far gone."

Alone in the room, she shut the door and began to cry. A prairie wind shook the windowpanes, startling her, and she composed herself and pressed the flat of her hand against her waist, expecting to feel some-thing inside, but she felt no different, she felt nothing at all. From the space between the bed and the wall, the mangle-faced grocer rose from the dead and pointed his fountain pen at her, and when he opened his mouth to accuse, out poured a river of blood black as ink. What would she tell her parents? Would they send her to jail? She shut her eyes and tried to clear all questions from her mind.

So long ago, it seemed, when he first told her of the Angels, Wiley's voice had intensified, the words spilling over like champagne foam in a flute, such rich passion that she ceased to receive the meaning of his sen-tences, the battering flow of his paragraphs, and heard only the sym-phonic rise as he worked himself into a kind of sexualized frenzy. They were to save the world by destroying corruption—especially the authori-tarian grip of the state, the church, big business. All they had done was rob a few people poorer than they had been. And shoot a small-town grocer in the face. The thought of Wiley as a father put her on the edge of feeling. Livid, dangerous, he was lit within as few boys his age were, and she had loved that great mane of curls, his earnest eyes, the way he walked defying wind and gravity, how he beat back the sea with chains, how his skin flamed at each touch. She remembered why she had fallen so hard and, once smitten, allowed herself to be subsumed by all that he said, though his words now seemed husks of someone else's thoughts, a screen for his anger and self-hatred. Bad as her father. She clawed at her doubts, pushed them away, and washed her face again, put on new lip gloss, ran a brush through her hair.

The sound of his singing preceded him by half a minute. Morrison and The Doors intensifying as each step drew near till the key clicked in the door, and he came in wired, happy she was up and dressed, swinging a bag of doughnuts by two fingers and grasping a coffee with the other three. Sugar and grease perfumed the room. "Good news, babe. I mapped the rest of the way. Sixteen hours to Vegas, and another eight or nine from there to San Francisco. We can be there by the end of the week and begin again like we planned." The aroma of coffee and heavy sweetness made the gorge rise in her throat, but she choked back her fears and offered him one last honest smile.

28

Paul was talking, but Margaret could not hear a word he said. The voice in her head overtook his speech, reducing it to white noise, and a part of her took perverse delight in watching his lips part and move, the animation of his features, and the grand sweep of his hands as he rambled. He never could still those doctor's hands as he spoke, how bound to his thoughts were the unconscious gestures, so that he was a mime, a clown making a dumb show, and all Margaret saw was the silent movie.

She counted the days, wistful at each one's passing. After the local newspaper ran a story about the teens' disappearance, she had expected more from the press. But time passed and there was nothing to report. The newspapers moved on to the next big thing. The police stopped coming round, the man from the FBI had not called since November. Erica did not come home for Thanksgiving. She did not come home for Christmas. For New Year's. Not on the second, the third, the twelfth day. She did not come home in January. She will not make it back in February. No valentines. Not tomorrow. Not next week or the one after. Not in time for spring and the tulips in the garden. Not in time to see the cherry tree blossom and bloom. She will miss Easter, Mother's Day, Father's Day, the whole Bicentennial. She will not be home for the fireworks, the barbecue, the swimming pool. She will not call on the telephone. No telegrams. There will be no letters, no more postcards. She will not see you in September. This whole year will pass without seeing her again. You will not know where she is. She will not be right back, see you soon. She will forget your birthday, his, hers. Nothing you do will bring her back. Jackson cannot find her. Linnet will not. Paul could not. Everyone shuns you, even the Delarosas don't come round with flowers anymore. Erica has hidden herself underground, in the stars, beneath the sea, up above the sky. You may look a thousand years, take a thousand steps, but you will not find her. She is back in the womb, beneath six feet of dust. She is with the angels in heaven. She is in hell.

Paul did not seem to mind that she was not listening, if he could tell. Someone something at the clinic, he said, and somehow some way I sometimes can say a real word. "Anyhow, I hope she's happy now," he said. "Now that's she expecting. I hope the baby does the trick."

"Expecting? I'm sorry, dear, I drifted off."

"Eve Fallon." He sawed off a hunk of steak and pierced it with his fork. "She thinks a baby might help tame that tomcat husband of hers, and I hope she's right, because the baby is coming, ready or not."

Ready or not, here I come, Margaret would holler from the other room. That girl loved hide-and-seek, didn't she? Remember how she would slither under the sheets and pretend she could not be seen till you tickled the bump in the middle of the bed?

Margaret watched him work his jaws, and the effort for pleasure obviously tired him, for he looked like a man living in slow motion. Picking at her salad, she asked about the lady and her baby, but his answer was little more than static. This will kill him. Not losing the girl—he has made his peace and believes that she will find her way back in time. But losing me, she knew, as he helplessly looked on. Snap out of it, go back to him. And it's been what, half a year since she left?

"Four months."

Setting down his empty fork on the edge of his plate, he scrutinized her face, knowing at once what she meant but mystified as to how and why she voiced her thoughts. "Do you think about her all the time?"

"Not her, so much as her absence. Not think, but feel the hole. The empty chair between us. No sound of a door opening when we two are alone in the house. No sudden good morning. No creak of the floorboards when she settles in for the night. Things that no longer happen."

"I miss her too."

She saw Paul now as an old man, his feelings slipping away with his faculties. The circles around his eyes looked like the entrances to a pair of caves. Hair white and thin as a cirrus cloud. Those lines across his brow looked carved by a mason, and she knew that constant tremor in his hands would drive her crazy. Why did he leave me alone, she thought, alone to bear my suffering while withholding his own? Where did he go? Why did he leave too?

The phone rang as she washed the dishes, and she madly dried the suds from her hands to reach the receiver before the caller gave up.

"Mrs. Quinn? This is Special Agent Linnet, sorry to be calling you so late. Is your husband home too? I'm over here at the Rinnick house and since it's so close, I'd like to talk with you in person tonight, if it's not too late. There's been a development in the case."

29

In Amarillo, she dyed her hair yellow. She had always longed to be someone else.

On the long straight drive through Oklahoma and into the Texas panhandle, Wiley talked about the need to be more careful, to disguise their identities in case the police picked up their trail after the shooting at Garrison's Creek. There could be no more messages home, no more accidents, no more meandering along back roads. A new car would be necessary and more cash and ammunition. "We have to erase ourselves and write a new story. We have to be able to disappear and change, like chalk on a blackboard, one quick swipe and you are gone. Hope the wind obliterates our tracks, and every trace of who we once were is blown away."

No trees provided shadow on the gray flatlands. The sun beat down on the window glass and the car felt hot even though it was cold outside. Erica fought to keep her comfort balanced by cracking her window and letting in some fresh air. Every few miles she pressed a hand against her belly. She wondered if the man they shot was someone's father. He had a gun, she told herself, a gun, and he shot first, and I thought the man was shooting Wiley. I didn't know what I was doing. Yes, just disappear.

"You should cut your hair short too, like mine, and maybe bleach it. Get some shades, maybe granny glasses, and change the way you dress. A whole new look, whatcha think about that?"

She gathered her brown hair in a ponytail and hid it from his sight.

"We will be strangers to all we have met on the road. Nobody will remember we were there. And we will forget our old friends and family back home. The Angels will know us, and we will be known only as Angels."

"Don't you think I'll be cute as a blonde?" She patted his leg. "Like having a whole new girl to screw."

Taking her remark as light-hearted, he laughed and beat a rim shot on the steering wheel. "Tell you what: we'll rob a wig store and take seven heads of hair. You can be a different girl every night of the week."

Amarillo, silhouetted by the falling sun, grew on the horizon as they approached, the squat office buildings resting like building blocks on the prairie. Erica thought of the Wild West of her youthful daydreams—cowboys in chaps and ten-gallon hats, the country sere and tan, the long-horn herds lowing on the dusty trail to the stockyards or railroads—but instead, the Texas landscape seemed bereft till they reached an airport dotted with Piper Cubs and an antique biplane. If she jumped from the car, she could roll down the embankment and sprint across the dust, make it to the runway, and some movie-star pilot—maybe Dustin Hoffman or who was the boy that played Billy Pilgrim in that Vonnegut film?—would rescue her and they would fly away, make it home or down to Mexico, where there could be a happier ending. Wiley pulled the Torino into the parking lot of the Wagon Wheel Inn and checked in for the night. When he jumped into bed with her, she showed him her back, complaining that the nausea had returned.

She went into the bathroom at dawn and chopped six inches of her hair, leaving the ragged ends to skirt the base of her skull. Using a peroxide kit Wiley had shoplifted, she bleached the remains, mourning in the shower. Dizzy from the sulfur smell, she sat in the bathtub and let the stream beat the top of her head, and closing her eyes, she waited until her scalp no longer burned from the chemicals. As she dried herself with the thin white towels, Erica could hear him through the closed door. Wiley was practicing again, posing in front of the mirror, first cocking the pistol and then snapping together the shotgun. The bloodied grocer moaned from behind the drawn shower curtain as she trimmed her wet bangs and the sides to frame her face, and he would not keep quiet, so she wrapped her hair in a towel and stepped into the bedroom. Trained on the entrance, the shotgun greeted her. For a brief second, she thought that Wiley intended to shoot her and wished that he would.

"Let's see," he said, motioning with the gun at her head.

Unwinding the towel like a turban, she murmured softly to herself the lines to a song her mother used to sing about a yellow bird way up in a lemon tree. Brilliantly golden, bordering on white, her hair stuck out in crazy angles like straw from under a scarecrow's hat. She fluffed it

further with the scruff of the towel and stood there beneath her bur-
nished halo.

"You did it. Your own mother wouldn't recognize you. You are a
whole new you."

In the lobby of their motel, the morning clerk stood behind the
counter staring at the vacant space, the landscape already beginning
to bake, deep in conversation with himself. He did not acknowledge
Wiley or Erica when they entered other than to flinch at the sound of
the door closing. Despite the hum of the air conditioner, he perspired
heavily, the sweat visible in twin arcs below his madras-shirt sleeves.
Drops dotted his forehead and clung like dew along his receding hair-
line. As the two neared the counter, the man stiffened and began to speak
in the practiced cadence of a radio announcer. "We're open Monday
through Friday. Monday-Tuesday-Wednesday-Thursday-Friday. Nine
to six. Drop on by and say hello. That's Haverty's Hardware on South
Cheyenne."

"We'd like to check out," Wiley said.

The radio man ran his fingers through his wispy hair and stared
through the window, as if he could see something invisible to the others.
"Tuesday-Wednesday-Thursday-Friday-Monday. Closed on weekends.
Wednesday-Thursday-Friday-Monday-Tuesday. Nine to six, so we can
be with our families and you can be with yours. Drop on by and say
hello. That's Haverty's Hardware on South Cheyenne. Tell 'em Hank
sent you."

Wiley leaned across the counter. "Are you going to take the key,
friend?"

The question caused a synapse to fire the broadcaster back to normalcy. He fiddled with the receipts and poked at the bell as if it were explosive. The nervous man made them nervous. At the axis of jaw and ear,
his skin looked beshot with blackheads, as if he, too, had been sprayed by
bird pellets long ago, and his lips trembled slightly, struggling to contain
a torrent of words. She wondered what station he was receiving now. Out
of some innate civility, she and Wiley waited, said nothing, gave him the
chance to start.

"Where are you heading?" he blurted out. "The maps, the maps."

"Las Vegas," Erica said.

"Viva Las Vegas. That's Spanish. Runaways?"

"Our honeymoon," Erica lied.

"And that's the way it is," the man said.

"We'd like to get us some breakfast," Wiley said. "Anyplace good around here? Maybe some pancakes."

"I saw Jesus once, the face of Jesus on a pancake."

"Must have been hard to eat," Wiley joked.

"You aren't the same one come in last night." He pointed to Erica. "What happened to her?"

She did not realize that he was referring to her hair until Wiley turned to stare at her head. All she could offer was a shrug of her shoulders.

"I run away," the radio man said. "Run away from the place they kept me, and you have to run away where they'll never find you. If they come looking. Your mom and dad. And the police. The maps."

"We're not running away," Wiley insisted. "We're on our honeymoon. We're married." He handed over the keys. The man searched the papers and receipts scattered now across the counter, finally handing them a napkin with a greasy bacon stain.

Wiley played along. "If there's no other charges, we'll be on our way."

"Stay off the main roads. Don't go where they expect you. The straight path is not always the fastest way. Look both ways before you cross the street. Do you have a gun?"

"Listen." Wiley spoke sharply. "We paid last night when we came in. Cash." He walked to the door, expecting her to follow.

As if he had switched stations, the radio man began talking like the newscaster, picking up some distant signal bouncing back in time from outer space. "Now we must be ready for a new danger: the atom bomb. Radiation is something we live with every day. If we know the facts and act intelligently, we'll be able to weather any storm that blows our way."

Fascinated by the man, Erica inched closer. He grabbed her by the wrist.

"The key to survival is adequate shelter." The man paused, looked at an imaginary explosion on the horizon. "The fallout shelter is the best defense."

"Let me go," Erica said. He was reminding her of her father and squeezing her arm so hard she wanted to cry out but was afraid.

"Stay off the highways," he whispered to her. "Watch the news and read the papers. They are looking for you. The little girl said."

"Who? What little girl?"

"You know."

"Please let me go." She circled her wrist with her other hand and tugged free.

"Don't talk to strangers," he shouted as she pushed open the flimsy screendoor.

On the western side of town, they stopped for breakfast at the Yellow Rose Cantina, a neon flower visible in the gray November light. Just like Mr. Delarosa's shop, she thought. The neighbors would not recognize me, and was the radio man right, a stranger to my own mother? Before they left the car, Wiley counted their remaining cash, scooped the coins from the holder next to the ashtray, and then reached across her lap for the pistol in the glove compartment. She put her hand over his wrist and said, "Not here. Not now." He withdrew his arm, and they went inside, trying to be inconspicuous, and seated themselves at an empty booth. Every surface— from the Naugahyde seats to the plastic menus—bore a slick of grease as fine as furniture wax, and while they waited for their server, Erica traced the AOD logo and wings with her fingertip on the table and slid a sugar canister to cover her handiwork.

The nine o'clock crowd had come and gone, leaving a few retirees in baseball caps swapping gossip in a corner booth. A solitary young woman in the corner tortured the pulp in her orange juice. She looked like the woman from Elmwood Cemetery back in Memphis, and her stare unnerved Erica until she turned away.

"You kids ready to order?" The waitress arrived dressed in mint green polyester with a glass coffeepot. Erica covered her mug with her fingertips, then turned it upside down. Though she dared not look, Erica could feel the woman's stare, knew that she was scrutinizing the crazy haircut, but orders were given and taken without pause. When she departed, the aroma of oranges lingered in the air, and from behind, her blonde hair looked like a haystack upon her neck.

"Wiley, I have something to tell you."

"Is it about that dude back in Oklahoma? Honestly, Erica, you gotta let it go. Into each war, some blood must flow. Besides, I might have—"

The grocer appeared behind Wiley's shoulder, his bloody face a mash of anger, a butcher's cleaver in his hand, and he lifted the blade above his head like an executioner.

"No!" she screamed. Faces pivoted in their direction. She offered the half circle a small smile, and the other patrons and the waitstaff looked away, the hum and clink of conversation and cutlery resumed. "Not that," she said. "Sorry, it was upsetting, and I don't want to upset you, not this morning, not when I have something this important I want to talk about."

"Is it about the money? We'll get more; we can last a day or two. Enough for gas. Why don't we shoot straight through to Vegas? It's only eight or nine hundred miles, and we can sleep under the stars. Then we'll get ourselves another car, something with better mileage."

"Not that. You remember that woman I met?"

"We met lots of people on the road, babe, and it could have gotten much, much heavier than it did. Remember that policeman when we were lost in Virginia, and those two dudes in Nashville?"

Angels had been warning us all along, she thought, telling us to turn back, go home, this was not working. Now it's too late. A man is dead, and we shot him down like an animal. She looked at the boy across the table, a hardness fixed to his features, twitching fingers tapping a staccato beat on the rim of his orange juice glass, hopped up on caffeine and Lord knows what. The baby's father.

"Wiley, I think I'm pregnant."

The waitress arrived with a plate of French toast for her, huevos rancheros and strips of greasy bacon for him. He did not seem to notice as she set the plate before him, did not glance up once at the bouffanted blonde, no acknowledgment when she topped off his coffee, asked if there would be anything else. Stare fixed on Erica, he was seething, holding his words inside through brute force. Up to Erica to offer a word of thanks, a gesture to send away the lingering woman.

"You think you're what?"

"Expecting a baby. Back in Shawnee, the maid found me out cold on the bathroom floor."

From the corner booth, the woman who had been watching stood suddenly as if to leave, but when Erica smiled at her, she sat back down and stirred her drink.

"You never saw her once, did you?" Erica said. "You never saw anything."

The people from the road appeared one by one. Through the din of the room, a voice croaked out: "When you see the flash, remember: duck and cover—" Two tables over, radio man nattered on to Carl over a stack of pancakes. Red and blue lights bounced against the walls, and the Virginia trooper entered the diner, began chatting with the gunshot grocer seated at the counter, who swiveled around on his stool to point out the murderers in the booth. Pushing through the swinging doors from the kitchen, their waitress morphed into Josie, laboring under a tray laden with night deposit bags filled with money, setting them down in front of Mrs. Gavin. Through the ceiling between two broad timber beams emerged the child, undulating softly to the floor and landing on her bare feet. Translucent, as she moved toward them, Una carried the light inside and gained brilliance with each step. The penumbra in the round glasses, who had been watching all along, loomed over all. Erica could no longer bear to witness. She cast her eyes away from these visions, stared at her cooling breakfast, the scoop of butter sliding to the plate, and looked again to Wiley, who was watching her, poised to explode.

"This woman Josie picked me up off the floor and gave me clothes and crackers and ginger ale. She told me she had seen it before, had kids of her own. The morning sickness, she knew right away." His blank, unblinking eyes revealed no evidence of listening, much less thinking of all she was saying. "Your eggs are getting cold. Eat."

"You expect me to have an appetite after you lay this on me?"

She glanced around the room to see if anyone was listening and leaned across the table to bring her face closer. "There's no reason to raise your voice. What will everyone think?"

He shouted at her. "I don't give a shit what everyone thinks!"

The patrons hushed at his outburst, and two burly men at the counter pivoted on their stools to face them, threatening to move farther at the next sound.

"Wiley, baby, it's all right. We'll get through this."

"How can you be sure you're pregnant?"

"I've missed two periods. I didn't notice because of how sick I was back in Tennessee. It must have happened before we left home."

"Missed? I thought you were on the pill."

"They're in my dresser back home—"

"God, Erica, how could you be so stupid?"

The mint green waitress reappeared and announced her presence by clearing her throat. "Everything okay over here, kids?"

Without a word, Wiley sidled out of the booth and brushed past her, sailing off toward the men's room, and Erica buried her face in her hands. Through the darkness, she heard the waitress's voice, and as she unknitted her fingers, she saw the woman seated where Wiley had been. "Are you all right, Pudding?"

Erica reached for her juice glass and drained it in one long swallow. The buzz in the diner dissipated, and the crowd melted into the periphery. They were alone.

"He bothering you, child? Because I'll have Mitchell come round give him a talking-to."

She shook her head. "We were having a spat. Everything's going to be fine."

"You say so, Pood, but girl, you look a mess. Who did that to your hair? Your pinkie finger stuck in the plug socket?"

Her hand flew to her butchered scalp, working the runaway locks back into place. "I did it. Does it really look all that bad?" She laughed nervously.

A toothy grin flashed at her. "Naw, I just said so to make you smile. Sure you're okay? That boy didn't hurt you, did he?"

"No ma'am, like I said, nothing but a lovers' quarrel. He loves me." Doubt colored the tone of her words, and she recognized at once the woman doubted her as well. "We are going to be married in Las Vegas and have a baby together."

"But you're just a baby yourself. None of my business, but don't seem to me he'll treat you any better after than he's treating you before. A man will show you his hand early on, if you're alive to it."

"I don't believe you."

"Ain't a matter of faith, Puddin'. They's belief and they's facts. This ain't the first time he shown his spots to you, is it? Best never put him in a cage in the first place. Just let him go."

"I have faith in him."

The waitress rose from the table and touched Erica's bare shoulder and the winged tattoo. "Ain't nothing too far gone you can't get back at your age."

"Thanks for your concern, but it's my life."

"Sure is, no one else's. Good luck to you and your baby. And when the color starts showing, just let your hair grow back the way it was." She tore a slip from her pad and laid the bill between their plates. "Y'all pay on the way out."

30

A light snow was falling as Agent Linnet arrived, covered in white. From the pocket of his overcoat, the pink edge of an envelope was puckered with moisture. Valentine, she supposed, but for whom? He stomped his shoes clean on the doormat, and when Margaret invited him in, he sent powdery showers to the floor as he wrestled free of his coat. Paul lurked in the archway to the living room, and Linnet cheered up when he saw him, extending his right hand like an old friend, and ushered him toward the sofa and chairs, and three cups laid out upon the table. Margaret hung up his coat and tucked his hat upon the shelf.

Don't be afraid, she told herself. This can't be good news at this hour and in person. Good news they tell you over the phone. Bad news shows up in person. Whatever you do, keep it together. No tears.

Linnet rose when she entered the room with the coffee, bowing slightly at the waist, and waited for her to take a seat before lowering himself to the easy chair. The February wetness soaked through to his suit, snowdrops sparkled in his hair, and he smelled faintly of sour wool. "I was just telling your husband, Mrs. Quinn, that we may have made a break in the case, but I want to tell you both right off that we have not been able to locate your daughter. Though we do have news about the boy, and good reason to suspect that she is somewhere in northern California."

A notion, a notion, you picked the wrong ocean.

He reached into his suit and took out a small manila envelope, opened it, and spilled out the postcard onto the coffee table. Margaret recognized at once this last word from Erica, the cryptic message from Memphis.

"It all started here, for we were otherwise lost as stray lambs. We may have tracked them sooner had we been notified when you first received it. A couple of days can make a big difference, so I want you to promise if you hear from her again, you get in touch right away."

Paul stole a look at Margaret. They had agonized and argued for three days when the postcard first arrived. She had wanted to keep it as tangible proof of her daughter's existence, while he had insisted it be turned over to the authorities as evidence. Without telling her, Paul simply took it one day to the Pittsburgh FBI offices. Margaret slipped it in her pocket while the investigator blathered on.

"When we learned she was in Memphis, we had our first clue. Our field offices sent out a bulletin to local law enforcement, but I suspected, and was proven out, that Wiley and Erica were no longer holed up there." He patted the breast pocket of his jacket, and realizing the object of his search was not there, he stood with a sheepish grin and excused himself to fetch his coat.

"What do you think he has to tell us?" she whispered to Paul.

"I'm no mind reader. News about Wiley Rinnick."

With the flat-footed walk of the forgetful and embarrassed, he returned to the living room and stretched a map of the United States across the table, doubling it over to the southern portion. "I put a pin here in Memphis," he said. "And drew a series of concentric circles, figuring that they either came from, or had to be heading to, one of these spots, but we had no idea of which direction. My first guess was New Orleans. Look how Memphis is sort of on the way between here and there, and you could disappear into the bayou, and no one would never find you. I always wanted to go to New Orleans. But turns out we heard from state and local police a couple of other places."

Margaret and Paul studied the map. A yellow line began in Nashville and ran along Route 40 to Amarillo, Texas, and then a dotted red line curved northwest to San Francisco.

"It's like a jigsaw. We had one piece—the postcard—but where are the others? Our first real lead was from a fast-food joint outside of Nashville that was robbed a couple of days after Rinnick and your daughter left town. The assistant manager worked with the police on getting a good sketch, and the state police thought to send it our way. Could've been Wiley, long hair and all. But it was just the boy by himself, no mention of a female accomplice. Though the night manager remembered the robber insisted on two milkshakes, one for a girlfriend somewhere. And the

Tennessee police had another unsolved mystery with a Pinto—we think that's Dennis Rinnick's car—that had been abandoned in a high school parking lot till the end of October. They switched license plates, and the girl whose car was stolen mentioned a boy and a girl who invited her to come along with them to California. But we didn't make the connection right away."

Where in God's name is Erica now?

"So we had two crimes they might have committed, but the timing is all wrong. A real pickle. If they're on the way to California, what kept them so long in Tennessee?"

The telephone rang.

"That's probably Shirley Rinnick calling now. Best not take it."

A dozen more rings, plaintive, then resigned, and the caller gave up.

"Maybe they got lost somewhere. A question I'll have to ask her if we find her. Our real break came later. Seems there was another robbery in Oklahoma, though we didn't make the connection at first. Man runs a general store in a flyspeck town, and these two kids come in one afternoon, and he starts jotting down a description, just before they rob him. Shot him twice, first by the boy in the shoulder, then he takes a load of buckshot in the face. Thank God, they didn't kill him. From his hospital bed, he told the tale to the Okie police, gave them a good description. The field office down there tracks them west, straight as an arrow, to Abilene, Texas. They hold up the Yellow Rose Cantina, and one of the waitresses there remembers talking to a young woman—though the description doesn't match your daughter—and her boyfriend who made a getaway in a red car with Tennessee license plates. Witness at a motel says they are runaways, though he can't be considered entirely reliable. The local sheriff finds a drawing one of the kids made in the waxed tabletop." From his pocket, he pulled an index card with a crude approximation of the AOD logo with the rampant wings. "You seen this before?"

"In the boy's room," Paul said. "Stenciled on the closet door."

"AOD—Angels of Destruction. The Bureau has been playing catch-up since then, and we knew their destination. To meet up with a dissident counterculture revolutionary cell in San Francisco, essentially the brainchild of a petty criminal named John Wesley Cromartie, aka the Crow. Of course our offices out there have been keeping an eye on the Angels for over two years now. If we count Wiley Rinnick and your daughter.

Now, we don't know if she went willingly or was kidnapped, but there were at least seven of these Angels—"

"Willingly," Paul said, "but she didn't know what she was doing. She's just a child."

"—before the accident. I'm sorry to have to tell you." He paused and waited for them to settle themselves. "We believe that this Cromartie and Rinnick were constructing some sort of explosive device—"

A hand clips a wire to the wrong post, and in that instant the light expands and diminishes all at once. The destroyer of worlds becomes clear. A thousand suns burst open. The flash penetrates his consciousness as the bomb rends them asunder and time roils and fastens to the certain knowledge of the glorious mistake.

"If there's any consolation, they died instantly, as sudden as a sneeze. Mrs. Rinnick took the news as well as could be expected." Beside her, Paul melted away into the sofa as Linnet ticked on like an alarm clock. "The other Angels have flown away, so to speak, maybe left the country or gone underground, we don't know. But we will keep looking, if she can be found."

After the rush of air, after the thought of flash and the fire, after the interrupted cry, after the last breath and beat, silence expanded to fill the void, and what had once perched in Margaret's soul took wing.

31

Racing away in true fear, she kept looking over her shoulder, expecting at any moment a phalanx of police cars to roar over the receding horizon, sirens blazing. He had come back into the Yellow Rose like a madman, the guns natural in his hands, a look of pure anger on his face, the shaved head beet red, demanding that they all get down on the floor. As usual, not enough cash in the register to justify the risk, and he put an angry hole in the ceiling with a shotgun blast. Pulled by the vortex of his emotion, she followed to the car, deaf to his laughter and exhilarated yell. By the time they escaped the Texas scrubland and were welcomed to the Land of Enchantment, she allowed herself a deep breath. Little traffic passed in either direction, and he drove possessed into the deserted landscape, the sagebrush and chaparral floating on a sea of orange dirt, the mesas to the west mutable shadows underneath the broad sky crowded with clouds as big and graceful as ocean liners. She could feel Wiley's angry energy in the way he steered the car, and he said virtually nothing until Tucumcari, with its curio shops and old motels lining Route 66, and they stopped for a late lunch.

"I have to get to a doctor's," she told him over enchiladas. "Take the pregnancy test, find out for sure."

"One step ahead of you, baby. That's why I got us some more cash. Next big city, we'll stop and kill the rabbit. We'll find you a clinic where they can check you out."

"Albuquerque is ahead," she said, studying the map. "Three hours."

They stopped for the night near Old Town, settling into a bed-and-breakfast, an enclosed group of rustic casitas facing a patio garden, fading to winter. Along the paths rows of luminarias glowed, and a string of red pepper Christmas lights had been woven through the slats of the central gazebo. Against the chilly night, they huddled together on a bench, staring at the small fires surrounding them.

"This is how I imagined it," she said. "Somewhere romantic and new and different, with you."

"An old-fashioned girl."

"You make it sound so uncool, but I just want to be with you. Get married, like we said."

"Is that why you joined the revolution?"

"I ran away with you, because you believe. But you've changed, somehow. The gun has become more than a gun. I'm a little scared, but I still believe in you—"

"And the Angels?"

She nodded against his shoulder and gripped his hand.

Wiley squeezed back. "No place for a baby." His face a mask of confusion, he rose to pace the courtyard, and then disappeared behind an adobe wall, leaving her alone for nearly an hour.

The lights flickered, their hypnotic dance carrying her back to the fires at the Gavins' cabin, then to childhood winters in Pennsylvania and the feeling of warmth and solace she felt so long ago. A breeze whipped through the courtyard, contorting a mad windchime and rattling the stalk of chiles drying on the lintel. He returned and sat next to her, a question on his lips.

"First let's see if there actually is a baby," she finally said.

As they readied for bed, she sensed a change come over him, the heavy fall of his boots on the floor, the callused hand against her face as he kissed her softly goodnight. Into the blue china teacup on the night table, she poured her prayers. Forgiveness, salvation. Late in her dreams, she thought of Una Gavin's plight of faith and doubt, in believing her grandmother's desire while knowing it could not be so. Her parents would not be coming back. Skeptical of her own fragile hope, Wiley tossed and grumbled, and once, before she fell asleep, Erica felt his open eyes watching her, waiting, a barely audible sigh when he realized that she stared at the timbered ceiling. She did not stir when he crept out of bed, and did not cry out when he bumped the table and crushed the doll's cup under his booted foot. Later, only later, did she realize that she had ever fallen asleep. In the dead hour before dawn, she was awakened by a woman crossing the courtyard singing, *". . . porque no puedo llorar."* By morning, winter had arrived, a frosty draft sifting through the adobe walls and pressing against the windowpanes. Erica burrowed beneath the blankets, aware at sunrise that Wiley had abandoned her hours before, yet she was unwilling to leave the bed and find pinned to the door the envelope stuffed with stolen cash and the note that explained *goodbye*.

BOOK III

February 1985

1

Margaret sat up in bed and switched on the lamp, knocking the shade askew. Beyond the circle of light, a figure stirred, opaque in the darkness, struggling to become manifest. A rush of weight filled her as though she had swallowed a wave, and the dread settled in her bones. Ever since Erica had run away, the vision had often appeared to Margaret—on her long solitary walks, she would see the figure pass like a fog over the next hill or its flash of movement buried deep in the forest, quiet as a doe. She sometimes thought him visible in the interval between the flick of a light switch and the rush to darkness. At first, the presence frightened her, but the commodious mind tolerates inexplicable phantoms as readily as the real people who wander in imaginary houses, the necessary angels and requisite demons, the memories and ghosts summoned to explain again just what had gone wrong. Margaret thought she had rid herself of such questions and could barely face her old conjecture, just as she had always pictured him, a man of her age, elegant and handsome, under a brown fedora. She sighed. "You are supposed to be gone."

"I never leave," the shadow said. "I am with you always. You choose when to acknowledge my ever-present presence, and quite frankly, I am hurt by your attitude. I'm here about Norah. Your angel?"

"Are you asking me if I believe in angels? You might as well ask if I believe in you. Every child exaggerates," Margaret argued. "Who hasn't stretched the truth to be seen as more interesting? It's just a phase."

"Let me ask you a philosophical question: how many angels can dance on the head of a pin?"

An image blossomed in her imagination: angels jitterbugging, pulling up their long robes to make way for flying feet clad in bobby socks and Mary Janes.

"Do you find me amusing this morning?"

"Not you, but the dancing angels. Just wondering if they knew the Lindy—"

"Notwithstanding the *kind* of dance, the number of angels remains the same. If God wills it, they may be infinite."

"And very, very small."

"Smaller than atoms, smaller than the atoms inside of atoms. Small to the point of nearly not existing at all, but they do. Blessed are they that have not seen and yet have believed. Once upon a time, atoms did not yet exist. There was no Dalton, no Rutherford. Albert Einstein was nothing more than a theorist, but you only have to look at Hiroshima and Nagasaki to know that things invisible exist and bear great power. The power to destroy. Or the power to create."

Margaret thought of her husband and the secret he tried to keep from her all those years.

"Atoms and angels, reason and faith," he went on. "One without the other is less than half as strong and can be a danger to our vitality. Reason is subject to the tests of logic and observable, demonstrable phenomena. Faith is tested by our desire and will. One cannot see faith, just as one cannot pour out hope or love from a beaker. Self-sacrifice and devotion escape the strongest microscope, but such qualities of spirit can be shown and known by us all, my dear. And so with God's messengers, more believed than seen, more felt than touched, our angels exist in open hearts, if we have but faith."

Dead silence followed, too many measures without a note.

He cleared his throat. "The question is: does the child believe what she says she is? And do you think she is a messenger of the Lord?"

In the next room, Norah slept without a sound. Margaret had checked earlier to make sure before readying herself for bed. They had spoken briefly of the incident at the school and the calls from her teacher and the principal, but she had not pressed the child for explanation. Truth be told, she did not want to know, but hoped instead that the notion would pass in time, that the girl would settle into the role Margaret desired.

"You lied to protect her, protect yourself. Lied to everyone, your sister. Thought you could keep her. What will you do for this perfect stranger?"

He held his gaze, and she looked into his eyes, expecting her reflection on the black pupils, but there was nothing but misery. Margaret snapped off the light, covered her ear with the pillow, and drew the blanket to her forehead to banish him from sight. Pain snuggled against her spine and shared an intimate hour wrestling in the darkness.

2

Watching the roseate clouds darken as the morning crept in from the east, Sean stood waiting for her in the yard, half expecting the bathroom window to part at the sash and Norah to fly through with white wings unfurled and land at his side. The winds had shifted from the southwest in the early hours, pushing warmer air over the Alleghenies, teasing at springtime. Sean opened his overcoat, unwound his scarf, wondering how much of this warmth could be attributed to the rising temperature and how much to his state of anticipation. Ever since he had heard her confession to the entire class, he had five hundred questions he longed to ask her. All night, from supper to bedtime and in his dreams, he carried on an imagined conversation with Norah, supplying both sides of the dialogue and providing the answers to all that plagued his mind. He stamped his feet in the snow, begging her to hurry, and his sudden motion startled a gang of crows, shouting alarms from a bare oak as they hopped and scattered to safer branches. From their new perches, they scrutinized the stranger in their midst.

Frightened by the birds, Sean did not notice how she arrived— magically, perhaps—red-cheeked from her exertions. Norah welcomed him with a wide grin, her face framed by the gray hood of her coat, her glasses fogged. She appeared no different than any other morning, though he felt they were meeting for the first time.

"Did you remember to do your math homework?" she asked him, and the spell was broken. He shrugged out of his backpack, unzipped the opening, and looked inside, hoping that some overnight miracle had occurred. "You might have time before the first bell, if we hurry." Looking back over her shoulder, she waved at Margaret and Diane watching from the window. He raised his hand, but they were already gone, the curtains closing like windblown ghosts. Norah pulled at his coat sleeve and they tramped off.

In the winter woods, the bark of the trees thawed and crackled, and water trickled where the ice had thinned and melted. Rags of bare earth revealed the brown leaves and rot beneath the snow, and the bike path was little more than a worn depression, slick with packed footprints. They moved as quickly as they could manage over the ruts, speechless as they picked their way out of the forest and into the sunshine. She threw a shadow across the road, the shape bold in relief and bisecting the lines cast by tree trunks and networks of bare branches splintering like tributaries off a river. The morning light banked and bestowed its energy, and he soaked in the radiance, felt a vertiginous happiness at the heart's core compounded by her presence. Other children struggled on their way, the adventurous daring to parade in the plowed streets alongside the heaps of dirty snow, and the rest hewing to the familiar path through the slush and muck. She had hastened a few steps ahead, so he jogged to catch her. He asked, "Are you afraid of what might happen today?"

Norah stopped to address him. "Afraid? Is that how to start the day? I am not the least bit worried about what others might say. If you mean am I anxious about how people might treat me now that they know the truth, the answer is no."

They walked on, and he labored to keep pace. More children joined the stream toward the building. "But why did you tell them that you are an angel?"

"Suppose you dip your big toe in a pool, there's no way to stop the ripple, or suppose you pluck a string on a guitar, the vibration has already begun. Everything is in motion."

"But why did you come here? Why now?"

"Sean, if I knew where the motion will take us, my job would be done. Hurry up if you are going to finish your homework on time. You know how long it takes to multiply and divide."

Judging by the stares and whispers, every child in every grade and every member of the faculty and staff at the Friendship School already knew of the incident in Mrs. Patterson's class on Valentine's Day. A few intrepid souls walked right up to them, said hello. One girl curtsied in a self-conscious way, cutting the gesture short. Their classmates stopped chattering when the pair entered the room, all eyes watching and waiting for another sign. Sharon Hopper looked for wings as Norah passed by her desk. Mark Bellagio snorted at Sean, wheeled around in his seat to sock him on the meaty part of his arm. Earlier that morning, Mrs. Patterson had taken down the cardboard hearts and cupids and lace, and in their place, flat cartoon drawings of Washington, Jefferson, Lincoln, and Reagan stared down from the walls. Pretending not to notice the commotion, the teacher fiddled with her attendance roster, checked off their names, and tried to gauge the climate of the classroom. She surveyed her charges: the Fallon boy scratched at an equation with a pencil stub. A pair in the back row whispered intimately. Gail Watts mumbled to herself, a recitation or a prayer. The rest of the children were poised for the morning bell, anticipating the beginning of the day and what might be said about the prior afternoon's outburst.

Mrs. Patterson could feel Norah Quinn watching with a leopard's unrelenting stealth and had to fight an overwhelming urge to flee, to leap from her post and sprint through the halls to the teachers' lounge and pour herself another coffee, smoke another cigarette. Muttering a curse beneath her breath, she began with her good mornings and the calling of the roll. "And I just want to say one thing about yesterday's episode after the Valentine's cards. There will be no more incidents, no more disruptions, and we will not be talking about angels or other matters inappropriate for classroom discussion. This is a public school. I have spoken with Mr. Taylor, and he has spoken with Mrs. Quinn, and we have all reached an understanding."

Norah's arm rose like a flag. Snickers from a few desks threatened the whole day.

"And, just a minute, and we have work to do, and we need team spirit, and do you know that teams are only as strong as the teammates and our respect for one another and our differences—"

Norah waved her fingers. "Mrs. Patterson? Mrs. Patterson? I have something to say to everyone."

"Not now, Norah. That's enough."

"I feel I need to say—"

"No apologies are necessary. Your grandmother apologized for you. You've been under a lot of stress—"

"—to tell the truth—"

"—the difficulty of starting a new school, new friends, feeling like an outsider—"

"—not to say I'm sorry, but to let everyone know—"

"Norah, please. Be quiet."

"—that no harm shall come to them."

Sean Fallon put down his pencil, gave up the futile attempt to solve his problems in time, and laid his head across his folded arms atop his desk. He waited for the room to stop spinning, for the bolt of pain behind his eyes to go away. Inside his head, their voices began as a low hum, white static as the dial rolled to the next station on the radio, and then the words came overlaid, bits and pieces distinguishable from the cacophony: Sharon's thoughts, Mark's, Dori's. The wandering mind of Lucas Ford. Gail Watts practicing an étude in her imagination. Mrs. Patterson, please just make them stop. All the children wondering, doubting, believing— until the sound of their ideas and feelings coalesced into a wall of music, measured and cadenced, like a symphony between his ears, and the music did not stop until Mrs. Patterson, straight-backed as a conductor, tapped a ruler on the desk and invited them to begin their consideration of the first subject of the day, history.

3

The eyes of Our Lady of Guadalupe betrayed an all-too-human emotion. Instead of looking upward to the heavens or downward in mercy to the earth, she focused on some object to the left of the frame of the *retablo*, and the wayward gaze made her appear contemplative, almost sad, mourning the viewer, or remembering her son, heartbroken over his early death. A mother pained for her child, full of despair over her powerlessness against fate and the child's stronger will. The primitive style of composition and brushstroke could not hide the merciless intelligence of the painter, who had captured in a single gesture the pathos of motherhood. Six other folk paintings hung on the walls of the café: Matthew, the scribe; Mark, the lion; Luke, the winged bull; John, the eagle; San Pascual, the patron of cooks; and one labeled *Angel de la Guardia*. In niches hollowed into the adobe, *santos* perched like puppets awaiting the breath of life or the master's hand, and by the cash register, *bultos* of the holy family stood like refugees from a Christmas crèche.

Diane sipped a coffee laced with piñon and stirred a bowl of blue corn *atole*. The time change between Washington and Albuquerque had thrown her, and she had risen earlier than the local hour, the late-winter light slipping over the city as she wandered past the closed storefronts and restaurants, searching for breakfast in Old Town. The Café de Santeros had the only open door, and for a time, she was alone with the beautiful young girl who had served her and then went back to idly sketching flowers in a spiral-bound notebook. After circling the room, taking in each of the paintings done by the same hand, Diane sat with her coffee and thought of her sister and the strange child she had left behind the week before. Protests were declared, but she had been forgiven for leaving as soon as she had promised to return. She told Margaret nothing of her travel plans. After a few days to take care of things at home in

Washington, Diane had packed for New Mexico, armed with an old photograph of Erica, a child's implausible claim, and an X on a map.

Norah's outburst at the school had compelled Diane to go, not so much for the girl's welfare, but for her sister's sake. She had seen what loss could do to Margaret—the stunning silences, how she seemed to shrink with each blow until diminishing to nothing more than a whisper, a feather, a sigh. As the only children, they had grown up as close as twins, just two years apart; each reflected the best and worst of the other. While the indeterminacies of fate pulled them apart as young women, sending Diane off to travel around the world with her husband while Margaret settled in with the doctor in their hometown, they remained committed to the idea of sisterhood. Summer family vacations together at the shore, long-distance calls, letters, consoling as no other could at the passing of Daddy, and three years later their mother. When Erica had vanished, Margaret had phoned her first, even before the police, and Diane watched her sister drown month by month and then float back to a kind of half-life. She could save her now by finding her missing girl. Or at least uncover the truth about Norah.

On the sidewalk outside the café, a flock of pigeons took flight en masse, wheeling to formation in synchronicity. The front door creaked open and in came two young men, dressed snug against the cold. Behind the counter, the girl laid down her pencil, waved hello, and braced to receive their orders. They appeared to be regulars, smiling back in a familiar fashion and not bothering to read the slate chalked with today's menu.

"*Qué pasa, Lupita?*" the one with the sweeping black mustache said. "Anything fresh today? Besides you?"

Lupita rolled her eyes in mock annoyance, but her smile gave away her pleasure.

"*Dos* cappuccinos. And *mi hijo* wants something to eat. His old lady kicks him out every morning with no breakfast 'cause he snores all night."

His friend bent to scan the baked goods in the glass display case and, rising, asked for a poppyseed cake. When the girl shifted to the espresso machine, the two men pivoted on their heels, mirroring each other, away from the counter to scan the room. Even as they arced their shoulders and swung their hips toward her, Diane wanted them to do it over in slow motion, for she was entranced by the unthinking grace of their bodies. In the dim light, the brightness of their faces disarmed her. She blushed over the look the men gave her and cast her gaze to her hands folded on the tabletop, to the slick on the surface of her coffee.

The men came over to her, the pale blue cups like toys in their hands, and stood patiently just beyond the edge waiting for her to look up, and as soon as she did, they took it as an invitation to sit and join her, though she had said nothing. No new customers had wandered in. The younger man took a big bite of his poppyseed cake and savored the crunch and grit against his teeth. The one with the mustache wrapped his long fingers around his cup, warming his hands. "Good morning," he said when Diane granted her notice with a wan smile. "I hope you don't mind us joining you. It just seems strange for you to be all alone and for us to be alone when there is no one else here."

"Not a bit. You're welcome."

The man eating the cake had poppyseeds stuck between his teeth.

"When you are alone, small company can often change the meaning of the whole day. Of course, there are times when you want to be by yourself, shut off with your thoughts." He spoke in a laconic tone, reluctant to part with each word. "Sometimes you just want another person to shoot the breeze with, shorten the burden of moving from A to B."

The poppyseed man blew on his cappuccino and took a hot swallow, leaving a milky brown stain above his upper lip.

"I just came in last night and don't know a soul." Laughing politely, she set down her cup. "My first time in New Mexico."

"Welcome, then. What brings you here, business or pleasure?"

With a laugh, Diane set down her cup. "I have no business. I'm here to . . . see my daughter." The white lie popped out to her immediate regret. She opened her purse and found the high school photograph. "Erica. She lives in a place called Madrid. Do you know the way?"

"A ghost town," the younger man said. "They call it MAD-rid, by the way, not muh-DRID. Not like the one in Spain. Used to be a coal-mining town, but the mine was shut down thirty years ago when all the Santa Fe trains switched over to diesel. Everybody used to go there for the Christmas lights. They say you could be flying overhead at night and see them from hundreds of miles, like candles in the dark middle of nowhere. But they're all gone, the people. Just a bunch of ancient shacks. Some dude even put an ad in the newspaper: whole town for sale."

"Where you been, *hijo*? When's the last time you been up the trail?

Fifteen years ago, yourself? There's plenty people in Madrid. Back in the Seventies all these hippies and artists came in and took over. What do you call it? Squatters? Homesteaders."

"Like trying to find a ghost." He was pressing his thumb against the plate, picking up black dots.

The other set down his cappuccino with an empty ring. "Don't listen to my friend, señora. His brain is fried."

"Más loco que una cabra."

"Chiflado. You look like you've been eating bugs."

"Te falta un tornillo." He ran his tongue over his teeth.

"Boys," Diane said, "I guess I'll have to see for myself."

"Drive east on old 66, and you'll see the signs. We'd show you the way, but we're heading up north to work."

"Where are you going?"

The man with the poppyseed grin leaned over and spoke in a low voice. "Los Alamos."

"That's why he is so crazy. Plutonium head." She thought of her conversation with Norah in the graveyard, the talk of the atom bomb and the destroyer of worlds. He stood and bowed slightly, and his friend repeated the gesture. "Good luck on your trip. I hope you find what you're looking for."

For a moment, she could not remember why she had come.

"Your daughter."

"One more thing," she said. "Tell me why all the icons on the walls?"

"Santos," the younger man said. "To remind us. The *santeros* carve or paint them on *retablos* and sell them where they can. The makers of saints."

"Thank you for having breakfast with me."

The man with the mustache buttoned his shearling coat. " 'Do not neglect to show hospitality to strangers, for by this some have entertained angels without knowing it.' Book of Hebrews. You'll find her."

"Adios," his friend said, shaking his head.

"He's *loco*, there's no such thing as ghosts."

4

The song came from above, a tuneless air that rode the vocal register in erratic fits. Margaret had heard such improvised singing years earlier, and she crept up the stairs, paw-soft on each step to prevent the telltale squeak, and then she carefully placed her ear against the bathroom door to hear Norah in the tub, happily composing the events of her day in syncopated rhythm. The discordant music filled Margaret with unexpected joy, remembering how Erica sang in the bathroom. And how, as little girls, Margaret and her sister used to harmonize in a cloud of soap bubbles, or late at night in the stillness of their darkened bedroom, or traipsing through the fairy-filled woods, or out on the sand with the roaring surf nearly drowning all human sound. Carefree summer songs at the shore.

A long line of pelicans played follow-the-leader nearly skimming the waves, one after the other diving into the chop not thirty yards from shore. Her father pointed excitedly each time they buzzed the surf, hunting for fish. And later that evening over dinner, face red with wine and sun, he scraped back his chair on the wooden deck of their rented house and recited:

"A wonderful bird is the pelican,
His bill will hold more than his belican.
He can take in his beak
Food enough for a week,
But I'm damned if I see how the helican."

"Oh, John," her mother chided him, and he gave her a look that begged an indulgence, and Diane and Margaret watched the unspoken signals seesaw between them until the tension was broken by their mother's mischievous laugh that signaled all was well and permitted the children to clamor for more. Listening to the girl sing through the bathroom door, Margaret felt complete satisfaction of the moment. What must they have been like, not as parents, but as a grown man and woman with two daughters sunbrown as nuts, a bottle of wine, the dying of another summer? Her father would have loved the singing nymph in the bathtub and understood, and her mother would have silently acknowledged the need to lie on Norah's behalf even when the child could not be believed.

The singing stopped, and she could hear the girl dripping in the tub as she reached for the towel. Margaret hurried away, cantered downstairs on stiff legs, and took up her book under the lamplight. She scanned for her place in the story, read again the page abandoned, and had just remembered the passage when Norah arrived bedraggled as a storm-drenched kitten, her ragged hair plastered against her skull, yet new again and clean and fresh, wrapped in Erica's thick robe. Margaret wished the girl would sing again. She longed to pull her close but feared the bone-ache of an embrace. "Norah, sit down beside me." The child wiggled round the coffee table, hopped onto the cushion, and squeezed into the corner between the woman's body and the arm of the sofa. She pressed against Margaret's side, all heartbeat and wet heat. "I had another phone call today from your principal, Mr. Taylor. I thought that was all over last week. He said your teacher had reports from some of the other children that you were pretending again in the lunchroom."

"Oh, that? Just a cheap trick."

Margaret sighed. "That's three times in two weeks, Norah. I can't have all this trouble from the school."

"I'm sorry. It won't happen again."

"People will talk, are talking. Parents fussing. I do not like to be the subject of so much gossip, so many questions."

Norah snuggled closer. "It won't happen again."

Hearing the sincerity of the child's apology, Margaret regretted the tone of voice she had taken with her, wishing instead that she could affect her father's disposition at the times when his wit disarmed ill feelings or burst like an explosion to cause them all to laugh when the situation called for sobriety. She longed for a way to bring about a consolation, and finally wrenched free her pinned arm and laid her hand upon the girl's shoulder. "So you're ready for bed now? Brushed your teeth?"

Close enough to kiss, Norah lifted her face. "Here, smell."

Margaret turned her head and nearly caught her ear in the girl's open mouth. Like listening to a seashell, she could hear the roar of waves and, more disturbingly, the wind blow across the sand, the laughing cry of gulls, as though the girl had swallowed the sea. The sound lasted no longer than the time it took Margaret to recover and position her nose to catch the scent of peppermint, but in that fraction, her mind reeled. Perhaps her senses had conflated the memory with the moment. But she was not certain, as she sent Norah to bed, not certain of any distinction between what she had heard and what she had chosen to believe.

5

Sean loved the panther best and nearly leapt with joy when he found one tensed for the attack. He was surprised by the bear—not the sitting circus bear, but the grizzly on the prowl. The zebra and the camel were acceptable, though one or both sets of legs frequently were missing. The broken ones disappointed, left him feeling somehow cheated. An elephant without a trunk was a catastrophe. Once in a while they came out misshapen altogether, a walrus glued to a kangaroo or the features of a moose puddled in horror. These he almost could not eat. But more than the crackers, the box fascinated him with its vibrant colors, the caged animals poised wild against the bars, the reclining gorilla, the snarling tiger, the mystery of the musk ox. On the bottom panel, instructions, lines to cut and fold, enabled the construction of the wheeled circus wagon and a top-hatted ringmaster holding a megaphone. Or, on alternate designs, a lion tamer with a whip. He never bothered to make the train of wagons, knew of nobody who actually destroyed one illusion to create another. Most appealing of all was the thin red cloth string along the top edge of the box. A handle, of course, that made the emptied carton a purse or a treasure chest for any collection of small valuables. One was filled with plastic army men and molded wild animals. Another held marbles, smooth stones, and a discarded jack. A third contained feathers from jays and robins, sparrows and wrens, the black ace of the crow, the white of some unknown flying thing. And nested nearby, the pale blue teacup Norah had given him.

His collection of animal cracker boxes was situated artfully among the books and magazines in the rough-hewn case of shelves his father had made when Sean was a baby. Hidden carefully within the books, tucked between the covers and title pages, were all the birthday cards from his parents, first signed jointly and later two separate notes. Norah's valentine he secreted, like a pressed wildflower, in the pages of *Birds of North America*, the volume missing a score of clipped illustrations. He stared at the spines of his library, hoping for the distraction of a good book, but every title left him slightly dissatisfied. He could not shake the image of Norah's deceit in the lunchroom earlier that day.

She had promised to be good. Ten days had passed uneventfully since Valentine's, for with Diane gone, there was no subterfuge to carry out. They played together like normal children, once going round to the Rosa Rossa Flower Shop to marvel at the finches. Another afternoon was spent drawing side by side, arguing over who was better—pirates or knights. Checkers and hot chocolate. Sunday on a sled. At first, Norah waved off any discussion of her confession in private or in school, content to bask in newfound admiration and popularity, but one by one, the temporary friends drifted away, bored by her ordinariness. The memory of the spectacle gave way to prayer conspiracies to conjure another snow day's vacation and to a general colloquy on the horrors of finding common denominators when confronted by more than one fraction. She was being forgotten. Matthew Mansur began taunting her at lunch, the ridicule pathetic and absurd. "If you are an angel, show us a miracle. Faker." And then the bully picked up Sharon's animal crackers and spilled them onto the cafeteria table. Without fuss, Norah brushed them to her with both hands, and the children watched intently as she lined the animals nose to tail along the surface and then held the open circus box in her lap.

"Happy are they who believe but need not see," she said. The table began to vibrate slightly as if from the shock of a faraway rumbling earthquake or lifted by a séance and an unseen force beneath the surface, and into the box the hippos and rhinos and giraffes fell one by one to the very last cracker. Nobody said a word during the entire performance, and soon after the finale, the bell rang. The children packed their bags and lunchboxes to hurry back to the classroom, murmuring among themselves. Sean walked three steps behind her and looked at the tiles between his feet when she glanced over her shoulder, wondering, if she was an angel was she also a girl, also his true friend?

At home in his room, waiting alone till the order came for lights-out, he replayed the scene on the stage of his memory but could not discover a secondary explanation no matter how many times he stopped or slowed the action. No wires or engines or wind. No evidence of tampering with the laws of nature. "You promised," he said aloud to the imagined space he had cleared for her. You scared the crap out of them, did you see the look on their faces? You promised no more angels, no miracles, nothing seen that cannot be believed. How could you, Norah? You promised that no one would be harmed.

He fought to stay awake. From the bookshelves, the animals paraded out of the circus wagon boxes, the panther and polar bear, the fox and the bison marched across the carpet trumpeting and roaring and out through his bedroom window into the snow-filled yard, leaving tracks so small as to be almost invisible. No proof at all of their existence, much less their travels through this lonely spot on the world. He groaned in his sleep, opened his eyes to darkness, the threat of the shelves cluttered with books and circuses, and wished he could have his father come to offer comfort, or his mother surprise him by checking in, or Norah drop by to say goodnight, before sliding under the dream again.

6

The road to Madrid rose past Sandia and twisted into the high country, bare and stark, dotted with sage and rock. The sky changed around every bend and corner, sunlit to heavily overcast threatening torrents, and back again to puffy cumulus against indigo. The rental car chugged over the mountains, and without any warning, she was there, so early in the day that nobody stirred, no cars, no people, only a stray yellow dog crossing her path, looking back over its shoulder before trotting away. Diane pulled off the highway just as it curved westward, and parked on the gravel in front of the Mine Shaft Tavern. Bits of broken glass clotted in the gutter along the wooden foundation, green and brown blasted smooth by the sun and wind. Off to the east, a short row of storefronts offered arts and crafts, jewelry in silver and turquoise, a dressmaker's dummy draped in handwoven wool and muslin dyed in muted earth tones. The cold air was thinner here, and she tired easily, resting on a wooden porch of a vacant building with a faded FOR SALE sign in the window. A hank of tumbleweed lay caught between the wooden slats and the ground, and she kicked and tried to set it free, unaware that she was not alone.

From over the eastern hills came a wraith. Or so she appeared at first, her elongated shadow stretched out in front of her, a corona glowing around her body before passing into the mountain's shade as she neared. Diane stood to greet her but lost her balance and tumbled off the porch. The woman hurried over, presented a bangled wrist for support, and with unexpected strength stopped her from falling. They stood close enough to dance, and Diane lowered her chin to thank her. A crown of curls, blonde fading to ash, spilled beyond the woman's shoulders, and her pale skin shone translucent at the sharp curve of her jawline and high cheekbones faintly speckled. Round glasses in rose-colored frames heightened the contrast with her pale blue eyes. Even in her plaid winter coat, too poor against the February morning, her body could not hide its birdlike form, spare and taut, both fragile and strong. A vision of Norah grown and matured.

"Are you all right?" the woman asked. "That was quite a stumble." Her voice was a strange mix of tones and rhythms, flat and broad as the East with an unexpectedly childlike earnestness in the slow cadence of the West, as if she, too, had been blown across the country. Diane muttered a solitary thank-you.

"You're out and about awfully early. Come on over to the Mine Shaft, and I'll make you an omelet."

"I've already had my breakfast, thanks."

"Then a cup of coffee. Can't say no to a free coffee. Everyone always has room for another cup this time of day. My name is Maya." She offered to shake again, and they sealed the deal.

Maya molded her hand into a megaphone and hollered back to the horizon: "Come on, boys. Breakfast."

From the lip of the world, two iron gray long-leggety wolfhounds trotted, big as ponies, fearsome as *los lobos*, and ambled straight for the women. The one on the left loped to greet Maya, and the one on the right hastened to Diane, tail circling with excitement, and sprang on her, its great flat forepaws heavy as fists which punched her shoulders and knocked her sprawling backward. She looked up to see the large square head staring back at her, thick tongue lolling, teeth worn as arrowheads. Maya scolded once, barked a command, and the dog retreated, its head bowed in repentance.

"Ah, you're a bad boy, bad dog. Don't mind Finn, he's just a pup and doesn't know his own strength. But that's a dog for you. Can't never hide its true feelings. I think he likes you."

They walked toward the tavern, the dogs jostling at their sides, with Diane watchful every few steps when one brushed against her leg. As Maya fished for the keys, the dogs stared at the doorknob, waiting for the magic, and then in they scooted like toddlers through the opening and moved through the dark table-cluttered room without so much as a single bump or scrape. The lights buzzed and flickered on, revealing a great mirror behind a bar that ran the length of the room. She was surprised by her own reflection and fixed her hair as Maya puttered behind the bar.

"I got the first dog twenty years ago when this was truly the Wild West. There were coyotes in the parlors in a couple tumbledown houses. Thought a wolfhound would be great protection, you know, they're bred to chase out the wolves. Called my first fella Cuchulainn after the great hero of Ulster, and he was a lamb. Never had a one since then, and I've had seven altogether, that's so much as snapped at a person drunk or sober, though Micky here will chase jackrabbits, flush a pheasant or quail, and Finn will tag along behind it. But he doesn't know what he'd do if he ever managed to catch one, isn't that right, you great Irish doofus?" With both hands she ruffled the wiry scruff of his big head. "How do you take your coffee?"

"Black." The inside of the Mine Shaft Tavern was nearly as dark as the real thing, wood discolored by age and abuse, the walls littered with broadsides for old and new plays and variety shows, a John Ford Film Festival, a buffalo's head, whimsical signs and notices to the customers: Ladies, mind your purses; No Expectorating; a painting of coal miners greeted by an angel holding a banner which, in Latin, read, "It is better to drink than to work." At the far end of the building a small stage had been set, props of wagon wheels and beer barrels, and a sepia-toned photograph of a woman in whiteface with ragged sheets, a theatrical ghost, announcing the upcoming melodrama. Through the window, morning cut the dimness, threw lines upon the floor. The dogs sought out the warm patches near her feet, the older hound curled into a compact ball of fur.

Dust danced in the sunbeams, shifting as the clouds outside sailed across the sky. The interplay of light and shadow reminded Diane of the August shore with her parents and Margaret, lolling away the afternoon, watching the light cross the beach-worn rugs and pine floors. Her parents napping on the deck, the heat-stricken house seemed to drowse, and they were quite alone, a quiet yearning, safe with her parents nearby. The rise and fall of the ocean, the breeze off the veranda, the quiet and un-planned time all leading to daydreaming of the future. They shared their big plans for husbands and travel, to see the world, take a turn on the stage, Sunday paintings, a book to write. And children of their own to take to this same place, to give to those imagined sons and daughters what they had been given. Now, Diane wanted desperately to bring back her sister's child.

Maya set a mug in front of her and joined her at the rail. Finn snored from below.

"How many people live here in town?" Diane tried to feign a disinterested air.

"Madrid proper, or up in the hills? Not many. Fifty-sixty households, many hermits and evacuees from reality. Maybe ninety souls in all. It was a ghost town or nearly so when I came here in the Sixties. Seemed like a good place to escape the madness."

"Crazy times. Vietnam."

"The whole thing, sister. JFK, Malcolm, Bobby, Martin. Water hoses and beatings on the bridge. Riots in the streets. Tune in, turn on, drop out. Some of us dropped pretty far." Maya set her elbows on the counter, leaned across to Diane. "If they live in these parts, I know 'em."

"Then you'll know my granddaughter." The lie possessed its own life. "Norah Quinn."

Maya frowned and tried to bring life to the name. "I don't think I know a Norah Quinn. There's not that many kids in these parts, barely enough to keep the school going."

"She's about nine. Blonde hair, glasses. Lives with her mother here, or at least, up until this past January." She leaned forward and whispered. "There was a fight. My daughter and her husband."

From the floor, Mick whined, shook his head, then shimmied from haunches to tail and paced to the front door as quiet as a cat.

"Quinn, you say?"

"Erica is her name. My daughter."

Mick barked at the door, having heard something stir outside. For a moment, Diane expected a knock and a visitor: Erica, Norah, legions of heavenly hosts. But the dog lost interest and retreated to his hot spot on the floor.

"I'm sorry to say, there's no Erica Quinn in this town."

Diane's hand rummaged through the purse, found the photograph. "Are you certain you haven't seen this girl? It's an old photo from high school but—"

Delight crossed Maya's face as she scrutinized the photograph. "Not Erica," she said, and tapped the image with her fingernail. "Different hair, but same eyes, that same look if I'm not mistaken. She lives out in the hills." A little belly laugh from a little belly. "That's Mary Gavin."

Word of the marching animal crackers spread through the Friendship School, and the children began to invent and circulate new accounts of similar miracles to heighten the lore of Norah Quinn. There were whispers that whenever she visited the library and passed the aquarium kept there, the little fishes would school and swim as one, following her movements from glass corner to glass corner. Another story asserted that she could divide a single peanut butter and jelly sandwich into enough portions to feed the entire student body. Rumors escalated: that she could walk upon the surface of the snow without leaving footprints, that in certain aspects of light a halo could be spied, that she bore on her back stubs of wings at the shoulder blades, that she had been seen flying over her rooftop in the moonlight, that you could put your hand right through her like a ghost, that she was no angel but a devil in disguise.

Gossip reached the teachers' lounge after a few days, and her fellow faculty members mercilessly teased Mrs. Patterson about her student angel and the miracle of the completed homework. She had been watching closely since the Valentine's incident, and in class, at least, the girl was circumspect and attentive, a model student. Bonhomie guided Mrs. Patterson's initial reactions and she laughed with her colleagues, but as the talk persisted, she felt compelled to defend her newest pupil, for the teachers' innuendo quickly became unseemly. Over bad coffee and stale doughnuts, arguments ensued, and she nearly came to harsh words with Miss Becker, and one morning she stubbed out a cigarette in Mr. Rocco's cherry Danish. In confidence she consulted with the principal in the dank and cluttered recesses of his office.

"You've heard the stories by now, Mr. Taylor. I'm afraid of it getting out of hand."

He pulled tighter the knot of his tie. "These tall tales usually peter out on their own accord if we do nothing. Let us leave sleeping dogs lay. If it gets any worse, I'll have a talk, but for now, the best thing we can say is to be quiet."

Shaking her head at his mangling of the language, Mrs. Patterson walked back to Room 9 more exasperated than when she had departed. The truth was that Norah did not belong in her class. The child smartly covered her tracks, but no amount of chicanery could hide the fact that she was too bright for her third-grade cohort. Mistakes were too obvious, of the kind that children usually do not make on tests and homework. On every assignment, she proffered exactly one wrong answer. An otherwise perfect math equation would be off by a single digit. A tightly constructed paragraph would be marred by misspellings of "nowledge" or "sosighity." Norah deliberately stumbled over pronunciations each time she read aloud—"inoxious" for "innocuous"—words that in other contexts Mrs. Patterson had heard her say quite precisely. The teacher had seen her kind a few times over the course of her career, the socially correcting child who, in an effort to appear normal and be accepted by the peer group, presented herself as less intelligent. But the girl could not fool her. She deserved to be skipped ahead, out of her class.

More troubling to Mrs. Patterson was the angel fantasy, not so much for the religious overtones, though she felt absolute in keeping matters of God out of the classroom, or for the complexity of the child's role-playing, but rather for what the outburst revealed about Norah's inner life. In nearly twenty years on the job, she had seen a number of similar reactions to stress, usually stemming from a familial or domestic situation. One girl would pee in her pants right before every mathematics test. Another boy insisted on talking to an imaginary friend named Jack-Peter every recess and lunch hour. Any number of boys and girls had claimed that when they grew up, they wanted to be something entirely inhuman: a dog, a house, the moon. Why worry about an angel, for such moments usually passed, often without elucidation or lasting harm. She was even more concerned about the boy, Sean Fallon, and how, since Norah's arrival, he had glommed on to her. This friendship allowed him to emerge from his cell, imprisoned as he was by feelings of anxiety and self-recrimination after his father left. In September, he had circled around the whirlpool, threatening to sink and drown, and by February, he could sail on. Norah had enchanted him and brought him back to normalcy, and Mrs. Patterson watched the transformation, the silent knowing looks, and all the stolen acts of two kindreds in a crowd that rewarded conformity. How obviously he adored her.

Chatter in the hallways shook her from introspection. The children, returning from the playground, were abuzz about the accident on the monkeybars. All through the winter, they had clamored to play outside for their morning exercise, but January had bitten cold, and February had been too snowy. A soaking rain and three days of abiding sunshine had cleared and dried the playing field, so Mr. Taylor had decided to herd them outdoors rather than stuffing them grade by grade in the cramped gym for half an hour. Most of the children ran free, chased after a ball or each other, or massed on the pavement to skip rope or etch their marks with hard stones on the macadam. A half dozen staked out the swings and flew into the sky, and a clump of kids perched on the jungle gym—Dori Tilghman, Matt Mansur, Sean Fallon, Lucas Ford, and in her crow's nest, Norah Quinn. "You can see over the tops of the trees. You can see the whole world from here. Look, there's a river and a bridge!"

Each child climbed the ladder of iron bars and took turns for the bird's-eye view, all except Lucas, the smallest in the group. Urged on by the boys, he inched to the rounded top, arms and legs stiff as a scuttling crab's, and from there he lost his footing, slipped and screamed, falling headfirst down the center space. Heads turned to the sound of panic. Some witnesses claimed that Lucas stopped midair, his head pointed like an arrow targeting the ground, others said that he seemed to be falling in slow motion, and later, not a soul disputed that there had not been time enough to rescue him. Norah reached through a square of space and grabbed his ankle in one hand, the weight of the boy wrenching her forward with such force that her face clanged into an iron pole as loud and sudden as a firecracker. The blow knocked her glasses to the bare ground. She managed to hold Lucas suspended three feet from impact until the others sprang to gather him into their arms like a frightened monkey fallen from the top of a tree. When she was sure the others safely had him, Norah let go and slumped forward, legs wrapped around the bars, and gingerly touched the welt thrumming across her left cheekbone. Blinking wildly, she seemed about to cry but was in fact searching for her missing glasses, and when Sean retrieved them, she put them on and peered through a lick of mud at the wallowing world. The bell called them in, and when she saw the bruise on the child's face, Mrs. Patterson asked her about the injury. Norah shrugged her shoulders. "We were playing."

By day's end, the teacher had pieced together a rough draft of the events, and as the third graders packed their satchels and bookbags, Mrs. Patterson requested that Sean Fallon stay behind. He signaled Norah to go on without him, and within minutes he was alone with his teacher, shifting from foot to foot at the front row as she wiped the blackboard. "I've heard all kinds of stories, Sean, about what happened out there on the playground. Some students have the crazy idea that Lucas floated in the air. At lunch, one of the children said to another that Norah put a spell on Lucas. Levitated him, so to speak, to fall not quite as fast, so that she'd have time to save him. What do you think about that?"

"How would she do that?"

"Impossible. You were there. What happened?"

He chewed his bottom lip. "He was going to fall, so she just reached for him—"

"By instinct."

"Right. And she made a lucky catch."

"Like a baseball player sticking out his glove and the ball lands in it?"

"Just like that. And then we grabbed Lucas as she was about to drop the ball."

Mrs. Patterson sat back on the edge of the desk and peeked at the clock on the wall. "You and Norah are good friends, right? You shouldn't let the other kids tell stories on her. You should tell them the truth like you told me. Lucky catch."

Sean did not reply but stood there, staring at her shoes and crossed ankles. Thinking back, he was nearly certain. Lucas had stopped, frozen in time. She needed a second to position herself to make the catch, and everything on the playground ceased—swings locked in flight, a kicked ball as still as the sun, everyone a statue, and in that instant freed in time as everyone else was trapped, Norah moved so that her arm was already through the space between the bars, her other hand wrapped around a pole, her feet crooked to brace for the impact, and he saw it all, his friends poised to resume gesture, speech, act. Blink and begin again, the lucky catch, the wonder, and in the aftermath, imaginations straining against the mechanics of an illusion. When the rabbit is pulled from the empty hat, the crowd is certain it must have been there all along. But where? How does a magician deceive our senses, trick all reason? He nodded once without looking up at Mrs. Patterson's inquiring face.

Her questions asked and answered, his teacher sent him on his way. He shuffled home like an old man searching along the path, mumbling, trying to remember what he had intended to say. When he cut through the Quinns' backyard, he dared not look up at the windows, afraid of his own sense of shame should her face appear in the panes, and when he unlocked the front door to his empty home, he felt certain he had done something wrong.

8

The mark on her face deepened from burgundy to plum, then blackened in a broad stripe tinged at the edges with a jaundice yellow. Ice first, a slab of raw steak, and then fresh air did nothing to deter the magnificent progression of hues, and Norah admired the bruise at every chance, looking at her face in the chrome toaster, the teakettle, the darkened windows, and the bathroom mirror, and she touched it often, pressing her fingertips against her cheekbone until she winced.

Margaret, too, cringed when she first saw the contusion, and lifted her hand to her own face to touch the skin stretched across the bone and assure herself the empathetic pain was real. The child's version of the playground event downplayed her own valor, briefly mentioning a boy who tripped and the collision with the cold iron bar, but Margaret, upset by the injury, paid slight heed to the particulars of her story. The first phone call came before dinner, Mrs. Ford to say thank you, requesting to speak directly to her granddaughter, and Norah wanting nothing more than to be off the phone. During dinner, another mother, Mrs. Tilghman, who wanted to know what really happened during recess, but she was dismissed with the promise to call back when they were not in the middle of a meal. Mrs. Bellagio called. Mrs. Mansur. Sharon Hopper to check on her friend. Intimations of some miraculous heroism accompanied every voice, but Norah would have none of it. "I don't know what they are talking about. You would have done the same in my shoes. If a body fell from the sky, wouldn't you hold out your arms to save it? Even if it meant a risk that you might be hurt? Suppose it was someone you love most in the world? What would you do to save her?"

"Anything."

"Lay down your life? Mine?"

"Child, do not say such things."

Long after they had both gone to bed, Margaret woke in agony. A bolus of pain knotted her shoulder, and she sat up, remembering her dream of Erica falling, falling like a star, and she chased the brightness with a butterfly net, well aware of the futility of her efforts. The image left her cranky and restless, so she went downstairs to hunt for a Valium stashed in her husband's study. Shortly after Paul had died, she thought to convert his office into a sewing room or a solarium but satisfied the urge by organizing his papers and pills, confirming and arranging his secrets, and allowing the rest of the room to remain as he had left it. The filing cabinets, the cherry desk, and his diplomas on the wall needed to be dusted now and again, but she ignored everything except his medical bag. There she stored her own medicines along with his stethoscope, a handful of ancient tongue depressors, an otoscope, and a small rubber hammer. She lit a lamp against the darkness and sorted through the prescription bottles, searching the labels for the friendly comfort. From the big chair, leather creaked, and she thought she saw the silk leaves of the artificial ficus stir in an imagined draft and a figure, hat in hand, pass between her and the light. She was startled by his tempered appearance. He was losing stark edges, fading in patches, as if she could no longer hold him in her vision.

"What do you think she meant by asking that ridiculous question? Sacrifice your own life, surely, but what of hers?"

"You scared me. She is an unusual, sensitive child. But not tonight, I'm tired and I have a headache."

The chimera spoke in an insistent tone. "There is a reason Norah came here to you."

For a moment, she considered engaging him further, but he was already weakening like a fading signal. "Let me go to bed," she said. "I just need a little sleep. I'm going to turn off the light, and you'll disappear."

In the blank darkness among her late husband's effects, a voice whispered. "Never forget, she isn't yours."

9

"Who is Mary Gavin?" Diane asked. "This is my daughter, Erica Quinn. She lives here in Madrid with her daughter, Norah. The girl pointed me right to this spot."

Maya spoke slowly, carefully. "I don't know any Erica, and I don't know any child named Norah. If that's your daughter in the photograph, she's a dead ringer for Mary."

"Maybe someone else can help me?"

"You're welcome to ask around. The rest of the staff will be here shortly, but I'm afraid you are mistaken." She busied herself with the opening chores, and Diane dropped her protest and questions and re-treated to a table in the corner of the tavern. Three times that morning the hounds pricked up their ears and lifted their noses when each new person entered. First came the cook, burly and bald and festooned with tat-toos, who inspected the photograph Diane produced and agreed with a shrug that it might be a younger version of Mary Gavin. The bartender, an older man with a single gray braid that hung to his belt, affirmed more confidently Maya's surmise. "Could be," he said, and began counting his bottles. The waitress, young and pretty and slightly hungover, immediately identified the girl in the photograph. "That's Mary," she said, and laid two fingers over both sides of Erica's long straight hair to cut it off from view. "You have to imagine a totally different do, but otherwise she looks practically the same. What's this from, high school?"

"Do you know a little girl around here named Norah? A third grader? Blonde hair, glasses?"

"Can't say, though there's only about twenty kids total in the ele-mentary school," she said. "Just down the road."

Around eleven the regulars began drifting in, some for takeout coffee, others for an early lunch or late breakfast. Diane watched the customers come and go, working up the courage to approach each stranger. Not a single one knew the little girl, either by description or by name. She fought the urge to flash the photo of Erica and ask for another confirmation, but instead held her place, repeating over and over the mantra Mary Gavin.

What's in a name? Her father would have made a game of it, rolling out the possibilities—Gavin, gave in, haven, heaven. Mistress Mary, quite contrary. Hold on to your name, girls, he'd say, it's the only thing you can be sure of to tell yourself who you are and where you've been. He used to call her Di, Diana, Diamond Lil, Didi, Dimples. Poor Margaret had it worse—Mags, Marge, Margie, Maggie, Meg, Peggy, Millie, Molly, Maghilla, Margarita, Mame. For some reason, his wife was only Peaches, and as she lay dying, Peaches confessed: he thought I was sweet and juicy. Then she returned to her morphine slumber and was heard no more. You become your name, he had told Diane, and not the other way around.

Shortly after noon, the tavern began to fill up with diners, and Diane stretched and walked to the bar. She needed to clear her head, to sift through the information which had distorted her vision of reality. "I'm going out for some fresh air, Maya. But I'll be back, and maybe we can sort this out."

"Take care crossing the highway, and always look both ways," Maya said and hurried the next order to an impatient table.

The wolfhounds rose and followed Diane through the door, unbidden guardians for the road ahead, and she felt oddly comforted by their presence. A number of strays and wanderers loitered by the screened porch, hoping for the chance to sneak inside. Cattle dogs, a pit bull, and a pair of border collie mixes, dirt-dull mutts that belonged to nobody and everybody. They wore lean and hungry looks, a natural sneaky submissiveness born of curses and kicks, just this wary side of their wild cousins. The yellow dog she had seen that morning slunk away, tail low, when the wolfhounds stepped outside. Crisp cool air energized her senses and swept away the lingering fatigue from her cross-country flight and the lack of sleep. She checked for approaching cars and trucks, tried to gauge the distance of the bend that curled around the next hill, but the road was empty, no sound except the huff of the hounds, the crunch of their pads on the gravel. They sauntered past a row of patchwork businesses and houses so baked they appeared almost flat and walked along a dirt berm fronting other reclaimed homes reimagined into colorful, eclectic shrines. The dogs kept pace on the packed ground, now and again bending their heads at an interesting smell, the mark of others who had passed this way. Finn lifted his leg and pissed into a brittle sage, the parched earth sucking in the liquid at once. She played out the two alternatives regarding this Mary Gavin: either Erica incognito or someone else altogether. In her staging of the meeting, the rescue went off without trouble. Erica would acquiesce and spare all queries. Lost in her thoughts, Diane did not notice that the houses had disappeared from both sides of the road and that the road itself veered off in an uncertain rising curve that promised only emptiness. "End of the line, boys."

To the left lay the shell of a derelict baseball park, the grandstand collapsing, the infield overgrown with thistles and clumps of stubborn grass. Stone dugouts harbored mice and the bones of a stray cat. Nothing else stirred on the winter's day, desolate and empty, the ruins of all that had once vibrated with life. A plastic bag skittered across the low hump of the pitcher's mound, and when she closed her eyes, she could imagine the bygone time, the young boys at play, the stands crowded with cheering fans. All vanished, ashes, dirt, memories, and those, too, disappearing. Beyond the outfield fence, she could see another road in the distance, the houses hanging on to the side of a small mountain, and as she crossed the arroyo, she began to pray in earnest, with the plaintive heart of a schoolgirl begging for remedy or reward, of a married woman desperate for a child, of an aging wife asking for her husband to be spared misery. In the deserted hills, quiet as a chapel, she prayed that Norah had told the truth, that the child's mother could be found and restored, that Erica would come home. A pair of magpies streaked across the sky toward a juniper tree, and her hopes lit out after them.

Mick and Finn straightened and pointed their heads to the crest of the road, sighting the approaching figure, and tensed to run. Diane clicked her tongue against the roof of her mouth and they took off, covering great swaths with each stride, kicking up clouds of dust, till they slowed and circled round the person in the distance, long before she recognized who it was. Maya drew closer, waved, and called out a greeting. From ten yards, she shouted, "How long you planning to be out here, nature girl?"

"I've lost track of time."

"It's after two thirty." Maya could read the disappointment on Diane's face. "Why don't I take you to her?"

"You know where she is?"

"Where she has always been. Right around the corner. You can see for yourself that it's Mary, not your daughter."

They veered off the road and followed an inclined path to a small wooden house hidden from view by a stand of conifers. An iron sculpture stretched across the front yard; peeling red and yellow paint covered two horned arcs welded and joined to a central pole. Judging by the height and breadth of a person, the figure could be a stylized cross, a tree, a man. The house behind the sculpture bore the wear of fifty years, the wood bleached to gray, but cheered by the trim around the windows in bright turquoise and the door deep burgundy. A string of feathers—hawk, crow, black-and-white magpie, the barred blue Steller's jay, roadrunner—hung down in a wreath and danced in the breeze with a sound bordering on silence.

Maya knocked, and in the time between the call and response, Diane panicked. Her exhausted heart pounded, a prickle of fear raced up the back of her neck, and intense pressure built in her chest, causing her breath to be rapid and shallow. A film of perspiration on her brow evaporated at once in the cold, thin air, and the frost of sweat gave her a second skin, a mask that hid her true identity.

The door swung open, and there she was.

Nothing had changed, nothing had ever happened. Diane had a fixed memory of her niece at age nine, and she was eternally so despite the young woman before her with the spiked blonde hair and the fine sun lines at her eyes. Familiar but strange in these alien surroundings, the discordant pictures on the walls, the blue jeans and yellow blouse she had never seen, thinner than imagined, but those same eyes, scent of jasmine, and the unabashed smile.

The door swung open, and there she was.

A ghost. An unexpected reminder of the life discarded. A shard of memory found like a lost keepsake, forming into wholeness. She had not thought of her mother in days, yet there was her echo, standing in the door, the least expected.

"Aunt Diane. How did you find me?"

"Erica."

They stood facing one another at the threshold, neither one budging. The hounds jostled for position and whimpered to be let in, and Erica opened the door wide to accommodate both dogs. Taking Diane by the elbow, Maya pushed her in after them. The wolfhounds trotted straight through the sitting room and headed down a hallway on a mission. The women stood in awkward silence like three points of a triangle that seemed to contain within its boundaries a host of secrets.

Maya spoke first. "This seems to be some kind of kin of yours, Mary; least you could do is say hello."

Freed from their traces, the other two broke toward each other and collided in an embrace. Diane exhaled the chaos in her body, and Erica allowed herself a moment's forgiveness. They held on, wordless, until Erica pulled away and took in her aunt at arm's length. "I'm so sorry."

"Erica, Erica, let me look at you."

"Is there something wrong with my mother? Is that why you've come?"

A decade's tension broke, and the story spilled as from a cracked dam. "So this is where you've been, this is what happened to you."

"Is it my mother?"

"No, it's not your mother, though God knows why you don't go home, and why you felt the need to call and be so mysterious. It's not your mother, she's fine. It's the little visitor you sent her way who has become too much for her. There's been trouble at the school, and I am concerned, we are all worried about the child. She stood up in front of the entire third grade and claimed to be an angel of the Lord. She said an angel of destruction, and we thought that . . . was long over." Reading the confusion in her niece's eyes, she turned to Maya. "Her mother does not know what to do with such a child."

Stunned and remembering, her eyes welling with tears, Erica spoke in a rueful tone, so softly as to not wake a soul. "My baby—"

10

Norah could not stop talking about the bridge. From the moment on the monkeybars when she first saw its twin arches and fretwork of cables, precise and beautiful in the distance, she wanted to be close to its splendor. Beyond the circumscribed boundaries of the neighborhood, the bridge funneled traffic over the Monongahela morning and night, leading away from home and toward the city. She pleaded with Sean to tell her all about it. He had made the journey across many times by bus and by car—his father's people lived on the other side—but not as often lately and never on foot. The danger of the bridge was legendary. Parents warned their children of falling, of drowning, of disappearing forever, and young boys and girls were forbidden to go anywhere near it. Only the older teenagers, the toughs who knew all about sex and drugs and the meaning of curse words, flouted the restriction. Yet the tall tales came as surely as summer vacation and ghost stories, of a boy who had been drinking too much beer, or a girl, full of shame and hopelessness, who slipped away into the waters by accident or design.

"Please, please," she said. "Remember that peregrine flying around here in January? I'll bet its nest is up under the steelwork. They like the vantage of the highest point around."

Sean studied the bruise on her face. "We'd get in trouble if they find out."

"There's something I want to show you, and I guarantee none of the grown-ups will ever know."

March brought mild temperatures, and on the month's first Saturday they escaped, announcing to Mrs. Quinn that they were going for a walk. Within an hour, they had strolled beyond the converted farmhouses with their small fenced yards, past the Craftsmen and half-timbered Tudors and Foursquares on more crowded streets, and on to the town proper. Built for the immigrant factory workers during the steel boom, the blocks of brownstones and storefronts now showed signs of neglect and early decay. The last of the mills ran only one furnace, and she was slated for demolition in the fall. Jobs had gone overseas, and only the old-timers hung around, drifting aimlessly between the VFW club and the cigar store where they bought lottery tickets and the afternoon's *Press*. Glass and cigarette butts littered the gutters, and scraps of paper blew across the cracked sidewalks. An Italian restaurant was shuttered and neglected. A toy shop that Sean remembered visiting with his father had been replaced by a job-training center. Across the street, behind the ornate scrollwork fencing of the Glass and Iron Workers Bank, a man sat against the brick wall with a brown bag between his legs, his face as vacant as a doll's.

Following the old streetcar tracks, they rounded a corner, and the bridge appeared all at once, much bigger and more imposing so close. The steel framework had been painted taxi yellow, and the capped rivets, big as a child's head, studded the beams and held it all together. The lattice arched into the pale blue sky, and as they crossed the street to its deck, the opposite shore momentarily disappeared from view. Norah hastened her step, bouncing with excitement, as Sean slowed, a queasy fear rumbling in his stomach. The walkway formed a narrow lane between two fences—a guard against the traffic, and a railing protecting travelers from the edge. She had moved six feet onto the lane before he realized she intended to cross.

"I can't do it," he hollered. "I don't like bridges."

"Have I ever let you down?" With one arm outstretched, she begged him to follow, and he ran to take her hand, making sure that she walked on the outside, nearest the edge. Norah led him past his anxieties and out onto the middle of the span. A line of cars crossed the bridge, the vibrations hummed under their feet, and at the base of each pole holding up a section of fencing, the worn and pockmarked cement appeared ready to crumble and give way. Fifty feet below, the swollen river rolled, the shadows from the struts and arc of the bridge rippling on the surface. He did not dare unclench his grip but slowly composed his nerves enough to glance beyond the structure's limits. Next to him, Norah stuck her toes beneath the fencing, and as she leaned tight against the railing, the fabric of her jacket poked through the spaces between the bars. He wanted her to back away to a safer spot but she seemed oblivious to the peril, happily suspended in the air, her face full to the breeze, the bruise on her cheek a red plum, her eyes hidden behind the sun in her glasses.

In desperation, he looked up at the elegance of cabling webbed between the arches. "I don't see any nest," he said. "Can we go now?"

"You don't believe me, do you, Sean?" She wrenched her hand away and stretched both arms from her sides. "What would it take to convince you? Shall I take off right here and fly away?"

"Don't even kid, Norah." A chill ran through him and he felt like crying. "Can we go? You're scaring me—"

"See and believe." She pointed over the river. Streaking from the treeline, a falcon appeared from nowhere. The bird's call echoed across the valley, and it lifted its wings for drag and spread its talons, landing on an iron support not twenty feet above their heads. "Cool," Norah said. "We have to bring the kids from class. Now do you believe?"

And seeing the doubt written on his face, she folded her hands in prayer. He pulled at her sleeve, anxious to be off the bridge. A dark mass formed on the southern horizon, a black legion over the water, and as the flock drew near, the sound became deafening, a cacophony of birdscream, and its rolling rhythm crossed above them and blotted out the sun, and over the dark center of her eyes beat their winged reflection.

11

Sharp aromas pervaded the kitchen. The smell of chile peppers drying on a string next to the window. Lemon in the tea mingling with the sandalwood hand lotion each time Diane touched the warm porcelain cup. Mesquite and hickory burned in the woodstove, around which the wolfhounds dozed like bears in hibernation, their rhythmic breathing marking the silence. Each woman searched in vain for a way to begin the conversation. They drank their tea. Confrontation was studiously avoided. Diane studied the whimsical curtains, repeating patterns of carrots on a yellow field, and the ancient appliances, the chipped avocado refrigerator, the dark brown oven, both rescued from Albuquerque flea markets. A simple daisy in a plain wooden frame adorned the whitewashed walls. She looked at her niece, revising her mental picture of the girl, and wondered if the cropped bleached hair was some disguise, a way to blend underground through such a bold stroke. Her friend Maya hovered around the tiny kitchen, as if she had been there many times before.

The women waited and hoped for the words to come. When Diane checked to see how much time had passed in this manner, she was surprised to find that her watch had stopped. Shaking the kinks from nose to tail, the dogs uncoiled and readied themselves to go the moment that Maya inched from her chair. She smiled, finally understanding the situational etiquette, and then rolled her eyes from one woman to the other. "I should have gotten those boys home hours ago, and let you girls catch up in privacy. You'll give me a call later, Mary? So nice to have met you—"

"Call me Diane." She rose from her chair. "It's Diane Cicogna, and I'm so sorry that I told a fib earlier. I just thought you would be more helpful if I came across as a mother looking for her daughter."

"Ask and ye shall receive." With her open palm, Maya tapped her thigh, and the dogs trotted to the front door.

Erica followed Maya and held her hands at the threshold. "I'm sorry for all the deceptions. Hers, and mine."

"No need to apologize for what you choose to conceal or to reveal. Everyone has a story they choose to tell. I have shames that I've never confessed to another soul, not even to Mick or Finn, and a dog will listen to you, no judgment." She kissed her lightly on the cheek. "Just be kind to your auntie."

Erica found her carting the teacups to the metal sink, idly rinsing dishes to stave off her curiosity. Laying a hand upon her aunt's shoulder, she apologized.

"Should I call you Erica? Or are you Mary?"

"Let me show you something." With no more than a nod, she led her through the back of the house, out a door, and across a yard cluttered with clay pots and pieces of twisted, rusting metal. Excavated into the side of a hill, a shed the size of a two-car garage provided a long southern exposure. Inside the building, Diane could see at once the vantage of the light, even at this weak hour, and the openness of space that reminded her of the windowed vista of the beach house of her childhood. In the center of the room, wrapped around a massive post that supported the roof at its apex, stood a crude round table. Bouquets of brushes and palette knives rested points up in coffee cans and glass jars of a dozen shapes and sizes. A handmade rack held small rolls of canvas, slats of hickory, and measuring tools, and along the table's surface ran a river of colors, paints in pots, tubes, powders. Splatters on the floor spread as wild and violent as a murdered clown. Gesso, varnishes, turpentine, and resins huddled in toxic confederation. A toolbox overflowed with woodprinting tools, menacing carvers, brayers, pine blocks, zinc intaglio plates, chisels, and pastes. Diane ran her fingertips over the strange tools as she circled the table, stopping in front of a new canvas, stretched and prepped, which faced an empty stool. She imagined Erica in action. "Let me see what you have made."

"It's all around you." She waved her arms like a game show model, but her voice deepened in tone. "What I don't like I sell in a shop in town where I work, or once or twice a year in Santa Fe or Albuquerque. What I can't part with stays right here."

The walls begged for slow contemplation, and Diane strolled as if it were Sunday in the museum and gathered in the pictures. In the far corner, another series. "*Retablos?* I just saw my first ones this morning in a coffee shop down in Albuquerque." She inspected them more closely. "But I see you have made them your own."

"These are the first things I painted when I was teaching myself how to paint. They're not very good, and I made many wrong turns before I found how I wanted to live my life."

Seven paintings clustered on the wall behind a table as simple as an altar. Nearest to her, a taciturn state trooper, wrapped tight in his dark uniform, stood in a bleak and arid landscape, the earth bleached to bone, the sky bleeding to dusk, and along the darkest edge at the top copper border, a buzzard circled black against black. Diane tiptoed and craned to take a closer look, spied the outline of Virginia painted on his peaked cap, and reflected in the twin lenses of his mirrored sunglasses the familiar mushroom of an atomic explosion. The expression on his face could easily be mistaken for joy. Second in the series, a hyperrealistic close-up of a counter scene at an old-fashioned diner. In the background, a mixer twirled and bubbled up a frothy chocolate milkshake. Stacked beside the machine, a half dozen hamburgers prim in their paper wrappers, and on the top, an unwrapped sandwich. Instead of lettuce protruding from underneath the bun, she had torn and glued in impasto scraps of twenty-dollar bills. An order of bullets stood in the French fry holsters. In the foreground, standing on a shiny counter, a salt and pepper shaker set, capped by the faces of two men, gagged and furious.

The only horizontal painting was worked in a deliberate style more primitive and traditional, like the folk art at the Café de Santeros. In imitation of a Madonna and child, a grandmother and granddaughter faced the viewer head-on. The child held a glass chalice filled with milk, and nearly invisible, etched on the white surface, were a skull and crossbones. Despite the simplicity of style, Diane recognized the girl at once by the glasses and toothy smile, the ragged crown of hair and beatific look in her eyes that gave her away as Norah, but Diane could not see her sister in the portrait of the older woman. Perhaps, she thought to herself, this is how Erica imagines her mother after years apart, but this woman was no Margaret. Too old, and crazed in the eyes. Escaping the frame, in the left-hand corner, a bare foot and ankle, the tip of one large white wing.

Protruding from the wall at the center of the group was a small shadow box covered in tin, and when Diane stepped in front of a sensor, a small light came on behind the surface and poured through a constellation of pinholes punched through the metal. Initially, the beam obscured the hammered face of a man and, above the hair like a sign, a pen with a trigger. Next to the shattered face was a cartoon drawing of an Indian maid, like the girl on the Land O'Lakes box, offering instead of the usual carton a new baby molded from butter. Beside her, a man with radio antennae sticking straight out of his scalp, his wasted eyes staring at a stack of pancakes, and above, obscured by a melting pat of butter and a lake of maple syrup, the face of Jesus burned onto the surface. The last *retablo* featured a uniformed waitress with a magnificent beehive hairdo spun three times the size of her head, and nesting in the tresses, seven blackbirds, a pistol, and a bus ticket stamped H-O-M-E. In the corner stood a wooden statue thin as a candle and three feet high. Diane took it for an ascetic santo, but on inspection, she saw that the cross on his chest was actually a bandolier packed with ammunition and the staff in his hand was a semiautomatic machine gun. "Who are these saints of yours?"

"They are the people I met ten years ago when I ran away, the people who tried to protect me or warn me that I was on the wrong path."

Diane put her hand on the statue and felt at once a deep sense of fatigue and despair. "And this one?"

"El diablo."

"You should come home and see your mother. She's not the way at all that you've pictured her." Diane crossed to the picture of the woman and the child. "Although I'd recognize the girl anywhere. This looks just like Norah."

"Who?"

Surprised by the answer, Diane faced her and pointed to the scene. "This picture of your mother and your daughter."

Erica put her fingers to her lips. "That's not who you think it is. That little girl is one of the people along the way—"

"It looks just like your daughter."

Her eyes searched Diane's face for some intent of cruelty, but she saw only that her aunt was sincerely puzzled. "There never was a baby. I was pregnant, yes, but I didn't have the baby."

"But what about Norah?" Diane insisted. "She said she was your daughter."

"I don't know anyone named Norah. Wiley ditched me in the middle of nowhere." Trembling, she sat on a stool and wrapped her arms across her waist. "When you first told me about the child, all I could think about was the one I was expecting, but not a real child."

"But I saw her, I talked to her. The girl in the picture."

"That girl's name is Una Gavin. A nine-year-old I met on the road. Her mother ran out on her. I had no baby."

"But she's with your mother and says she is your daughter. Why would Margaret lie about such a thing? The girl calls her Gramma and knows where you live, what you did. She told me how to find you. Your daughter knows all about the Angels of Destruction—"

"I tell you," she said in a forceful tone of voice, "there is no Norah."

12

Hair still wet from the bath, Sean Fallon stood at the stormdoor, watching the sun set on another weekend. Barefoot and ready for bed, he savored the fresh air on his skin and was transfixed by contrails pluming across the empty sky, reflecting the reds and oranges of the disappearing star. The pants crept up his ankles, and the shirt was too small and tight, but he would not part with the cowboy pajamas that his father had given him on his seventh birthday. Outside on the street, an older boy flashed by on a bicycle, trying to beat the darkness home. In the kitchen, his mother checked the bubbling casserole and swore softly when her forearm grazed the oven rack. Sean dreaded Sunday evenings, for this last hour marked the end of freedom from school. Macaroni and cheese, apple pie, a half hour to read or watch TV, and so to bed. He would lie there alone in the dark while she puttered or listened to the radio, and then after she performed her nightly rituals, the house would go quiet before the creaks and moans and ticks and knocks that threatened to never end.

Venus appeared on the horizon, just as Sean had nearly run out of hope waiting for the chance to make a wish, though he did so with some reluctance, knowing that so far every talisman had failed to gather the desired result. Testing his faith in such notions risked inevitable disappointment and raised questions of fate and circumstance that he would rather not trust. They said grace together over two plates with frugal servings. His mother smiled at him, and he wanted to believe. In her tired eyes, some hope that he would fall asleep early this night.

Over dessert, Sean asked, "Mom, you know the bridge in town? How high is it to the water?"

The question caught her with a swallow of milk. "Forty, fifty feet I'd guess."

"And how deep is the river?"

"Scan, why do you ask?"

"A report for school." He pretended to change the subject. "Do you know when the birds come back in spring?"

She attacked her pie. "When the weather's warm enough. A week or so, middle of March. I've seen robins in a snowstorm around here, so maybe they get fooled and come back earlier."

He longed to tell her about the incident on the bridge, and the boy who froze in the middle of the monkeybars, the march of the animals, that afternoon when the sun refused to set, the origami birds, the balancing toy, her command of the crows and sudden appearance in two places at once and all the signs and wonders in his life since Norah arrived, but he felt that his confession would cause only greater troubles. His father was disappearing beyond reach, and even if Scan could find him, he would not share such secrets now. Teachers were out of all consideration. Classmates would make a joke of the evidence, or worse, torture her with their teasing. Norah was the only soul he could tell his troubles to, but the trouble was Norah.

Later, in the sanctuary of his room, Sean heard an airplane pass overhead, and though he had never flown anywhere, he longed to be up in the air and press his face against the glass above the mountains and the forest, the river and the bridge, the fading rooftops and toy cars, the ant people heading home, the doors and windows of the houses, and he would see through his own window and into his own dark eyes. When Norah said jump, he would leap off the bridge, he would fly. The falcon that first morning had stopped in midair, spread its wings, and floated still, riding the steadying current, and then, on a pendulum, tipped one feather, swept across the sky, and hurtled mercilessly toward the earth.

13

"Poor old thing, she's exhausted. We were up talking till three in the morning, and what with the trip out here and so emotional." Erica kept her voice low. "She's in the back still asleep. And tell the truth, I'm not so hot myself."

Maya dumped the leftover wine down the sink, into the red-stained metal, the glasses rimmed with lipstick, and the dishes caked with rice and beans. Shaking two fingers under the running water, she waited for the cold stream to change temperature.

"Leave those. I took a long shower this morning, and it'll be a couple hours for that old water heater to work." Erica let the dogs out, and they crossed the patio into the open studio. Cold air filtered in through the ajar door. "I should have told you long ago, Maya, what brought me here. This boy and I ran off from home when I was still in high school. We were headed west to this . . . cult. To join the revolution, but the revolution never came. The Angels of Destruction were going to save the world by destroying all that was evil, but we got lost along the way. We had some trouble with the law. And later, I found out I was pregnant in Albuquerque, but he had split. Abandoned me with a couple of dollars in a strange place. I felt like an alien landed in the middle of nowhere. A knocked-up Martian."

She crossed to the refrigerator, filled a glass with carrot juice, and drained it in one swallow. Maya sat at the kitchen table, the light filtering through her fine hair.

"I couldn't have the baby. I wasn't even eighteen, and I couldn't go home, because of what we did on the road. We did a horrible thing, and that's why I'm here, why I changed my name. My real name is Erica Quinn, like she told you."

"So she's here to take you home?"

"I can't go back. If the police knew I was there, they'd arrest me. Lock me up in jail, or worse. I couldn't even risk contacting my friends, my mom and dad—" With a sigh, she stopped herself and waited for the feeling to pass. "My aunt told me he died about five or six years ago."

"That boy?"

"No, yes. Him too. But she said my father is dead, just like that. You sit in a spot and don't realize everything you left is changing too, and you think that maybe someday you'll get the chance, but then it's too late." A tear rolled down her cheek and she wiped it away with the back of her hand. When she was a child of five, Erica thought her father a giant, for he could circle her wrist between his finger and thumb. The last time she saw him, she had to bow slightly to kiss him goodnight on his whiskered cheek.

"You miss him, Mary?"

"When I left home I was furious with him for all he withheld, terrible secrets, but time goes by, you see them from a different perspective, what they had to do just to live their lives while hiding it all, even from themselves. He was right, at least, about Wiley."

"The boy you ran away with?"

"Aunt Diane said that he blew himself up trying to make a bomb. Just a couple of months after he ditched me. I'm not glad it happened; on the other hand, I'm not sad he's gone. He hurt me. I had nothing, you understand. Some money he'd stolen, but that lasted me precisely one month, and I spent another three on the skids till I found a job waiting tables at the Waffle House out by the airport, and I'd still be there with a child. Took me another two years to save up enough money to come up here and find this place—remember what a hole in the wall it was?"

"First time we met, you were on your hands and knees scrubbing this floor. More like praying." Maya smiled at the memory. "Praying for me to come along and help you."

Erica grabbed her hand. "That's right."

The click of nails across the ceramic tiles heralded the arrival of the dogs. Pausing to sniff the disturbed air in the kitchen, they wagged their tails out of politeness, then moved to the hallway, having heard a stirring in the spare bedroom long before the humans, to await Diane's entrance. She emerged, momentarily taken aback by the sudden strangeness of her situation, weaving through her overtired memory to place them, and herself. "Good morning, you devils." They lifted their noses, and she scratched one bearded chin and then the other.

On the way into the kitchen, Diane tripped over a flat piece of pine that marked the threshold, lost her footing, and flew, paddling the air like a double-bladed windmill to catch her balance, banging the meaty part of her thigh against the table's edge. The teacups separated from their saucers. A dish fell to the tiles and shattered into a hundred little pieces. The dogs barked at the new game, and Maya jumped up to steady her while Erica shooed them away from the shards.

"Jesus, Mary, and Joseph," she said. "You'll send the whole house down upon our ears. Are you all right, Aunt Diane?"

"Who would nail a board there, right in the middle of the one room with the most traffic? A person could break a neck." She hobbled to a chair. "I'm fine, though this leg will never be the same. And good morning to you, Maya, and to you, Erica or Mary, whichever it is."

"Just catching her up on our conversation last night. The saga of Mary Gavin." She swept the pieces into a dustpan and dumped the mess into the trash. With a twist of the wrist, she put the kettle on to boil.

Her aunt rubbed the sore spot and sat down next to Maya. "We're used to switching names. Most of my childhood, I'm Diane Mullins. Along comes Big Joe Cicogna, and all of a sudden everyone thinks I'm Italian."

Tracing a signature on the tabletop, Maya said, "I was born Sophie Voorsanger in Brooklyn, New York, but I haven't even *said* that name in thirty years. Left it all behind with the past." She looked up from her invisible writing. "Maya is a Hindu concept for the ways we allow the material world to disguise the reality of the spiritual. That's why I chose the name. *La vida es sueño.*"

Through the open curtains, Erica watched the man out by the fir trees grab the sculpture to hoist himself to his feet. Older now, his hair gone white, he was thinner and slightly humpbacked, but still the wound suppurated, his eye had swollen shut, and the stain on his shirt rusted and spread into the shape of a panhandle. In his right fist, he grasped the blunderbuss of a pen, dripping red ink, and seconds after she first conjured him, the dead man took the first lurching steps toward the house.

"And I'm Mary Gavin because Erica Quinn once killed a man."

"Killed a man?" Diane asked.

"In a grocery store in Garrison's Creek, Oklahoma. Wiley told me to wait outside with a gun and to come in if there was any trouble, and there was trouble. He looked like he had a gun too, and was going to shoot Wiley, and Wiley fired, then I fired, and we were so scared we ran out."

Diane stood and reached out to her. "You poor thing, don't you know? That man survived. We heard from the FBI that he was one of their best leads. The man was wounded, but he lived and gave the police a description of you two, but you must have been long gone—"

"He was dead."

"No," she insisted, heartbroken at the girl's anguish. "You never heard?"

In the yard, a breeze twirled the wreath of feathers, and the sun baked the ground. Slumped against the counter, Erica slid to the floor and stayed there, voiceless and motionless, while her aunt rambled, telling her over and again that the dead man was actually alive. Guilt had plagued her for ten years, seeped into her bones and infected her nervous system, spreading into the muscles, the brain, the heart. Remorse for the dead man in Oklahoma, for all she had lost, all she had failed to do. The knot in her stomach loosened, and she felt as if her insides had been scoured. She began to weep for her father, her mother, herself. Puzzled, the dogs strolled over to Erica seated on the tiles and stuck their noses in her face, trying to discover the scent behind her sadness.

OVER THE HILL they traveled, three weird sisters: the oldest hobbling on an injured leg, her pink coat flapping in the wind; a stick-thin witch accompanied by two panting hounds from hell; and in between, the refugee from her own past, stumbling over ruts in the road, crushing underfoot the tiny cacti which sprouted like toadstools wherever water collected. Two dusty caballeros rode by on quarter horses and tipped their broad-brimmed hats. A herd of Harleys roared down the curve of the mountain, headed for the Mine Shaft. From a ramshackle house, a door exploded open and two toddlers escaped into a dirt yard, followed immediately by a barefoot woman who stepped out into the bright light to lasso them in. Blind to all but her thoughts, Erica put one foot in front of the other and kept up only at her companions' insistence. They linked arms and saved her from collapsing on the march and melting under the late-winter sun. Now that there was a second chance, she wanted nothing more than to curl up and sleep for another decade, but her aunt was prattling on about a strange girl.

"This child," Diane said, "is obviously an imposter. First, she claims to be your daughter sent from New Mexico. Then she claims to be an angel of the Lord. Your mother is in on this somehow."

"But is she an angel?" Erica asked.

Diane snorted and Maya laid a hand upon the girl's shoulder, and together, they let the matter pass.

They reached the steps to the tavern, and the yellow dog sunbathing on the porch creaked to its feet and scampered down the road. When they were inside in the darkness, Erica felt much better. The brutal sunshine had pierced her skull and given her a headache. Maya held up two fingers and said, "*Dos* margaritas," and then added her thumb. "Make it three. I'm in." Close to the tiny stage, they found an empty table, and as soon as the glasses were set down the women began drinking and licking the salt from their lips.

"Let me be the practical one," Maya said. "You want Mary to come back with you to see what this girl is all about—"

"And to be with her poor mother."

Erica's eyes shone with tears, for she was gazing into a distance beyond the present, visiting again the entangled past.

"But what about this shooting?" Maya asked. "Can she still get in trouble for that if someone recognizes her and turns her in to the police? What's the statute of limitations on such a thing? Is anyone still looking for her?"

Erica set down her nearly empty glass. "That's not all we did. We stole a couple of cars—we even lost one entirely—and Wiley robbed four places I know about."

"A regular Bonnie and Clyde," Maya said.

"Not as bad as all that, but still I don't want to end up in jail for what I did when I was young and foolish. I'd like to help you, help my mother, but—"

Putting a finger to her lips, Diane leaned forward and motioned them to form a triangle. Foreheads nearly touching, she whispered, "I know a man in Washington who can tell us if there's any danger, if the Feds are still hunting you. He's an old beau of your mother's."

When Erica laughed, a hiccup escaped with a bang. "My mother with a boyfriend? I can't imagine."

"There's a lot you don't know about your mother. She almost ran away with him, just like you, when she was your age. His name was Jackson, and he was so in love with her, but her sense of propriety held her back. There's a great deal you don't know about all of us."

Erica thought of her father, bent over the hospital cots, the needle poised above his suffering victims. "But I can't run the risk of someone turning me in."

"Jackson can be trusted, and besides, I'll make up some excuse for the call and just casually ask about your case. But the authorities must not be looking very hard. You've been missing ten years, and they probably think you are dead or left the country."

"But the other Angels of Destruction?" her niece asked.

"All captured, except for you, and none of them mentioned your name. Two were caught trying to sneak into Canada on the Vancouver ferry. Another one arrested at Berkeley for threatening President Ford. The others got away for two or three years, but they're all gone, done their time I expect, probably out of jail already."

"I don't want to go to jail. I'm worried about getting caught if I go home."

Maya raised her glass. "It could work, you know, if you're careful. Follow the rules. Stay low, keep to yourself, don't talk to strangers. You've been underground so long they have you buried. You've become Mary Gavin, and for all anyone knows that's who you are."

"To Mary Gavin." Diane joined the toast. A sip remained in her chalice. The three glasses chimed, waking the dogs beneath the table.

· 14 ·

A note and accompanying flyer had been sent home with the school-children announcing, in rhetoric bordering on the hysteric, a case of head lice in the first grade. Precautions were spelled out in graphic detail, complete with a close-up illustration of a louse, so Margaret made Norah wash her hair, rinse and repeat, and sit under a strong light for a thorough combing and inspection of the girl's scalp. Norah knelt and fidgeted with her nails while the teeth glided through her still-wet hair. From the easy chair, Margaret concentrated on the simple task, taking care not to snag the comb on the tangles of split ends and marveling at the ragged lengths. With each stroke, the pain in her hands flared, but she persisted. "Who attacked you with the scissors, darling? This is all hacked and uneven back here."

"I cut my own hair."

"We'll get you a proper haircut." She smoothed the girl's head with her free palm. "Maybe in time for Easter. When the weather gets warm, you won't be able to hide under a hood."

"I never pay much attention, just snip and you're done."

Margaret cupped her hand around the nape of the girl's neck and bent around to peer into her pale eyes. The bruise on her face was fading and had split in two. Barely touching a fingertip to the cheekbone, she traced the contours of the mark, remembering through the smoothness of her skin, remembering a girl through the whiteness in her eyes and the specked irises, remembering through the fineness of her hair, the delicate fretwork of bone and musculature. She was not resurrecting Erica, but lost in her own childhood, beholding her reflection. As a child, she had an ardent faith, said her prayers before every meal, before bedtime, prayers of thanksgiving or supplication. As a child, she readily believed in angels, guardians at her shoulder, Gabriel to Mary, avenging Michael, the angel of Exodus, sent ahead to protect the chosen people. But she had not thought about such things for decades, only the twisted version of Wiley Rinnick's delusions. And then, the one who visited her in her grief, the man in the fedora, who seemed at times to her an outcast from heaven, now that heaven had closed. Nothing left to believe, faint echoes of a forgotten faith until this girl, Norah, dropped from the sky. She was new and freshly scrubbed. The bottoms of her feet were puckered with ripples of loose skin. A scab on her ankle had fallen off in the tub and left a clear pink spot the size of a dime.

Margaret folded back the collar of the child's robe. "What do you say we go shopping soon? You could use some new clothes, and I'd like to take you downtown to Pittsburgh, maybe go to the zoo or the children's museum." She pictured them holding hands as they crossed the street. "And maybe this summer, I can take you to the beach where I went when I was your age."

Norah interrupted her reverie. "Where I come from, there was no one to cut my hair, so I just reached around with the scissors. I learned to take care of myself."

"You certainly did, and you did a good job. But I'm here now, and I'd like you to feel at home, and if you need a haircut or want to get a proper dress for Easter, or maybe go somewhere for a special occasion, you just let me know."

"Easter is a long way off."

"Not so long at all. Spring will be here before you know it, and summer. Maybe we could ask your little friend along."

"You have been very kind to me, Mrs. Quinn. I wish I could stay with you."

"You must call me Gramma, like when my sister was here. All the time now. My home is your home."

The child threw out her arms and hugged Margaret around the neck. The scent of baby shampoo filled the air. Margaret spoke cheek to cheek. "I want to tell you something, not because I expect any answer, but because sometimes you just need to say it, do you understand? I love you."

The girl squeezed more tightly, nearly choking her, and said something that Margaret could not hear, she could not hear any sound but the pounding of her own heart, and the whisper of the oceans from the girl's lips into the shell of her ear.

15

Through the tiny window, Erica watched the western mountains disappear as the airplane rose and floated over a sea of clouds. In every direction but up, the unbroken surface shone brilliant white, cleaner than snow, to the horizon where, well met by a deep and lasting blue, the universe became circumscribed by what could be seen through an oval porthole spidered with frost.

Over the course of a week, Maya, Erica, and Diane had worked out the details for traveling under an assumed name, for tending to Mary Gavin's life while its owner was away. Erica and Diane left Albuquerque for Washington two months to the day from Norah's sudden appearance. Diane would make the necessary phone calls, find out from Jackson whether anyone was still looking for the fugitive, whether she was still in trouble with the law, and then they planned to drive to Pennsylvania to see Margaret and the strange little girl who had invaded her life.

"Would you believe I've never been above the clouds?" she told her aunt, sitting beside her. "I always imagined heaven was here. Golden gates and angels. I met a girl named Una, and she lived in the middle of a dark forest in a magical cottage, and I got sick there. Sick enough to die. They fed me on a weak soup and a nightly dose of sleeping potion. I think she wanted me to stay because she knew the trouble ahead."

"What happened to her?"

"Una's parents abandoned her. Took off for Canada instead of Vietnam. Ending up in hiding like me, I guess, or dead or lost. And they left the baby in the cabin in the woods. The grandmother thought we were her son and his wife come back for the little girl."

"This is when you were with Wiley."

"Wiley, yes." She traced the circle on her fold-down tray. "Love makes you crazy. For the one and only time, I lived in a kind of trance, always wanting him—not just for the sex, though that was insane—but for his presence nearby, which somehow softened all else. He could be in the next room, or just outside the door, and I would feel better knowing he was close at hand. Have you ever been in love this way? Where you feel just uncorked, your mind and body and spirit open and you want to give back that same sensation to him? But he didn't want me, not that way. And the worst part is they can hurt you with impunity, refuse your very soul, yet part of you goes on loving."

"Sounds like your mother."

"My mom and my dad?"

"Your mother and you."

"Right. I guess we've all broken hearts without intending to."

Diane chuckled softly to herself and stared at the seats fanned out in front of her. A businessman sipped a black coffee and checked yesterday's stocks. A row of teenagers dealt another round of cards and laughed the time away. A young mother held an infant in her lap, the boy's eyes wide with curiosity, his fingers entwined in her hair. Lovingly she bent and kissed him on the forehead and turned the page of her novel. "Some people are quite capable of extraordinary forgiveness," Diane said.

Erica pressed her skull against the cold window glass. "Maybe that's why she latched onto me and tried to keep me there. Una. What will my mother think when I come home? Why didn't you tell her you were coming to get me?"

Laying her hand upon her niece's arm, Diane pulled her to attention. "I had to do this on my own. If I make it, I earn her trust. I've never told another person this, not even your mother, but your uncle was, how can I put this, a skirt chaser. Flirting with waitresses and shopgirls right in front of me. But didn't I know about the affairs? What did he take me for? Once he even made a pass at your mother, down at the shore. You remember those summers? Who knows, too much sun, too many beers, and I was supposed to be asleep in the hammock in the shade, but I saw him, saw her, his big hairy hand sliding beneath the strap of her bathing suit as he leans over to nuzzle her neck, and she just hauls off and slaps him smack on the face. I can still picture him, his paw holding his cheek where she hit him, like he was stung by a jellyfish. A look of stupid wonder, how could she do such a thing? Of course, he never mentioned it to me, probably forgot about the whole incident. Man like him, not the first time he was refused, I'll bet. But your mother never said anything either, not a word, and you know, I was hurt at first and didn't completely trust her for some years after that, because you're supposed to tell your sister. But when you vanished and later when your father passed, I came to understand her nature better, the secrets and silences. She lives in a different world, Margaret does, a world of her own desire to live free from conflict. Joe was forgiven the moment she swatted him. She began to put things back in place when she pulled up her strap."

"I can't picture Uncle Joe making a pass at my mother. I'm sorry for you, of course."

"So hard to believe? But this isn't about Joe, his brains were in his pants. And it isn't even about being a good sister and confiding in the one person who loves you unconditionally. It's about secrets and your mother and your daughter—"

Erica glared at her.

"The one pretending to be your daughter, or, should I say, pretending to be her granddaughter. Margaret is using her to put her world back in order. She's concocted some ruse as a way of finding forgiveness."

"But who must be forgiven?"

"All of us seek forgiveness." The baby boy in the row ahead stood on his mother's lap and peered over the top of the seat. Searching the faces swirling in his ken, he locked onto Diane and smiled, attempting to elicit smile in return. When he was rewarded with not one but two admiring looks, his face lit with joy, and he bounced and clapped and shouted his wordless hosanna. Diane turned to her niece. "You . . . for leaving, and your mother for letting you go."

"And what does this Norah have to do with it? How did she know where to find me or find my mother? Where do you suppose she came from?"

The boy was squealing, cooing, begging for their attention. "I'm afraid to guess," Diane said, and gave herself over to the happy child.

16

In later years, when the incidents passed into legend, the acts became known as the Week of the Miracles and the Seduction of the Innocents. Each school day, Norah told stories about angels and the afterlife, luring a small clot of children to the radiant sound of her words, the inspiration of her very breath. On a damp March morning, a cluster gathered round her on the sidewalk in front of the school ahead of the first bell.

"The time is at hand," Norah said on Monday. "I will tell you all my secrets if you will believe. I will answer every question and show you the way."

Five third graders were there: Sean Fallon, Mark Bellagio, Sharon Hopper, Dori Tilghman, and Lucas Ford. They huddled close, noses red from the cold, vapors exploding from their open mouths with every breath. Teachers and students streamed by this knot on the walk, too busy to take notice.

"First you must understand what eternity is. Calendars and clocks are modern inventions to track time. Long ago, people watched the moon to tell the month and week, and used sundials and followed the stars to mark the hours. But these are measurements of what you cannot measure. This day, March fourth, is just one of many days that stretch out behind and forward in a line. This minute is but a point on a line."

Sharon yawned and covered her mouth with the back of her hand.

"You believe in the immortal soul, don't you, Sharon?"

"After you die," she said, "your soul goes on forever in heaven. Or hell."

"Forever stretches both ways. No beginning, and no end. If you are eternal, you have no end, or no beginning."

Lucas asked, "What about your birthday? The day you were born?"

"I know," Dori said. "You live in your mother's stomach for nine months before you are born."

"Right," Norah said. "But where were you before that?"

"Nowhere?" Lucas offered.

"If a line extends in two directions from a single point, and it is called eternity, there can be no beginning, if it has no end. It simply is. You is. Are. My first secret is that you have always existed and will continue to exist."

The bell rang and they entered the school in a daze. The morning snailed by: Mrs. Patterson talking without saying a thing. Problems on the blackboard, the messy business of fractions, piled up one upon the next. At the break for lunch, the six children grabbed their paper bags and lunchboxes and went to their table in the corner of the cafeteria. Small talk accompanied sandwiches and chips. They waited for Norah to finish her cup of peaches and begin again. In the waxy film of the tabletop, she pressed her fingertip to create a point and drew a line that ended in a final point. "Those who truly believe must conquer time. It's not the length of your life that matters if you will always be—"

"Conquer time? You can't stop time," Dori said.

Sean looked down at the remains of his tunafish sandwich and felt ill.

"Don't be so stubborn," Norah said. "Who is good at counting off the time?"

Sharon raised her hand. "Like counting to sixty seconds to make a minute?"

"You have to say Mississippi or you'll go too fast," Sean said. "One-Mississippi, two-Mississippi . . . like that. My dad taught me how." He blushed, and Norah patted him quickly on the hand.

In the center of a stage that ran the length of the cafeteria, a large clock ticked away the passing seconds. Norah pointed to the sweeping arm. "When the red hand gets to the top of the minute, start counting."

Pushing their chairs from the table, they all faced the stage and concentrated on the dial, and at the moment she had instructed, they whispered the chant in unison. Five seconds in, Dori and Mark stopped counting and were afraid. Sharon and Lucas checked their own stilled wristwatches and did not get past ten. Only Sean counted off the full minute as the pointed hands remained frozen in position. Most of the children in the cafeteria took no notice, but three or four souls nearby, curious at their schoolmates' rapt attention, were caught up in the failure of the clock. Nothing else happened. All around continued the din of slurping and chewing, the clink of silverware, bursts of laughter and shouts of recrimination. At sixty-Mississippi, the second hand jerked to a start and time began again.

THERE WERE SIX further signs that week.

After school that Monday, they were joined by two more witnesses. Norah led them to the path through the woods, and there on the causeway between the street and the trees, she huddled the children around her and asked them to close their eyes. On her command, they looked and beheld her outstretched hand. Atop each splayed fingertip glowed a small white flame. She folded her fingers into a fist, extinguishing the fires as quickly as windblown candles. The children were astounded and burst into spontaneous applause. When the others headed home, Mark said to Sean that he hadn't seen such a cool trick since the time on *The Tonight Show* when a magician made a whole cage of doves disappear.

On Tuesday morning before they awoke, she appeared to the seven in their separate dreams, perched at the foot of their beds and passed judgment on the seven sins of their respective parents. When comparing stories at school throughout the day, each nine-year-old affirmed the details of the dream, and they were struck dumb by the similarities and the accuracy of her knowledge. Even those who only suspected their parents of greed or adultery acknowledged that their worst fears and most secret thoughts had been mined, that she somehow knew the struggles of their souls.

Three more children heard the rumors and joined the group for lunch on Wednesday and then followed her on the road that afternoon, listening to her stories of faith and foreboding. She led them on the path through the woods, and a plague of summertime midges rose up and swarmed around the group, a cloud so thick and sudden that the insects fouled the children's mouths and noses and sent them speeding home, hands flailing against their faces.

Thursday, she and now twelve followers snuck into St. Anne's Church, and in the dark and hushed nave, Norah raised a pencil, declaiming like Moses with the rod, and cracked it against the finial of a pew. Statues all around were seen to move: Saint Joseph flexed his fingers holding the crosier, a plaster angel blinked, baby Jesus squirmed in his mother's lap, and half the children fled frightened and in disbelief, not trusting their own witness. The others stayed to see Mary weep, the wounded Christ appear to bleed, and other visions of inexplicable terror and wonder.

Reports of these mysteries rekindled the talk in the hallways, and the phone calls from worried parents of the twelve and from those who received the gossip secondhand. Earlier claims had been dismissed as the fantasies of a troubled girl new to the school and the community, but now her tale bore the weight of the parents' malice and exaggeration. The most ardent churchgoers protested the most loudly, and those who believed in nothing at all were their temporary allies. Fourteen messages awaited Principal Taylor upon his arrival on Friday, and another dozen complaints were transferred before nine o'clock. The non-Catholics scoffed at the weeping statues as some papist hocus-pocus, the literal Bible was invoked, and charges of blasphemy were bandied. The Catholics, though anxious to believe, were offended by the children's trespass. The agnostics and atheists wanted to know why such nonsense was allowed to continue at a public school. Several parents insisted that Norah Quinn was the problem, and one father thundered that he would bring in the American Civil Liberties Union if Taylor could not prevent the exposure of his daughter to this kind of religious talk.

Over the intercom, Mr. Taylor summoned Norah to his office, and she left the classroom during a discussion of prime numbers. Two dozen faces, fascinated by the spectacle of the condemned, watched her exit. Sean imagined her long walk down the corridors, mentally counted her steps past the second graders' self-portraits hanging on the walls, the shamrocks and leprechauns taped to doors, past the music room and its shelves cluttered with recorders and timpani, past the quiet library and around the corner to the cafeteria. Then on to the principal's office she would tread softly and slowly. But before she arrived, the emergency alarm bells clanged. The students stirred with enthusiasm. Mrs. Patterson looked at the clock and sighed, arranged a single-file line at the door, and mustered them out to the schoolyard in the morning sunshine. By magic, Norah joined the group, smiling at her reprieve.

"Do you think it's just a fire drill?" Sean asked.

She did not answer. Unlike the rest, who stared at the empty building, she looked toward the faculty parking lot and seemed to be counting

softly to herself, the numbers trailing down, seven-six-five, barely percep
tible on her moving lips. Sean watched the countdown, three-two, his
gaze shifting from her mouth to the object of her attention as she neared
the end. At zero, a loud metallic explosion caught the crowd's attention
in time to see the beginning of smoke curling from the front of a white
sports car, and then with another bang, the flames forced open the hood.

"My baby!" Mr. Taylor shouted. He took two steps toward the beloved
Mustang and then halted. The fire roared to life, and near the heart of
the flames, a bird rose like a phoenix, a huge crow beating its broad wings
and cawing madly as it escaped into the sky. Each of the disciples searched
for fellow believers, exchanging looks that touched upon the central mystery of their nascent faith. When the firetrucks rolled up their hoses and
the drama of fire and water ended, a dozen children encircled Norah, curious to affirm her role in the blaze.

"How did you do it?" Mark asked.

"There's no way," Matt said. "You were miles from the car like the
rest of us."

Dori broke the ranks. "Funny way of getting out of having to go to
the principal's."

The children pressed closer, and Norah waved them back, creating
an invisible boundary around her body. "Best not tick off an angel," she
said, with a wink and a grin.

"I don't believe you had anything to do with that fire," Lucas said.
"My mother says there's no such thing as angels and that you are a crack-
pot or some religious nut—"

"Don't you remember how I saved you? I see the hesitation in all
your hearts, and so I will show you once more." She lifted her eyes to the
glassy sky, warm and foreshadowing spring. The others took notice too
of the fine day, the greening of the grass and budding in the trees. "The
wrath of angels falls upon a doubt-filled world."

As the firemen cleaned up the mess, the teachers and students filed
back into the building and did their best to restore normalcy to a Friday
afternoon. During the final class of the day, the windows began to vibrate
and hum. The wind began to blow and the tall trees outside swayed and
bowed their crowns. Rolling clouds blackened the sky and cast shadows
across the classroom. Bits of debris flew by—forgotten dry leaves, napkins,
wrappers, lost homework, and mislaid notes. A jump rope skipped by like

a downed telephone line. Returning to her desk from a stint at the black-board, Sharon Hopper laid her palm against the window and withdrew when it burned, and then tentatively touched the glass again, stunned by its fragile coldness. Bigger objects lumbered about the grounds—trashcan lids, a soccer ball spinning madly, a lunchroom tray, a shattered maple branch. They expected a flying cow, a spinning farmhouse come to rest upon the striped feet of a witch. The hour darkened, near pitch, and in the windows, the children saw their worried reflections.

Stepping outside after dismissal, the children squealed and screamed when the cold wind hit them. Few were prepared for the fallen tempera-ture, and jackets billowed, sweaters made tails as stiff as those of mock-ingbirds. They wrapped their arms across their chests, bent their heads against the gales, and struggled homeward. Those with the wind at their backs felt they could be airborne at any moment. A bird beat its wings against the rage, made no progress, and then pinwheeled back to a secure haven. Over the wind-whipped roar, the children hollered their good-byes. Norah's followers clumped at the edge of the sidewalk, freezing, mystified, and afraid. Tendrils of hair swirled around Norah's face, and the air fogged her glasses, but she alone seemed oblivious to the storm. A handful of children walked with her like a band of explorers braving the open tundra as the wind howled in their faces.

The trees at the edge of the bike path home formed a break, and it was calmer, but the shush of branches and the restless waters of the creek denied any normal level of discussion. As she reached the fork, Norah stopped to confront them all. "So do you believe now?" she shouted.

Dori's black eyes were wet with tears. The boys sniffed runny noses and stared at the ground. At her side, Sean tugged her arm and shouted back, "Make it stop."

"Meet me tomorrow," she said above the wind. "At three o'clock, and I will show you even greater wonders."

The apostles raised their hands farewell, nodded their assent. Norah and Sean split off from the others, traversing the path through the forest to the Quinns' house. By the time they reached the fence, Sean noticed the winds had subsided, and when he finally made it to his own home, he realized that they had all but died.

17

*M*other. *Mom. Mommy. Mum. Ma. Margaret. My mother.* On the drive from Washington, D.C., to Pennsylvania, Erica chanted to herself in time with the wheels upon the highway, the air whistling through the opened window, the on-and-off radio, the bites of conversation with her aunt. *My mother, my mother, my mother.* Such memories that jostled for dominance were confined largely to that last year of enmity, the discovery of her father's wartime past and the emotional wall surrounding each of them. She tried to remember them in earlier and more pleasant times. A chase over the dune to be the first to catch the long-anticipated expanse of summer ocean. The unexpected wit, fringed with sarcasm, which stunned the dinner table. Her hope welling in the moment before her gifts were unwrapped. But mostly, her mother listening patiently to some worry or woe, offering up the solace of prayer or a cliché of received advice. "All part of the plan," she was fond of saying by way of consolation. But Erica knew there was no plan, only accidents and deceit, and such bromides lost force. By adolescence, she could no longer talk to her without departing emptied of emotion, but perhaps homilies were all that Margaret could say when letting go. There is no proper goodbye between daughter and mother.

"She's older now, of course," Diane said. "When you disappeared, she aged all at once and just seemed to skip the middle part altogether. One day the big sister I remember got up and walked away, leaving behind a hollow shell. Until Norah came along—"

My mother, mine.

W HEN ASKED WHERE he was hurrying to that Saturday afternoon, Sean shouted "Out" as he raced past the living room and "Bye,

Mum" as the stormdoor slammed behind him. Perhaps if she had been less weary Eve would not have hesitated, but by the time she stepped out onto the porch he was nowhere to be seen. She looked both ways along the street, but he had flown away.

"WHAT DO YOU know of this child, really?" the watcher asked, hat in hand, his face and hands now translucent. "All the talk around town of her strange behavior and the innuendo of a holy delusion. Caution, your mother would say. Safety first."

Margaret spoke in a soft tone. "My mother was all about propriety. The worst sin of all was that the neighbors would talk."

"She disapproved of your wildness. Your choices in men. Jackson—"

"Please don't talk to me about love. It is a disappointing thing."

"This child is not your daughter. You may not have this angel Norah." He was slipping away, breaking apart like a broadcast charged with static.

"What would you have me do? Wake up every morning not knowing what happened to my child? Miss her every day till I die?" She addressed the space he had occupied, empty of all but the atomic shadow of memory. He was gone for good, and she began to worry what his disappearance meant in terms of the other who had entered her life.

Luminous in the afternoon sun, Norah appeared before her in the living room, stepping between Margaret and her shadow. "I've done all my chores," she said, "and don't want to be late. Can I go now?"

18

Ѕhe led them to the bridge, to the river.

Passersby thought nothing of the pilgrimage of a half dozen children on their way to a Saturday matinee, or to play some game in the park, or wandering aimlessly on a sunny afternoon. Norah, Sean, Sharon, and Dori walked while Mark and Lucas trailed in lazy circles on their bicycles. No one stopped them. No one inquired as to their destination. The children moved invisibly among the men and women busy with their quotidian cares, mired in the Steel City blues.

The boys parked their bicycles at the corner, and the group stepped single file onto the bridge, Norah on point and Sean bringing up the rear. At the apex of the span the apostles stopped and leaned their arms against the railing to stare out at the river rolling underfoot. Birds on a wire, they perched and waited. In the distance a coal barge looked like a toy boat pushing dirty trays downstream. A station wagon slowed, the driver staring their way before moving on. Limber as a spider monkey, Norah lifted her body until she was seated on the rail and facing the others, her feet dangling in the air, her fingers wrapped around the bar for balance. Blind to the open sky, the fall behind her, the river at her back. A breeze caught her hair and sent it spilling across her eyes, and she let go with one hand to push the stray locks behind her ears. "If you have existed," she said, "since the beginning and shall be forever, then the cares of this life are little more than a sigh in time. And yet, we worry over every problem large and small. Instead of trusting our troubles will pass as we will continue."

The five faces below her twisted with uncertainty. Sharon winked into the sunshine, and the others shielded their eyes against the blinding light with salutes. Below, the river darkened like spilled ink. The wheels on another passing car clipped a pothole and made a sound like the pop from a gun. "It's a perfect day," Norah said. "For flying."

In the first vision, Sean saw the others join her, steady themselves like tightrope walkers on the rail, arms twirling; and balanced in a line, heads cocked to the middle, they listened to her instructions. Backlit, the five silhouettes stood stark against the whiteness, and at her command, every child leapt out into the void, hovering momentarily as the wind pushed against their outstretched limbs and bowed chests, still and perfect and beautiful for one moment before plummeting, silent and swift as stones, into the water, striking the surface with knifing explosions, sinking to the bottom, slowing, bobbing, coming to rest in the silt, a look of disbelief written in their eyes, their bodies borne by the cold undercurrent. In the second vision, they lined up again like fledglings, spread their arms, and glided up, full of bliss and surprise, spiraling into the deep blue sky until, like the angels, they disappeared into the heavens and were gone forever. In both cases, he stayed behind on the bridge, watched them sink or swim the sky, powerless to join them and fixed to the spot by his doubts and fears.

Like a swimmer crouched to dive into a race, she had brought her feet to the rail and was holding on by her fingers and toes. The other children on the walkway were poised to rescue her, but no one moved. A delivery van with a rose painted on the door squealed to a halt, and Norah turned her head toward the sound. Sean reached for her, grabbed her arms. Blood pulsed through her veins, the echo of her frightened heart. "Stop," he said. "Just stop and come down. I believe you—"

She cried out and let herself collapse to the walkway, her wrists cuffed in his fingers. The driver of the stopped van had opened the door and stuck his bald head above the window, too stunned to abandon his seat. He knew these children, his neighbor's granddaughter and the boy. "Are you crazy?" Delarosa yelled. "You kids get the hell off this bridge. What are you doing up here anyway?"

"We're learning how to fly, mister!" Mark yelled.

"From an angel," Sharon added.

"Get offa here before one of you breaks your neck or falls off."

After Sean let go of her wrists, his grip left a red welt against her skin where she had been bound and now was unchained. Pat Delarosa waited until the group, following Sean's lead, made it to the corner, and he opened the back door, releasing the perfume of bouquets just as the red and blue police lights began to flash against the steel framework of the bridge. Without complaint, they surrendered.

19

They ate dinner in silence, eying each other between bites. After the police brought Norah home and explained what had happened on the bridge, Margaret was so distracted that she nearly forgot to cook anything at all. For the first time, she was frightened by the girl and her dangerous stories, wary of asking too much and of the truth that might spill out. Late in the evening, they sat down to table, avoiding a single wrong word. She scrambled some eggs, burnt some toast, and laid out two jars of preserves. There had been a scene at first, a confrontation immediately after the uniforms departed, a lecture on the need to stay out of trouble. The Delarosas called, traces of panic in the voices on the wire, spouting some nonsense about a stranger who had visited their store asking about Norah, but Margaret dismissed the connection as superstitious paranoia. She gave Norah a warning on the dangers of high places, an admonition against the telling of stories, and a plea to drop once and for all this talk of angels. Norah refused to engage and promised only to be good and careful. "The time is at hand," she replied to a question of why, and for the first time, Margaret was impatient with the cryptic nature of her foundling. Food served as their temporary truce. She resolved to speak to the girl again in the morning, but at dinner she was more grateful that no harm had come. The child was safe, licking the peaches off a jelly spoon.

Three big knocks at the door were pursued by the creak of the hinges, and a familiar voice called out hello. "Aunt Diane," Norah shouted, and raced from her chair, nearly slamming into her full force in the foyer. Throwing wide her arms, she nestled her head against Diane's chest and hugged her tightly. "I knew you would come."

"Behave yourself, child," Diane said, patting her head. "Where is my sister?"

At that moment, Margaret turned the corner to find her lost daughter standing before her.

"I should have called first," Diane said, "but I wasn't sure until right now that she would actually go through—"

"Mom." Erica brought her hands to her mouth and wept.

"And I wanted to see your face when I brought her home. Maggie?" Norah stepped into the shadows.

Stunned, Margaret could not move, though every muscle twitched with reflexive energy. A ghost not six feet away, her baby. "Erica?"

Her daughter swept past Diane and embraced her, held on so tightly that when they finally parted to look again, kiss, and embrace again, she left a sore spot on Maggie's cheek where bone met bone. They did not speak for a long time, content to cry and touch, to prove that the other was real.

"Is it you?" Margaret asked. Her daughter was a stranger, though closer to her than anyone in her life. She had willed her return for so long that she was stunned by the answer to her desire, and it was as if Erica had left to spend the night with Joyce Green and returned the next morning. Had fallen down the rabbit hole and popped up like a groundhog, shadowless. She was seven years old the night before and twenty-eight the next day. She was a crocus in the snow. The summer of cicadas. Here and gone and here again. Changed, but still the baby in the cradle, brave child diving into a pressing tide, teenager laughing at a lucky draw at cards. She had blown away and come back after the wind had circled the globe. Erica was hers once more.

"I'm so, so sorry about Daddy. I was afraid I'd never see you again." Erica glanced once at the child, but held in her mother's arms, she could think of nothing but their reunion. Aunt Diane was right; her mother looked older than her years. Careworn, time-trodden. The fine lines of sun and worry, gray hair at the temples, the slackening of her skin. Margaret was crushed and beaten. Mangled by worry. Tied by a deep pain coursing in the bones. Slow to realize the fact of her daughter's presence. Yet she was ineffably her mother, had cheated the grave. She was steadfast as sorrow. She was forgiveness.

Allowing mother and daughter some privacy, Diane led Norah into the kitchen. They, too, did not speak to one another for some time but stared at each other in deep regard. "Surprised to see your mother again?" Diane asked. "Or should I say, for the first time."

"How did you find her?"

"You should know. I went to New Mexico, like you said. The question is how did you know she would be there?"

"Gramma," she began, and thought better. "Mrs. Quinn had an old letter but never went to get her. I couldn't go because nobody asked. I knew you would go if shown the way. You are brave."

"Lionhearted."

Norah capped the jelly jars and set the dirty plates in the sink. "I knew you would go the moment we met."

"And just how did you know that? Another one of your heavenly powers?"

"No. You are her sister, and you were the only one left."

ALONE AT THE kitchen table, Norah drew intricate scenes of hunting cats, leopards in the shadows, tigers pouncing, a pride of lionesses gang-tackling a zebra. Filtered through the walls, the adult conversation flowed like the murmur of a faraway stream, and she listened to the music of their voices in three parts, daughter echoing mother, sisters in counterpart, bursts of laughter in harmony. Once, in her solitude, she thought she heard someone at the back door, but when she pressed her nose against the glass, sheer darkness prevented her from seeing beyond the panes. Whatever had been was no longer there. The symphony of voices changed measures and tone. Every so often the word "Norah" floated from the living room, but nothing would tempt her to eavesdrop. They would have to remember eventually that they had left her alone.

At half past nine, Erica came into the kitchen, filled the teakettle, all the while sneaking glances at Norah, who kept her pencil moving, intent on her drawing. "What have we here?" Erica asked, and took the chair across from her to consider the pictures one by one. "Those are really good."

"Thank you." She continued her line till the end and then laid down the pencil.

"Pleased to meet you, Norah. I'm Erica, but you already know that. You must call me Mary. Especially in front of your friends. Do you think you can pretend that I'm Mary Gavin? Here for a visit. It will keep us all out of trouble."

"Don't worry. I can pretend."

"I'm sure that you can." She studied the child's face, clicking her tongue against the roof of her mouth. "Once upon a time, I met a girl like you. She even looked like you, same glasses and eyes, same hair. Her name was Una, and she had no mother or father, just like you, and she lived in a cottage all alone in the woods with her grandmother."

"What happened to her mom and dad?"

Pressing the pads of her fingers against the table, Erica retrieved a few stray crumbs. "We don't really know. They may have run away. May have been in an accident. In any case, they left her there in her grandmother's house and never returned."

"That's a sad story," Norah said. "Was she lonely?"

"A little. But she was smart, like you, and had a vivid imagination. Una was good at pretending too."

Behind her glasses, Norah blinked several times in rapid succession, her efforts magnified by the thick lenses. She wavered slightly like an object gone temporarily out of focus. Lost in her thoughts, she offered a curt smile, and then considered her unfinished drawing. "Are you going to send me away right now?"

"Of course not. My mother and I need some time to sort out things."

"Where do I sleep tonight?"

"In your own bed. We'll talk more later. Why don't you run and kiss the ladies now, before you go to sleep?"

"Goodnight, Mary."

The name put a smile on her face, and then patting the child's hand, she rose to answer the singing kettle.

20

The mothers came to save their children, to reel in the long strings, the kites and balloons threatening to float away forever. They were resolved to rescue their sons and daughters from the bridge, to leap into the waters far below, if necessary, and scour the bottom if any chance remained to hand them out of trouble, panting and gasping, back into sensibleness. All weekend, telephones relayed the news of the police, the children on the bridge, the little danger living among them—not only at their school but in the community itself. Norah Quinn put in peril their unspoken shared values and the order they insisted upon for their children. By late Sunday night, the protest had been planned. The mothers would marshal to speak to those in authority, to give a piece of their minds to the unguarded listener, to root out and remove the virus spreading from family to family. In the breaking light of Monday morning, the posse gathered outside the school, hands gripping the shoulders of their beloved charges, waiting to ambush Taylor—for the respect of "principal" and even "mister" had been abandoned—to make him do something to ensure that this talk of angels among them would be scrubbed like obscene graffiti marring the school walls.

Taylor did not know what to do with the phalanx of mothers and children gathered on the front lawn beneath the flagpole, and the mere sight of the women deflated his already sunken spirits. He was driving his sister's Volkswagen, mourning the loss of his sports car, and swore at the group from the parking lot, muttering foulness till he met Mrs. Ford, coiled with anger, halfway up the walk. The boy pinched under her arm was white with terror and shame.

"You have to do something about that Quinn girl." Froth gathered in the corners of Mrs. Ford's mouth when she spoke.

Mrs. Tilghman rushed to join. "A menace. My daughter coulda drownded."

Soon he was surrounded and could progress only by slow steps and the shuffle of the circle. Mrs. Hopper, petite as a mouse, thundered like an elephant. "She's making them think about things they shouldn't be thinking about," she said. Mrs. West wagged her finger, even though her boy was already in fifth grade. Mrs. Paddock, Mrs. Harper, and Ms. Grimalkin formed a Scottish coven, bubbling with trouble. Gull-eyed as her son, Mrs. Mansur appeared slightly crazed and desperate to find a single right word. They howled at him. Cornered, they protected their cubs.

No fathers were present, for the few lucky enough to have jobs could ill afford the hours away from the mill to yell at a school administrator, and none were inclined to flaunt any authority in these hard times. Those waiting for the steel industry to rise up from the dead dreamt at home abed or nursed the day's first boilermakers at the union hall. But though they absented themselves, the fathers bristled at the threat to their children as soon as the mothers told them about the episode above the Mon River. Some secretly knew that their sons and daughters were ripe for such a pied piper, were too thick or simple to resist, would say yes to any hint of magic. The fathers wound the string on these children when the mothers were not looking. Their corrections were more oblique—the distraction of football or hunting or fishing with sons, the utter confusion of what to do about their daughters while they were still young enough and beholden. The glory days before their children thought them helpless idiots. Time would come when the fathers would be reduced to stealth, bribery, and angry hectoring at their children to stay put and not float away a moment too soon. Fathers know from the beginning the string will snap, and they mourn a bit each passing day. Mothers keep their eyes fixed on their children in the bright blue sky and are dumbfounded when they break their hearts.

The mortified children chafed at their parents' involvement, shrank under the mothers' complaints. Five of the six disciples bore the double burden of an uncertain faith and the inadvertent trouble they had caused. They hid in their mothers' shadows, more fearful of scorn from their peers than of anything the adults might say. After the police had stopped them on the bridge, the followers betrayed Norah one by one. Lucas Ford and Dori Tilghman recanted. Sharon Hopper fell to tears and did not know what to believe. Mark Bellagio held out the longest, trusting the empirical sensory evidence and his long training to accept the possibility of miracles. But even he was cowed when his parents began talking about sacrilege and blasphemy and the gall of anyone claiming to be closer to God. "Those Quinns," his father spat out. "First the goddamn crazy daughter, and now the granddaughter, mad as a bumblebee."

On the school green, promises were made and an accord was reached. After allowing an appropriate amount of parental huffing and puffing, Taylor agreed to talk with the student and, later, her grandmother. "On my calendar," he said, "as soon as you let me into the building." In the interest of peace, he consented to meet with all interested parents one evening that week, hear their grievances, and explain what steps he would take regarding Norah Quinn. With each capitulation, he scanned the horizon beyond the mob, carefully watching the other children and faculty arrive. He wanted nothing more than for the parents to stop shouting at him and to simply go away, and the thought of a larger rabble filled him with dread.

The mothers released their sons and daughters, and free from their talons, the children hastened into their classrooms. Some lingered for a final approving hug or look goodbye, but most spun away as fast as they could, anxious to discover the truth as told by the actual participants. Was it true you were trying to fly? Do you honestly think she's an angel? Did they really take you to jail? Their mothers remained behind to invent and embroider a group narrative and a consensus on what must be done. A remnant of eleven stayed long enough to see Norah Quinn and Sean Fallon arrive.

Despite his mother's caution, Sean had called for her as usual, slipping onto the Quinns' porch as softly as a cat. He knocked, but the whole house seemed to be asleep. The rental car in the driveway alerted him to a visitor, so he was not completely surprised to see Diane's bewildered face at the door, though she was taken aback by his presence, as if she had forgotten to decide upon a proper question. A cloud in the memory lifted when she finally remembered his name and ushered him inside. He sensed at once the difference in the household, old troubles vanquished, new ones in their place. Tightening the belt of her robe, Diane hurried off to find Norah, clueless as though she had misplaced a shoe or set of keys. She looked at the coat hooks, the dining table, and even the closet beneath the stairs. She called for the girl in a hoarse whisper usually reserved by those desperately hoping not to wake a sleeping baby. When Norah finally appeared from the kitchen, she seemed altered too. More subdued, less luminous, dark circles around her eyes.

"Up late?" he asked.

"Quiet, they're still in bed."

He wondered for a moment if she had fallen ill or had suffered some dark consequence from the incident with the police, but when she flung her bookbag over her shoulder and raced past him, he knew he would . have to struggle just to catch and keep up with her.

When she saw the women clustered in front of the school like sheep in a glen, Norah slowed to a normal clip and stopped Sean to talk before they were noticed.

"She's come back," she said. "Last night. Just as I hoped. Mary Gavin."

"Who is Mary Gavin?"

Incredulous, she rolled her eyes. "That's what she calls herself now. Mrs. Quinn's daughter, Erica. She's in seclusion."

"The one that's been missing?"

A face in the crowd stared in their direction. A hand pointed, an arm drawn erect as a rifle. Above them, the flags beat against the flagpoles.

"The one. The time is here."

The mothers spotted her in unison, raised their heads across the plain, and tensed.

Sean took no notice. "Mrs. Quinn must be so happy. How did she find her?"

"You and I showed her the way. Listen, you cannot tell a soul. If anyone knew she was here, the police would come and take her away. They think she is guilty, but she has paid for her sins. Promise you will not tell."

With one finger, he drew a cross over his heart.

The women huddled on the lawn.

"You ought to go on ahead," Norah said.

Hands balled into fists, the scowling mothers hastened toward them.

"I'll stay with you."

"You'll wish that you hadn't."

And the mothers fell upon the children and tore the pair to pieces with their words.

21

All morning long, after absentmindedly sending the child to school, Diane watched the dance between mother and daughter. Margaret could not keep from touching Erica each time they passed, to assert her claim on her daughter's reality and continuity. To say you are mine once more.

Diane kept the conversation going, kept the music playing to push them past their awkwardness with each other. She put on the kettle, buttered the skillet, toasted the bread. "Talked with an old friend of yours, Maggie. Very discreetly, of course, he'd do nothing to hurt you after all these years. More than a friend, eh? Jackson. He's still as handsome as ever, would rock your rocking chair. He says that Mary here—that is, Erica Quinn—is still a wanted woman. The choice is to turn herself in and pay her debt to society or keep hidden."

"I can't stay too long, Mom. Too many people here remember me." The reality of her statement rolled across the kitchen table and struck Margaret in the chest. She drew in a deep breath and studied her hands vined round a teacup. Her daughter leaned forward. "You could always come with me to New Mexico."

A second wave washed over her. She slumped back in her chair. "But what about Norah?"

Diane cleared her throat and set two plates of eggs before them. "I spoke with Jackson about her as well, hypothetically of course. He seems to think, from what I described, that she has got to be some sort of runaway, and I agree. Maybe a foster child. An orphan."

The thought seemed to stun Margaret. Erica rose and went to her side, crouching like a child at eye level. "Tell us the truth, Mom. How did you find her?"

"She arrived in the middle of the night, freezing cold and hardly a stitch on her. I only meant to keep her for the night and see to it in the morning to send her back. I let her sleep in your room, Erica. Just so she'd have a warm place to stay. If you'd seen her, poor thing, you'd have done the same."

"Did she ever say where she came from?" Diane asked.

"She said she had lived all over and that she had no parents and asked could I keep her for a while. I'd been so lonely—"

Erica wrapped her arms around her mother's shoulders. Margaret nestled her head against her daughter's chest and felt the thrum of her blood. "I don't know why I did it, but I had fallen and she saved me."

"But there is something wrong with the child," Diane said. "She is . . . delusional. All this business with the school and now the police. Maybe she's escaped from an institution. Maybe she needs help."

"I'm her help."

"And she is saying she is an angel. Messenger from God. Hello?" She towered over her sister and her niece. "You yourself said she was going to fly off a bridge. Someone could have been hurt, or killed. If you want to help, take her to a doctor at least. See what's wrong. She's not one of us, and we cannot keep pretending forever."

22

During the broadcast of morning announcements, he filled the doorway to Mrs. Patterson's room and hooked her to him with one curled finger. As the teacher turned her back on the students, she heard the first whispers, and all of the children knew at once why Mr. Taylor had come. Norah stood quietly and waited to be called. As she passed Mrs. Patterson, she felt the woman reach out and lightly brush the crown of her hair. For the next hour, Mrs. Patterson's fingers tingled as if frostbitten.

The principal and the child walked side by side down the corridors in grave silence, exchanging glances at each corner to make sure the other was following the same path. Behind the closed door of his office, Mr. Taylor loosened his tie and undid the top button of his shirt. He cast off the stern demeanor he wore in public and forced a smile. Norah grinned back at him and knotted her hands in her lap.

"Miss Quinn. Norah. You have made quite an impression here at Friendship in the time you've been here."

"Two months."

"Is that all? It seems much longer. How are you finding our school? Everything to your satisfaction?"

"I love it here, Mr. Taylor, though I am sorry about your car."

"My car?" For the first time since the incident, he allowed the possibility that the explosion was no accident. The demure child in front of him chased away such speculation. "Yes, never mind about the car. I've wanted to speak to you about another matter. I'm sure you noticed the group of ladies outside school today—"

"You mean the ones who yelled at me and Sean Fallon? One of them called me a name I'm not allowed to say."

"So you know how angry they are. I want you to know I am not angry with you, per se, but just concerned about this whole business. It's become a disruption to the school, and when I spoke to your grandmother when it first happened, she said it wouldn't happen again, but it has happened again, and as I say, I am a bit worried about you. And your feelings."

She fidgeted in her chair. A scarlet streak flashed by the window, a cardinal.

"Norah, if you and your grandmother agree, I'd like you to talk to a doctor—"

"A psychiatrist, Mr. Taylor?"

A jay landed in the branches outside and screamed angrily.

"Yes, no. A counselor. Someone trained to discuss some of the thoughts you've been having. The things that you've claimed."

"But I'm not crazy."

His voice rose and quickened. "Nobody said you were. This is just someone who could help you understand what you've been thinking."

"Is this about being an angel?"

Three sparrows hopped across the outer windowsill. He breathed in deeply and exhaled a long sigh. "You can't keep going around saying such things. You are jeopardizing your place at this school, not just among the other children, but with Mrs. Patterson, and the parents too. Do you realize what people are saying about you and your grandmother? That stunt on the bridge could have been far more serious, young lady, than you might suppose. What if someone fell into the river? Mrs. Mansur says you should be suspended, and Mrs. Tilghman threatened to go to the school board if you weren't immediately expelled. They say you are teaching their children to think dangerous thoughts."

All the birds flew away. She no longer stared through the window but gave him her full attention.

"Now, I'm trying to be reasonable here. I've called your home a number of times but nobody answers, so I have a note for you to give to your grandmother to come see me. Maybe we can talk this through and meet with some of the other parents, explain the situation. I'm sure if you apologize and agree to counseling, they will be understanding. But you must tell the truth. I don't want to see you in any more trouble, Miss Quinn, but I can't have this kind of disruption any longer in my school, and I hope you will give some serious consideration to seeing this doctor."

"The truth is never as simple as it seems, and people will believe what they need to believe."

He stood and walked to the door, opening it for her. "I'm sure it isn't, Miss Quinn, but you have to understand I have a job to do here. Make sure I see your grandmother tomorrow. Make sure she gets that note."

AT OUTDOOR RECESS, Sean did not notice that they had been shunned, for they were too busy hunting the first clues of spring. As she pushed through the doors, Norah pointed out a line of bloodroot blossoms peeking along the fence, and they made a game of counting flowers and other plants pushing through the detritus of dead leaves and mulch. Sean found a green frog in a wet patch of ground behind the baseball backstop, and Norah discovered the ferns coiled like snail shells next to the maintenance shed. A flock of robins landed in the yard, flashing their ocher breasts, and they tried to count them all. With their shoes muddy and reeking, they went inside happy as explorers.

The banishment continued through lunch. Sharon and Mark picked up their trays and moved silently to another table when Sean and Norah approached. The other children wound through an obstacle course of chairs and tables so as to avoid the slightest contact. Exile lasted the entire day. Nobody spoke to them in the classroom, and the slightest word from either one drew a cold stare and quick rebuke. In the breaks between classes, the whispers began. Notes circulated. A malicious plot hatched by signals and shorthand.

As they packed their knapsacks to go home, Norah took the letter from the principal intended for Mrs. Quinn, folded it in half, and placed it between the leaves of her grammar book. Then she opened the lid to her desk and buried the grammar inside. "I don't like it that nobody's talked to us all day."

"They're only mad because their parents are mad at us," Sean said.

"But on Friday they believed—"

"Sometimes adults can get you to believe or not believe in things."

From a departing schoolbus, the first taunts came. A boy rolled down his window and yelled "crazy" at the passing pair. "Why don't you just get out of here?" another said from the front steps. A pack of fifth graders flapped their arms as Sean and Norah walked by, and she looked over her shoulder to see one of them sneering and holding up his middle finger. The space between the school and home provided a calm interlude, and as they neared the end of the bike path and the Quinns' backyard, they flushed a covey of mourning doves. The birds cried and beat their wings to launch themselves higher and disappear into the treetops. Because he was distracted by the birds flying away, Sean did not see the figures emerge from their hiding places until the gang of boys had encircled Norah. He stepped to her side.

Strangers, mostly, bigger boys, but two of the followers—Lucas and Matt—and a few other faces from their class. "Why did you do it? Why did you get us all in trouble?"

"You belong in a lunatic asylum. They're going to take you away in a wagon."

"Crazy bitch." A boy spat at her.

"Why don't you just fly back to where you came from?"

"Angel. Where are the other angels to protect you now?"

Sean stepped in front of the accuser. "Leave her alone."

"Show us your wings, if you're an angel. I don't believe you. Liar."

"Show us your wings, freak." The boy edged closer, sneaker to sneaker. He was a head taller than the rest, but Sean pushed him back.

"She's telling the truth. Just leave her—"

"Faggot," the boy said. "Pussy. Hanging out with girl angels—"

"Show us your wings," a voice came from behind, and two boys stepped forward and grabbed at her blouse. Sean moved to help her but the boy who had spat and cursed him jumped and wrestled him to the ground. Others pounced upon him, punching and kicking till he had to cover his face. Crumpled on the pavement, he flailed about blindly, striking out with his elbow and bloodying the boy's nose. Someone lifted his boot and stomped on Sean's hand. The others, angry for their comrade, struck more viciously, and from the tangle of limbs and fists, he could hear Norah crying, her books being thrown and scattered in the woods, and the ugly rending of her clothes. And then a woman's voice hollered out a warning, and a clump of dirt landed like a grenade and exploded on the tarmac, scattering the attackers like a pack of stray dogs. The boys ran off, scared and helpless. Head bowed, her blouse torn in two, Norah bent at the waist, revealing her naked back, the sharp bones of her shoulder blades heaving like wings against her skin as she wept. From the Quinns' backyard, a young woman sped to save them both.

Upstairs, Margaret and Diane tended to Norah. The sound of water coursing through the old pipes indicated that a bath was being drawn. Downstairs, at the kitchen sink, Erica saturated an old dish towel in cold water, and with gentle pressure, she wiped clean Sean's face, stanched the blood from the corner of his lip, and winced as she pushed the dirt from the pebbled lacerations at his cheekbone and chin. They could hear Norah slip into the tub, cry out that it was too hot, and the singsong reparations from the two sisters. Finished with her ministrations, Erica stepped back to consider his face the way an artist might move to gain a different perspective. "You'll be all right," she said. "You clean up nicely."

The remark seemed a kind of gentle joke, so he returned a weak smile. She reached for his hands, and he let her wash the wounds on his palms and knuckles. Clean again, his hands seemed less alien, and the balm of her touch restored him after the violence. The woman said at last, "I am Mary Gavin."

"I know who you are."

"You must be Sean. I've heard a lot of good things about you from Norah and Mrs. Quinn."

"Your mother."

She brushed an escaping strand of hair from in front of her eyes. His words felt like an accusation, but she realized at once that of course Norah would have told her only confidant. A story existed below the surface of sudden angels and lost daughters, and this poor boy was caught in the vortex. She wondered what other secrets he kept.

"You can trust me," he told her. "I won't tell." As he made the promise, his lip began to bleed again, and she held the cloth against it like a kiss.

"Is there someone I can call to come get you? Your mother or father?"

Through the dish towel he mumbled, "My mother's still at work, and my father doesn't live with us anymore."

She reached out and laid her hand against the side of his face, and he tilted into the warmth of her touch. He closed his eyes and rested there. Upstairs, the water drained from the bathtub, a door opened, and the girl emerged to the muffled strains of two comforting voices.

Norah descended. She came down from her bath a different person, her wet hair combed close against her scalp, the scent of jasmine shampoo in the air, and the light gone from her eyes. Trailing her, worn by the shock of the attack, were her attendants: Diane, limping from step to step, for her foot had fallen asleep, and Margaret, anxious and fretful, pulling at the hems of her sleeves to hide her reddened hands. Wrapped in a thick robe, Norah crossed barefoot over the floor and put her arms around Sean, rested her head against the shoulder she had once bitten, and left a wet patch on his shirt. He accepted the gesture with good grace, blushing.

Erica watched her mother watch the girl and could see that Margaret was grieving already before the child was gone. Grief had become the handmaid of hope, and she whose life was also bound by heartache and desire understood all too well what must be done.

The five gathered at the table, and Norah and Sean circled back to how it began with the protests of the mothers and how it ended with the attack by the children. Telling the story released its internal tensions, for it is an old tale of misunderstanding that ends in violence. A comfort of tea was brewed and served, a pan of hot chocolate for the younger souls. A deck of cards appeared by sleight of hand. Tricks were realized with shouts of triumph, and laughter resounded over improbable bids risked and made. In this way, they assuaged their anger and disappointment. When the hour came for Sean to go home, they had willed themselves back to equipoise, found a route to one another.

"Your mother will be worried," Margaret said. "I'll walk you home, Sean, and be there to help explain those bumps and bruises."

Diane stood and bowed. "We'll take my car. A hero deserves to ride in style with at least two chauffeurs. Your chariot awaits."

Diminished by the oversized robe, Norah walked him to the door, a child again spent by fear and hope. Her hair had dried to a tangled mess, and her eyeglasses must have been chipped earlier that day. Facets caught the falling light and broke it into many colors. "Thank you for sticking up for me."

"It's okay."

She lowered her voice to a whisper. "And for believing. I'll never forget it."

He looked away. "Okay, see you tomorrow."

Norah waved goodbye, and on the drive home, he began to miss her and wish he had lingered awhile.

After watching them get into the car, Erica sat on the bottom step and patted a place for the child. She sidled in close enough to touch, and the woman leaned into her, pressed her shoulder against Norah's head. Alone in the house, each became acutely aware of the other and their roles in bringing about the reunion. "Would you like to talk now?" Erica asked. "Tell me how I can help?"

"No, I can take care of myself."

"How long have you been on your own?"

"All of my life. Since I was little."

"I can't stay here, you know."

Norah cleared her throat. "I guess not."

"I have to go back to New Mexico, and I want to take my mother with me."

"You'll want to be with her as long as you can. She's not well."

"She would want you to come," Erica said. "And I would have you, but you and I both know that isn't where you belong."

"I want to stay," Norah said. "For her sake, my own, and the boy's. He has let sorrow carry him away."

"He's strong. He stood up for you. He'll find a way out of what he's feeling."

"Are there really coyotes and roadrunners in New Mexico?"

"Not like the cartoon."

"Then I wouldn't want to go." Through the stormdoor, the sky darkened, far away a flash of lightning.

"Tell me, how long have you been an angel?"

She had no reply.

Erica lowered her head so she could see directly into the child's eyes behind the forlorn chipped glasses. "Did you run away? Is it far from here?"

She gave no answer but turned her face to the wall.

"Did you come to save my mother? To bring us back together?"

"Hope is not about tricks and miracles."

"Norah, if you stay, there will be no end to your trouble. They think you have imagined it all. They think you are a danger to yourself, to the other children. Not even the true believers want to see an angel in their midst. They will take you away to God knows where."

Black against black, the shadows streaked across the sky, barely legible. Birds heading to roost for the night in the tall trees. Extinguished stars shooting across the heavens. Ranks of angels sent to destroy, or beckoned to console, or called to guard the angry and the innocent. Prayers, becoming answers. Erica wound an arm around Norah's shoulders and pulled her closer, a score of possibilities playing in her mind. "Are you ready to go back to where you came from?"

The child nodded. "Will you tell Mrs. Quinn? Will you tell her that the time has come?"

24

When Sean arrived on Tuesday morning to accompany her to school, he was met at the door by Diane, who told him that Norah wasn't feeling well and would be staying in bed that day. On Wednesday, he found a note taped to the front molding informing him not to wait and to please not wake the house. Thursday no one answered when he knocked, and the aunt's car was no longer parked in the driveway. A rumor ran through Friendship that Principal Taylor had reached the limit on angels and suspended her, and the punishment had escalated into outright expulsion for refusing to follow his orders, for Mrs. Patterson had found the principal's note to Mrs. Quinn hidden in the grammar book in the girl's desk. A rebuttal challenged the premise that she had been kicked out. Among third graders, it was said that a gang of bullies had attacked her that day after school and that she was in the hospital, or dead in the morgue. This tale spawned the further counter theory that she had not been killed by the children but, rather, had thrown herself off the bridge in town and the body was lost downriver. Her erstwhile disciples, shamed by their own lack of faith, put forth the fable that she had departed on the wing, ascending into the heavens, saddened and sobered by the viciousness of life on earth.

Such stories did not bother Sean, for he knew that people often make up the most outrageous tales to explain what they cannot understand. All of them—the children, Mrs. Patterson, Mr. Taylor, the parents—granted him a certain solicitude, for the cuts and bruises on his face reminded them of all that had happened and their complicity. The boys guilty of the attack in the woods stayed clear of him, skulking in the corridors and classrooms, fearful that he would turn them in. More than the wild speculation and the presence of bullying cowards, he was bothered by the return of his ordinary life and the uncertainty and emptiness of the Quinns' house. Each time he passed, morning and afternoon, he longed for some sign, and on Friday after school, he thought he saw the kitchen curtains part and close as he cut through the backyard. Summoning his courage, he circled round and knocked on the front door.

Mrs. Quinn answered and stood on the threshold, her hand clasping the open door, worry knit across her ashen brow. She seemed tired and distracted and looked at Sean as though he were not real, but some spirit child.

"How is Norah? I haven't seen her since Monday, and I've been wondering."

Stepping onto the porch, she allowed the door to close behind her with a bang. Clouds swollen with rain had accompanied him there, and she lifted her eyes to gauge the proximity of a storm. "Sean, I was planning to come see you and your mother this weekend."

"I just stopped by to see if—"

"She's not here, Sean. That's why I was coming to visit. She's not here."

"What happened? Is she okay?"

"I don't know how to tell you. She wasn't my granddaughter. We were just pretending—"

"I've known that for a long time."

Margaret cleared her throat and looked over his head. "When she started to go around claiming to be an angel, I was concerned at first, but not too much so. Lots of children imagine things, like to pretend."

"But I saw her, Mrs. Quinn. I saw what she can do. She made the clocks stop. She drew fire in the sky. She made whole flocks of birds appear."

"You know what you think you saw, Sean, but maybe you were imagining too." She moved to put a hand on his shoulder and then reconsidered. "Ever since your father left. I'm sure it's difficult."

"It isn't about my father. She showed me the stars in her throat."

"She is a sick child, Sean. A runaway. I'm not sure how she got here, and I wasn't in my right mind either. Seeing things that were not there. I wasn't myself, not till my daughter came home."

He checked the urge to cry. "Can I see her when she gets back?"

"What I'm saying is, she's gone. She asked me to tell you—"

"You sent her away? How could you?"

"For her own good." She paused as if not quite believing her own words. "Where she'll be better off."

"But she isn't crazy. She is an angel."

Margaret looked past him to the horizon.

"She saved you. She brought your daughter back. How could you?" He ran down the steps and out into the yard.

"Sean, please," she called after him.

"How could you? I hate you! How could you not believe in her?"

"Son—"

"I hate you!" he shouted again and again, and then he ran all the way home.

THE DAY WAS ending, the light weakening, and outside his window a crescent of birds took flight, heading to shelter for the night, propelled toward darkness. Sean rolled over on his side and looked at the cardboard circus wagons, the feathers, the blue teacup. He wondered how she had departed. The man from the State—sinister beneath his fedora—coming to bind her in a straitjacket and drive off in a wagon with the other caged runaways. Mrs. Quinn, her sister, and her daughter standing on the front porch waving goodbye, their handkerchiefs fluttering in the breeze, and when they could no longer see her, turning back to the house like mourners leaving a funeral.

Or this time Norah did not hesitate. Climbing onto the rail, she steadied herself above the blue river and stared into the brightness of the sun. Like a bird she bent her knees into a crouch, unfurled her gigantic wings, and leapt into the air. The wind rushed beneath her as she beat higher and higher into the sky, and within minutes, she was small, then smaller, like a balloon floating away, and he followed with his eyes till she vanished into a point and then nothing at all.

Around dinnertime, his mother came to check on him, and when he claimed not to be hungry, she laid her hand upon his forehead, and he wished she would stay longer, stay forever, for the coolness of her touch was the only balm against the fire in his mind.

25

The For Sale sign went up the week before Easter, but he did not see it, for he took the long route to and from school, avoiding the shortcut and the Quinns' home altogether. Her absence in the classroom was burden enough to bear, and the sight of that house each day would have tortured his memory. Sean also took no part in the sacralization and mythmaking that arose among her third-grade apostles. Those who had turned away now crafted a gospel of their fragmentary remembrances, conflating episodes, granting her powers she did not have, neglecting the significance of those she possessed. Days after the confirmation of the Quinns' departure, new stories began to circulate. Some, mostly children, accepted her claims and in retrospect regretted how Norah had been treated. Others, particularly the adults, were glad to see the Quinns leave town. No one knew where they went or why, not even the Delarosas next door. It was reported that the owner had left the rooms furnished, vanishing without so much as a goodbye to neighbors or friends or anyone at all. The house, furniture, and land were being sold by one Diane Cicogna of Washington, D.C.

As one season gave way to the next, the legend of Norah Quinn faded. By May, the schoolchildren were x-ing out the remaining days until summer vacation, their minds preoccupied with swimming pools and trips to the shore, Little League and the seemingly endless nirvana of doing nothing at all. In time, they largely forgot about the girl that had once graced their lives, forgot the animal crackers and moving statues, the burning car and the lost minute. She was put away with the Easter decorations, the sweaters, and the rain slickers. From time to time, another child invited Sean to play, but he was so sullen at Monopoly, so bored by cowboys and Indians, that he was rarely asked back again. Skimping on his schoolwork, he barely passed. He wanted nothing more than to be alone.

In summertime, his wish came true. His mother left him by himself when she went to work, and there was nobody who ever came around. He spent his days in idleness, trying to forget Norah, but he still missed and thought of her often, for it had never occurred to him that she would ever leave. When Father's Day arrived, he remembered a conversation with Norah about his missing father. "He hasn't abandoned you," she had said, "but lost himself. Pray that he may find himself again."

On an evening in late June, Sean rode his bicycle past the Friendship School and sat awhile staring at its utter emptiness. Dusk crept up unexpectedly, and fireflies began to flash like thousands of stars across the playground. Along the edge of the woods, a chorus of peeper frogs and crickets filled the silence with their music, and he felt a kind of panic at getting home after dark. His mother would be angry with him, so against his instincts, he took the path that ran past the Quinns' yard. Under a quarter moon, he stopped at the fence bordering their property. Next door, the lights were off at the Delarosas'; he had not dared to say a word to the flower shop man since the incident on the bridge. The grass had grown high and wild due to neglect, for nobody was buying houses around there any longer, nobody was moving in, only moving out or dying off. Looming like a black box, the house was more shadow than substance, but he could still picture Mrs. Quinn watching from the kitchen window and Norah hopping the split rails as nonchalant as a cat. He closed his eyes to better picture her, and in the instant he opened them again, he noticed a flicker from her window as if a shadow had crossed the room. No light had been on when he first pulled up, he was certain, but now the window shone like a star. Inching closer, he saw the luminous spill from the second story, the curtains flapping gently in an intermittent breeze. Lured farther, he parked his bicycle against the fence and waded through the grass to the back door. One unanswered knock proved empty and ridiculous. He turned the knob and found the door unlocked.

The kitchen was largely as he remembered. The pictures on the walls were gone, but everything else looked the same—the scarred oak table and chairs pushed back as though a family had just gotten up from a meal. Going room to room, he found himself in an abandoned museum. In Dr. Quinn's study, the medical books stood steadfast and a stethoscope curled like a snake on an old hat rack. A few personal effects were missing from the living room, but left behind were the old sofa covered in a faded afghan, the reading lamp silted with dust, and beneath the coffee table, their old Monopoly, Tip It, a magazine from the middle of March. For a brief moment, he expected Mrs. Quinn and her sister arriving home from a late dinner, but the idyll passed. Staleness hung in the air, an odor particularly strong and sharp at the bottom of the stairs, where he debated whether to investigate further the source of that mysterious light. Along the bottom edge of her bedroom's closed door, the faintest shimmering line appeared through the darkness. He called out her name.

Something stirred at the sound of his voice, a surprised cry and then a fluttering scurry. Sean took the steps, pausing at each riser to listen again, but he could not be sure if the noise emanated from above or came from inside his own pounding chest. On the top step, as he was about to reach the landing, he risked her name again. "Norah," he whispered hoarsely, and the response was unmistakable: drumbeat of wings, dozens flapping in panic, a rush of wind pulling at the closed door.

Angels, he decided. Angels behind the door and Norah among them. Or the seven Angels of Destruction come to end time, led by the angel in the hat and overcoat he had summoned in his nightmare. The wingbeats grew furious and crashing. *Just don't hurt me,* he said to himself as he turned the knob.

The sudden opening sucked in the air and sent feathers undulating in the cross-breeze, as though he had just walked in upon a fleeting pillow fight. The bed was a mess, the brocaded covers and blankets ripped and unraveling at the seams. A lit lamp lay knocked over on its side, the shade brown where the bulb had scorched the cloth. White droppings coined the bookshelves. Colorful strands from the blankets were threaded into a nest atop the bureau. Birds, he realized. Gotten in through an open window. Knocked over the lamp and bumped the switch. No angels present. He laughed at his foolishness, laughed at how afraid he had let himself be. He picked up the lamp and set it back in place, and as he pushed down the sash, he saw in the glass the reflection of Norah. Soft as a wingtip, something brushed his shoulder, and he pivoted quickly expecting by some miracle to find her there, but just as quickly, the prayer vanished and he was alone in an empty room facing his own image in the black window.

26

Her mother began calling her Mary as soon as they had settled in New Mexico, as if Margaret herself chose the name for her new child. As a gift for Mother's Day, her first in a long time, Mary hand-colored the black-and-white photographs they had taken on their picnic in the woods. A little work to hang in Margaret's room. With soft pencils, she filled in the white and gray, changing her own blonde hair to brown, adding roses to her mother's cheeks. Aura of gold emanating around Maya. For Diane, tincture of green to brighten her eyes. Birds were added to the junipers and piñons, the clouds tinted with a blush of brown, and the endless sky made bluer than heaven. Each time she sat to work on her gift, she would recall their trip into the Carson National Forest and go back in time to the day of her full forgiveness.

The foursome had piled into Maya's jeep that weekend at the beginning of spring, a spontaneous jaunt north to show Diane another part of New Mexico before she would be heading home for good and to quench Margaret's restlessness at the upheaval in her life. Her aches and pains had gone into remission; the reappearance of her daughter made her feel whole and healthy again. They spent the night in Taos, shopping with the tourists, snapping shots of San Francisco de Asis, made famous by O'Keeffe, and wandering the pueblos north of town proper. Skiers had abandoned the Sangre de Cristos a week earlier, but the snow still clung to the mountain face, and after the sun set, the cold air put them all in mind of winter. They woke on Sunday invigorated and, at Maya's suggestion, bought provisions for lunch and drove into the Carson National Forest for a noonday hike.

Bundled in sweaters and jackets, they took a novice trail through the evergreen forest, the jagged firs pointing to the morning sun hiding behind a veil of high clouds. Maya led the way, wielding a hawthorn walking stick, and in single file followed Mary, her mother, and her aunt. Despite the cool temperatures, the brush and wildflowers, spurred by the lengthening days, had begun to bud and sprout. Songbirds announced their mating melodies, and once, a tawny jackrabbit flinched against the stony background, hopping away at the women's shouts of joy. They rested often in deference to Margaret's age and condition, though she protested, having not felt so good in years.

A black wave rolled over the mountain with alarming speed, and when a snit of hail and snow began to fall, the foursome dashed for cover. Maya and Mary hid under an outcropping of rock fifty yards ahead of Margaret and Diane, who sheltered beneath a juniper, laughing like schoolgirls.

"I wish you didn't have to go," Margaret told her. "I'll miss you."

For the first time in their lives together, Diane lifted her hand and stroked her sister's cheek. A gesture so brief that both sisters nearly misunderstood its meaning.

"Thank you," Margaret said. "For bringing my daughter back to me. For being so strong and brave."

"I would do anything for you."

"After I was such a horrid big sister? Picking on you, blaming you for everything when I got in trouble."

"You aren't so bad," Diane shouted over the clack of hail. "You could have trusted me more. Let me inside."

Margaret raised her hand to her sister's face, repeated the gesture she had been taught. Gathering her sister in her arms, she felt the sigh of ages escape. "You're right. No more secrets."

"And I'm sorry about the little girl." She bent her head to Margaret's shoulder.

"Norah? I know, I know," and she patted her back as if soothing a small child.

As quickly as the storm gathered, the clouds blew on to the next mountain, and the air cleared, the sun reappeared. An hour's march later, they stopped, spread the blanket on a flat rock, and shared a cold picnic. By magic, a bottle of wine appeared, was opened and divided into four plastic cups.

"It's so beautiful here," Diane said.

Mary said, "I wanted to show you why I love it here before you head home."

Stretching out her legs, Margaret leaned back into the bright air. "I could stay here forever. Puts me in mind of Emerson. 'In the woods, we return to reason and faith. There I feel that nothing can befall me in life . . . which nature cannot repair.'"

"How is it you remember stuff like that, Mom?"

"I went to college once upon a time, young lady, filled my head with poetry and philosophy and art. Saw the hand of God in everything. Where do you think you got your natural talent?"

Whether from the wine or the fresh air that flushed her cheeks, Maya brightened, as if lit from within. "A transcendentalist," she said. "And a theologian. What do you make of the angels sent your way? Mary told me all about your otherworldly visitor."

"Oh, I've thought about her every day since we left, and worry about her too. I can't find a rational explanation for Norah. Or for the other one."

Diane sat up, alert. "There was more than one?"

"Not the same as Norah, more like a bad dream, an annoying hallucination. A man in a fedora and camel hair coat used to appear to me over the years. Sounds crazy, doesn't it? But a kind of presence to compensate for absence. Someone to talk to, so I wouldn't talk to myself." She finished her wine, closed her eyes, and raised her chin toward the sun. Mirroring her gesture, the others turned their faces skyward. To any wayward pilgrim, they would have seemed penitent, at prayer, worshipping something felt but not seen.

"The bodhisattva," Maya said, "a holy being about to enter nirvana, refrains from so doing out of compassion for others. In order to save others. There are angels everywhere, strange angels, and every faith accounts for intermediaries of the lost. A little girl, an old man, a stranger on the road, your friend. Best to be safe, always, and assume anyone may be."

One by one they opened their eyes to the bright spring day. Light-headed from the wine, they packed the empty bottle, stowed the trash, and headed back, leaving no sign of having passed this way. Except for a few photographs.

Mary finished coloring the last of them, her favorite; the hues brought out the currents circulating through them both. Just Mom and Me. Into a frame, then wrapped and beribboned. Switching off the studio lights, she left to surprise her mother.

June 2005

Heartbroken when the young woman he loved told him she was soon to be engaged to someone else, Sean asked his boss for two weeks' time off and headed southwest. He longed to circle back to his childhood dreams when he had helped an extraordinary little girl re-create out of modern myths—books and postcards and bits of television shows— a place neither one had ever seen. A Land of Enchantment, with its cartoon canyons, wind-carved stone arches, and the mesas with anvil-shaped boulders balancing on precipices. New Mexico meant the insouciant roadrunner and the hapless coyote and schemes bought COD from ACME Co. He remembered the name of the ghost town—Madrid—that he and Norah had resurrected from a pinhole on a map and knew that once it had been home to a woman that he and the girl had restored from the past. Mary Gavin lived there.

He found her easily, unlike the searchers years before who lost her somewhere in America, unlike her mother's emissary who did not know which name to call out. The path was certain. In Albuquerque, he rented a car and drove into the hills, following the signs to the Turquoise Trail. The sun glowed like a blinding eye, and when he parked and got out of the car, he felt the brain-boiling heat of three in the afternoon. People kept to the dark and cool spots, and even the stray dogs would not budge from their patches of shade. A string of shops in a long adobe gallery afforded him the chance to query several clerks and owners, but he had no luck.

He went into a small café where two customers had laid out a winding path of dominoes. As if they had been at it forever, the men lingered over each placement, calculating the odds, their tiles arranged in front of their coffees like picket fences. The older of the two, a graying mustache hiding his mouth, noticed Sean at the door and with a nod invited him to their table.

"Sit down, brother. Have something."

The younger man showed him a dazzling smile, bright as sunshine. "I'm looking for someone."

Pot in hand, a waitress appeared and poured him a cup of coffee. Sean offered to treat the gents to something, and the younger ordered a poppyseed cake.

"We're all looking for someone," the mustachioed man said. "Tell me, if I'm not too forward, is it someone who's broken your heart?"

His friend leaned over his black fortress. "Forgive him. He's a romantic and thinks he can spot a fellow heart-on-your-sleeve."

Sean thought of the girl he had left behind but shook his head. "This is someone I know from my childhood. Who lives in Madrid."

Leaning back in his chair, the older man paused to consider his next move. "My mistake, though I'm a pretty good judge of the soul. A man's desires stir just below his words. Who are you looking for, amigo?"

"Do you know an artist named Mary Gavin?"

The poppyseed cake arrived and the younger man stuffed a bite in his mouth.

"*Peregrino,*" the man said to his young friend. "*Busca la verdad sobre los ángeles.*"

His teeth peppered with seeds, his friend answered. "Show him the way."

They gave him directions and on the face of a napkin a hand-drawn map to her house. "Strangers kinda spook those monsters she's got up there," the young one said. "Two wolfhounds, big as tigers, and they'll sniff out the difference between friend and foe."

"I'm a friend," Sean answered. "From way back when."

"Don't listen to him, they're pussycats. *Mi hijo* has spent too much time staring at the sun. He is blind and crazy."

Wearing a broad-brimmed slouch hat he purchased on a whim from the next-door haberdashery, Sean hiked the trail to the Gavin place, past the shops painted lilac and butterscotch, their wares baking in the sun, past the old and faded Spanish church, into the tattered hills, anxious with each step. He had allowed himself the illusion that they had lied to him as a child, and pictured the three of them in the hacienda: Mrs. Quinn, her daughter, and Norah. The heat radiating from the bare ground bent the air in waves, and the hounds sprinting toward him

seemed at first a mirage, some trick of the harsh light and his imagination. The pair closed fast, split, and circled round him like hands on a
clock, taking his measure. Sean stood perfectly still and waited.

"Boys," a woman called, and they pricked up their ears and returned
to her side. From the brush, she emerged in a white cotton dress that
nearly touched the ground, one hand shielding her eyes against the sun.
"Sorry, mister," she called out. "Are you lost?"

He did not recognize her at first, forgetting that she, too, had aged,
but there was no mistaking the resemblance to the person he remembered. The spiky blonde hair had grown out to its natural brown, but in
every other aspect, she remained the picture in his memory. He yelled
back to her. "Mary? Mary Gavin?"

The woman in white stepped toward him, the dogs flanking each
side. "Do I know you?"

He took off his hat and raised his chin. "I know you. I know your
mother—"

"My mother?"

"Margaret Quinn. From back home, Pennsylvania. When I was a
kid, I knew your mother. And Norah. Do you remember her?"

She strained against the light and shadows to recognize his face. "I
can't—"

"Sean Fallon." He lifted his arm to shake her hand, but she was
upon him in a firm embrace, surprising in its intensity.

"Norah," she whispered in his ear. The dogs whined and nuzzled between them to separate. "Look at you, Sean, all grown up. What's it
been, twenty years?"

"I came to see you—"

"Come out of this sun. I can't believe it."

Two young children straightened their posture and lifted their gaze
when she ushered him inside, pausing from their game of blocks
arranged like a faraway imaginary city on the cool stone floor. Sean
squatted to inspect their architectural engineering as introductions were
made. "This is my boy, Cole, he's six. And this Miss Josie here likes to be
called Jo." The four-year-old girl stood and clung behind her mother's
protective leg. "And this here is Mr. Sean Fallon, who has come all the
way from Pennsylvania to meet you guys. Wait in the parlor, won't you,
and I'll get us something to drink."

The boy quickly scanned the stranger's face, then went back to constructing a ramp for his toy cars. The girl tried climbing up to her mother's arms and hid her face from the stranger. With a sheepish grin, Sean stood and straightened the pleats of his pants, allowing her to lead him to the next room, a dark parlor, crowded with art and the exotica of her years in the West. The requisite longhorn skull beaded in a mosaic of lapis and green turquoise. Landscapes of mountains and unending sky. A framed baseball jersey, "Madrid Miners," hung next to a painting of a holstered nude woman brandishing two revolvers. Roped around the mantel, a chain of feathers, and resting against the wall an infrared photograph of a pueblo, Indian dogs glowing white in the bare yard. On a table next to shelves crammed with books were pictures of the children and their father, he presumed, a man clearly happy in the company of his kids. There was a hand-colored photograph of a woman thin as a reed and wreathed in a corona of wild gray hair, two dogs at her side echoing the two beasts resting on the mosaic tiles fronting an adobe hearth. Next to this portrait, the familiar face of Margaret Quinn, radiant in the light, cheek to cheek with her smiling daughter under the limbs of a juniper. He was staring at their faces when Mary returned with two tall glasses.

"Your mother? Is she living with you?"

"Yes, that's my mother. That's up north, beyond Taos in Carson National Forest. We took a trip in the springtime, the year she came to live with me. Aunt Diane was here too. And my friend Maya. Some trip. She was a big-time hiker, did you know, my mother? Loved to be in the outdoors, while she could still get around. Said it renewed her sense of wonder. Up in the high country with nothing but evergreen and hills and sky stretching as far as the eye can see. Mom loved it there." Mary handed a glass to him and they sat across from one another, a beatific grin pasted on her face.

"When we went out into the woods, it seemed like she just cast off the years and the troubles and was a child again. A day when we could be our perfect selves, just kind of vanish into the landscape." She paused as if reliving the event and then set down the frame. "You know, I missed her for ten years, and we only had ten months together after she came out here. This was taken a couple months before we found out about the cancer. Still, I treasured the days. A blessing."

"She passed away?"

"That next February, around Valentine's, 1986. But we had the chance to make up for lost time, and I think she forgave me in the end."

"Of course she forgave you. You were all she thought about."

The boy yelped in the other room, and she excused herself to investigate. Alone, Sean looked at the photo of Mrs. Quinn and her daughter, his heart filled with regret. Mary came back, shaking her head. "Kids will keep you young. Do you have any yourself?"

With a shrug of his shoulders, he indicated there were none.

"Don't wait too long. You know, I never fully understood what my mother went through until I became a mother myself. Like I was saying before, we had a second chance. Don't get many of those in this life."

"You're right, and I was hoping against hope that Mrs. Quinn would still be here. Last thing I ever said to her was 'I hate you.'"

"I'm sure she forgave you, too, whatever you might have said."

"I was so angry. On account of Norah. After you left, all kinds of stories went around town about her. Some people said you took her back to an orphanage, and others said she jumped off the bridge—"

"People are crazy, make up all kinds of things."

Jo squalled into the room, her brother behind in close chase and a blur of noise.

"I don't really know what happened to Norah. We were supposed to take her—"

From the opposite direction, the chase resumed, the little girl screaming with joy, her brother growling, and the two dogs, anxious to join the game, racing one after the other through the parlor.

"Those kids. Norah vanished in the middle of the night, left a note saying she was going back home. Of course, my mother was in a state. For a few days, she could not bear the thought of leaving without her, not knowing where she was. Coming out of nowhere and going back the same way. She never—" A curdled scream rang out from the other room. "She wanted us to look for her, but there wasn't time. And besides, what could we tell the authorities? 'We're looking for a girl whose true name we do not know, and we don't know where she came from or where she might be going, and by the way, I'm Erica Quinn. I'm on your fugitives list.'" Calls for Mommy bounced off the walls. "Give me a minute."

While peace talks were under way in the imaginary city, Sean drained his glass and set it on the table. Like a magic potion, the drink loosened his tongue, and when she returned, Josie in tow, he spilled out the story, a tale of miracles and visions, recounted the signs she had shown, the angel's ability to be outside of time, the night he found her transported and praying on the cold ground. In his telling, he searched for a logical response to each act, but could not account for the mystery of Norah. Mary took in every word, interrupting only to have him clarify his account. Absent Margaret Quinn, her daughter was the only person he could trust with his confession. "I always wondered if she might have somehow been telling the truth," he said. "If that's possible. I don't believe in fairy tales, and the only angels around these days are on calendars and greeting cards. But I always wondered what she was and why she came into our lives."

"*Perdido en los sueños.*" Stiff from sitting, Mary stretched like a cat, and her daughter slid down her legs. "Lost in our dreams." She spoke to her child. "Go get Cole, Jo-Jo, and come out to the studio with Mama. Follow me."

The wolfhounds got their legs underneath them and, shaking off the dust, led the way. Sean trailed, caught in the sail of her white skirt, the weight of his secrets lifted and blown to the four winds. As she threw open the shutters, columns of light penetrated the darkness section by section until the whole room burst into being. Thrilled by each aspect, he questioned her about the studio, the tools and brushes, the rolled canvas and stretchers. Mary gave him the grand tour while her children played in a corner brightly colored. A current of assurance and contentment changed the tone of her voice as she described the steps in her processes, and he felt the joy her work had brought to her.

"And these are my old angels," she said before the wall of dusty *retablos.* "My first try. I don't know how much of my story my mother may have told you."

"I only know the story Norah invented for school, how she lived with you out here in New Mexico and was only at her Gramma's because you and your husband were fighting."

She stared at the bandoliered santo in the corner. "Wiley."

"Norah had me expecting coyotes and roadrunners overrunning the place."

Beginning with the long-ago night that she and the boy snuck out of the house, she told him about the Angels of Destruction and their plans to save the world by destroying it and starting all over. She told him of their encounters with the strangers on the road, ending with her abandonment and the baby who never arrived. "They were warning me," she said, sweeping her hand to the figures on the wall. "Warning me away from perdition and back to grace. They were trying to get me home while still possible, but I didn't listen."

She sat at a stool and picked up a brush. "All kinds of angels, something missing in our souls, we re-create when we are awake and in need. Like your Norah."

Hanging on the wall behind her shoulders was a series of abstractions, life-size canvases each dominated by a single color in different hues and shadings. Each piece featured a dark figure reminiscent of the human form—a splayed hand, the pear of a derriere, flattened circles with bull's-eye nipples, a face, a nose, lips. The bodies in the paintings struggled to escape from the blues and reds and greens, or perhaps to meld into the canvas, or transcend this world for another. Desire, coming into being.

"And these?" he asked.

"I call them the Nagasaki angels, a long story."

Sean walked over to the paintings and considered them one by one. "Norah told me about your father, what he did for those poor people after the atom bomb."

The figures in the paintings strained to the surface, between imagination and reality, waiting to be borne into another world. He could see their pain at letting go of this life, caught between here and there, nowhere.

Mary chewed on the end of the brush. "If Norah knew, then my mother must have told her. My mother must have known all along and never said a word to my father."

"Maybe that was her way of letting it go, her way of forgiveness."

"Maybe my father was their angel, caught up in the chaos between mercy and pain."

One of the dogs padded into the room and settled in front of her. Mary reached down and scratched the coarse hair between his eyes. "They were Maya's dogs. The last pups in a long line of wolfhounds my friend Maya used to keep. She passed away too, and told me to watch over them, but they really kind of watch over me. And the kids."

"Maya." He smiled. "From the Upanishads. The veil thrown over the world."

Mary laughed, and then drew her hand to her mouth. "I'm sorry, Sean. Who knows? Maya could have been right. Norah could have been right. Who's to say what's real and what's an illusion? Why do we believe in things we cannot see?" From the corner her little girl laughed and called to her mother to come look at what she had made.

BEFORE DAWN, SEAN woke and dressed and tiptoed past the rooms where Mary and her husband, Dan, slept and past the two children nestled in their beds. He could not bear to wake them. At the kitchen table, he scribbled a note thanking them for the hospitality. For her boy Cole, he left the slouch hat, "for the dusty trail." From his bag, he took a small parcel swaddled in layers of tissue paper. He unwrapped the gift and left it atop his postscript: "This is all Norah left behind. For your little girl." The wolfhounds lifted their shaggy heads and thumped their tails against the floor, goodbye. As the sky faded to plum, he found his way back to the car, pointed north, and drove away.

Blue as a robin's egg and suited for a child's hand, a child's imagination, the teacup seemed too small to hold more than a whisper. When she woke an hour later to find the cup on the table, Mary drew in a deep breath, recognizing the lost token, and then she bent to listen to the echo of a thousand prayers.

Past Santa Fe at first light, he found the road toward Taos, the mountains filling the windshield, the air blowing cool and clean. He followed the signs to Carson National Forest and arrived late in the morning. From the vacant parking lot, he climbed into the quiet hills, alert to the sound of the land, and the silence of nothing when he stopped. Murmuring softly to himself, Sean made his goodbyes to Mrs. Quinn, whom he had hoped to find in this lonesome place. In her own way, she was more mysterious to him than Norah Quinn, and he had wanted to ask her why in the first place she had opened her door to the girl, why she had lied so carefully and created the fiction of a long-lost granddaughter. Perhaps she, too, realized the necessity of the angel, a creature born from desire. He hiked to a break in the treeline, and from the high overlook, the piñons and junipers appeared to stretch endlessly to the horizon, and he had never been more alone. In the ancient sunlight, a blackbird sang a tune without words. Perched on an outcropping of granite, Sean listened awhile to the sound of the wind and watched the ever-changing skies, fearing what might come, hoping for its return.

ACKNOWLEDGMENTS

Thank you to Peter Steinberg, extraordinary agent. Thank you to John Glusman, my editor, and everyone at Shaye Areheart Books. I am grateful as well to Lauren Schott Pearson, Markus Hoffman, Ellen Bryson, and Amy Stolls for their suggestions, and a special thank-you to Melanie for her close reading and patience. You make a better book.

KEITH DONOHUE is the author of the acclaimed novel *The Stolen Child*. For several years, he was a speechwriter at the National Endowment for the Arts in Washington, D.C., and he now works at another federal agency. He lives with his family in Wheaton, Maryland.

ABOUT THE TYPE

THIS BOOK was set in Adobe Garamond, a typeface designed by Robert Slimbach in 1989. It is based on Claude Garamond's sixteenth-century type samples found at the Plantin-Moretus Museum in Antwerp, Belgium.

1. Who are the strange angels that appear to Margaret Quinn, and what role does she play in their materialization?

2. Images of birds fly through the story. How do they correspond to the epigram from Emily Dickinson, "Hope is the thing with feathers . . . ," at the beginning of the novel?

3. "The Snow Man" by Wallace Stevens opens with the line "One must have a mind of winter. . . ." Why is *Angels of Destruction* set in wintertime?

4. How is childhood portrayed in the novel? Clearly, Norah stands apart from the other children, but why is Sean Fallon susceptible to her force and vision? Who else bears witness to the miracles and wonders?

5. In the Valentine's Day scene in the classroom on page 115, Norah cites "the seven angels who serve the terrible will of the Lord to punish the faithless," drawing upon the *Malake Habbalah*, and there are traditions from many religions about punishing angels. How does this proclamation—and her later acts in Book III—serve to push the adults into confronting their beliefs?

6. At the beginning of Book II, we are suddenly swept back ten years to the story of Erica and Wiley. In what ways does the author connect their story to the events of Book I?

7. As they pull out in the middle of the night, Erica and Wiley fail to see the girl watching from the side of the road. Who is she and why is she there? How are the other people on the road changed through Erica's later perspective?

8. How are Una and Mee-Maw alike and different from Norah and Margaret?

9. Several of the characters talk about having to change their names. How does Erica's new identity and pursuit of art and painting play with her desire for redemption?

10. Faith and the desire to believe in things unseen play an important part in the lives of virtually all of the characters. How is Sean's journey to find Mary Gavin like a pilgrimage? How are the other characters—Norah, Diane, Paul, Wiley, Maya, Erica, and Margaret—engaged in some quest for grace?